I0778024

Oliver Bell and the Infinite Multiverse

© Jake Swan, 2025
All rights reserved.

First Galleon Edition, February 2025
ISBN 978-1-998122-134

Published by Galleon Books
Moncton, New Brunswick, Canada
www.galleonbooks.ca

Cover design by Jeep Jones.

Author disclaimer: This book is a satire, written by an idiot. Try not to take it too seriously.

Publisher addendum to the author disclaimer: If offered several strawberry daquiries by a washed-up author claiming to be a "caster" in sketchy Key West tiki hut in preperation for a trip to another realm of existence, please drink repsonsibly. And call your mother first.

Check out www.jakeswan.ca.

Library and Archives Canada Cataloguing in Publication
Title: Oliver Bell and the infinite multiverse / Jake Swan.
Names: Swan, Jake, author.
Description: Includes index.
Identifiers: Canadiana 20250152630 | ISBN 9781998122134 (softcover)
Subjects: LCGFT: Novels.
Classification: LCC PS8637.W363 O45 2025 | DDC C813/.6—dc23

GALLEON

OLIVER BELL

and the

INFINITE

MULTIVERSE

JAKE SWAN

For Jack—
You're one in a billion, kid.

One

Oliver Bell shoved his glasses up the bridge of his nose and squinted at the flashing column of equations.

Worried he might miss the problem on first pass, he grabbed a legal pad and quickly jotted down each set of figures as they scrolled by.

He could have taken screenshots, but screenshots were not part of his problem-solving method. This was how he hunted for bugs. It was the way he had learned, and so it was the way he would always do it.

To relearn a process that already worked was inefficient, and Oliver loved efficiency. By consequence, he was a creature of routine.

He wrote in his own version of shorthand—a note-taking custom he developed while trying to keep up with Dr. Ishaan Mehta, a professor who spoke so quickly the students had nicknamed him "Machinegun Mehta."

While his pencil danced across the paper, Oliver kept his gaze fixed firmly on the screen. The university library's quiet study room was unusually warm, and beads of sweat popped on his forehead. He swiped them away with his sleeve.

The consequences of this exercise were significant in the sense that they pertained to Oliver's thesis, and specifically, the computer program upon which its fate rested. He had to figure out why, after six months of nearly flawless testing, the algorithm he designed had decided to glitch.

Nearly four years earlier, in a bout of what he could now recognize as overconfident naïveté, he had set out to achieve what seemed impossible. He wanted to build the perfect practical realization of theoretical mathematics and to present it as his doctoral thesis. His goal was to construct the first universal instruction language.

It would be no simple translator. His would be a quasi-intelligent, deep-learning program that could mathematically predict exactly how to turn any set of instructions into accurate code in any computer language, past, present, or future.

With almost no computer language experience, he had set out to build the holy grail of coding.

Perhaps he had felt there was something to prove. Circumstances at the time dictated that he turn down a scholarship from Stanford, and while he was intentionally aloof to the academic rumor mill as a rule, there had been no way to avoid hearing the volleys of whispers. His colleagues' speculations ran from "He couldn't hack it," to "He failed the entrance exam," to "He was caught cheating."

To the same extent that Oliver loved efficiency, he despised attention. He was a fiercely private young man, and knowing that he was the target of such conversation deeply troubled him.

Though he was far from proud by nature, as time went on, and his colleagues' curiosity failed to ebb, the importance he assigned to his upcoming dissertation had swelled in proportion until the program and its accompanying presentation and materials grew into an all-consuming monster.

Mediocrity was not an option. His thesis had to exceed everyone's expectations. He would throw a wet towel on their burning questions with finality.

For the better part of four years, Oliver lived his thesis. He breathed it, slept it, and dreamed it. He thought about it while he ate. He thought about it while he walked. He thought about it in the shower. He thought about it while he attended lectures, and while he marked undergraduate papers.

The idea of mathematically predictable instruction was a puzzle, wrapped in an enigma, deep-sixed in a sea of mystery. But over time, as he worked at the problem and worried it, attacked it from every angle, it became increasingly simple to understand, until he finally conceptualized it not as an ever-shifting four-dimensional multifaceted structure, but as a rudimentary door that needed only a key to open. At that point, to his complete surprise, he opened it.

Alone in his apartment, on Thanksgiving Sunday, he came up with the idea that the solution lay in the classic problem of P versus NP. Since he had nothing better to do, he tried adding a few lines of instruction to his code, essentially telling the autoencoding subset to check and correct its own programming, and when he subsequently ran a test, for the first time, it ran to completion, and produced a result.

It was stunning. But it hadn't been a particularly difficult task. In fact, had he known it would be a moon-landing moment (or as close to a moon-landing moment as could be achieved by an academic theoretical mathematician) he might have written something more meaningful than "Draw a fifty-pixel by fifty-pixel blue square."

Nonetheless, in every language he could think to check, the program had drawn a fifty-by-fifty-pixel blue square.

It might have been a fluke, of course. After all, "Draw a square" wasn't exactly rocket science. But as he subsequently crafted increasingly complex challenges for the software, it succeeded in producing results time and again.

The variability in which the different languages solved his problems was a beautiful thing unto itself. Watching his creation at work had been like watching the first brushstrokes of the different impressionist masters.

It was when he finally had program work on the really complicated stuff, the DARPA challenges and the Millennium Prize problems, that Oliver first began to understand the magnitude of his accomplishment. He had unlocked what was sure to be mankind's next great technological leap.

And while he was viscerally opposed to more personal attention, he suspected that once his dissertation was complete, like it or not, he'd be in for some. The silver lining would be his ability to leverage such buzz into an interesting career.

He was tired of the status quo. Having spent his whole life on the East Coast, most of the strings that had previously tethered him to Halifax had snapped, and the ones that remained were badly frayed.

He yearned to start anew, in a new place, with new people. He imagined working in Seattle, and pictured the mountains of the Pacific Northwest, sparkling like emeralds after a rainstorm.

He imagined California, and pictured a bank of fog rolling over the Golden Gate Bridge.

He imagined the Gulf of Mexico, and pictured the turquoise surf stirring up the shell-laden white sand as it washed against the pilings of a fishing pier.

He imagined all those places, and imagined forging meaningful friendships in them, and becoming part of someone else's story, and someone else becoming part of his.

When the program had succeeded, he allowed himself, for the first time as an adult, to imagine having a life.

The thesis could unlock it for him. It was the key to his entire future.

Unfortunately, in the homestretch, with only days to go, he had somehow broken it.

That morning, when he cued a routine test, the software stopped, mid-calculation, and had spat out an error. He spent an hour hunting through a Linux reference PDF searching for the fault reference, before slapping his forehead in exasperation when he realized that whatever the error was, it would be, by definition, the first time it ever happened.

Now he was in geek hell, running the most basic calculations through the software, hoping against hope that whatever the problem was, he would be able to sniff it out based on the numeric problem-solving test he'd devised, called "Five Equals Five."

Five Equals Five essentially instructed the program to offer mathematical proof that every whole number up to one thousand was equal to itself.

The first time he'd run it, his desktop had bluescreened. Operating a diagnostic from the bios, this appeared to be due to a hardware error—specifically, a corrupted drive.

That was no matter. He still had an up-to-date version of the code on his laptop. He started the diagnostic again, but with his anxiety running overtime, Oliver had been distracted by the neighbors fighting next door, and a student protest marching down Spring Garden Road, and blaring car horns, and his dripping faucet, and finally he had given up, thrown the laptop in a backpack and booked it to the Killiam Library, where, with midterms in the rearview mirror, but finals still a month away, he knew a quiet study room would be easy to find.

At ten o'clock in the morning, he parked himself in the study room and vowed not to leave until the issue was fixed.

He glanced at his watch. It was seven o'clock.

He wished he had thought to bring a bottle of water.

Without looking, he tore another sheet off the pad and flipped it onto a pile on the floor before continuing his paper copy at the top of the next page.

A droplet of sweat that formed at his eyebrow rolled down his eyelid and hung, momentarily suspended, off his eyelashes. Before he could dab it, it dripped onto the lens of his glasses and blurred the last three values of the column. He shook his head to direct the liquid away from the center of his vision, and another droplet fell on the opposite lens.

"Oh, come on," he muttered.

When he snatched the frames from his face and used his shirt to pat dry the offending effluent, the screen changed.

"Dang it!"

He had missed the end of the column. He knew the chance of the error being in those last lines was infinitesimally small, but as a hopeless obsessive, ignoring it would drive him crazy. To do so would mean introducing a new variable.

He paused the program, and dropping the mechanical pencil, stretched his aching fingers. Beside his chair, a sizeable pile—four pads worth of yellow legal paper—had accumulated.

Oliver yawned. His mouth was dry and his lips felt like they could crack.

He had been sitting there for nine hours. It would be dark outside.

Shaking his head at his lack of progress, he tore off the last sheet he'd been writing on and examined it. On the last line was written:

Accepting that 7=6+2

He blinked.

"Seven equals six plus two," he whispered aloud.

Understanding dawned.

He remembered his nightmare, and grinned.

Two nights prior, Oliver had experienced a dreadful dream in which the value of known numbers had been redefined to correct for the Heisenberg Uncertainty Principle. This had forced him to relearn a numeric data set from zero to eleven (the new number system worked in base-eleven for some reason) that would persist outside of human observation. In turn, he'd learned to redefine the meaning of the number seven. Seven had been eight because zero was one.

He must have sleep-walked, or rather, sleep-coded this lucid fallacy into his thesis. The fix was as simple as running a find and replace.

"Oh, thank God!" he said.

A crash reverberated through the building, and the floor shook. Oliver's breath caught in his chest.

The lights flickered, then went out, plunging the quiet study room and the foyer outside into a near-total blackness.

A chorus of angry shouting followed.

Or, had people been shouting all along, and Oliver was just now taking note of it? He suspected this could be the case.

He strained to make out the words, but they were smeared in echoes and competing voices, and the details were swallowed up in the study room's acoustic tile.

Illuminated by the light of his computer monitor, he felt very exposed. He gently closed the laptop, cloaking himself in darkness. Now sitting in the darkened room, he realized just how hot it was. He would have guessed it was thirty-five degrees Celsius, which, by anyone's standards, was too hot for the interior of a library. It was no wonder he was sweating.

The blue-hued emergency lights flickered in a staccato, stroboscopic burst. A woman—a very naked, rail-thin woman wearing only a ski mask—stood in the adjacent common area. In one hand, she held what appeared to be a compound hunting bow. In the other, she gripped the shaft of an arrow, that, if Oliver were to believe his eyes, had been tipped with a flaming tennis ball. Her slender body stood perfectly framed in the window, and Oliver stared, wondering what on earth could possibly be happening.

The thin woman's skin was covered in a full-body, Wabori-style tattoo that appeared to depict the twelve stations of crucifixion of famed author Ernest Hemingway, by famed author Margaret Atwood. Colorfully dyed dreadlocks poked out from the fringe of her mask.

In the binary flash of the wall-mounted, sealed-beam halogens, her motions played out as a slideshow. In one frame, she raised a compound bow. In the next, she nocked the blazing arrow. Next, she took careful aim at some unknowable, out-of-frame target. In the ensuing moment of blackness, a soft *twang* emanated from the place where she stood. Finally, when the lights flashed again, she had raised her arms in triumph. A feral war-cry pierced the gloom. In the next flash, she was gone.

The struggling backup electricity failed, and the foyer went dark.

Oliver smelled smoke. It was not the pleasant aroma of a campfire; rather, the dirty, sooty, unhealthy aroma of a structure fire. Specifically, he guessed, a university library fire.

He shimmied around the desk to look out the window.

Through a faint orange, incandescent glow, he saw septuagenarian librarian Doris Langley kick off her Denver Hayes orthopedic flats, hike her pencil skirt above her knobby knees, and clamber up a stack of periodicals to avoid an incoming Molotov cocktail that exploded across the reference desk. Despite the horror of the situation, Oliver was impressed by the senior citizen's dexterous display of evasive maneuvering.

Somewhere along the library's western wall, the backup generator attempted a reboot. The overhead fluorescents flashed crazily, out of sync. They revealed a scene of chaos, somehow evocative of a Hieronymus Bosch portrayal of hell combined with a documentary about Woodstock '99.

Naked people were everywhere. Some wore ski masks, while others not only showed their faces, but were proudly capturing themselves on video as they toppled stacks of books, or set fire to shelves of scientific journals.

It was the way those rioters embraced the documentation of their crimes that clued Oliver in, that this must be related to the protest he'd heard on Spring Garden Road earlier. Lately, campus uprisings had been turning to property damage in order to garner attention. Whether paintings were being defaced to draw eyes to the anti-oil movement, or statues of ancient explorers were spray-painted to alert the public to the anticolonialism movement, it seemed a game of one-upmanship amongst the main players in the near-constant civil unrest was at play in order to acquire those precious few seconds of coverage on the national news.

Normally, Oliver found such methodology to be in poor taste, and tried to ignore the demands of the actors involved in such shenanigans. But burning down the library was a whole different kettle of fish. The library was close to home. In fact, it *was* home! He was in it!

The fire alarm finally sounded, a blaring, disharmonic klaxon that only added to the melee.

The lights failed again.

A sharp *slap* resounded through the quiet study room, and Oliver jumped.

When the auxiliary lighting finally clicked on, he saw that a naked man had backed into the floor-to-ceiling glass window that separated him from the unfolding riot. The naked man's buttocks were pressed hard against the glass such that the cheeks resembled pale, fleshy pancakes. Suspended from one of the man's hands was what appeared to be a can of paint. Oliver adjusted his glasses and crouched to read the label. It was, indeed, a one-gallon bucket of Benjamin Moore Color Code 2007-20 "Shy Cherry" semigloss latex paint.

What the man was planning to paint amidst the fracas, Oliver could not begin to imagine.

While he crouched there, wondering exactly what shade "Shy Cherry" was supposed to be, the man turned, giving Oliver a full-frontal view. Oliver tumbled back and, gazing upward, locked eyes with Huang Chen, vice president of Student Operations and Finances, and co-captain of the university's debate team. Huang raised a fist in the air and made an angry face. Oliver, not knowing exactly what he was supposed to do, meekly raised his own fist.

"Hi, Huang," he said, though not nearly loud enough to be heard.

Huang nodded his approval before turning and bolting toward the scientific archives, where he swung the can of paint round and round like an Olympic hammer throw champion, then releasing it into the Psychology subsection. Shy Cherry, Oliver noted, was red.

Two perfectly round grease-impressions were left on the glass, marking the place where Huang Chen had staged his assault against the annals of psychological study.

Oliver got to his feet.

A splintering *crack* echoed through the common area, followed by a chorus of laughter. The sound had come from the trellis-work that some long-ago administration had commissioned in a doomed attempt to grow ivy in the atrium. Oliver adjusted his glasses. A nude male student with a shaggy head of blonde hair had climbed through a broken third-floor window and was attempting to staple a banner to the ancient, brittle, wood frame. Satisfied with one corner, the man shuffled across the lattice to affix the opposite side. Just as he pressed the stapler against the fabric, the trellis-work failed, and the screaming young man tumbled gracelessly, crashing through the canvas awning of the Second Cup coffee kiosk. The blank banner stayed in place, stapled backwards to the remains of the wooden lattice.

A fireball erupted from somewhere in the North Learning Commons.

Oliver had seen enough. He squeezed his way around the desk to collect his things, perched himself on the chair and stuffed handfuls of notes into his backpack. It felt obscene to just let his work burn. After all, there was a chance he would need it, should his find-and-replace plan fail.

He was transferring the final stack of papers when the plate glass window to his study room exploded. A potted palm tree smashed against the oversized desk, showering him with earthenware shards and soil.

Oliver kicked it away, only to slam the back of his head against the wall and nearly topple off his seat.

With the window gone, the shouts and screams were much louder. The fire alarm was absolutely deafening.

Something just outside the small room toppled over with a *crash*. Enthusiastic cheers followed.

Oliver scrambled to get up, but a large, exceptionally hairy man wearing nothing but a ski mask and white cotton briefs barged in through the broken window.

"No more meat!" the hairy man yelled. "No more... uh... meat books!"

Meat books?

Smoke wafted through the broken window. A blast of hot air filled the room.

Oliver's instincts screamed. The building was burning! Escape!

The library was jampacked with kindling in the form of paper, wooden desks and chairs. To stay a minute longer could prove fatal. But the hairy man blocked his exit from the study room.

"Excuse me," he said, raising a hand in what he hoped was an anodyne gesture. "I think you might have the wrong room."

The hairy man thumped himself in the center of the chest, and burped loudly. He noticed Oliver's computer and swiped it from the desk. He tucked the laptop under a very damp-looking armpit.

Oliver's heart leapt into his throat. That computer had not just the code, but his entire dissertation. His future was on that machine! The desktop drive was corrupted, and he hadn't backed up to his server in weeks!

Even over the smoke, he could smell the man's sour body odor of onions, marijuana, and stale beer.

He needed his computer back, but had no idea how to convince the hairy intruder.

Then he saw that the back of the hairy man's hand bore a blue mark. Oliver squinted. The mark was a sweat-smeared, ink-bled logo stamp from The Grawood Student Union pub. It was reasonable to assume, therefore, that the hairy man was a student.

Perhaps he could appeal to the man's own academic anxieties.

"Hey, dude! My thesis is on that. I really need it."

The hairy man wobbled on his feet. He turned to face Oliver. He covered one eye in an apparent effort to focus his vision.

"Is it vegan?" Every inflection was off. His voice was inappropriately loud, as though it were emanating from a television with the volume turned all the way up. The hairy man was obviously drunk.

"My thesis?"

"Yeah!"

"Uh... no, not really. It's a computer algorithm. I study theoretical mathematics, and..."

The hairy man hoisted the computer over his head and hurled it.

Oliver dove out of the way. He had never once imagined a scenario that might require him to dive out of the path of an incoming projectile with such agility. For a moment he marveled at how niftily he'd managed it, and with no prior practice. Then the laptop struck the wall, and exploded into fragments.

A dull, twisting pain shot through his gut. He wasn't normally quick to anger, but as he calculated the amount of progress he'd made over the past two weeks, he had to grit his teeth to keep from swearing.

The laptop's hard drive had settled in the corner. It appeared to be in one piece. He scooped it up, and picked himself up. Turning, he dusted himself off. The hairy man was bigger, and much stronger. But Oliver was upset.

"Now listen. I've been more than reasonable. But I have half a mind to go file a complaint with Mrs. Langly, and..."

Oliver looked to the place where the Senior Librarian's desk was supposed to be. One of Mrs. Langley's Denver Hayes orthopedic shoes smoldered on the carpet, next to a burning copy of *Fahrenheit 451* by Ray Bradbury. The combined circulation reference desk itself was entirely engulfed in flame.

"Oh right," he said.

His attention was then drawn to the microfiche viewing section, which was now nothing more than an infernal blaze. Thick, brown, and undoubtedly extremely toxic smoke boiled into the adjacent common area.

"You're gonna what? Tell on me? Ha. Try telling on me after I kick your ass, you intolerant fascist!" the hairy man yelled.

Not one for physical confrontation or violence of any kind, Oliver quickly came up with a plan.

"The microfiche!" he said, pointing.

The hairy man turned to look.

Oliver had intended to use the momentary distraction to escape, but he was trapped on the far side of the big desk. He crouched down, thinking maybe he could scoot underneath, but a particle board partition blocked his path.

He slowly stood back up.

The quiet room was small and cramped. It had been designed for serious study, and its architect had given next to no provisions for the possibility of a violent takeover by a hostile force of disenfranchised, nude, young adults, hell-bent on destruction.

The hairy man stood completely still, watching as flames consumed the first floor, apparently transfixed by the Brownian motion of the smoke.

Trapped as he was between the oversized desk and the far wall, Oliver stared at his shoes, and tried to conceive of a new escape plan. He was distracted by the heat—the air had grown so hot it hurt his throat just to inhale. Finally, sensing that death was likely imminent, he inched his way around the table. The hairy man stood like a statue in the doorway. Outside, black smoke billowed from the adjacent Chemistry and Physics Scientific Journal Room.

"Excuse me," Oliver said as he squeezed past. The hairy man's skin glistened with oily sweat, and his body odor was oppressive, but Oliver tried to exude non-judgmental calm. His crinkled nose betrayed him.

"You got a problem?" the hairy man drunkenly growled from behind the ski mask. The man swayed on his feet, and Oliver wondered whether he was succumbing to the alcohol or the heat.

"Ah... no!"

"I think you got a problem with the way I smell. With my natural musk."

Oliver decided his best chance was to bluff. "Oh, is that your natural musk? I just thought I'd caught a whiff of the unique soap you were using, and

I was wondering what brand...."

"Soap? *Soap!* I suppose you're one of those pro-corporate brown-nosers. You know, the ones who don't care how many animals get subjected to cruel science experiments. You're probably just like the guy who rubs shampoo into the eyeballs of helpless little New Guinea pigs."

"It's 'guinea pigs,'" Oliver said.

"What?"

"Guinea pigs. You said 'New Guinea pigs.' That isn't a thing. It's just guinea pigs."

"If I say they're 'New Guinea' pigs, then they're New Guinea pigs! You'd better learn to respect that! Respect my preferred lexicon!"

"Hey man. You can call them whatever you want, OK? It's just that 'New Guinea' pigs aren't a real thing. I was just trying to help."

"Fascist bastard!" the hairy semi-nude man roared.

He cocked his arm back, and the blast of stink from his axilla was so powerful it nearly made Oliver swoon.

Oliver couldn't believe it. Was he in a fistfight? He was a mathematician, for heaven's sake. Mathematicians weren't supposed to get into fistfights. They were supposed to get into bland arguments about the cube root of unreal numbers. Nonetheless, as a pragmatist, he understood he was just going to have to deal with the situation. He took a deep breath and tried a few quick triceps stretches to ready himself.

"What the hell are you doing?" the hairy man demanded.

"I'm readying myself for what seems to be an inevitable fistfight."

"Oh," the hairy man said. "Good."

Without another word, the hairy man took a fully telegraphed drunken swing, which Oliver easily sidestepped.

The man's fist struck the doorframe with a crunch. He howled in pain.

"You hurt me!" he shouted.

"You punched the doorframe!"

"Yeah, but you *made* me punch the doorframe. That punch was meant for you, Adolf!"

Oliver, who was nothing at all like Adolf Hitler, found this accusation fundamentally bothersome and in extremely poor taste. That he should be considered a Nazi for his rejection of the forced false-binary demands of an extremist protest group was really the epitome of why he treated exposure to modern society with the same principle he would apply to radioactivity— namely—ALARA (As Low As Reasonably Achievable).

The whole campus had taken a black-and-white approach to social issues. You had to be one hundred percent with whatever cause was at the forefront or else you were considered to be one hundred percent against it. It was stupid. It left no room for nuance, or for the grey areas where bridges could be built. Such polarization would never lead to anything productive. And yet, it was all the rage.

People, Oliver decided, and not for the first time, were frustrating.

A cluster of hot embers rolled through the door on a column of smoke. One landed on Oliver's shoulder and he brushed it away.

He had had enough. The protest-turned-riot had almost nothing at all to do with him, and if he stayed any longer some poor arson investigator was going to have to collect his remains with a Dust Buster.

He was done arguing. The hairy man might be bigger, but he was obviously, and completely, uncoordinatedly drunk.

Oliver pushed roughly past. "Excuse me."

The hairy man lurched after him, only to trip over a burning copy of *Sense and Sensibility* and fall face-first on the carpet.

Oliver waited a breath, expecting his opponent to stagger to his feet, but the hairy man was apparently down for the count. Even over the blaring of the fire alarm and the roaring cacophony of hundreds of thousands of books being reduced to ash, he could hear the man's snores.

This, of course, raised an ethical question. The fact that the hairy troglodyte wanted nothing more than to put a dent in Oliver's forehead didn't necessarily mean the man deserved to die in a fire. At the same time, Oliver wasn't entirely sure he could save his own hide, let alone the big brute's. He knelt beside the unconscious hairy man and patted him lightly on the polyester mask's cheek.

"Hey," he said. "Wake up."

The man didn't move.

He patted him harder. "Hey!"

Nothing.

He slapped the man's face with every ounce of strength he could muster. "Wake up!"

A resounding snore was the only reply.

"Fantastic," Oliver said aloud.

Closing his eyes, he tried to imagine which exit route would pass through the least amount of flammable raw material.

North or south?

He was having trouble thinking. Alarmingly, he was also having trouble breathing.

He decided the north exit was his best bet. It was farther, but much of the route was through a concrete-enclosed hallway.

He grabbed the man by the slippery, oily forearm, and tried to drag him toward the north corridor, but the sheen on the man's skin may as well have been Vaseline. Oliver lost his grip after moving the body less than an inch. He examined his palms, and to his dismay saw they were coated in grease. He wiped them unceremoniously on the man's ski mask.

He was in the process of deciding whether there was anything else to be done, when a metal cylinder pinged down the hallway and stopped at his feet. He squinted at it and made a vow to see an optometrist and update his prescription.

The cylinder was perforated with evenly spaced holes, and even in the dim flicker of firelight, Oliver could see a pale blue stripe running around the circumference. At each end was what appeared to be some kind of oversized hex-nut. At one end was a small metallic mechanism that looked like the top of a Bic lighter.

Briefly, he thought he must be looking at a pipe bomb, but that didn't make sense because why would someone perforate the sides of the bomb to allow gas to escape?

"Huh," he said.

The flash-bang exploded, knocking him to his knees and punching all the air from his lungs.

Hands clamped over his ears, he struggled back to his feet, spinning in the direction the grenade had come from. He rapidly blinked, trying to get rid of the bright turquoise afterimage of the blast.

A dozen nude people raced his way from the end of the hall. As his vision returned, the fact that some of the nude people were female did not escape his notice.

Trying his best to be a gentleman, Oliver turned and looked away from the naked women. He was immediately struck in the small of his back by an impossibly heavy object.

"Oof!"

He tumbled back to the carpet, and found himself staring at a fourth edition copy of *The New Annotated Lovecraft*. One of the nude people must have thrown it.

Wheezing, he got to his knees. The rioters hurried past, roughly jostling him aside. A few of them trampled over the hairy man, who continued to not wake up.

Oliver felt like screaming in pain and frustration, but then he remembered he was in a library. He held back his lament. Someone, he figured, should stick to decorum.

Leaning against the oven-hot brickwork, he managed to get to his feet. The small of his back bulged against his belt, the tissue pregnant with a growing hematoma. He was going to be sore come morning, assuming he survived the next five minutes.

The fleeing nude people were followed by a dozen police officers in riot gear, charging down the hall in pursuit. Oliver stepped aside to make way, but when they reached him, a short, female officer swept his legs with a nightstick and tackled him back to the floor.

"Humph!" Oliver said.

"Don't resist!"

"What?"

He could barely hear her over the fire alarm, the growing roar of the inferno, the flash-bang grenades, his ringing ears, and the incredible snoring of the unconscious hairy man.

"I said *don't resist!*"

"Resist what?"

She secured a zip tie around his wrists. "Um. Anything, I guess."

"OK."

She was probably only talking about the current situation, but for all he knew, she could have been a Buddhist. In either case, her instructions came across as judicious advice.

Once she had him securely zip tied, the officer relaxed. She grunted, standing slowly under the weight of her riot gear, and then helped him to his feet.

"Just why in the hell did you think it was a good idea to burn down the library?"

"Oh," Oliver said, "I think you might have the wrong person."

"That's what they all say." She rolled her eyes.

"Could you fix my glasses?" he asked. "I can't tell if you're rolling your eyes."

She straightened his glasses.

"Thank you."

Upon properly seeing her for the first time, he briefly stopped breathing.

She had smooth, olive skin. She worried at her bottom lip with her perfectly white teeth in a way he thought had been the exclusive domain of the sultry models on teenage boys' bedroom wall posters. He had never considered that a person under duress might worry their lip that same way. Her bright, intelligent eyes flashed as they darted wildly up and down the hallway, searching for threats. In Oliver's humble estimation, she was somewhere in between hauntingly beautiful and knock-out gorgeous. He leaned toward the latter.

She turned him by the elbow. He noticed his hard drive on the carpet next to the sleeping, hairy man. It was partially concealed by a Fifth Edition copy of *Introduction to Organic Chemistry* by Brown. He must have dropped it when the flash-bang went off.

"Wait!" Oliver said. "Would you mind grabbing my hard drive? It's on the floor over there."

"Your hard drive?"

"Yes. It's right there," he motioned with his chin. "It has my thesis on it."

"Thesis?"

"I'm defending next month. It's about applied number theory in public key cryptography and reverse code extrapolation, and—"

She held up a hand. "You lost me."

A flaming beam crashed down on the librarian's desk, sending up a shower of sparks and cinders. The embers kindled a dozen new fires on the carpet, shelves and adjacent stacks.

The sprinkler system finally engaged, and Oliver had to shout to be heard over the racket. "You see, I theorized that since computer language is essentially binary, one could design an intelligent algorithm to reverse engineer any coding language to match a desired result, and thus code could be written across all computer languages. It's really coming along; only, a lot of my work is on that hard drive over there—"

She pressed her gloved hand to his desiccated lips to stop him from talking. She was about to say something, but her fellow officers came rushing back around the corner. "It's all about to come down!" one man shouted over his shoulder.

She stooped to pick up the drive, then, grabbing Oliver forcefully by the elbow, she hustled him down the hallway.

"What about..." he was going to mention the sleeping hairy man, but a cloud of pungent smoke rolled over them and prompted a coughing fit.

Flames licked the walls of the exit corridor, and poured through the gaps in the acoustic-tile ceiling.

A rending *crash* split the air just behind them.

Oliver craned his neck to see a red-hot steel I-beam thump down to the floor. A thick wall of noxious black smoke roiled upwards from the place where the beam landed on the industrial polypropylene carpet. A wave of intense heat roasted his back, instantly vaporizing the moisture from the sprinkler system.

He felt his eyebrows singe. He smelled burnt hair.

They ran faster, sprinting hard, and with almost no oxygen to feed his pumping muscles, the edges of Oliver's vision went grey.

The air was cremation-furnace hot. The fire ate up the atmosphere, starving him of breath. When colorful spots swam before his eyes, he knew he was soon going to pass out.

They rounded a corner, and the glass exit door came into view. They hit it together, the officer slamming her shoulder and sending it hurtling open, only to have a second steel beam crash to the floor at their heels.

Then they were in the cool night.

Oliver collapsed on the grass, gasping for breath. The officer knelt next to him, panting hard. She gently slapped his head a few times.

Too winded to speak, he looked at her questioningly.

"Your hair was on fire," she said.

He nodded his thanks and she leaned against him. Oliver realized that she, too, must be exhausted.

He cleared his voice. His throat felt raw. He spat a wad of soot onto the grass. "Are you OK?"

"I think so."

After a moment, she staggered to her feet, then bent and took him by the forearm, helping him up.

The fire alarm sounded distant and unimportant from outside, but when he looked up to the sky, a curtain of smoke obscured the stars. Distant sirens peeled through the night and echoed off the campus buildings.

"That guy in there," he motioned back to the library, "do you think he's dead?"

She was about to answer when a flaming potted palm smashed through the glass door. The now-even-more-naked hairy man, clothed only in the charred waistband of his underpants and the smoking remnants of his ski mask, sprinted out. He didn't pause to consider the shards of glass that skewered his bare feet. He simply ran, hell-for-leather, away from the conflagration.

"I think he's still alive," she said.

Oliver tried to make a comprehensive assessment of the situation. The library was burning. His laptop had been smashed. All along the horizon, columns of smoke rose skyward and the city lights twinkled with an eerie orange tint. The library riot was obviously not an isolated event.

"I'm sorry to ask this," he said, "but what, exactly, is going on?"

"Are you really not involved?" she asked, but the way she was looking at him, Oliver guessed she already knew.

"I swear."

"And you say you're a mathematician?"

"A number theorist, yes."

"Prove it."

"Why?" he asked; then, considering her proposal, "How?"

"I have this theory that you can classify campus riots by the degree path of the students involved. For instance, when STEMS students are rioting, people end up duct-taped to monuments in ways that seem to defy gravity. We might encounter tear-gas-absorbing robots. That kind of thing. Do you follow?"

"Sure."

"This riot has more of an arts and humanities feel. Would you agree that's a fair assessment?"

He thought of the nude woman with the compound bow and the Margaret Atwood tattoo. "Yes."

"So if you can prove you're a number theorist, I'll let you go."

She pulled out her phone and used it to search something up, while shielding the screen from his view.

"OK, here we go. What are the first four numbers of a standard Fibonacci sequence?"

Oliver didn't hesitate. "Zero, One, One, Two."

She produced a small knife from her pocket and cut his restraints.

"Thanks."

He rubbed his wrists.

"Don't mention it."

Oliver wanted to say something sophisticated and interesting that would potentially make for a conversation starter, but he was absolutely terrible at approaching the opposite sex. He knew, in theory, that if he made an advance and she turned him down, he would be no further behind than he was the second before they'd met. But he didn't think he could handle the rejection. It was stupid, of course, but he couldn't get around it.

She was attractive. She was obviously smart. He willed his brain to say something that would make her smile. Instead, he said, "Whelp... I should probably mosey on home."

Had he really just said "Mosey"?

God, he sucked at this.

His face flushed and he turned away, hoping she hadn't noticed.

"Oh," she said. "Well, it was a pleasure restraining you today."

"Yeah," he smiled, turning back to face her. He was hoping for redemption. He did not, however, find it.

"You too. I mean, uh... it was a pleasure being physically restrained by you. Oh my gosh... this is coming out wrong."

Hot blood rushed to his face again, and he turned away a second time. He sounded like such a dweeb!

She laughed. "Alright, see you later Copernicus."

"See you," he said.

She *was* smart! That was a really clever nickname. Why was he so cursed when it came to talking to women?

He made to leave, but she held up his hard drive.

"You forgot your thesis."

"Oh. Right."

Water dripped from one corner. She handed it over and grimaced.

"I hope you have a backup."

"I have a home server. I mean it's been a few weeks since I backed it up, but..."

He stopped, mid-sentence, and wondered if she thought he was bragging about owning a home server. The last thing he wanted was for her to consider him a braggart.

"But it's no big deal," he finished.

"Are you OK to get home?" she asked, seeming to notice for the first time just how unathletic he was. "It's a bit of a war zone out there."

He watched her gaze move from his narrow shoulders to his skinny arms. He self-consciously puffed out his chest. "I'll be OK. I play intramural badminton against the foreign exchange students every other Tuesday."

Again, he thought this might sound a bit boastful, so he added, "But they always win."

The corners of her mouth twitched. "Where do you live then?"

"Just down the road a few blocks." Oliver waved his hand in the general direction of a nice part of town that was entirely unrelated to where he lived.

The deception raised a small twinge of guilt, but he didn't imagine she would be particularly impressed by the details of his living situation. Specifically, he thought it was best not to mention that he inhabited a very cheap, one-bedroom apartment above the Old Dairy Deli and Donair—a favorite food joint amongst the inebriated, three-a.m. pizza and donair crowd. She also didn't need to know that the restaurant beneath his home was renowned for having the largest cockroaches of any food establishment within city limits.

She probably had some of the trappings of adulthood, such as a pension, and presumably a comfortable, insect-free abode. Frankly, he felt pretty juvenile.

"Well," she said, extending her hand, "good luck with your thesis."

He shook. "Good luck with the riot."

"Thanks."

They parted ways.

Ambling along the footpath that subtended the flaming library, he could not help but ruminate on the interaction. His shortcomings played out over and over in his memory, and he kept wondering if he'd just been a little bit more forward, would he have gotten her name and contact info, or might she have asked for his? He should have thanked her. He should have offered to send a glowing review to her department.

Instead, he totally whiffed it.

As a mathematician and an introvert, it was exceedingly rare for him to meet single women, let alone women as clever, and as apparently nice, as the one who'd tackled him, before pretty much saving his butt.

In the four years since he'd started his PhD, he'd been on exactly one date. He had gone to dinner with the niece of one of the post-doctoral fellows in the Math Department. Halfway through, she'd admitted she was only seeing him as a favor to her uncle. She'd spent the rest of the night checking her Instagram feed and ignoring him.

He felt cursed.

Oliver stopped walking. Leaning on a cool steel railing, he closed his eyes. He had lost his notes, his backpack, and his laptop. He'd been, more or less, in a fistfight. He'd almost died in a fire. He had screwed up a chance at a romantic encounter with a very nice person.

He wanted to feel better about the trajectory of things.

At least, he incorrectly reasoned, the evening couldn't get any worse.

From the edge of the campus, he heard a shrill voice shouting over a bullhorn. A roistering crowd answered back.

The words were unclear, but he recognized the syncopated rhythm of call and answer—a very classic 6/8 time signature. After years of studying number theory, his brain was tuned in to such patterns. The typical protest chant of What-do-we-want? -X-Pause, When-do we-want-it? -Now-Pause, could have synced perfectly with any number of classic rock songs, including "Norwegian Wood" by the Beatles, and the ever-popular "We Are the Champions" by Queen.

Turning a corner, he nearly walked face-first into a ten-foot-high plywood wall. It blocked the street that led to his apartment. It had definitely not been there when he'd made his way to the library earlier.

"What in the world?"

He stepped back.

The wall was roughly two stories high, and appeared to be continuous as far north as the Commons and as far south as Gorsebrook Park. There was one gap at the intersection of Robie and Spring Garden. As far as Oliver could tell, it was the only way in.

A naked man, with long orange hair and a scruffy beard, stood at a cement traffic barrier that filled the break in the wall. The man had what looked like an AK-47 rifle slung over his chest.

Oliver gawped.

Was this part of the same protest he'd seen in the library? The nudity angle was certainly consistent. But the gun represented a concerning development. The guy was just casually standing there, naked as a jaybird, cradling a Soviet-era assault weapon.

Where were the police?

He didn't need to look far.

Across the street from the shaggy militant stood a half dozen uniformed officers. They warily faced the wall gap, hands on their pistol butts. While they were obviously keeping an eye on the armed nudist, they did not appear intent on engagement. The place where the officers had taken position at the end of the Public Gardens was called "The Writer's Alcove," and was basically a decrepit collection of statues that had been commissioned as a gift to the city in the 1970s and had never been maintained since. Due to the accumulation of pigeon excrement over the decades, sculptures of J.D. Salinger, and Virginia Woolf now looked uniformly, more or less, like Grimace, the purple McDonald's blob monster.

Should a firefight erupt, Oliver suspected the police officers had chosen the spot due to the cover offered by the collection of bronze and concrete effigies.

He inspected the tall plywood wall and remembered a few summers before, when a protest in Seattle had turned into a downtown occupation. Was that what he was looking at?

Unsure of how stable the situation was, he decided he would ask one of the police officers. He picked up his pace, not wanting to be caught in the crossfire, should it all kick off.

He approached a smooth-faced young man.

"Excuse me."

The man tensed and looked him up and down. Oliver held up his hands and the man relaxed.

"What can I do for you, sir?"

"I'm just wondering what's going on? My apartment is in there, and..."

"Your apartment's in the zone?"

"The zone?"

"Yes sir. The student protestors have set up an autonomous protest zone in this neighborhood. They're refusing entry to anyone they consider to be part of the fascist state that refuses to remove... hold on a sec..." he turned to a colleague. "Hey, Ray, what is it they're trying to remove this time?"

"Books or something," Ray said.

"Right. They want to remove books."

"But... wouldn't removing books be kind of fascist?"

"They claim no," Ray said from the base of a Grimace-version of F. Scott Fitzgerald. "Because they're on the right side of history."

"Oh."

"Yeah." Ray sauntered over and joined them. "It kind of stuck in my craw, being called a fascist by people who are trying to remove books. But what can you do? It isn't like anyone's going to take time to reflect on these things in this day and age. We figure it's our job to stay here, and make sure nobody gets shot, while trying not to do anything embarrassing that might later be circulated as a meme. It's the department's opinion that eventually they'll run out of steam, so unless they start firing, we're to stand here and keep an eye on things."

"How do you know they'll run out of steam?"

"Well, they'll literally run out of steam pretty soon. They don't have a water supply."

"You cut off their water supply!?"

"They cut it off! They said they didn't want to share their water supply with... what did they call us, Ty?"

"Crypto-fascist meat whores," the younger officer answered.

"Right. That was it."

"So... how do I get in?" Oliver asked.

"Are you sure you *want* in?"

He thought of his home server. He definitely needed to collect it. He could get it, and then get out and find a hotel. "Yeah. My thesis is in there. It's due in a couple weeks. I've been working on it for four years."

"Just go talk to that naked fella." Ty nodded in the direction of the man with the rifle on his chest.

"What if he shoots me?"

Ty and Ray both shrugged. "Hopefully it won't come to that," Ray said.

Oliver crossed the street, keeping his hands raised in a gesture of capitulation.

"Ah. Hi."

The shaggy man squinted at him, doing a pretty good impression of a naked, extra-scrawny Clint Eastwood.

"My apartment is in there," Oliver said, pointing to the city blocks behind the barricade.

"Oh yeah?"

"Yes."

"It's inside the Vagisil Autonomous Zone?"

Oliver slowly lowered his hands.

He pinched the bridge of his nose, hoping to ward off a headache that had suddenly bloomed behind his left eye. "The... Vagisil Autonomous Zone?"

"You heard me," the naked man with the rifle said.

"Why is it called 'The Vagisil Autonomous Zone'?"

"They're our corporate sponsor. You can't pull off a major protest that includes the establishment of a self-governed and policed autonomous zone without a corporate sponsor. So, we let them put their name on our movement. They get good corporate cred for supporting a progressive cause, and we get plywood and Kalashnikovs."

"Vagisil bought you AK-47's?" Oliver asked.

"If they didn't we'd call them out for being fascist and anti-progressive, and they'd lose business. Failure to support progressive causes like ours is absolute marketing poison. Especially for their target demographic. And think of all the advertising they're getting. By midnight tonight, hashtag Vagisil Autonomous Zone will be trending on Twit, I mean X! Then everyone will have Vagisil on the brain. Sales will sky-rocket."

"I see," Oliver said, though the logic-pretzel one would have to twist oneself into in order to actually *see*, was insurmountable. Ultimately, though, it was really someone else's problem.

"Listen, would you mind letting me through? It's been kind of a long day, and I have a headache."

"First, tell me this..." The naked man with the rifle held the firearm up a little higher on his chest. "Are you a believer in the cause?"

"Umm..."

"Do you believe that our bookshelves need to be de-carnivorized, man? Do you support that? Or are you against us?"

"De-carnivorized?"

"History, man... history was written by meat eaters, bro. That ain't history. That's agenda. That's propaganda. That's the purposeful exclusion of historical vegan voices! That's fascism, dude!"

The naked man with the rifle seemed to be getting upset. Oliver didn't like the idea of an upset naked man with a rifle. It seemed unlikely that such a situation would lead to anything positive.

"I... I study number theory," he said, as though his professional devotion to mathematics might somehow excuse his inability to sympathize with whatever it was the naked man with the rifle was talking about.

The naked man huffed, and shook his head. His level of agitation increased. His right eye twitched. "Numbers, man? *Numbers?* Numbers are, like, a social construct designed to oppress vegans, who tend to veer toward the creative arts. Did you know that the Roman numeral for five is a V because it represents the pits in the ground where the centurions would throw vegans who refused to eat beef? Five vegans in each pit."

"That's not true," Oliver interjected. "The *V* actually represents the V-shaped space between your thumb and forefinger when you hold all five fingers up. See?" Oliver extended his fingers, and pointed at the V-shaped space.

The naked man's eyes went wide, and he began to raise the rifle. With an index finger curled tightly around the trigger the naked man was not, Oliver couldn't help but notice, practicing safe firearm discipline.

"That's bullshit, man! You're a fascist! You're a fascist meat-whore!"

Oliver understood he was about to be murdered over the brief history lesson he'd tried to share. He closed his eyes in preparation for the shot, but then a very calm, very deep voice made itself known.

"Is this man trying to get inside?"

Oliver opened his eyes. A tall, mustached man wearing a trench coat over a shirt and tie, now stood at his side.

The naked man with the rifle lowered the Kalashnikov.

"He's a fascist..." the naked man said, though the way he said it was more of a question than a statement. "He... does stuff with numbers."

"Do you live in there?" the man asked Oliver.

"Yes, sir."

Trench Coat flashed a badge on his belt to the naked gatekeeper. "Detective John Jennings. This young man needs to get to his home. Could you please let him in?"

The naked man lowered his head. He looked ashamed of himself, and stepped aside without further objection.

"Son," the detective said to Oliver, "if I were you, I'd grab your essentials and come straight back out. Let things settle in there for a day or two, you understand?"

"Yes sir," Oliver said. "I'll do just that."

"If you'd like, I can wait here." The detective pointed across the street. "I'll wait over there by those statues."

Bizarre as it was, it occurred to Oliver that if Detective Jennings were to walk away, the armed naked man would most likely shoot him in the back. He was certain that Detective Jennings also knew that that was what would happen. And that the detective knew that Oliver knew.

Oliver couldn't explain it, and he didn't want to push his luck by asking questions, so he nodded his thanks and walked around the barrier and into the Vagisil Autonomous Zone.

He jogged double-time down Spring Garden Road, and compiled a mental list of the things he would have to take. First and foremost was the backup drive from his home server. Then, of course, he would need some underwear and socks, and a few clean shirts. Then came a toothbrush, toothpaste and toiletries. His backpack was long gone, lost in the library fire, but he kept a carry-on roller bag at the back of his hallway closet. He would stuff everything inside and then hightail it. He had six hundred dollars in his bank account. He could stay in a hotel for a few nights.

From somewhere behind him a woman shouted. Oliver turned, but only saw the naked gatekeeper, whose face had turned skyward, and who stood at ease, arms by his side. He didn't blink. He looked like a man upon whom a great truth of the universe had just been bestowed. The guy was creepy as hell.

Beyond the naked gatekeeper, Oliver saw that Detective Jennings had joined the other police officers in the literary alcove. He'd taken a spot under one of the only non-excrement-deformed statues—a tall bronze sculpture of George Orwell.

Oliver waved, and the detective waved back. There was something so unusual about the man—specifically about his voice and the way it had placated the scruffy gatekeeper. It reminded Oliver of the Jedi mind trick.

The autonomous zone might have been the set for a film about a dystopian, post-apocalyptic future. All the windows lining the street had been smashed. Graffiti tags marked every building. Groups of naked and nearly naked young people staggered between smoldering, burned-out vehicles.

He kept to the shadows as much as possible. "Get in, get out," he whispered. "In and out."

Anxiety came naturally to Oliver, and the close call with the naked rifleman had him on edge. Making his way deeper and deeper into his shattered neighborhood, his breath tightened. His mouth was dry and wouldn't make any spit, leaving the coppery taste of adrenaline to mix with smoke and ash.

"In and out," he hoarsely whispered. "In and out." It was his new mantra.

The further he walked, the thicker and hazier the atmosphere became. Muffled shouts and screams pierced the night, punctuated with the occasional *crash* of shattering glass. From somewhere further into the zone, the rat-a-tat thump of successive gunshots rang out and echoed between buildings, followed by a cheer. Oliver turned to see if the police would be drawn by the small arms fire, but his view of the gate was obscured by smoke.

He was almost home when a naked woman with dreadlocks turned a corner and bumped into him.

"Sorry," Oliver said, trying very hard to avert his eyes.

"That's OK, man," she said in a gruff smoker's voice. "It's cool."

Since she was alone, and didn't seem particularly unfriendly, Oliver took a chance and asked, "Just out of curiosity, why is everyone naked?"

She gave him a look of disgust one might reserve for a person caught him in the act of public defecation. Just then, however, a man on the other side of the road squatted and began defecating next to an overturned police cruiser. The naked woman with dreadlocks did not give the public defecator the same look of disgust.

"It's about the animals, man. Like, animal byproducts are used to make clothing dude. How do you not know that?!"

"You mean... like leather?" Oliver asked. "Because couldn't you just not wear stuff made out of—"

"Wait. Are you some kind of fascist?" she asked.

"No, no... not a fascist," Oliver said quickly.

"That's exactly what a fascist would say."

"I'm not a fascist. Honest. I just thought maybe everyone was using the nudity angle to... I don't know, garner more attention or something, I guess."

Her eyes popped. She turned and shouted, "Fascist! I've got a fascist here!"

The man who had just finished defecating next to the police cruiser jogged in their direction, clearly ready for a fight, now that his excretory business had been tended to.

Oliver, desperate to avoid another fight—especially one with a public defecator who hadn't washed his hands—sprinted toward his apartment, darting down a side street. The defecator momentarily pursued, only to cry out in pain and hobble to the nearest curb. Oliver slowed, turning to watch the defecator extract a long sliver of glass from the sole of his foot. The man had clearly failed to recognize the inherent dangers of running nude in riot zones.

When he reached the Old Dairy Deli and Donair building, Oliver was dismayed to discover that the restaurant, and by extension his second-floor apartment, had been reduced to a smoking heap of embers. The fire must have been intense, as even the building's frame had collapsed. Charred beams stuck out of the rubble at odd angles.

"It's... gone," he said aloud.

The weight of his situation hit him like a fist in the belly. He sat on the curb and brought his hands to his face.

"Oh man," he said. "Oh man, oh man."

The corner of the hard drive dug into his hip, and he pulled it from his pocket. The sodden, dented device was his only hope for recovering the fruits of his last four years of labor. If he couldn't recover the program, that was it. No doctoral degree. No travel. No exciting job. No friends.

"Dang it!" He pinched the bridge of his nose again. The headache was unrelenting.

He tried to imagine what advice his father might have offered. His dad would have told him to take a deep breath, and to gather his thoughts.

He took a deep breath. He gathered his thoughts.

After a minute of intensive thought-gathering, he decided that a pragmatic approach was his best hope. Emotional thinking would get him nowhere.

He systematically thought through his problems.

First, there was the immediate issue. The Vagisil Autonomous Zone was not safe. He had to leave.

After that, he could deal with the next most pressing problem. He would find a place to stay.

Then, with those things dealt with, he could deal with the thesis. He could search computer repair and hard drive recovery from his phone.

It was a simple plan, but he felt a little better.

He got to his feet, feeling foolish for having sat down in the first place, and took stock. He'd lost a lot, but he hadn't lost everything.

He had his walking sneakers. That was good. Sneakers alone meant he was better off than roughly one-seventh of the world's population.

He wore a pair of blue jeans and a plaid shirt. They weren't his favorite clothes, but since the rest of his wardrobe had been incinerated along with all his other earthly possessions, they would have to do.

He had the hard drive, of course. Yes, it was a little beat up and a bit wet. Regardless, he figured there was still hope. He had seen a *Case Files* episode, wherein the crime scene investigators were able to recover data off a hard drive they'd retrieved from a house fire. Surely, if the technology existed for that scenario, it stood to reason that someone could work with a drive that had suffered some moisture and a few bumps.

He patted his pockets. He still had his phone. That was good. He inspected it and discovered it only had twenty percent of its battery power remaining. That was less good, but it could be worse. Phone chargers weren't exactly a rare commodity.

He pulled his wallet from his back pocket. There were two twenty-dollar bills, along with his Visa card, his debit card and his driver's license.

He was going to be OK. Losing the laptop and the apartment was a setback, but it wasn't the end of the world. He'd been planning to leave for greener pastures anyway. Maybe, when all things were considered, this would end up being a good thing. Maybe it would give him the impetus he needed to make the move.

A young man wearing a Speedo bathing suit and a ball cap with a stick-on label that read "Vagisil Autonomous Zone Official Peacekeeper," snatched the wallet from his hand. Oliver hadn't seen him approaching.

"Hey!"

"There's a fine for wearing clothes in the VAZ, bruh," the man informed him. "It's..." he checked Oliver's wallet and retrieved the two bills, "forty bucks."

A man and a young woman, also sporting makeshift peacekeeper hats, approached.

"Hey," Oliver said, "I think this guy is trying to rob me!"

They snickered. The first peacekeeper handed the other man one of the twenties.

"I need that," Oliver said. "My home just burned down."

"You don't need money," the second man said. "Money's just a social construct to repress the disenfranchised."

"Then why do you need it?"

"Because we're disenfranchised," the young woman said. She rolled her eyes as though this were the most obvious fact in the known universe.

"Did your home burn down too?"

"This isn't your home, bruh," the man in the Speedo said. "This is the unceded territory of a proud Mic Mac tribe. The truth is that home is just a social—"

"Yeah, right," Oliver said, holding up his palms in surrender. "Got it."

The mock indignation of the protestors was demoralizing and exhausting. To argue was pointless. They only understood binary. Black and white. One and zero. With us or against us.

They were so high on their sense of moral superiority that there was no point in trying to forge an inroad. Their egos were propped up by everyone's newfound fear of causing offense. Their excitement over the power they wielded, in Oliver's opinion anyway, made them more than a little bit insufferable.

Did they all really believe in the de-carnivorization of bookshelves, whatever that meant? Or, was it possible—perhaps even probable—that many of them were just stuck in an addictive loop of positive social media feedback that encouraged them to join such bandwagons?

"Look. I'm out of here. Just give me my wallet."

Oliver held out his hand.

"I'm not sure I like your attitude," the man in the Speedo said, sliding Oliver's driver's license out of the card slot and inspecting it, "Mr. Bell."

"Hey, Ronnie, is that wallet made of leather? Like leather, from an innocent animal?" The young woman's eyes went wide. "Do you know how offensive that is to me?"

Oliver imagined it was not at all offensive to her, since she must know that leather wallets exist. He chose not to say anything, however, because he was being pragmatic.

"Fascists like you are the scum of the earth," Ronnie said, his tone burdened with outrage. He hurled Oliver's wallet into the smoking ruin of his home.

Oliver could take no more. The pragmatic approach to this situation, he knew, was to escape it. In and out. Wasn't that his mantra?

He felt incredibly stupid for wasting so much time beside the smoldering remains of his home. He should have turned on his heel and made for an exit right away.

Ignoring the shouted insults of the trio of peacekeepers, he headed back toward the gate. He would have to find a hotel—preferably one that would allow him to recite his credit card from memory, now that his wallet was being roasted by the red-hot remains of his living quarters.

He was careful to avoid any and all naked arts majors. He ducked into buildings, and hid behind dumpsters to dodge the roving groups of disenfranchised and outraged vegans.

At one point he had to circumvent a group of four naked protestors who were spreading a layer of topsoil less than an inch thick on the asphalt in front of the burnt husk of a McDonalds. He squinted to read the cardboard sign they had erected. It read "Community Vegetable Garden."

Picking his way back through the rubble to the entrance of the Vagisil Autonomous Zone, Oliver was surprised to arrive at the gate and find no trace of the naked man with the Kalashnikov, or anyone else.

At least something was going his way. He walked briskly through the exit and turned north, toward Quinpool, where he hoped the Atlantica Hotel might have a vacancy.

A terrific crash came from the alcove across the street.

He whipped around, expecting to see an automobile accident in progress, but instead saw a cloud of dust rising from the statue garden.

Somebody screamed.

A panicked crowd dispersed in every direction and uniformed police officers took chase. When the dust settled, it was apparent that one of the statues had been toppled. George Orwell was down.

A naked protestor, looking over his shoulder as he fled the scene, ran square into Oliver and they both went sprawling.

The man had matted blonde hair tied back in a ponytail. His eyes were wild. He tried to stand but when he did, he wobbled, winced, and sat back down. Oliver suspected a broken ankle.

He offered the ponytail man a hand and helped him sit up on the cement traffic barrier.

"What's going on over there?" he asked, nodding toward the alcove.

"We brought down the Orwell statue," the man said, trying to adjust his ponytail. "Only it landed on some cop."

Oliver immediately thought of Detective Jennings. "Oh God. Is he OK?"

"I don't think so, dude."

Oliver jogged across the street. To his dismay, Detective John Jennings, the nice man with the mustache and the gentle voice, lay pinned under the mammoth bronze effigy.

"Detective Jennings?" Oliver said, crouching.

The detective opened his eyes and locked them on Oliver.

It was glaringly obvious that Detective Jennings was in a bad state. For some strange reason that might have made sense in the 1970s, the sculptor had chosen to portray Mr. Orwell drinking from a coffee mug. The writer's pointy elbow had penetrated deep into the detective's chest. A pool of blood was quickly expanding across the paving stones.

Jennings reached out with his right hand, offering Oliver a small cardboard rectangle. "Take it," he whispered. Blood bubbled from under his mustache.

Oliver grabbed his phone from his pocket. He was going to call 911. But the detective weakly slapped the phone down and held up the card.

"Mayhem," the detective whispered. More blood dribbled down his chin.

"Right?" Oliver said, trying to sound calm despite feeling sick to his stomach. "It's pretty nuts!"

He grabbed the statue by the head, and squatting, strained to lift it.

"Orwell is too heavy," he said.

"That attitude," the detective sputtered, "is what got us into this mess."

John Jennings closed his eyes, and died.

"Oh no," Oliver said. He put a hand on the man's shoulder and gave it a gentle shake. "Detective? Uh… Mr. Jennings?"

Oliver stopped moving. Something was happening. Something weird.

A warm, fizzy sensation ran up his back. His arms and legs tingled, and his vision blurred. A sparkler went off in his brain, sending brilliant glimmers cascading across his vision. He thought he might faint, but then the feeling passed just as quickly as it had come on. He shook his head. "I'm in shock," he said. "This must be what shock feels like."

He stood, tucking the small card into the pocket of his pants. He turned to see if there were any nearby emergency responders. Earlier, he had seen a half dozen police officers in the statue garden. Where were they? Where were the paramedics? He realized with horror that he was alone.

He dialed 911. He waited for the call to connect. After a second he got a busy signal.

"Frig!"

He felt a hand on his shoulder and was roughly pulled around. A police officer pointed a pistol at his head.

"Give me the code, and give me the charm."

"I'm sorry?" Oliver said, so surprised that he didn't have time to be terrified.

"The code and the charm! Now!"

Oliver had no idea what he was talking about. He shrugged and cocked an eyebrow. "Look, Detective Jennings is in a bad way, and..."

"The code and the charm!"

"I don't know what..."

"Fine," the man said.

He thumbed off the safety and was clearly making to pull the trigger when a ferocious voice bellowed from behind the downed statue.

"Die, Legion bastard!"

A second man charged from the shadows. He wore army pants and a sleeveless T-shirt. A delicate silver chain dangled around his neck. His muscles bulged. What struck Oliver most, was that the man was a spitting image of Dwayne "The Rock" Johnson.

The hulking stranger jumped over the downed Orwell statue. At the apex of his impressive arc, he swung a baseball bat directly into the face of Oliver's would-be murderer.

The impact sounded like a coconut being dropped onto pavement from a sixth-story balcony.

The gunman crumpled in a heap.

Oliver stared at the carnage in horror. The man's face had been thoroughly caved in. Lying on his back, his bulging eyes blinked crazily, pointing at one another across the inverted bridge of what used to be a nose. His legs kicked spastically while his arms hammered at the pavement, like those of a child in the throes of a temper tantrum. Blood fountained from the man's forehead, ruining the uniform and forming an expanding puddle that Oliver crazily thought would soon be big enough for a duck to swim around in.

"Whoa!" he said. "Oh... holy hell!"

He turned away, covering his mouth, trying not to upchuck.

His giant muscle-bound savior was up from the ground as quick as lightning. He kicked the thrashing corpse, then stooped, swiping the handgun from the ground before smoothly stuffing it into the waistband of his pants.

He turned to Oliver. "I'm giving you an injection," he said. "It will make you sleepy."

"*What?*"

"An injection."

"Like... a lethal injection?"

The big man smiled and appeared to be genuinely amused. His teeth were shockingly white. "No. It will make you sleepy."

Oliver hated drugs. Even more so, the idea of being drugged by a homicidal stranger. Nothing good would ever come of such a thing. He certainly didn't want an injection that would make him sleepy. That was serial killer stuff.

"What if I resist?" he asked, staring at the baseball bat tucked under the giant man's arm.

"I wouldn't."

Oliver offered his arm, and the man gripped it in an enormous, calloused hand. The big man tore open an alcohol swab with his teeth and used it to clean a patch of skin. He tossed the alcohol swab aside, and fumbled in the cargo pocket of his army pants.

"Just a sec," he said.

"Take your time."

The brute produced a syringe. It was tiny in his big mitt.

"I'm not very good at this, so it might sting. Sorry."

He used his mouth to uncap the needle, before gently sliding it into a vein and depressing the plunger. He then recapped the needle and pocketed it.

"Wouldn't want anyone to step on it," he said.

The giant crouched to face Oliver. Oliver got the feeling the man was waiting for something.

"One can't be too careful," Oliver said.

His voice sounded hollow.

He felt his neck muscles relaxing, and he looked down and eyed the horribly disfigured corpse at his feet. He felt detached.

He had the overwhelming sensation that this was all meant to be.

"Will I vomit?" he asked.

"You'd better not," the big man said.

The drugs were quick. He was overcome by weariness.

"I'd better... sit," he said. He felt almost too tired to talk.

He absently wondered if the big man had adjusted the dose for himself and failed to account for the fact that Oliver was roughly one-third his body weight.

"Oh well," he said to himself aloud.

He was dizzy. He made to grab the Orwell statue, but before he could the big man lifted him as easily as one might lift a bag of groceries. He threw Oliver over his shoulder, and jogged into the darkness of the public garden.

A moment later, Oliver Bell was dreaming about numbers.

Two

THE GREAT BALANCE

Oliver woke up with a headache for the ages. His tongue felt like sandpaper, and his eyeballs battered in concrete dust and deep-fried.

Once, during his freshman year, in what would prove to be his only attempt to reinvent himself as an enthusiastic bon vivant, Oliver went to a dorm party. He bought a case of beer for the occasion, which he fully intended on sharing with the other young people who lived in his residence. Despite his social plans, however, he was shy and self-conscious. To fill the void of conversation directed his way, he took nervous drink after nervous drink, until, to his surprise, he awoke on the sidewalk the following afternoon, wearing a lampshade on his head.

This felt worse than that.

Oliver tried to calculate exactly how much worse. He was a mathematician, after all, and he figured he should be able to come up with a number. Carefully weighing variables such as headache intensity and oral mucosal surface desiccation, he settled on twenty-seven point six-six-six (repeating) times worse.

Mottled sunlight flashed against his eyelids, the dancing beams skewering his brain like red-hot knives. When he tried to move his hand to shade himself, he found his arm was stuck. Slowly and methodically, he ventured to open his right eyelid.

His glasses were missing and the world was a blurry smear, but he nonetheless perceived a green foliage canopy beneath a brilliant cobalt sky.

In Halifax, plants had yet to bud. Spring had been cold. He was, therefore, elsewhere.

As his right eye strained to focus, he purposefully directed his gaze toward his right wrist, which, as it turned out, had been wrapped in galvanized chain.

He furrowed his brow, causing tremendous pain to cascade through his head.

Focusing harder now, he followed the length of chain from his wrist and discovered that the other end appeared to be fixed around an elm tree.

There was no possible scenario in which this was a good development.

When Oliver had trouble sleeping, he would often listen to a true-crime podcast on low volume. He found the background voices calming. Having just now realized that he was chained to a tree, however, he couldn't help but reflect on the wide variety of serial killers who would bind their victims before dispatching them. He wondered if he himself was scheduled for termination at the hands of such a lunatic.

His instinct was to panic, but when he tried, he felt far too terrible to do it effectively. More gentle evaluation and quiet introspection was apparently in order.

The headache thrummed between his temples. No matter what else happened, he vowed to keep all movement slow and methodical. Any quick action, he guessed, might cause his brain to explode.

He closed his right eyelid again and very slowly, ever so methodically, began the delicate task of turning his head to the left. Then, like the centuries-abandoned rusted hinges on the hatch of an ironclad ship in a Clive Cussler novel, he pried his left eyelid open.

His left wrist was also wound in chain. A heavy-duty padlock affixed two thick links. This chain led to a different tree. He believed it was a silver maple. It was hard to say for certain without his glasses.

He tested both his legs, and felt heavy, hot metal against his skin.

Someone had bound him in a spread-eagle position.

A cool breeze raised a rash of gooseflesh. This was distressing for the fact that he perceived the breeze all over, and without any dampened intensity.

He was naked.

The evidence was compiling. His situation was definitely not good, but he reassured himself that things could always be worse. Then he spent almost a full minute trying to guess how, exactly, things could be worse, until he settled on the fact that it could be raining.

He tried to panic again. Again, his headache intensified, so he stopped panicking.

He closed his left eye and felt some relief. Perhaps it would be best to never open his eyes again.

Who had done this to him, and to what end? He remembered the big man with the baseball bat, who had injected him with some kind of sedative. The man didn't strike him as the type of person who would protest books written by meat-eaters. He didn't strike Oliver as a vegan at all, though, of course, Oliver had only spoken to him for a minute. Still, he couldn't even begin to calculate the sheer volume of plant-based protein one would have to consume to build such a physique.

He decided his confinement was most likely unrelated to the protests and riots. Which left motives such as "murder spree" on the table.

Being murdered, now that he thought about it, would at least mark the end of his headache.

He lay still, half-wishing for death, trying not to hear the chirping birds, and trying desperately not to hear the gentle breeze through the trees. He tried not to feel the soft grass against his bare skin, and especially tried not to wonder why he was naked. More than anything, he tried not to remember what had happened to his apartment, and his thesis.

When it became obvious that he was going to have to suffer through his current circumstances, he cleared his throat and tried to get his captor's attention. He needed water. He was resigned to the idea that he was probably going to die, but he hoped it wouldn't have to be from kidney failure.

"Hmmph," Oliver said.

He felt a tickle in his mouth, and opened it to allow a fat black ant to crawl out.

"Hmmmmph!" he said, louder this time.

"Oh, are you waking up, hon?" a woman asked in a sweet southern drawl.

She sounded pretty but Oliver dared not open his eyes to confirm this. He'd opened them before, and had learned his lesson. To see was to suffer. Even in distress, he was a quick study.

"You look a little parched. Why don't I get you something to drink."

Oliver nodded slowly and tried to thank her, only managing, "Hmph hoo."

"I'm going to pour just a little capful of water over your lips, OK? I don't want you to choke."

Oliver nodded, and as he did so, she poured the water. It went up his right nostril.

"Hmph!" he exclaimed.

"I'm sorry, hon," she said. "I wasn't expecting you to nod like that. Let's try again, shall we?"

The lukewarm water cascaded over his lips and teeth and seemed to evaporate entirely before getting anywhere near his throat.

"Ohh," he said, meaning more.

"I can give you a little more, but not too much. I don't want to upset your tummy. You understand?"

Tummy?

She poured another capful into his mouth. The relief of moisture against his parched throat was incredible.

"Thanks," he said.

"You can open your eyes, darling."

"I'm really not sure I can," Oliver said. "I tried earlier. It didn't work out very well."

"Just a sec," the woman said. He heard her walk away.

He was alone again. He knew he should be trying to escape. But the woman with the water had a nice voice. She didn't sound like a serial killer. Of course, if serial killers sounded like serial killers, there wouldn't be any serial killers, since the police could just round up anybody who sounded like one.

He heard footsteps again.

She had returned. She used a wet cloth to wipe the sand and dirt out of his eyes.

He asked for his glasses. When she fitted them on his face, he blinked a few times to focus and then fixed his eyes on her.

Dappled sunlight danced across her mocha skin. Her impish smile held no trace of unkindness. She appeared at once regal and humble, a fantastical princess secretly mixing it up with the common folk. Her countenance—her nearly angelic brightness—betrayed maternal concern. The way her lip curled—the slight downturn of her eyes—the way her thumb worried the cloth in her hand—every gesture spoke of empathy and grace. She was, perhaps, the most beautiful human being Oliver had ever seen.

Her long hair was tied back in a ponytail. She wore brightly patterned yoga pants and a grey tank top that showed off her slim, athletic build. Oliver quickly felt ashamed of his nakedness.

He knew not to judge a book by its cover. But every instinct he had told him that she was good. Still, her relaxed nature raised a concerning question.

"In the movies, when the kidnapped person sees their captor's face, it usually means they're about to be killed," he said.

"Darlin'," she knelt next to him and offered another capful of water, "I am very much hoping it doesn't come to that."

She leaned in close and whispered, "I have a pretty good feeling about you."

"I, on the other hand, fully expect to smash your head in."

Oliver recognized the voice from the previous evening.

He had to crane his neck to an extreme angle—such that his forehead was nearly touching the ground—in order to see an upside-down version of the brute, the same muscle-bound man who had drugged and abducted him. The man still carried the wooden baseball bat.

Oliver, having watched hundreds of episodes of *Law and Order*, figured holding onto a murder weapon was just about the absolute worst thing you could do with it. He wasn't about to say anything, though. He'd seen the big man in action.

His captor casually swung the bat in swift figure eights. He wore the same khaki army pants, but now sported a white Bass Pro T-shirt that was stretched taught over his bulging pectorals and biceps. The muscles in his right arm twitched rhythmically as he swung the Louisville Slugger round and round.

"Would you mind making it quick, please?" Oliver asked. "And maybe notify my mother?"

"You aren't going to beg for your life?" the big man asked.

"Would it do any good?"

"No."

"Well, then I guess I'll skip that part."

"Come on now, Teddy," the woman said, "there's no need to terrify the poor guy."

"Teddy?" Oliver asked.

"This is Teddy, and I'm Emma," the woman said. "May we ask your name?"

"Oliver," Oliver said.

"See, Teddy? He's going to tell us the truth. Aren't you, Oliver?"

"How did you know I was telling the truth?"

"Your name's written on the waistband of your underpants, hot shot," Teddy said.

Oliver blushed. He felt the need to explain why his name had been written on the tag of his undershorts. Especially in front of Emma. For the first time, he realized that his devotion to pragmatism could make him appear quite immature to the opposite sex.

"We have... Well, we *had* a shared washer-dryer in my building," he explained. "Sometimes the laundry would get mixed up. I didn't want someone inadvertently making off with my boxer briefs."

In the silence that ensued, he wondered how best to broach the subject of his nudity. A direct approach was probably the ticket. "Since we're on the topic of my underwear, would you mind helping me put them back on? I'd prefer to die clothed, if it's all the same to you guys. And this is a little embarrassing."

With the practiced professionalism of a scrub nurse, Emma covered his crotch with the cloth she'd used to wipe his eyes. "Soon, Hon. We just need you to answer a few questions. It's very important."

Teddy ambled around so Oliver could plainly see him. "Oliver, did you kill the man under the statue?"

Oliver jolted. Did *they* think *he* was a killer? That would be quite ironic.

"Detective Jennings? No... I tried to help him."

"Who killed him then?"

"The rioters, I think. It sounded like it was an accident."

"I saw you speaking with him."

"Yes."

"What did he say?"

Oliver tried to think, which only caused the pulsating orb of throbbing pain to intensify between his eyes.

"He said something about chaos," Oliver said.

Teddy stiffened.

"And...uh...something about George Orwell."

"Did he give you anything?"

Oliver remembered the card.

"Yeah," he said. "It's in the pocket of my jeans."

Teddy strode back out of Oliver's line of sight. A car door opened somewhere nearby.

"Do you need some more water?" Emma asked.

"Please."

Before Emma could bring the water to his lips, however, there was a crash from behind. A moment later, Teddy reappeared, holding up metal fragments for him to see.

"You are a liar!" he exclaimed. The big man was red in the face.

Oliver squinted. He could make out the word "Hitachi" on the dangling protective housing that had once cocooned his hard drive.

His heart sank. His brain short-circuited, sending rapid-fire waves of confused emotion ricocheting around his skull. He felt a jumbled mess of grief, terror, misery, and to his great surprise, a small measure of relief. Whatever else this meant, one thing was for certain—the thesis defense wasn't happening.

He took a breath and silently counted off several decimal points of pi until he felt some semblance of control returning. All that work. *Gone.*

If he could avoid crying in front of his captors, he would consider it a small victory.

"Did you just smash my hard drive?" he asked.

"Yes," Teddy said.

"It had my thesis on it."

"Your thesis?" Emma asked.

"I was supposed to defend next month. Two and a half years I spent working on that."

"But you said the detective gave it to you," Teddy said, looking almost concerned, and ever-so-slightly ashen.

"The business card. He gave me the business card in the other pocket."

"Oh," Teddy said.

"You must have made a backup copy," Emma offered helpfully.

"It was on my home server."

"Well, that's good, then," Teddy said. "All is not lost after all."

Oliver shook his head. "It was incinerated last night, when the militant wing of the vegan movement overthrew a few city blocks, renamed the area 'The Vagisil Autonomous Zone' and decided to burn down The Old Dairy Deli and Donair, presumably to protest cheese."

Emma knelt beside him and rested her palm on his shoulder. The tears he'd felt threatening to overspill receded. He wasn't sure if it was her touch, or his own severe dehydration that kept him from crying, but he felt stronger for holding back the waterworks.

"This won't be much consolation right now," she said, "but things generally happen for a reason."

"Be careful," Teddy warned her.

"He's not going to hurt me—are you, Oliver?"

He couldn't imagine hurting something so beautiful. It would be like setting fire to the Mona Lisa.

"I don't think I could if I wanted to," he said, rattling the chains on his wrists to emphasize the point.

Teddy strode out of sight and returned with the rectangular card Detective Jennings had handed to Oliver.

"Is this it?"

"Yes."

Teddy leaned the baseball bat against the trunk of the elm tree, and gripped the card in both hands. He grunted, trying to tear it. The card did not yield.

"What the hell?" Oliver asked. "Why isn't it ripping?"

The big man then produced a silver Zippo from his pocket, and flicked it. He held the card over the flame, but it didn't light.

"Interesting," he said, putting the lighter away.

Emma took the card and inspected it. "Oh my!"

"What's going on?" Oliver asked, but they were both ignoring him, staring meaningfully into one another's eyes.

"We're going to have to do it," Teddy said. "If there's any chance whatsoever that it's him, we can end this now."

"No!" Emma said. "Then we're no better than Legion. He could be a host. He could be what they were after. We don't even know if they carry charms. We don't even know if he *can* come here! We don't do it if we aren't certain. We talked about this! Do you *think* it's really him? Be honest."

"He said it himself," Teddy protested. "Chaos."

"Look at him!" she exclaimed. "He's practically a child, for God's sake!"

"He's a man-child at best," Teddy said, dismissively waving a hand, but Emma's eyes flashed.

"No, Teddy. Not yet!"

Oliver was listening intently, hoping for a clue as to what was happening, and why he'd been kidnapped, undressed, and bound to deciduous trees. He was able to deduce that it would probably be better for his health if Emma were to win the argument.

"Guys," Oliver said, "what's going on?"

They continued to ignore him, which he took to be a bad sign.

Thinking back on the plotline from *Silence of the Lambs*, he remembered it was always best to try to humanize oneself to one's captors.

While they argued back and forth, and Oliver considered possible ways to humanize himself to his captors, a plump horsefly landed on his thigh and began creeping its way toward his scrotum. The fly paused for a moment, rubbed its back feet together, and then continued its northward march.

"Ahh!"

Casually, in mid-conversation, Teddy stooped to pick up the baseball bat. Without so much as an off-the-cuff glance, he swung it, one-handed, at Oliver's groin, swiping the fly off his skin and just brushing the hair on his thigh.

Despite his current predicament, Oliver couldn't help but marvel at the skillful fluidity of that swing. What did it say about Teddy? Had he been a circus performer before his kidnapping career? A professional baseball player? Or was he well-practiced with a bat for a different, scarier reason?

"How'd you do that?"

Emma held up her index finger, in a "give us a minute" gesture one would typically reserve for a toddler. Oliver refocused on their discussion.

"We have to see the old man," she said to Teddy.

"What old man?" Oliver asked, trying very much to sound like a relatable human being. Once again, he was ignored.

Teddy looked like he was going to protest, but then bit his lip and nodded. When he returned to the car, Emma knelt next to Oliver.

"You obviously have some questions," she said. "I'll answer what I can."

Oliver specifically had twenty-five questions he would have liked answered, with a new one cropping up, on average, every forty seconds. These included "Where are we? Why are we here? What's happening to me?" and, of course, "What's with the chains?"

But he decided to start with what he considered to be the most pressing of the bunch. "Why am I naked?"

"For our safety."

"I don't think my underpants posed a threat."

She smiled. "You'd be surprised."

Oliver furrowed his brow. The act caused him great pain, but a horrible thought had come to mind. "Does that mean I pooped my pants?"

Emma said nothing, only rolled her eyes.

"Did I poop my pants?!" he asked again, the sheer awfulness of the notion raising his voice an octave.

"No," Emma said, "OK?"

"OK," Oliver said, trying to calm himself.

"Anything else?"

"Where are we?"

"Connecticut."

Connecticut was over a thousand kilometers from his home in Nova Scotia.

"Connecticut! How long was I out?"

She checked her watch. "About thirty hours."

That explained the dehydration.

"How did we get across the border?"

"We drove."

"You drove across an international border in the middle of a pandemic with a naked man with no passport in the trunk of your car?"

"Oh no," she smiled, "it's a minivan. And you were in the back seat."

Oliver tried to imagine the scenario, and found that he couldn't.

"Aren't you wondering why you're here?"

"Now that you mention it..."

A warm smile creased the corners of her eyes. "It's complicated."

"I figured as much."

"Be patient, OK?" she said.

She placed a cool hand on his forehead, and he felt a little better.

Oliver remembered his encounter with the picturesque police officer in the library. "Resist nothing," he said to himself.

"Good plan," Emma said.

Teddy returned with a key and started opening the padlocks that secured the tight coils of chains around Oliver's wrists. He moved to the ankle chains, and hunched to unlock them. Waggling a warning finger at Oliver, he said, "Don't run."

"I don't think I can move."

"Good."

The big man helped him to his feet. For a moment, Oliver thought he was going to fall over. His joints had stiffened and pins and needles numbed his hands and feet. He stretched awkwardly, feeling hot blood rush to his extremities.

Teddy handed him his boxer shorts, which he put on slowly, so as not to fall down. His enormous captor then helped him with his jeans and plaid shirt.

"I have some good news and some bad news," Teddy said as Oliver rubbed at his wrists. "The good news is, we're not going to kill you yet."

"The way you said 'yet' kind of made that sound like bad news."

"I'm sorry."

"So then what's the bad news?"

"The bad news is we think you might have inadvertently been possessed by a powerful demonic entity known as 'Amon,' or 'Chaos,' and that means we're going to have to keep you restrained somehow."

Oliver considered this.

His captors were likely suffering from a specific type of shared psychosis he'd once read about, called "Folie à deux," wherein two people share a complex delusion. The classic example of shared psychosis was the case of Bridget Cleary. Her husband, Michael Cleary, was convinced that she had been possessed by fairies. Her friends and family were then similarly convinced, and she was tortured and ultimately burned to death. No fairies, Oliver remembered, were forthcoming.

Despite having made his amateur diagnosis, he had more pressing issues to address. "Can I use the washroom? It's been thirty hours."

Teddy led him across what turned out to be an empty campground.

Oliver he had been chained up no more than ten feet from the dirt road that led between the campsites. His mathematical mind couldn't help but question the thought processes of his abductors. Since they had been willing to take such a massive risk of being observed, would their propensity for risk-taking lend him a chance to escape?

Strangely, however, the thought of escape was not as appealing as expected. There was something about Emma—something about the way she made him feel like everything would be OK—that made the thought of running away seem stupid.

He believed she was being genuine when she said she didn't want to kill him. He guessed that if it came down to it, and Teddy decided to cave his head in due to demonic possession, or whatever it was, that she might even intervene on his behalf.

Then there was the card that Detective Jennings had handed him. There had been nothing special about it. A plain piece of card stock. Yet Oliver had watched Teddy, a three hundred-pound stack of pure muscle, straining to rip the unyielding item. Was the man an exceptional actor? And the card didn't burn when he held the lighter to it.

It was a curiosity. Further investigation was warranted.

The campground had a fairly modern public restroom, and Teddy waited at the door while Oliver made use of it, then washed himself as best he could using the hand soap and paper towels at the small sink.

"Do you have any deodorant I can use?" Oliver asked. "I'm afraid I'm a little ripe."

"In the minivan," Teddy said.

The minivan turned out to be a silver Honda Odyssey. Emma was loading bags into the back when Oliver and Teddy returned.

"That's a nice vehicle," Oliver said. "My mom's best friend has one."

Emma grinned. "I'm glad you approve. Teddy's very fond of it."

"Check this out," Teddy said, producing a key fob from his pocket. He pressed a button and the passenger rear door slid open using an electronic mechanism. "Incredible right?"

The big man beamed.

"Yeah," Oliver said. "Totally."

"Hop in!" Teddy made an elaborate motion with his wrist, one that brought to mind a gameshow host welcoming contestants to a spinning glitter money wheel, and Oliver climbed into the second-row captain seat.

Teddy leaned down, out of Emma's line of sight. He spoke in a hushed tone. "Are you planning to struggle?"

"No," Oliver said. "Should I?"

Teddy shook his head, produced a zip tie from the cargo pocket of his pants and fastened Oliver's right wrist to the handle from which one would typically hang one's dry-cleaning. Oliver suspected that this was going to be an uncomfortable trip.

"Uh, how long is the drive?" he asked.

"I can tell you exactly," Teddy said as he climbed into the passenger seat.

He turned on the standby power and fiddled with the navigation system. A map appeared, showing a blue line that ran from just north of Hartford to the tip of Florida. "It's going to be twenty-three hours and forty-three minutes. It could be a little more or less, depending on traffic and gas stops."

Teddy smiled broadly. He gave Oliver a look that suggested Oliver should also smile broadly.

Oliver smiled broadly.

Apparently satisfied, Teddy nodded and turned back to the infotainment system.

"Do you like DVD movies?" he asked.

"DVD movies?"

"Movies that are on DVDs," Teddy clarified.

"Oh, ah, sure," Oliver said.

"Watch this!"

He reached back and opened a small screen that hinged down from the headliner. After an FBI warning, and a series of previews for decades-old movies had played through, the 1996 Pauly Shore film, *Bio-Dome*, began.

"It's a classic!" Teddy said enthusiastically.

"But you can't see it," Oliver said.

"I can hear it." Teddy then tapped his temple and winked. "I see it with my imagination."

"*Bio-Dome* again?" Emma asked, climbing into the driver's seat.

"Yup," Teddy said.

"He loves this movie," she said to Oliver.

"Who could blame him?"

"You comfortable enough back there, hon?"

"To be honest, I'm a little worried that if I fall asleep my hand will require amputation."

"Well, try not to fall asleep for now," she said. "Watch *Bio-Dome*. It'll help you relax."

Oliver's body was still reeling from the effects of the sedative and the subsequent thirty-hour pharmacologically induced coma. He was sore, headachy and anxious, in the specific way that a terrible hangover makes a person anxious. In his current state, he was unable to conceive of a reason not to heed her advice, so he went with the flow.

He soon found, to his surprise, that just as she had suggested, he was able to relax. Better still, by gripping the handle with his right hand, he was able to alleviate the pressure from the zip tie.

The complexities of the situation, which had spiraled into stratospheric levels of improbability and unpredictability, would have to wait. For the time being his focus was on keeping circulation open to his hand and watching *Bio-Dome*.

They drove for a little over an hour and a half, and when the movie ended, Teddy turned and smiled. Oliver thought his smile was rather similar to the smile of a hungry alligator.

"I really hope we don't have to kill you," Teddy said.

"Yeah. Me too."

"You're a good movie-watching companion. You don't talk too much."

Oliver nodded. He closed his eyes and allowed himself to think.

For two years, his thesis had been his entire reason for being.

To his surprise, now that his magnum opus—the culmination of his life's work—was gone, and his elaborate, life-consuming code was effectively erased from the face of the earth, he felt, in a weird way, as though a weight had been lifted.

"You know, it's funny," he said aloud to no one—"I didn't store it in the cloud because I was worried about security."

"Are you talking about your thesis?" Emma asked.

"Yes."

"Remember how I said sometimes things happen for a reason?"

"Sure."

"Tell me—what was your thesis about?"

"It was a new type of computer code—a universal language that could reverse engineer itself to apply to, or be written from, any other existing computer language. It was very close to finished."

"Like before the Tower of Babel," Teddy said.

Oliver was taken aback. Teddy didn't strike him as a biblical scholar. Biblical scholars should have grey hair, and shuffling gaits. They should spend years planning their dream trip into the Vatican archives, only to arrive late for their appointment because they were swarmed by Roman street hucksters selling postcards featuring old, grainy photos of the Coliseum. Biblical scholars should not smash people's brains out with baseball bats, and should definitely not look like Dwayne "The Rock" Johnson. Most of all, Biblical scholars should not watch Pauly Shore movies in their minivan while transporting kidnapped mathematicians in the back seat.

He tried his best not to sound surprised. "Yeah. In fact, I was going to call it Babel-Fish after the translator fish in that Douglas Adams book, but the name was taken, so I called it BBL."

"It's good that it was destroyed," Teddy pronounced. "People need barriers."

"Now Teddy, that's a bit harsh," Emma said. "The kid spent years of his life on that project."

"It isn't harsh at all," Teddy said, turning to Oliver.

"You say this code can, in turn, write computer code in other languages? That there's no need for people to learn any code other than this one?"

"That's more or less the gist of it, yeah."

Teddy faced Emma and seemed to be speaking only to her. "Imagine the security and military implications of something like that falling into the wrong hands. All of a sudden, some lunatic can overwrite machine language and cause a nuclear reactor to melt down or something. Terrible idea."

Oliver felt his heart rate quicken. It wasn't that the big man had insulted his thesis concept—he could care less about that. It was the fact that he, *himself,* had never so much as considered what his code would mean for machine language and national security. He thought of the Ian Malcolm character in *Jurassic Park.* Had he been so focused on the "could" that he failed to adequately consider the "should."

"I was thinking more about teams of programmers with expertise in different languages coming together to make better video games."

"Still," Teddy said. "Barriers. They're important. Good fences make good neighbors."

They drove in silence for a while, and Oliver contemplated Teddy's words. Could his code really have been used for cyber-terrorism? He thought the answer was that, yes, it could. How strange was it that he had never even contemplated the possibility?

When they stopped for gas, Teddy bought Oliver a bottle of Gatorade, which he drank gratefully. His headache subsided as the first tendrils of pink sunset slithered their way across the distant clouds.

He wasn't sure how to raise the subject of his abduction. He spent a few minutes screwing up his courage before clearing his throat.

"You seem like nice people," he began.

"Thanks," Emma said. "We try."

"You don't seem to be..." he hunted for the right phrase, "complete weirdos."

"Right," Teddy said.

"So, forgive me if this seems like I'm being judgmental, because, believe me, that isn't my intention. But why, exactly, do you think I've been possessed by the devil?"

Teddy laughed heartily. "The devil!" he said. "Yeah right!"

"Well isn't that what you were saying? You chained me up because you thought I was dangerous—possessed by the devil."

"Not 'the devil,' Oliver," Emma said. "A *demon*."

He waited, expecting them to elaborate, but no elaboration was forthcoming. "So you think I'm possessed by a demon?" he prodded.

"Maybe," Teddy said. "It's hard to know. Demons can be deceptive little bastards."

"Its name is Amon," Emma said, "or Chaos."

"It's a Marquis of Hell," Teddy expounded, as though that explained everything.

"I, uh, don't think I'm familiar."

"You know," Teddy said, "Amon. Governor of Forty Legions? Supreme Deity of ancient Egypt? Reconciler of infernal feuds? Head of a bird, tail of a serpent? None of this is ringing a bell?"

Oliver blinked, and continued to shake his head.

"Didn't you go to Sunday school?" Teddy sounded shocked.

"They never really covered a lot of demonology," Oliver said in his defense.

"Well, what did they teach?"

"You know... being nice to one another, and stuff."

Teddy sucked his teeth in disapproval, and turned again to face the road. "Soft," he mumbled. "They've gone so soft."

"Wait," Oliver said. "Why do you think this...*Amon*... is inside me?"

Teddy produced the cardboard rectangle that John Jennings had given to Oliver.

"Do you know what this is?" he asked.

Oliver inspected it. It was not, as he had originally guessed, a business card.

"It's a library card," he said, "under the name Doris Hutchens, for the Cumberland Public Library in Pugwash, Nova Scotia." He turned the card over. "And it says it expired in 1927."

"That's a charm," Emma said.

Oliver thought back to the aggressive police officer—the man who had meant to shoot him at the Orwell statue. Had he not said something about a charm?

He realized there was a remote chance that Teddy and Emma were not living in a Manson-esque LSD-induced schizo-paranoid nightmare fantasy. Still, he was unwilling to write off the possibility just yet.

"I think the guy with the gun said something about a charm, just before you, uh..." Using his free hand, Oliver pantomimed the act of caving in a human head with a baseball bat.

"Yes, I heard," said Teddy.

"So are we, like, wanted now?" Oliver asked.

"Wanted by whom?" Teddy said.

"Well...like...by the police. You know, for killing that guy. I mean, he was probably a cop. He was wearing the uniform and everything."

"Oh no," Teddy said and laughed.

"Why not?"

"It's just how it works. The police never catch us. They never even suspect us."

It was clear that neither Teddy nor Emma were concerned about it. It was also becoming clear to Oliver, who, unlike so many of his generation, was capable of reading between the lines of dialogue, that Teddy and Emma were not new at this.

"So what's a charm?" Oliver asked.

"It's like a calling card for the Host," Emma said. "And maybe for the bigger demons."

"The Host? As in, like, I'm hosting a demon? Like a parasite kind of thing?"

"Yes and no," Emma said "The Host is a little hard to explain."

"Is it a bad thing?"

"It has its ups and downs," she said.

The conversation was making his head spin.

It wasn't that Oliver couldn't believe that things like demons existed. He just couldn't believe that one would have any interest in *him*. He also couldn't believe that demon-fighters crisscrossed the continent in a Honda Odyssey, watching Pauly Shore movies.

"I'm feeling a bit beleaguered by all this," he admitted. "No offense... like

I said, you seem like lovely people. But this seems a bit," he had to search for the right word again, "crazy."

Emma turned to him. "Do you remember what you said, when you were first waking up in the campground?"

"I think I said I was thirsty."

"You said, 'Resist nothing.' Do you remember?"

"Sure."

She turned to face the road. "Take your own advice."

Since he didn't seem to be in immediate danger, he decided that, for the time being, that he would do just as she suggested.

He watched the landscape darken as they glided southward.

"Do you like trivia?" Teddy asked.

"I do, actually," Oliver said, perking up.

As a number theorist, he very much enjoyed learning unusual facts that didn't coalesce well with human experience. He found them mathematically curious, and often wondered if trivia followed a yet-undiscovered algorithm.

Teddy turned in his seat, reaching back with an open hand. "Pass me your phone."

Oliver handed the phone to the big man. "The battery's pretty much dead," he warned.

"Check this out," Teddy said, producing an iPhone charger from the center console. He plugged the phone in and turned the device so Oliver could see the battery box with the lightning bolt that filled the screen. His eyebrows danced. "The minivan can charge your mobile phone! Incredible, right?"

"Yeah," Oliver said, trying to match his captor's enthusiasm.

Teddy played with the phone, and after a minute handed it back to Oliver on its charging cord.

"Open the app I downloaded."

Oliver browsed to the end of his app icons and found one titled, "Incredible Daily Facts."

He opened it. A screen of plain text appeared. It read:

The Canary Islands are named after dogs, not birds.

"Interesting," Oliver said.

"It gives you a new incredible fact every day," Teddy explained.

"I see," Oliver said.

"Yesterday's fact was that Oscar the Grouch was orange for the first season of *Sesame Street*."

"Great," Oliver said. He hoped that by emulating Teddy's enthusiasm for things, he might form a personal bond with the man and perhaps dissuade him from caving his head in with a baseball bat.

"You know," Teddy said, "there's a pretty good chance I'm going to have to cave your head in with a baseball bat, despite this personal bond we're forming."

"Right," Oliver said.

"I just want you to know, that if that turns out to be the case, it will very much sadden me."

"I appreciate that," Oliver said.

"Check the settings," Teddy said.

Oliver arched an eyebrow.

"On the app."

"Oh."

He clicked the settings icon.

"Now click languages," Teddy said.

Oliver did as instructed.

"Now click 'Old German,'" Teddy said.

When Oliver clicked 'Old German,' the tinny speakers made the sound of a trumpet playing a short fanfare.

The screen changed. The text read:

The Comprehensive Guide to Hosting a Celestial Entity

The title page faded leaving Oliver with a search bar.

"Cool, right?" Teddy asked.

"What am I looking at?"

"Well, as the title screen suggests, that is *The Comprehensive Guide to Hosting a Celestial Entity.*"

Something inside Oliver went weird. His gut felt like an energetic trout was trying to wriggle its way through.

Sure, shared delusions could be elaborate. But could they be "There's an app for that" elaborate? Could they be "Hide an easter egg app within the Old German language setting of a trivia app" elaborate?

"Did you guys program this?" Oliver dreaded the answer.

Teddy, so impressed by the USB cable in his Honda, was probably not a computer programmer. Emma, Oliver thought, would likely have set Teddy up with some kind of streaming service instead of an old-fashioned DVD player if she were tech savvy.

"Oh, no," Teddy said. "We're not good with computers."

Oliver eyed the screen and cold tendrils of fear sent waves of goosebumps up the back of his neck. The words "Celestial Entity" stared right back at him.

"When this refers to a celestial entity..." Oliver asked, trying to sound casual.

"Transdimensional beings," Emma said. "The term 'Celestial Entity' has always sounded like a bit of a marketing exercise, if you ask me."

"And we can host these, uh—transdimensional beings?"

Teddy nodded at the phone. "It's all in there."

"So, what do I do?"

"Ask it a question."

"Like any question?"

"Yeah."

Oliver typed, "What is a Celestial Entity?"

A page of text appeared.

"Celestial Entity" may refer to a number of entities from the spirit dimension, from sprites, nymphs and seraphim up to and including The Creator, disagreement over the exact nature of whom has been cause for significant earthly conflict.

While rarely observed in the physical dimension, Celestial Entities called "spirits" are known to inhabit the physical universe in the form of the Host.

"The Host" was a hyperlink and Oliver clicked it, bringing up a new page.

"The Host" (written with a capital "H") refers to celestial spirits who roam the physical dimension, serving to maintain the Great Balance, but the term "host," (written with a lowercase "h") is common shorthand for the humans who bear these spirits in the physical world.

Human hosts may be identified by a charm or talisman, an indestructible physical article carried in order to prove their affiliation to the society of the celestially involved.

Human hosts of celestial beings can be referred to in the plural, while Celestial Host, is typically singular, as all Host beings are felt to stem from the same entity.

While the term "Host," in reference to human beings, suggests a parasitic relationship between spiritual being and physical being, this is something of a misnomer, as the relationship is usually symbiotic.

The Host serve to repair, restore and maintain the Great Balance, and do this on Earth, by directing their human hosts through compulsions.

Complicating matters, "the Host" can also refer to the sacramental bread consumed in Christian communion.

The article went on to offer several hyperlinked categories for further exploration:

Transference of Host
Getting to Know One's Host Spirit
Charm / Talisman / Totem
Host Behavior
Host Compulsions
The Host and The Great Balance
The Host in the Spirit Dimension
Examples of Host Spirits
Bright vs Dark Host
Advantages of Being a Human Host
Disadvantages of Being a Human Host
The Host and Legion
History of the Host
Famous Human Hosts

Oliver put the phone down and stared out the window.

The app was yet another unexpected development in a week that had already provided a lifetime supply of surprises. Its existence forced him to reevaluate his assessment of his captors. It also meant he might have to reassess his survival strategy. Whatever these people were, they weren't your run-of-the-mill, easily fooled nutcases.

"This is very elaborate," he said.

"It's pretty comprehensive," Emma replied. "Be careful you don't go too far down the rabbit hole."

The app presented a fascinating predicament. Was it a guide to an elaborate fictional universe, or was it real, verifiable evidence of a secret society—an entire subset of humanity that had managed to hide a vast compendium of knowledge so potent it could unlock life's greatest mysteries?

Out of curiosity, he clicked on "Transference of Host."

The Host spirit can pass between human carriers at the time of a human's death. This may go entirely unnoticed by the new human host, but some subjects describe a sensation of warmth, of well-being, or of immediate compulsion at the time of transference. The physical sensation of "briefly becoming a carbonated beverage" has been widely described.

Often, the dying human host will be compelled to pass their charm to the new human host. This is felt to be the compulsive act of the Celestial Spirit itself, and as it is such a common occurrence, the act was offered as the third of four proofs to the existence of the Host at the Council of Yid meeting in 470 AD.

Since "Council of Yid" was hyperlinked, Oliver decided to click it.

The Council of Yid was a meeting of religious scholars from Europe and the Middle East that occurred in 470 AD at the request of Roman Emperor Anthemius and Pope Simplicius who understood the Roman Empire to be on the brink of collapse. The Council was called to determine the existence of the Host on Earth and to question its purpose.

In establishment of the Host, four proofs were offered.

1) The secret scrolls of St. Peter, which described in detail, the transference of power from early disciples to their followers, likening it to the transference of Host. The scrolls were said to be lost during the sacking of Rome by Visigoths in 410 AD, but a fragment that survived in the Vatican crypts described the transference. This sacred fragment was presented to the Council.

2) The totem of Saint Simeon—it is said a colorful square of cloth had been given to Simeon when he was visited by an angel. Simeon has been recorded as having been at least two centuries old at the time of his encounter with an infant Jesus in the Gospel of Luke. The cloth was presented by Marcello, who claimed to have received it from Simeon himself. It would not tear, or burn in flame. Marcello claimed to host the celestial spirit, Joy.

3) The passing of charms at the time of transference. This event was described by Marcello, Hadriana, Felix and Domitia, who were human hosts, present before the Council. The Scroll of Antiphany, which described transference, and passing of a charm, was also taken as evidence to the phenomenon.

4) The spirit light was said to be briefly observed between the present Host.

The Council of Yid concluded that there was sufficient evidence to determine the existence of Host, but appeals to Host present, for the salvation of Rome and for political interference, were unheeded. It was thus decided to maintain secrecy regarding the council and its findings, and to execute the attendant human hosts to prevent them from aiding enemies of the Roman Empire. For obvious reasons, this marked the last formal attempt to publicly recognize the phenomenon.

Oliver looked up, surprised to see the sun had fully set. Teddy was snoring in the front seat.

"Did you go down the rabbit hole?" Emma asked.

"I guess I must have. I was reading about the Council of Yid."

"Hmm," Emma said, "I don't know that one."

"Really?"

"That guide has something like four million entries. I tend to use it mostly for recipes these days."

"Recipes?"

"Sure. It isn't all just interdimensional stuff. There's recipes and drink mixes in there too. Pretty much anything the contributors thought was worth-while sharing."

"What... like Wikipedia?"

"I don't know what that is."

"Wikipedia?" Oliver was incredulous.

"I'm really not into all that *Star Trek* mumbo jumbo," she said.

Oliver rubbed his forehead.

On a whim he typed "Tom Collins" into the search bar. He was linked to an entry titled "Earth's Best Tom Collins."

2 oz Botanical Gin
1 Full Lemon
Club Soda
Simple Syrup
Elderflower Liqueur
Lavender
Ice

(Squeeze the juice of an entire lemon into a cocktail shaker, over plenty of crushed ice. Add two ounces of botanical gin, and half an ounce of simple syrup that has been brought to a boil with sprigs of lavender, and then refrigerated. Add one half ounce of elderflower liqueur. Shake vigorously and strain into a highball glass containing one large ice cube. Fill remaining space with club soda, and serve.)

"What are you looking up now?" Emma asked.

"A Tom Collins recipe."

"What do you think?"

"I think the guide is quite comprehensive."

"You don't know the half of it," she said, half-smiling at him through the rearview mirror. "It used to be a book, you know. It had fifteen volumes. Weighed about a hundred pounds. They've only added to it since then."

"So I'm guessing that you're hosts?" Oliver asked, then cleared his throat. "I mean, is that what you perceive to be the case?"

"Still struggling, huh?"

"It's a lot to digest," Oliver admitted. "The idea that there are these celestial spirits living in humans, and what, presumably interfering in the name of balance or something? And that this has been kept a secret for thousands of years? I hope you won't think less of me if I admit I think it's far-fetched."

Emma's eyes took on a faraway look. "'The Great Balance' is what the guide calls it."

"But if the world is in balance on account of all these 'celestial entities,' and 'hosts,' and what have you, why was my apartment burned down by nudist vegans in the Vagisil Autonomous Zone last night?"

"First of all, 'The Great Balance' hasn't been achieved. A lot of us suspect that it might never be achieved, but its restoration is our goal nonetheless. To restore the Great Balance to the world is supposedly to literally create heaven on Earth. I'll yada, yada, yada over some of the intricacies of the theoretical physics involved in our comprehension of the matter, if it's all the same to you. Suffice to say, to me, the Great Balance means the end of the barrier between the human race and eternity.

"The opposite of balance, of course, is chaos, and that is the goal of Legion—to create and encourage chaos. In terms of the riot, and what forces of balance might have brought me and Teddy there, my best guess is that it had something to do with your thesis."

"Really?"

"I've seen how these things work, Oliver. There doesn't seem to be any rhyme or reason to it at the time, but then later... well... let's just say I'm guessing it was the thesis that had to go. Teddy has a point. People need barriers."

"Like the Tower of Babel? Too much organization is a bad thing?"

"Exactamundo, kid."

He wasn't sure how he felt about being called "kid." He would have kind of preferred a manly nickname, like "Maverick" or "Rib Eye," but he realized such nicknames would be a hard sell to a woman who knew his name was written on the waistband of his underpants.

"I could be wrong, mind you," Emma said. "It could have been something else. It's just a hunch."

They rode in silence for a few minutes, then she spoke again. "Have you ever heard of Sir George Airy?"

"No."

"He was an astrophysicist. I studied under him for a while. Do you know about blue-shift and red-shift?"

"Sure," Oliver said, a little surprised. "A light-source moving away from you looks red, and a light-source moving towards you looks blue. It's like the Doppler effect, except for wavelengths of light instead of sound."

"Did you know that red-shift is the basis of the proof that the universe is constantly expanding?" she asked.

"Yes. Makes sense."

"Do you know what would happen if the universe were to contract? Or just to stop expanding?"

Oliver pictured the scenario—he'd heard the term "The Big Crunch" applied to models of a finite universe that would, one day, collapse under its own gravity. By his understanding, if the universe were to stop expanding, and start contracting, it would generate heat and pressure as it returned to a singularity. That would happen over billions, or perhaps trillions of years.

"I suppose it would be quite unpleasant near the end."

"It would be unpleasant almost from the get-go, Oliver. Picture the disruption of solar systems and galaxies. Galactic collisions. Rogue planets colliding with habitable planets. Mass casualties. Solar collapse. Chaos. And then, ultimately, the winking out of existence as we know it."

Oliver nodded. "Yeah. That's unpleasant, alright."

"So why does the universe expand?" she asked.

"Something to do with the Big Bang? A cosmic force we don't fully understand?"

"Maybe," she said, "but do you know what Sir George thought? He thought the universe was expanding to protect us."

"That's comforting. I mean, impossible to prove, but comforting."

"It really is," she said. "Now, would you like to watch *Bio-Dome* again?"

"No thanks. I might rest my eyes for a bit. Would you mind letting me know if I let go of the handle and my hand starts turning purple?"

"Sure."

"One last question," Oliver said, "if that's OK."

"Fire away."
"Why are we going to Florida?"
She met his eyes in the mirror. "You need to meet Death."

— *Three* —

The sun was high when Oliver awoke, his right wrist still zip-tied to the Honda Odyssey's grab handle. He yawned.

Gone were the budding trees and farmers' fields. The ocean filled the view on either side of the van. They were on what appeared to be an endless highway bridge.

He assumed they were in Florida, and tried to guess whether he was looking out over Tampa Bay or whether this was one of the bridges that connected the Florida Keys.

He was going to meet "Death."

There were so many references to death in *The Comprehensive Guide to Hosting a Celestial Entity* that he had eventually given up looking, and had gone to sleep after reading about "Death as a Construct," "Death, Taxes and Inevitability," "Spiritual Death and the Rise of Social Media," "Ego Death, and Why Your Host Would Prefer Restraint when Experimenting with Hallucinogenics," and "Death and Disease: How to Avoid Both while on a Cruise."

He assumed that he was going to meet a person, and that Emma and Teddy were not simply driving him south to kill him. He did remember an old saying about assumption, however.

"It makes an ass of you and me," he said quietly to himself.

"Mornin' sunshine," Emma said from the driver's seat.

He rubbed his face with his free hand, and felt a few days' stubble. He needed a shave. And a real shower. And to brush his teeth.

"Have you been driving all night?" he asked Emma.

"We stopped for gas a few hours ago," she said.

"You must be exhausted."

"I'm fine."

Oliver couldn't imagine that was true, but her eyes were indeed bright and perky in the rearview mirror.

She looked like a million bucks. Oliver knew for a fact that *he* looked like something the cat dragged in.

"She doesn't sleep a lot," Teddy said. He winked at her.

"Why did you just wink at her?" Oliver said.

"Oh, no reason." Teddy chuckled.

"Did you guys... uh... never mind." Oliver decided he didn't want to know if they had been copulating.

"We copulated," Teddy said, and laughed.

"Teddy!" Emma said, feigning shock. But she was also smiling her impish smile.

"Oh Lord."

"What?" Teddy asked.

"This is information I don't need."

"Copulation is wonderful," Teddy said. "We copulate three times a week."

Oliver wondered whether he was receiving some kind of cosmic punishment. Since having his laptop destroyed, he'd had his apartment burned down, his thesis erased from existence, he'd been kidnapped, drugged, chained naked in a public park, zip-tied to a Honda Odyssey, had every assumption he'd ever made about the physical universe called into question, and perhaps worst of all, he'd been made to listen to his captors as they discussed their sex lives. It was a topic that made him uncomfortable at the best of times.

"Teddy, stop. He's embarrassed!" Emma said, but Oliver could tell she took some delight in his torment.

"He shouldn't be," Teddy said. "Copulating is part of the human condition."

"Can we please stop saying 'Copulating?'" Oliver begged.

"Fornicating, then," Teddy said. "We fornicated on a picnic table outside the gas station. It was great."

"I wish you would just cave my head in already."

At Teddy's insistence, Oliver watched the Pauly Shore classic *Son in Law*, while the big man lip-synched all the dialogue from the front passenger seat. By the time it ended they were nearing Orlando, and Oliver was absolutely desperate for a bathroom break.

They stopped at an IHOP.

"If I release your wrist, do you promise not to create havoc?" Teddy asked.

"I promise," Oliver said.

"Do you swear this isn't just a clever ruse?"

"I swear that if you don't let me go to the bathroom, it's going to ruin the seat of your minivan."

"OK," Teddy said, "you have the upper hand."

He cut the wrist restraint and followed Oliver into the washroom.

The muscle-bound giant waited just outside the stall. Oliver had a very clear memory of his father doing the same thing on family vacations when he was a little boy. Of course, his father hadn't been trying to prevent him from escaping and calling the police. Add to that, as far as Oliver knew, his father had never caved a person's face in with a Louisville Slugger. So perhaps drawing on that memory was his way of creating a false equivalency. He wondered whether he was suffering the initial stages of Stockholm Syndrome, and decided to look up the symptoms once he had his phone back. He was alarmed to realize was subconsciously planning to look it up in *The Comprehensive Guide to Hosting a Celestial Entity.*

He had to get a grip.

Washing his hands, he asked, "Teddy, is there any way we could stop at a pharmacy or something, so I could get deodorant and a toothbrush? My mouth is feeling really gross."

"You can use my deodorant again," Teddy said. "It's Mitchum. Very good stuff."

Oliver didn't love the idea of sharing deodorant. Especially given the overall lack of shower-access they were experiencing. But he didn't want to offend his captor.

"And the toothbrush?"

"No," Teddy said.

"No what?"

"No, I don't want to share it with you."

"I mean, can I buy one? Actually, I guess what I mean is can you buy me one since my wallet was thrown into the embers of my burned-down home?"

"Let's wait and see if there's any point," Teddy said.

"In brushing my teeth?"

"Yes."

"Well, of course there's a point. I want to freshen my breath and avoid cavities and gingivitis!"

"I understand," Teddy said. "Only, if I have to smash your head in this afternoon, it will have been a waste of money."

"Oh. Right."

He'd somehow forgotten that Teddy believed he was possessed by a demon. He had a crazy thought that it would be a real shame if Teddy killed him just as his headache was finally starting to get better. He actually laughed.

"What is it?" Teddy asked.

Oliver told him.

"Don't worry," Teddy said, "if I have to destroy your brain, I'll make it quick so you don't feel anything."

"That's, uh, very kind of you," Oliver said.

"If I don't have to kill you, and we become friends, I think you'll find that I'm a very kind guy."

"I'm sure."

Standing in line for a table, a very odd thing happened. Oliver was overcome by an urge to walk outside. He had a strong hunch—a certainty, really—that there was a man outside in a black baseball cap, wearing an army jacket. He was sure of it. He didn't know where this *hunch* came from. It wasn't an intuition, or a premonition. It was more like the sensation you get the moment before you sneeze, the moment you know it's going to happen and there's nothing you can do to stop it. And he was just as equally certain he had to speak to the man.

"I...I need to go outside," he said to Emma. "Right now."

"OK," Emma said. "Come on, Teddy."

"The line," Teddy complained.

Emma whispered, "Didn't you say you were *craving* IHOP, and we *had* to stop here?"

"Oh, yeah," Teddy said. He put his arm around Oliver's thin shoulders and hustled him out the front door.

In the parking lot, the man Oliver knew would be there stepped out of the driver's seat of a rusted hulk of a pickup truck. He had deep, dark bags under his wild eyes. He twitched when he saw Oliver approaching.

"Hey," the man said in a shaking voice. "Stop there! Don't come any closer!" His cracked lips trembled.

Oliver sensed danger. It came off the stranger in waves. He wanted to turn and run. Every fiber of his being told him to get away from the man. Instead, he stepped closer! He spoke in a soothing voice that definitely wasn't his own. Neither were the words that came out. Someone, or some*thing* was speaking *through* him.

He tried to fight it. A bolt of pain ripped through his body. He relented.

"I know how difficult this must be," Oliver said in that other thing's voice, "but you're going to hand me that gun and go directly to the hospital. Tell them you need an MRI... that there's something wrong with your brain."

"Wh— What?"

Oliver spoke again, in the same calm voice. It was a voice he'd heard before. It was Detective Jennings' voice.

"The gun," Oliver said, his hand out. "It's really for the best."

The man lifted his shirt revealing the butt of a semiautomatic pistol tucked in the waistband of his pants. The guy was nothing but skin and bones.

"Take it," the man said.

Oliver gripped the pistol butt and slid it out. It felt heavy. The metal was warm from being against the stranger's feverish belly.

"The hospital, you say?"

"Yeah."

"Something wrong with my brain?"

"That's right."

"OK."

The man turned and got back in his pickup truck. He drove away, leaving Oliver holding the pistol.

Teddy gently took the firearm, then examined it. "Sweet—a nineteen-eleven."

He tucked it into the back of his own waistband, and slipped the Bass-Pro shirt over it for concealment.

Oliver had just done something that was completely outside of his control. It wasn't like being blind drunk, where you simply make disinhibited decisions. This was zombie movie, hivemind stuff. He fought back a wave of nausea.

"What the hell was that?" he said. His voice was tight, and cracked with adrenaline. "What the hell just happened?"

"It looked like a compulsion to me," Emma said.

"A compulsion?"

"It could have been a ruse." Teddy stared at Emma, his eyes full of warning.

"A ruse?" Oliver was incredulous. "Did you do that? Did you two do that to me, somehow? What was it... mind control? The power of suggestion? Don't give me that... that... *baloney*! What did you do to me? That was a gun! That guy had a freaking gun! He was here to shoot somebody. He could have shot us! How did you make me do that?"

"We didn't do anything," Emma said. "You had a compulsion. You acted on it."

"Or you came up with a ruse to deceive us," Teddy said, though he sounded less certain. "Amon is a master of deception, after all."

"A master of deception!" Oliver stammered. "Do I look like David freaking Copperfield?"

"The Charles Dickens character?" Teddy asked.

"The... the *what*? No... the illusionist."

"I have no idea who you're talking about," Teddy said.

"He made the Statue of Liberty disappear!"

"No he didn't. I just saw the Statue of Liberty, not two weeks ago!" Teddy said.

"It wasn't permanent! It was a magic trick!"

Somehow, the idea that Teddy didn't know who David Copperfield was freaked Oliver out even more. As if the mind control wasn't enough.

It occurred to him that for all he knew, he might have been kidnapped by aliens from the Alpha Centauri system. And why the hell not? Celestial hosts? Aliens? Sasquatches? What did he really know about anything, anyway? He could feel his face reddening. Tears, once again, threatened to spill.

"I think he's about to flip out," Teddy observed.

Emma put a hand on his shoulder and said, "Calm down, Olly."

His panic subsided. It was like magic. Had she called him "Olly?"

"I'm... I'm sorry," he said. "I don't like to lose control."

"Come on... let's talk about it over pancakes," Emma said. She gave his shoulder a gentle squeeze.

"Pancakes?"

Emma led Oliver back into the IHOP. Teddy followed.

When the waitress came to take their order, Teddy asked for two Break-Feasts, which were the highest-calorie item on the menu. He chose his meals, he explained, specifically for their caloric density. Emma ordered a half-stack of pancakes and a black coffee for both her and Oliver.

Once the waitress left them alone, Emma rubbed Oliver's forearm in a maternal, comforting gesture. "The first one can be pretty disconcerting."

Disconcerting wasn't the word. Oliver remembered a time in high school, when as "the nerdy kid" he'd been challenged by two hippy kids to explain what they described as "An LSD-induced psychic experience." In this recounted story, Jim, the hippy kid who smelled like patchouli, would picture an object in his mind, and Greg, the hippy kid who always had a deviled egg in his lunch, would guess what the object was. "The crazy thing was, he guessed it every time," Jim explained. Oliver had explained that they, themselves, already gave away the answer. The answer was that they were on drugs, and imagined the whole thing. Now he wondered if that was entirely true. Weird things, it seemed, were possible.

"Just so we're one hundred percent clear, that wasn't me talking to the guy with the gun in the parking lot," Oliver said. "I tried to stop and I couldn't."

"It was a compulsion," Emma said. "You get used to them."

Oliver remembered something about compulsions from the guide. He'd assumed it was hokum.

"It's the Host acting through you," she explained.

"Use the app," Teddy suggested. He handed Oliver his phone.

The fact of the day read:

There are twelve times more trees on Earth than stars in the Milky Way.

He clicked through the menu to open the guide, then navigated his way to the section on compulsions.

A compulsion refers to an action taken by the Host, which requires the use of its human carrier. This act often gives the human host a sensation of loss of control, similar to the premonition of a sneeze. Compulsions may be pleasant, or unpleasant, depending on the degree to which the human host attempts to resist.

"Pre-compulsion" typically refers to the period leading up to the compulsive act, during which the human host may find themselves traveling without necessarily knowing their own destination, visiting an unfamiliar location, or otherwise acting somewhat out of character. While there is ongoing debate as to whether the pre-compulsion period is truly related to the subsequent compulsion, established long-time human hosts tend to agree that it is a frequent, but not universal part of the phenomenon.

"So, I have no free will," Oliver said.

"Don't be so dramatic," Teddy said.

"Teddy," Emma interjected, "he's trying to process it."

"Oh baloney," Teddy said. "Look, you prevented a disaster. You should be happy."

"A disaster?" Oliver asked.

"Yeah—that guy was going to shoot up the IHOP. You prevented it. Good job."

"I didn't do anything," Oliver said. "This parasitic celestial thing, according to the guide, apparently took control of my brain and body. I had no choice in the matter!"

"Technically, you're right," Teddy said. "Oh, good. Here come our pancakes."

The waitress placed what could only be described as a mountain of food in front of the big man. She smiled at Oliver when she handed him his much smaller stack of pancakes, and then topped off Emma's coffee.

"Anything else for you, hon?" she asked Oliver.

"Me? Ah, no thanks."

"Well, my name is Susan. You just come grab me if you want anything, OK?"

"OK."

Susan winked before turning and walking back to the kitchen.

"Ooh," Emma said once the waitress had moved to the next table, "she likes you."

"Me?" Oliver said.

"Oh yes."

"Assuming we don't have to kill you, you should ask her on a date when you come back this way," Teddy said. "Some fornication would be good for you."

"Oh God."

"What!? You're tightly wound. Intercourse would help with that. You need to ejaculate at least ten or eleven times, by my estimate, before you're going to be able to relax and properly enjoy life."

Oliver groaned.

"What?" Teddy asked.

Emma gave Teddy a reproachful look.

"He does!"

Oliver, wanting very much to avoid any further discussion about ejaculation, stuffed a large forkful of pancake into his mouth. He was grateful for the food and hoped it would provide a significant enough distraction that he could veer the conversation back toward the topic of compulsions and hopefully (since he had to admit, they seemed to exist) how to avoid them at all costs.

A few minutes later, he thought he was making good headway with his pancakes until he looked up and saw that Teddy had finished the first "Break-Feast" and was half way through the second. The man ate methodically and quickly, reminding Oliver of a video he'd watched of Keith Moon playing the drums. The sequence of eating, which happened at roughly one hundred beats per minute, went as follows: fork to plate, fold and spear pancake, fold and spear bacon, use knife to collect egg, smear egg on pancake, fork to mouth, chew once, swallow, repeat.

"Wow," Oliver said.

Teddy didn't look up. "Wow, what?"

"How do you eat so fast?"

"I'm not fast," Teddy said. "I'm efficient."

Oliver nodded. He had never realized that a human being could swallow like that without choking.

He wanted to get back to the business of compulsion aversion. He figured he was going to have to accept the possibility that everything Emma, Teddy and the guide had been telling him was at least an approximation of reality. He steeled his mind for a second, took a deep breath, and against all probability, managed to accept it.

Next, he decided to see if he could find a loophole through which he could avoid this reality in its entirety.

He turned to Emma. "So, in all seriousness, have I lost my free will?"

"Sort of," she explained. "But try to look at it this way—you never really have free will over your essential biology. You can't just decide not to sneeze, not to go to the washroom, not to eat or drink, etcetera. The compulsions are like one more biological function you can't control. You really will get used to it. I know that sounds hard to believe, but it's true."

"Hmm," Oliver said. "I can't conceive of a universe in which that is possible."

"You say 'hmm' a lot," Teddy said. "It's kind of annoying."

"I say it when I'm processing something," Oliver admitted. "My mom says it makes me sound pretentious. She says I should just say what I'm thinking out loud, if I want people to get to know and like me. But I think that's ridiculous. I mean... you can pretty much tell what I'm thinking through basic intuition, right?"

"No," Teddy said. "What are you thinking?"

"You mean right now? About what Emma just said—how my brain and body will randomly, occasionally, and unpredictably come under the control of an otherworldly being?"

"Yeah."

"I'm thinking that it sucks."

"Really?" Teddy said. "I was thinking that you thought it was kind of cool."

"What!? No! I think it really sucks!"

"Well then... I guess you should listen to your mother more."

Oliver was unable to decide whether Teddy had poor perception, or whether, as his mother suggested, he was simply a terrible communicator of inner thoughts. He decided the truth might be a combination of those things.

"All that aside, do you want to hear some good news?" Emma asked.

"Sure."

"If it wasn't some kind of ruse…"

"We don't know that for sure," Teddy interjected.

"Right," she said, "but if it wasn't, and if you're genuinely as surprised by your first compulsion as you seem to be, that means that you probably aren't possessed by Amon after all."

"And that means I'm what exactly?" Oliver asked.

"A regular human host," Teddy said, "like us."

"Like you guys?"

"Surely you'd figured that out by now, smart guy like you," Emma said.

"Truth be told, until about ten minutes ago I'd kind of been hoping we were all experiencing some sort of LSD-induced psychosis that happened to have an accompanying iPhone app. Just now, I decided to accept that some of the things you've been telling me are true. Having said that, my acceptance could also be part of the psychosis."

"Did you take LSD?" Teddy asked.

"No."

"Well that rules out your theory."

"Yeah, but you gave me drugs," Oliver said. "In my arm."

"Diazepam," Teddy explained, "A mild barbiturate."

Oliver considered that for a moment. He didn't feel stoned at all. He discounted the idea that the "compulsion" he'd experienced had been related to the medication they'd given him. That left two possibilities. The first was the shared delusion theory, of which he, by definition, was now an active participant. The delusion was reinforced by the bizarre phone app that had been programmed by some stranger to an uncertain end. The second possibility was that Teddy and Emma were telling the truth. He decided that in either case, in the spirit of resisting nothing, he was probably going to have to assume that his captors were, in fact, being truthful.

"So, uh, which celestial entities are you guys hosting?" he asked.

Emma smiled. "Well, we're both brights," she said. "We don't actually know the proper celestial name of the Host, you understand, but we have been able to determine the subtype. Teddy hosts Goodness."

"It's a very important one," Teddy said, before emptying his steaming mug of coffee directly down his esophagus in one slurp.

"And I host Forbearance."

"How many are there?" Oliver asked.

"Thousands," she said. "Including multiples of the same subtypes. We ran into another Forbearance a few years ago in Mexico."

"A real bitch," Teddy said knowingly, through a mouthful of buttered toast.

Emma sighed.

Oliver leaned forward, "How did you figure it out, when it happened to you?"

"Well, I met Teddy almost right away," Emma said. "He recognized me for what I was."

"And you, Teddy?"

"My father," he said, "that's who transferred to me. He'd already told me pretty much everything before it happened."

Oliver took a sip of his coffee. He was genuinely intrigued. "How long have you guys been doing this?"

"Just under a thousand years now, personally," Teddy said.

At that, Oliver inhaled a mouthful of coffee and a sizable piece of pancake. He was immediately wracked by a violent coughing spell.

Teddy jumped to his feet and pounded him on the back. Oliver folded under the enormous power of the slap, and nosedived into his plate.

Other customers stared.

"I'm OK," Oliver gasped, hoping to avoid another pounding. "Really."

"I saved your life," Teddy said. "Even though there's still a small chance I'll have to kill you!"

"Thanks," Oliver said.

"Can I have the rest of your pancakes?" Teddy asked.

Oliver looked at his plate. His remaining two pancakes had a hole through the middle, where his nose had gone through. He used his napkin to wipe syrup off his eyebrows. "Be my guest."

Teddy sat back down, and, using the tines of his fork, greedily slid Oliver's plate across the table. He ignored the morsels that Oliver had coughed onto the plate and resumed eating with gusto.

"Dare I ask how long you've been doing this?" Oliver asked Emma.

"Promise not to choke?"

"I'll do my best."

"Two hundred twenty-three years."

He tried to imagine what two and a quarter centuries on Earth would do to a person. To have that much wisdom and experience, only to watch history repeat itself over and over, he guessed, would drive a person stark raving mad.

Then quadruple that! He observed Teddy, who was folding an entire pancake into his mouth at the end of a fork. He shuddered.

"That can't be true, right?"

"I'm afraid it is."

"So what's the deal then... do human hosts, like, live a long time?"

"Sometimes, but not always. It's complicated. Remember the transference? Human hosts can still die—but it's usually a violent death. We don't age the same way most people do. There are some other perks as well. Wounds heal fast. We don't seem to get infections. We don't get arthritis."

"We still get headaches," Teddy chimed in. "And colds."

"You have hay fever," she chided. "We do not get colds."

Oliver marveled at this. A subset of the human race that was immune to the cold virus!

"In exchange for all this, you get the occasional compulsion to stop a crazy person with a gun?" he asked.

"There are some other significant downsides," she said, and her expression changed.

"You outlive your children," Teddy said. "Well, my father didn't, I suppose."

"But you did?" Oliver asked Emma.

She nodded. Her eyes turned down. "That was a long time ago."

"How did they handle it? Them getting older, and you staying the same?"

"Well, when they were old enough to notice, we had a family meeting. Teddy and I explained everything as best we could..."

"Wait, you guys had kids together?"

"Three of them," Teddy said, smiling.

"When?"

Teddy furrowed his brow. "William, our youngest, was born in 1802. He passed in 1874."

"He was a good man," Emma said. "Very kind."

"Could you have more children?" Oliver asked.

"I'm sure we could," she said, "but we were foolish to do it in the first place. Can you imagine how complicated life was, between the kids, and the Host, and the compulsions and then plunk the Civil War onto the tail end of that? We don't recommend it."

"I use condoms now," Teddy said. "Three times a week."

Oliver tried his best to ignore this.

"You said we tend to die violently?"

"Sure," Emma said. "Beheadings, stabbings, shootings, that kind of thing can obviously kill you."

"A statue fell on Oliver's guy," Teddy said. "That was a new one."

"But you said your father transferred to you..." Oliver began.

"Battle of Hastings," Teddy said. "Took an arrow through the head."

"The Battle of Hastings!" Oliver nearly shouted. "In 1066?"

"Yup."

"An arrow!"

"Uh huh."

"Through the head?!"

"Right through." Teddy pantomimed an arrow going in one side of his head and out the other.

Oliver felt himself starting to freak out again. He fought to maintain composure. "I think I'd like to go home how."

"You don't have a home," said Teddy. "It burned down. Remember?"

"OK," Oliver said. "My mom's house, then."

"You can't," Emma said. "It's not safe."

"Not safe?"

"We don't know what you're hosting," Emma said.

"Assuming this isn't a clever ruse, it's a golden mouth," Teddy said.

"A what?" Oliver asked.

"A golden mouth," Teddy said. "You talk to people. It's how a golden mouth intervenes."

"That sounds like something out of Harry Potter," Oliver said.

"Harry what?" Teddy said, cocking an eyebrow.

"Potter. You know... the wizard... from Hogwarts?"

Teddy gave him a blank look.

Oliver turned to Emma. "Harry Potter!" he exclaimed.

She shrugged.

"Witches, and wizards, and... I don't know... Dumbledore! England!"

"Is this some kind of Dungeons and Dragons thing?" Teddy asked.

"What?!" Oliver exclaimed. "You're having me on, right?"

Somehow it was more incredible to Oliver that Teddy and Emma had never heard of Harry Potter than the idea that they were hundreds of years old, hosting celestial entities in a symbiotic interdimensional relationship.

"Huh," Teddy said. "Sounds pretty weird."

"It's a famous series. There were books... and movies. They're probably some of the highest-grossing books and films in history!"

"Never heard of it," Teddy said. "I'll have to remember to check it out."

Oliver sat in stunned silence. How was it even possible?

"I feel like we're getting sidetracked here," Teddy said.

Oliver nodded. He was just going to have to add the Harry Potter thing to the compendium of unlikely realities he was now facing.

"OK, how do I figure out what it is? This thing inside me, I mean."

"It isn't inside you," Teddy said.

"OK, this thing that isn't inside me then," Oliver said.

"It shadows you," Teddy said.

"Right then. This thing that's shadowing me. How do I find out what it is?"

"You have to see Death," Emma said.

"I'm a little vague on this 'seeing death' thing. I mean, I saw death the other night. The detective..."

"That's not what we're talking about," Emma said. "I'm talking about Death in Key West."

She put her hand on his shoulder once again and squeezed, "Bear with us, OK?"

Oliver felt himself relax. He wondered, almost absently, which celestial entity would be shadowing him for the rest of his life.

Then he startled and jerked. "Wait—are you—uh—golden mouthing me?"

"Uh huh."

"Is it like, a compulsion?"

"No—I can do it on cue," she said, her smile returning.

"So I'm going to see Death."

"Yes."

"In Key West?"

"Yes."

"And then you'll take me home?"

"Maybe."

"OK... let's go see... Death."

"Not quite yet," Teddy said, eyeballing Emma's plate.

"Oh just take them," Emma said, pushing her half-finished breakfast across the table to him.

Teddy grinned like a pit bull. His smile was all teeth and appetite.

— *Four* —

It was late afternoon by the time Emma pulled off the highway. She wound the van through a subdivision, taking a series of side streets. She had obviously done this before.

Finally, just north of Key West, she drove through the open iron gate at the entrance of the Sunshine State Fifty-Five-Plus RV Resort and Marina.

The outdoor thermometer read ninety-five, and the air was thick with haze. Oliver wondered if the anomalous atmospheric conditions of southern Florida were such that humidity could possibly exceed one hundred percent without creating rain. He tried to savor the minivan's air-conditioned atmosphere.

For the last leg of the trip, he'd been only loosely restrained to the child-seat U-bolt via a zip tie that simply ran through one of his belt loops. Teddy must have abandoned the idea that Oliver was up to some kind of trickery, though the big man still rode with the baseball bat between his knees.

Emma parked in front of a clean, white, double-wide mobile home that was cheerfully decorated with stained-glass windchimes and brightly colored cottage-craft sculptures of tropical fish and sea turtles. Teddy opened the back sliding door and cut Oliver free. The hot, wet air assaulted the van's interior, and Oliver instantly felt sticky.

"The people you're about to meet are very important," Teddy said.

"I wish I could have brushed my teeth."

Teddy ignored this. "I'm going to have to restrain you again. Please don't take it personally. It's for their safety."

Oliver passively offered his wrists.

"Um," Teddy said, "it would probably be better if you followed me to the back of the van."

Five minutes later, Oliver was cocooned in layers of chains and padlocks. His arms were lashed tightly to his sides. He looked very much like Harry Houdini about to perform an escape routine. He was only missing the lock pick tucked under his tongue.

It seemed he'd quickly grown accustomed to physical restraint and he wondered what it meant about his personality. Did he have some deep-seated flaw in his psyche that manifested as extreme passivity? It was probably best not to dwell on such things. He felt claustrophobic, and the weight of the restraints was so burdensome that he was forced to take short shuffling steps. If he were to lose his balance, even a little, he would fall and hit his head.

This is kind of ridiculous," he said. "I can barely walk."

"It's safe," Teddy said. "That's what matters."

"It isn't safe for me. What if I fall and hit my head?"

Teddy smiled. "You look out for *your* safety, I'll look out for everyone else's. Think of it as the needs of the few versus the needs of the many, if it helps. For clarification, you are the few."

Oliver couldn't argue. If he had to go on the attack, his only option would be falling on his opponent's feet in hopes of breaking their toe. The many were certainly safe from him.

Teddy helped him up the steps to the front door, where Emma was waiting. She knocked, and they heard rustling from inside.

A heavy-set woman with grey hair tied back in a loose ponytail answered. She smiled wide when she recognized the couple.

"Emma! Teddy! I can't believe it!"

The woman made no mention of Oliver. With his arms pinned down the way they were, he felt like a big metallic grub. The chains rattled loudly when he tried to nod hello.

She didn't freak out at the sight of him. That meant this kind of thing was probably normal for her. Oliver shuddered.

Emma and the woman embraced. "How are you, Carmella?"

"Better now that you're here! Come in! Come in!"

Oliver wasn't sure if he was supposed to wait on the porch or go inside, but Teddy nudged him and he shuffled over the threshold, clattering and clanking as we went.

Despite being ignored by his hostess, he got a very homey sense from the place. The inside of the doublewide mobile home was surprisingly roomy, and a mini-split air conditioner kept it cool and comfortable. Everything was clean, if not necessarily new, or modern. A wide window at the far end offered a view of the marina. White and blue center-console powerboats bobbed gently at their berths.

The woman—Carmella—busied herself for a moment in the kitchen. "Bert's just across the way at Ed Maloney's. He should be back anytime now. Can I get you some lemonade?"

"Please," Teddy said.

Teddy and Emma sat on a worn sofa, while Oliver remained standing, feeling invisible. He looked at his feet just to make sure he hadn't somehow gone translucent.

He briefly thought of a day exactly one week previous. It was an extraordinary day in its normality. Nothing at all interesting had happened. In a million years, that version of Oliver Bell from a week ago could not have imagined his present circumstances—chained and padlocked in a Florida mobile home, wondering if he was opaque.

Emma leaned close. "Don't worry, Olly. As soon as we confirm that you aren't hosting the demon, we can get those chains off."

He nodded.

It was like she'd read his mind. Heck, at this point it wouldn't surprise him to learn mind-reading was a thing too. He guessed she was just empathetic.

Two and a half centuries old or not, Emma was the only woman, other than his mother, who had ever paid any attention to him. It was kind of sad, in a way—it required possession by an otherworldly entity for a nice woman to talk to him.

Still, he couldn't help but like her. He had to admit, he kind of liked Teddy, too. They were a lot different from him, sure, but aside from forcibly confining him, they were pretty great people.

They certainly weren't the programming team he'd imagined playing such a pivotal role in his future. He realized, to his surprise, that he kind of thought of them as his friends.

Carmella returned from the small kitchen with a tray, upon which rested a pitcher of lemonade and four glasses. It was only after she poured all four that she turned and finally addressed the Jacob Marley-like presence in her house.

"I'm afraid I don't know you," she said. "I'm Carmella."

"I'm Oliver. Nice to meet you."

He rattled the chains over his right hand in a gesture that spoke of having the intention, but not the ability, to shake.

"Would you like some lemonade?" she asked.

"I'd love some," he said, "but at the moment I don't have the use of my arms."

"No," she said, "I suppose you don't."

Oliver remembered his manners, and looked around appreciatively. "This is a lovely home."

Carmella's eyes twinkled. "Thank you, dear! We certainly like it."

She handed lemonade to Teddy and Emma, then took her own glass and eased into a loveseat that was kitty-cornered next to them.

"So is he hosting some kind of demon?" she asked, motioning toward Oliver.

Oliver couldn't help but admire the way she just came out with it. Life, it seemed, was determined to slap him in the face over and over until he accepted this new experience.

"We thought so at first, but we're doubtful at this point," Emma said. "We hoped Bert could tell us."

Though Oliver had been half-heartedly clinging to a vague hope that this entire experience would end with Emma and Teddy receiving psychological help and himself returning back to some kind of academic routine, such an outcome was becoming increasingly unlikely. In this improbable fantasy, he would attribute his willingness to accept the unknown and weird to the shock of having been abducted, combined with a drug-induced suggestive state. Whatever tenuous remains of that possible outcome dissolved when Carmella mentioned the demon. In a way, it was like pulling off a band-aid. It was better done quickly.

Having accepted that he was not experiencing a psychological phenomenon, maybe he could better address the new realities of his life, or whatever remained of it. He allowed himself to hope so.

"If you're having doubts, why is he still trussed up like that?" Carmella asked.

"Better safe than sorry?" Teddy offered.

The door banged open and a deeply suntanned man with a shock of white hair burst in.

"Whose minivan is that?" the man asked in a cantankerous, New York accent.

"For heaven's sake, Bert," Carmella chided, "it belongs to our guests."

Bert squinted as he eyed Oliver, then Teddy and Emma. His mood visibly brightened. He smiled, showing off a perfect set of pearly-white dentures.

"Teddy! Emma! How are you?"

They rose and took turns embracing.

"What's with this?" he asked, motioning to Oliver.

"I'm Oliver Bell, sir," Oliver said. "There's a theory that I'm hosting a demon, intent on destruction. Pleased to meet you."

"Oh!" Bert said.

"We were tracking Amon," Teddy explained. "The Host have been disappearing."

Emma chimed in. "We followed them to that riot in Halifax. We saw Oliver take transfer, and Amon's Legion were swarming the area. Since he took transfer, and Legion usually can't, we thought he could be hosting Amon.

Oliver said the man he took transfer from talked about 'chaos.'"

Bert held up his hands and shook his head. "Wait, wait, wait! Are you saying that you're tracking Amon? Chaos incarnate? The Demon Lord? You're looking for him? And now that you think you caught him, you brought him here!?"

Bert took a step back from Oliver.

"Well... yeah," Teddy said.

"Is this a compulsion, or is this of your own volition?"

"It's by choice, as far as we can tell."

"Why in the hell would you do that? Do you know how dangerous that thing is?"

"Sure," said Teddy.

"What's your plan if this is Amon?"

"I figured I would hit him over the head with a baseball bat," Teddy said. "You know, how I do."

Bert sat down hard in an old brown recliner, and pressed his palm to his forehead as though trying to ward away a migraine. Oliver could sympathize.

"Let me get this straight, Teddy," he said. "You've been tracking a demon that specifically destroys human hosts. A demon that can physically carry the underworld with it. The same demon who commands forty legions in hell and has almost endless resources it can deploy to kill you and collect your Host. And your idea was to get close enough to it that you could kill it with your baseball bat?"

"That's about the long and the short of it, yes."

"I see," Bert said. "And you think this guy is Amon? You're under the impression that one of the most powerful demons in the underworld would... what? Let you chain up his physical embodiment, and drive him to the Florida Keys in a minivan?"

"Probably not," Emma said. "I guess it seems kind of farfetched, when you say it that way."

"He could be lying in wait," Teddy said. "He could be here for you. He could have known we would bring him to you."

"I don't think so," Bert said. "I mean... look at him. He looks pathetic."

"Hey," Oliver said.

"Lots of pathetic-looking people can wreak havoc," Teddy said. "Look at Kim Jong-un! He looks like a Korean version of the Gerber Baby with a side shave.

Bert waved Teddy away.

The old man climbed out of his recliner, and cautiously approached.

"Open your mouth," Bert said to Oliver.

Oliver opened his mouth. Bert squinted. "Aw geez! When did you last brush your teeth, son?"

"I'm sorry. They wouldn't buy me a toothbrush," Oliver said, shooting a glare at Teddy. "They said it would be a waste of money if they had to cave my head in."

"He isn't a demon," Bert said.

Teddy slammed a fist into his open palm. "Rats."

"What do you mean, 'Rats'?" Oliver asked.

"No offense, Oliver. I'm very glad you aren't a demon. But it would have been extremely convenient if you were Amon, and we could kill you and be done with it."

"You—you were *hoping* to kill me? You can't preface something like that by saying 'No offense'!"

Teddy looked confused. "I'm pretty sure I just did."

Emma produced a set of keys and began unlocking the padlocks and removing the chains.

"There's a brand new toothbrush in the bathroom vanity," Carmella offered. "Why don't you freshen up?"

"Thanks," Oliver said. "Hey, can I log in to your WIFI?"

"Sure," Bert said. "It's Homestead. The password is zero, capital 'O,' then two zeros and two more capital 'O's'."

"That's the most insane password I've ever encountered," Oliver said.

"Great, right?" Bert smiled.

In the washroom, Oliver inspected himself in the mirror. He looked bedraggled. His hair was greasy and unkempt. He had coarse stubble on his cheeks. His eyes were red-rimmed and bloodshot.

He looked like a drug addict on a methamphetamine binge.

He should have been overjoyed at the news that he was no longer slated for brutal execution, but he found himself wondering again about Emma and Teddy.

Due to Teddy's resemblance to Dwayne "The Rock" Johnson, it was easier to imagine him crusading around the country hunting some type of murderous hell-spawn. But Emma was different. She was sweet and compassionate. She was maternal, and beautiful, and yet, she was out there too, chasing a lord of the underworld.

Oliver considered her almost supernatural empathy. He wondered if she could sense all the fear and doubt constantly rattling around in his brain, despite his best efforts to bury those thoughts under a mountain of pragmatism. Somehow, the idea of it was even worse than the fact that she had seen him buck-naked.

After brushing his teeth, he opened his mouth and inspected his tongue and tonsils in the mirror, trying to guess just what, exactly, Bert had been searching for. What part of his oral cavity said, "I'm not possessed by a demon lord"?

"Who the hell knows," he whispered.

He checked his phone and saw he had an email from his mother. She'd seen the news footage of the riots, and pieced together that his home was inside the Vagisil Autonomous Zone. She wanted to make sure he was OK.

He loved her dearly, but their relationship was complicated. Ever since his father died, he felt a tremendous responsibility for her happiness and well-being. Responsibility—and a good dose of guilt, since he chose to live two hundred miles away. He could not escape the fact that he'd pursued his academic career over staying home. He tried to make up for that choice with daily phone calls and emails, but now they hadn't communicated in three days, and the old guilt began to churn out its familiar pang, flaring up like heartburn of the soul.

He quickly wrote her back:

Bit of a long story. I'm in Florida, but heading back shortly. Will call as soon as I am able.
-Love Olly

Next, he checked the news and discovered that the Vagisil Autonomous Zone had collapsed. A schism had arisen between the occupants when it was revealed that celebrated progressive writer Margaret Atwood still consumed chicken and fish. Half the population had demanded the removal of Atwood's work from the compendium of published literature, while the other half had insisted on granting the author of *The Handmaid's Tale* an exception. A brief, but bloody civil war had ensued, leaving the VAZ in ruins.

It all seemed very distant and unimportant.

Oliver considered writing to his doctoral supervisor to explain why he would be unable to defend his thesis, but he always had to be careful with those emails. He and his supervisor, Gerald Leger, had a strained rapport. This was doubtlessly due to the fact that Oliver was significantly more intelligent, but Gerald was much better at politicking. About a year earlier, when Gerald realized just how much impact Oliver's work could have on the coding world, in fear for his own tenured position, he began a personal campaign against his subordinate within the faculty. As always, academic politics were especially vicious due to the stakes being so small.

He decided not to write to Gerald after all. Pocketing his phone, he returned to the living room.

He felt a little bit sad. Weird though they were, Teddy and Emma were the first friends he'd had in a long while. He could hardly believe it, but he would miss them.

"So, I'm going to get going," he announced.

"Where?" Teddy asked.

"My mom's house, I think. It should be OK, now that I'm not a demon."

"You live with your mother?" Bert asked, "A young man like you?"

"His apartment was burned down in a riot," Emma explained. "Something about cheese and bookshelves. You know how those things are."

"A young man like you should be out gallivanting," Bert proclaimed, "sowing your wild oats, if you know what I mean."

Bert made an obscene gesture, poking the index finger of one hand through a ring made by the thumb and forefinger of the other. The sight of the leathery old man, in turquoise Bermuda shorts and a pale-pink golf shirt making such a gesture, put Oliver off, and the fact that Teddy sat grinning and nodding wasn't helping.

Oliver always found sexual innuendo embarrassing. He suspected this might be due to his own near complete lack of experience, but he preferred to think he was simply committed to etiquette.

Oliver's obvious discomfort only made Bert thrust the finger in and out faster. "You smell what I'm cooking here, right?"

"Oh Bert," Carmella said.

"I told him he needs to fornicate more," Teddy said, "but he doesn't listen."

"Don't you want to stick around and find out what you're hosting?" asked Bert.

Oliver hadn't realized this was an option. "You can tell?"

"Sure."

"I'd like to know," Emma said. "He's some kind of golden mouth."

"Interesting," Bert said. "I think he's a dark, but I can't tell for sure. Rare to have a dark golden mouth."

"How could you tell he's not Amon?" Teddy asked.

"Trade secret," Bert said. "You guys want to go for a boat ride?"

"I really should be going," Oliver said. "Also, I need to borrow some money."

"You don't have to go, Hon," Emma said. "Now that we don't have to kill you, we can be friends."

Despite the way she'd worded it, the idea was appealing. Having now accepted that he was a new awakened inhabitant of a universe of demons, and celestial Host, and who knew what else, he figured it might not be a terrible idea to at least try to learn from the experience of the seasoned professionals in his company. For all he knew, there could be knife-wielding Chucky dolls, or aliens armed with blasters, or werewolves or something waiting for him around the next corner. Since learning that the world wasn't what it seemed, maybe it would be best to learn just how different things really were.

Still, he had a life to return to.

When he spoke, his voice was uncertain.

"I think I should probably get back to the university. I have a lot of work to do, you know? I mean, I lost everything."

"Oh, you can't go back," Bert said, matter of fact.

"Sure I can," Oliver said, his voice betraying sudden doubt. "Right?"

He looked to Emma, who pursed her lips and shook her head.

Oliver had imagined there must be all kinds of human hosts around, doing mundane jobs and just waiting for a compulsion to strike. He'd begun to think of his condition in medical terms, like Crohn's Disease. Sure, there might be inconveniences and flare-ups, but there would be lots of normal periods in between, when he could be a productive member of society.

"They'll kill you," Teddy said.

Oliver didn't much care for the unsentimental way Teddy delivered this belated piece of important information.

"Who, exactly, will kill me?"

"Who do you think?"

"Amon? He doesn't even know who I am!"

"Do you remember," Teddy asked, "the cop who was about to shoot you after the statue fell on the detective?"

"Yes."

"How do you think he knew to ask for your charm?"

Oliver startled. He hadn't thought about it.

"He was hosting Legion... a devil... one of Amon's foot soldiers, so to speak," Emma said. "He witnessed you take transfer of the host. That means they know."

"Yeah, but he's dead," Oliver said. "Teddy smashed his head in."

"Sure, but whatever possessed him isn't dead. It's moved on. It's networking with its buddies. And it knows what you are."

"That's ridiculous," Oliver said. He was, once again, unable to sound even remotely confident.

"Amon hunts human hosts," Emma said. "He kills them. And when he does, he collects or somehow destroys their Celestial Host as well. That's our theory, anyway. It's why we're hunting him."

"Why would he do that?" Oliver asked.

"Because," Bert said, "his goal is chaos. To upset the Great Balance. The Host maintain the balance. Legion destroys the balance. It's how it works."

"No offense intended here, but this all sounds kind of cheesy," Oliver said.

"Oh, it's real," Carmella said. "It might sound like it falls a little on the sci-fi-fantasy side of pulp fiction, but make no mistake—you are in a dangerous predicament. Why do you think human hosts like Teddy and Emma have to go around living like nomads? Legion recognizes them. If they stayed in one place, they'd make for an easy target."

All this time, Oliver had just assumed that Teddy and Emma had a home base somewhere. He'd simply been too absorbed in his own drama to ask about it. But when he pictured the odometer of the Honda Odyssey—the mileage number was a *big one*. He believed it started with a four.

"I...I have to live like a nomad?"

"For the time being, it's probably best," Bert said.

"For the time being? How much time are we talking?"

"Oh, it's hard to say," Bert began.

"Five hundred years, give or take," Teddy said. "You make it five hundred years, you'll probably fall off their radar."

Oliver recoiled as though he'd been kicked. Overwhelmed to the point of stupefaction, he squeezed the bridge of his nose and tried to process this newest revelation. *Five hundred years!*

"Let me take you for a sunset boat ride," Bert said, getting to his feet. "We'll find out what you're hosting, and I can show you some things that will help you understand. It'll take an hour—unless we see some Spanish mackerel, in which case we're also going to fish for a while. I just picked up a new reel. A Penn Spinfisher Six!"

"Come on, Oliver," Emma said. "What's the hurry? Why not spend one more night with us. You have a lot to learn, and we're at your service. If you still want to go in the morning, Teddy and I can drive you wherever you want to go, to start carving out your own path."

"You should take them up on it," Carmella offered. "Teddy and Emma are exceptionally good at what they do."

"We are," Teddy said, his tone matter of fact.

Oliver was drowning, and here they were offering him a life preserver. He needed to find out what it was that he was hosting. That went without saying. But he needed something else too.

He turned back to Emma. "Can you do it on cue?" he asked. "You know, that thing where you make me feel like my head isn't going to explode?"

She smiled, and put her hand on his shoulder. "Your head won't explode," she promised.

He felt better. He also happened to really like fishing.

He would stay. He would sleep on it. Things would feel less chaotic by morning. He never liked to make major decisions when he was upset, so for now, it was settled.

He had to admit, he was going to need guidance. After all, what did he know about 'carving out his own path' or living a nomadic lifestyle? He'd been lonely before, living above the Old Dairy Deli and Donair, and spending all his spare time in a computer lab, but the idea of driving aimlessly back and forth across the Great White North without Teddy, or Emma, or any companionship whatsoever for the next five centuries was terrifying.

He had managed his loneliness in Halifax by promising himself better times to come. Accepting that such times were out of the question, and that he would have to endure so much of himself for so long was a very bitter pill to swallow.

So while he wasn't happy about his circumstances, he was beginning to understand his new companions as life preservers in a sea of aloneness that would otherwise drive him gradually insane.

As they walked down the path to the floating dock, they saw an ambulance enter the RV park. Its lights were flashing, but the driver didn't sound the siren.

It parked at the beige mobile home across the street from Bert and Carmella's.

"I wonder what that's all about," Teddy said.

"Oh, I had to kill Ed Maloney just before you guys arrived," Bert said. "Nice guy—nasty colon cancer though."

Oliver stopped.

"You killed him? You killed Ed Maloney? Your neighbor?"

"It's kind of what I do," Bert said. "Didn't you guys tell this kid anything?"

"You kill people?"

"I don't think he quite gets it yet," Emma said, taking Oliver's hand. "Oliver, Bert is Death."

"Death? Like the Grim Reaper?"

"Not *the* Grim Reaper, more like *a* grim reaper," Bert said.

"You're really not all that grim," Teddy said.

"No, I'm not. I suppose you could say I'm a not-so-grim reaper."

Oliver was stunned. Hosts, Legion, Demons, Grim Reapers... What the hell?! Bring on the Demogorgon from *Stranger Things*, and have it do a square dance with Spock and Sulu!

Acceptance, he reminded himself. *Acceptance was the key to surviving this.*

"How does it work?" he asked.

"Another trade secret," Bert said. "Sorry."

"But you're a host, like these guys?"

"Not exactly," Bert said, "but I suppose you could say that we operate in the same dimensional spectrum."

"He's kind of a celestial scholar," Emma explained. "They often get appointed death duties."

"OK," Oliver said. "What about Carmella?"

"She was the secretary at my clinic," Bert said, "but you know how things happen." He made the obscene gesture with his fingers again, then high-fived Teddy.

They arrived at Bert's boat—a center-console twenty-four-footer called *Code Blue.*

Emma laughed. "Clever," she said.

"I'm a retired cardiologist," Bert said to Oliver. "It's sort of a double-entendre. I picked her up a few months ago. Always wanted one."

They embarked and found their seats. Bert kicked the twin outboards to life. A moment later they were cruising out of the mouth of the harbor into a brilliant sunset, the open waters of the Gulf of Mexico stretching endlessly ahead. On the horizon, distant lights twinkled, marking the locations of a half-dozen offshore oil rigs.

Oliver couldn't hear much over the drone of the engines and the slap of the waves against the hull, and he felt OK about that. He sat on a padded bench seat and watched the sun set over the turquoise waves.

His life had turned so suddenly from one thing into another thing, it was giving him a kind of mental whiplash. He couldn't seem to build momentum in any direction before being forced to take a new turn. And yet, he had to admit, he was not entirely unhappy. This new existence was at least interesting. And his old life, now that he had some time to consider it, was pretty bland.

The idea of living like a nomad had a silver lining. He was sure to see a lot of the world. He wondered if he would be able to see his mother again. He was about to ask, but then noticed Teddy and Emma holding hands, staring into the sunset. He didn't want to interrupt their moment.

He smiled. Aside from drugging him, stripping him and chaining him to a campground, had they really treated him all that badly? The toothbrush issue was a minor quibble, but for a kidnapping and possible murder, the entire experience had been relatively civilized.

Watching them casually embrace gave him hope. There could be someone out there for him, too. Someone who accepted his soon-to-be bizarre lifestyle and idiosyncrasies. Someone who enjoyed his company.

As the sun kissed the horizon, Bert slowed the boat and killed the engines. "Beautiful, isn't it?" he said.

Emma leaned into Teddy. "It never gets old."

Bert took Oliver by the hand and helped him to his feet. "Alright, Mr. Bell, are you ready to find out what you're hosting?"

"Will it hurt?"

"Only if you resist." Bert's eyes sparkled with the kind of mischief particular to kind old men.

"I have no plans to," Oliver said. "In for a penny, etcetera."

"Terrific."

Emma and Teddy had found seats at the stern, but Bert motioned for them to come closer. "I'll need you near for this part to work," he said.

He cleared his voice.

The retired cardiologist concentrated for a moment. Oliver wasn't sure whether it was real, or simply his imagination, but the pocket of air around them seemed to grow darker, as though the light had thinned. The sounds of the waves and the breeze grew distant.

When Bert spoke, his voice was like wind through ancient reeds, and Oliver got the distinct impression that Bert was, in fact, no longer there at all. He spoke in a Latin dialect, but somehow Oliver understood the gist of what the old man was saying.

"Tu exaundi me spiritus?"

(Spirit, do you hear me?)

Oliver had no intention of speaking to that terrifying primordial voice.

Something inside him, however, had different ideas. A compulsion to answer rocketed through his brain.

"*Ego operor.*"

(I do.)

The creeping sensation of being spoken through gave Oliver such a jolt that his knees buckled. Teddy grabbed his arm and steadied him.

Emma wrapped a surprisingly strong arm around his waist.

Bert continued.

"*Quid enim tuum est nomen, spiritus?*"

(Spirit, what is your name?)

He couldn't help it: for a moment, Oliver resisted. An indescribable bolt of pain exploded in his head, sending molten shards of agony ricocheting around his skull. He groaned, and stopped resisting. When he did, the pain disappeared.

"*Vicium Mehemmi!*"

Bert let go of Oliver's hands and the illusion of darkness and seclusion instantly shattered.

"Whoa," Oliver said.

"Mayhem," Bert said. "I wasn't expecting that."

"Mayhem?" Oliver asked.

"You're hosting it," Bert said.

"Wow!" Teddy sounded impressed. "That's a rare one."

"You know," Oliver said, "I think Detective Jennings said that, before he died. He said 'Mayhem.'"

"What!?" Teddy exclaimed.

Emma stiffened.

"Yeah, when the statue fell on him, and he gave me the library card. He said something about mayhem. I thought he was talking about the riot."

"Oh, for the love of Pete," Teddy said, shaking his head in disbelief.

"What?"

"You told us he said something about 'chaos.'"

"Hey, you drugged me," Oliver protested. "You can't expect me to remember everything under duress. I thought you were about to smash my head in. Chaos. Mayhem. They're practically the same thing!"

"It's OK, Oliver," Emma said, her voice soothing, "It might have saved us some worry, that's all. No harm done."

Oliver turned to Bert, who was in the process of tying a lure to the end of a fishing line.

"All this stuff is real, isn't it?" he said.

"Oh yes." Bert didn't look up from the job at hand.

"Host. Legion—the Grim Reaper? All of it?"

"Did the scales fall from your eyes?" Bert asked. "Because it sounds like the scales just fell from your eyes."

The old man cast the lure into the waves.

Oliver turned to Teddy, "And you're really a thousand years old?"

"Don't remind me," Teddy said.

"And you..." Oliver looked to Emma, "you're the embodiment of Forbearance? A celestial entity that lives inside a human host?"

"Uh huh," she confirmed.

"This is all real," he said again. "All of it."

"Afraid so," said Bert, who jigged the lure back through the water. "Grab a rod... fishing will make you feel better."

Oliver, a quick study in the abandonment of resistance, grabbed a rod.

"There are some lures in that tackle box." Bert pointed. "Pick a shiny one."

Oliver did as instructed and took a spot against the gunwale beside the not-so-grim reaper, while Teddy and Emma talked in hushed tones on the bench seat in the bow.

"How old are you, if you don't mind me asking?"

"Me?" said Bert, "I'm seventy-three."

"So not hundreds of years old?"

"Oh no—like I said, I'm not a human host. Death is different. It's just a job."

"Do you get paid?"

"For being Death? Sort of. The reward is illumination."

"Illumination?"

"I'm a curious man. I get to learn things."

Oliver hooked a Spanish mackerel that zigged and zagged, pulling line off his reel. The drag screamed, and he intuitively tightened it to prevent a bird's nest.

"Like riding a bike, huh?" Bert said.

Oliver grinned.

After a brief fight, he flipped the fish into the boat.

"That was great," he said. "Ever since I started my PhD, I've been promising myself I'd come to Florida. That I'd go fishing."

Bert slapped him on the back. "And here you are."

"Here I am."

"Can you guess why?"

"Why I'm here?"

"Yeah... why you're in Florida."

"I suppose it's because you're here," Oliver said. "They brought me so you could, uh, inspect me."

"Sort of. Before now, you've been living in a world of *if*—you know computers, right? Back in the day, basic programming was done in something called *if/then statements*—the user presses the 'w' key, then print 'w,' do you follow?"

"Of course."

"Right, but when you live in the 'if,' you are reacting to events around you. What you need to learn now, is how to live in the 'why.'"

"OK," Oliver said. "Why?"

"See! You're off to a good start," Bert said, then, "Holy Moly!"

A fish had taken his lure and was quickly stealing line.

"That's no mackerel!" Bert cried. The old man's excitement was contagious.

"Probably a Jack Crevalle," Teddy said, joining them at the rail.

"How do you know?" Oliver asked.

"I spent two hundred and thirty years as a fisherman," Teddy explained.

"Oh. I was hoping for something more normal."

"It's the way it takes the line straight out without any head-shakes," Teddy said.

Oliver smiled. "Thanks."

Warm, gentle darkness settled over the Gulf of Mexico. The quiet waves slapped the hull in a rhythmic, aquatic lullaby. Lights from the shore twinkled. Oliver watched them, and wondered, in the decades or even centuries to come, how many of those lights he would see again. He thought maybe some. He thought this was a very good place to be.

With the moon and stars lighting their way, they returned the *Code Blue* to its berth in the marina. On the way home, Bert taught Oliver the controls, and though it was really quite simple, Oliver was gracious, because it seemed to mean a lot to the childless retiree, and because Oliver was, despite his aloofness, compassionate.

As they made their way along the path to the double-wide, Emma rubbed Oliver's shoulder. "Are you feeling better now?"

He did a quick self-assessment.

"Yeah. I guess I am."

Carmella met them at the door and took Oliver's two fish from him. "I'll just pop these in the fridge," she said.

She ushered them through to the screened-in patio, where she had prepared a large Caesar salad, a vegetable tray and a heaping plate of sandwiches.

"This looks lovely, Carm," Bert said, pecking her on the cheek.

They found their places around the table. Bert bowed his head, and everyone else followed.

"*Barukh ata Adonai Eloheinu melekh ha'olam borei minei mezenot.*"

He raised his head and grabbed the salad tongs.

"Was that Hebrew?" Oliver asked.

"Yup."

"You guys are Jewish?"

"Indeed," Bert said. "You want beer?"

"I want beer," Teddy said.

Bert excused himself and returned a moment later with a dozen Coronas in a bucket of ice.

Teddy popped the cap off a bottle using only his thumb, and offered cheers, then tilted the beer and drained it in a single swallow.

"Oh, to have a self-healing liver," Bert lamented.

Oliver realized he was going to have another opportunity to observe Teddy eating. He was actually looking forward to the show.

"So, Oliver, what are you hosting?" Carmella asked.

"Mayhem, apparently," Oliver said.

"Oh dear."

"What?"

"Well, I don't know that I should be the one to tell you," Carmella began.

"Mayhems don't tend to last very long," Teddy said, sounding only half-interested. "It's a very dangerous Host."

"*What!?*"

"They're drawn to major drama," Bert said. "By which I mean war, riots, terrorist attacks. You know, that kind of stuff."

"I'm a mathematician," Oliver said, feeling a little weak. "Can I, like, swap with someone?"

"That's not how it works," Carmella said. "You get what you get."

Bert cleared his throat. "You being a mathematician is probably no coincidence. Just like the Host can protect you from all kinds of ailments, maybe you'll be able to protect your Host by thinking logically and pragmatically. A

Mayhem Host paired with a human that tends toward spontaneity would be an explosive combination. This is just a theory of course, but perhaps you and your Host will be able to mitigate one another's weaknesses."

"In time, you'll come to think of it as a privilege," Emma said. "Since you're almost certainly going to die in service of the Great Balance."

"That sounds extremely cult-like," Oliver said.

"Sorry."

"So you think Mayhem *decided* to transfer to a guy like me, who spends his whole life hunting for order? That it was a conscious decision? Are they, like, aware of what they're doing when they transfer to a person?"

"Sometimes it's just whoever's closest when the human host dies," Bert explained. "Other times there's some intelligence behind it. That could be the case here. I mean, hosting Mayhem doesn't necessarily mean you're going to be out causing mayhem—for the most part, you'll probably be trying to quell it. You're a golden mouth, after all. That's what we call a 'pacifying gift.' So maybe in that sense, having a mathematician committed to order as a human host is intuitive."

"How often do you get these compulsions?" Oliver asked Bert.

"Me? I'm different. I'm not like you guys. But you? I'd guess, once a week or thereabouts."

"So I'm going to be in some major drama once a week for the rest of my life?"

Bert showed his palms, "I don't really know. I'm just guessing."

Oliver could accept a great many things. He could accept the nomadic lifestyle. He could accept the occasional outburst of his Host entity. He could *almost* accept what had become of his life. But could *not* accept constant, prolonged drama.

"I'm not sure I can handle this," he said.

"My advice? Don't resist. Just go with it."

"You know," Oliver said, "that's kind of been a theme over the last few days."

The sandwich platter had a little of everything. Oliver chose roast beef, and it was shockingly good, the bread was soft and fresh, the meat, perfectly moist. Bert explained that the deli counter at the nearby Publix was the best he'd ever found.

"Terrific meats there. I have a guy, Bruce. If he doesn't have what you're looking for, he'll order it in. Great guy."

Everyone but Teddy nursed their beer, and Bert and Carmella talked about the weather, and retirement, and Florida, and their boat, and for a while, Oliver could almost imagine that his universe hadn't just been turned upside down.

He allowed himself some financial curiosity. How could they drive around the country, living like nomads, and still pay for things like gasoline and food? When there was a momentary lull in the conversation, he decided to do some digging.

"How are we supposed to make money?" he asked. "I mean, we still have to exist in society, right?"

"Oh, that's actually pretty cool," Teddy said. "I'll show you."

Teddy had drunk five bottles of Corona, but if he was feeling the alcohol, it didn't show. He stood easily and walked with his usual lumbering, muscular grace. Oliver followed him out to the driveway.

Teddy opened the trunk of the minivan and retrieved a duffel bag from the back. He handed it to Oliver.

The bag was heavy. A long, metallic structure ran along its length, and Oliver pictured a rifle. Surely they weren't about to stick-up a 7-Eleven.

"Go ahead," Teddy said, "open it."

Oliver set the bag on the grass and unzipped it. He reached in and pulled out a metal detector.

"Huh?"

"Look, it goes together like this." Teddy snapped the pieces together and adjusted the search coil.

"Since these things came along, life has gotten infinitely better," he said.

"What's happening?" Oliver asked, alarmed. He imagined his life as a bum, sweeping public beaches with a metal detector to find aluminum beer cans that he could take to the recycling depot.

"You asked how to make money. This is how."

"You take a metal detector around, and... what? Collect scrap?"

"Try it."

He handed Oliver the device, then flipped a switch on the control box.

"Look around," he instructed, "and try to guess where something of value might be."

"I mean, the van is probably worth fifteen thousand dollars," Oliver said.

"That isn't what I mean. Concentrate."

Resisting nothing at all, Oliver decided to play along. He did a visual search of his surroundings until he found himself staring at a patch of grass on a corner of the recently deceased Ed Maloney's lot.

"How about there?" he said pointing.

"Give it a sweep," Teddy suggested.

Oliver clumsily ambled over to the place he'd picked. Unlike Teddy, he *could* feel the effect of the alcohol from the single bottle of beer. He ambled, instead of walked, because ambling just felt better.

He swept the patch of grass until he heard a high-pitched beep. He stooped and felt through the grass with his hands, but found nothing.

"Here." Teddy offered him a garden spade.

"Is this, like, OK?" Oliver asked.

"I don't think Ed Maloney is going to complain."

"Right."

Oliver dug down into the lawn where the detector had indicated. After a few moments the spade struck something firm. He widened the hole and extracted a plastic laundry detergent jug. This was *not* what he was expecting.

"Hmm..."

"Let's see." Teddy took the jug. He gave it a shake and something rattled inside.

"Ooh!" he said. "Good one."

He unscrewed the top. "Hold out your hand."

When Oliver did, Teddy dumped nearly a dozen heavy coins into Oliver's palm. The coins were heavy, and when he inspected them in the streetlight he saw that they were one-ounce gold Eagles. "No way!" Oliver said.

He turned one of the coins over and over, feeling its weight. "We can't keep these—they belong to his family."

"Hey, Bert!" Teddy called to the back yard, "Did Ed Maloney have any family?"

"Nope!" Bert shouted back.

"Looks like they're yours."

"Seriously?"

Teddy nodded.

"What do I do with them?"

"If it were me, I'd take a few to one of those gold exchange places and tell them you want the 'employee rate.' They'll give you spot price minus one percent."

"You mean those greasy cash-for-gold places know about the Host and Legion and all that?"

"Know about it? I'm pretty sure human hosts invented them!"

"No kidding," Oliver said.

"Anyway, if you're ever short on cash, just pick up one of these." Teddy stuffed the metal detector back into the bag.

"And it works every time?"

"When you need it to, it does."

"Incredible!"

"You get used to it."

Oliver did not believe that he would.

After coffee and key lime pie, Bert and Carmella offered Oliver the couch. They gave Teddy and Emma the spare room. While it wasn't particularly late, Oliver was exhausted.

Before turning in, he had a long shower. When he washed his hair, he thought he could still smell the smoke from his night in the Autonomous Zone. As it rinsed away and circled down the drain, the soot seemed to carry with it his previous plans for the future.

He pondered the twists and turns of his fortune, and wondered if there might be a mathematical model to be found, despite the superficial chaos. As a fresh graduate student, he had chosen one of the least probable paths to his PhD, and at that time, guessing the long game was peering through a glass, but darkly. Then he had stumbled upon success, and all the vagaries had clarified into bright, certain hope. With that hope dashed, the upcoming was once again dim and cast in shadow.

"It's cycloidal," he said to himself. "Certainty is cycloidal."

After washing up, the stench of ash in his clothing was even stronger. Making a mental note to buy some deodorant, and some fresh clothes, he shimmied back into his boxer shorts, felt his way through the darkened living room, and taking his place on the sofa, laid his head against a pillow and pulled a blanket up over his eyes.

— *Five* —

"You should probably get up."

Oliver strained to open his eyes.

He'd been dreaming about the riot in Halifax. His dream must have been triggered by the nearby shouts and screams, or, perhaps, by the smell of smoke.

The air was hot. Everything glowed. Flickering orange flames filled the windows.

Teddy gave him another shake. "The mobile home is on fire."

He came wide awake. "What's going on, Teddy? Another riot? In a senior's trailer park?"

"Looks that way," Teddy said. "Hop to, Mr. Mayhem."

"Oh, that sucks."

He rolled off the couch and quickly slid his jeans on over his boxer shorts. The air was acrid and it made him cough. He fumbled for his glasses and strained to see out the window, but the view was obscured in fire. A crowd was chanting. Somebody was shouting incoherently into a megaphone. Oliver made out the words "taxation" and "administration," but nothing more. As far as chants went, it wasn't very catchy.

His exhaustion had left his brain in a fog, and it took a second for him to reassemble the complicated web of events that had ultimately placed him in a burning Floridian mobile home.

Smoke stung his eyes and tore at his throat. Something whistled past his head, and hit the living room wall with a loud crack. It bounced across the floor, fluttering as it tumbled, then came to rest against his bare foot. He squinted to examine the thing—a charred, hard-cover copy of *The Wealthy Barber Returns* by David Chilton. Oliver had a moment to briefly wonder what David Chilton had to do with this latest conflagration, then inhaled a particularly bad lungful and fell into a coughing fit.

He went to his knees on the carpet to get below the smoke, the way a firefighter had shown his Grade One class when he was six years old. It worked. He could breathe much better.

He fumbled with his shoes, and crammed them over his bare feet. His shirt was missing.

"Teddy!" he called.

"What?" Teddy said from the guest room, where he too was fumbling to get dressed.

"What's this about? Why are they rioting?"

"I think it's the S.C.A. They've been protesting in gated retirement communities all month. This one obviously turned violent."

"What's the S.C.A.?" Oliver shouted.

"The Society of Communist Accountants!" Teddy shouted back. "They're airing their grievance about the inherent inequality of America's 401k system, which, according to their manifesto, lends double advantage to those with well-paying jobs by creating a retirement savings vehicle that leads to a tax-deferral, thus providing, in their opinion, an unfairly fiscally healthy position to those who save aggressively!"

"Accountants?" Oliver shouted through the smoke and flame. "Are they dangerous?"

"Extremely!"

Oliver had never imagined that such militant accountants might exist. All the accountants he personally knew were so docile and sedentary, one could almost mistake them for pieces of office furniture.

Emma crawled, army-style, out of the bedroom and shimmied up beside him. "We need to get Bert and Carmella," she said.

She wormed past Oliver toward the master bedroom.

He tried to emulate the way she was crawling, but found he was terrible at it. It clearly required some measure of core strength. He decided, instead, to crouch-walk, stooped over at the waist.

He finally caught a glance through the smoke outside the broken kitchen window. A crowd surrounded the minivan in the driveway. They rocked it side to side. A massive column of shabbily dressed men were bottlenecked along the cul-de-sac toward the trailer park entrance. They all seemed to be heading in the direction of Bert and Carmella's burning home.

Many in the crowd waved signs that read "Allow me to Bene-FIT my Fist Down Your Throat!" and "Why Don't You Come Closer and Discover My Arm's Length Range."

"We're way outnumbered," he said.

"Outnumbered?" Emma said. "Is that an accounting joke?"

"Maybe. In the future, assuming we survive this, would you mind pretending I did that on purpose?"

"Sure," she said. "Look, I don't want you to worry. This is nothing. We just need to get everyone out safe."

"How?"

"We'll think of something."

The wall-mounted flat-screen television crashed to the floor. The wall behind it was aflame.

For the second time in a week, Oliver was acutely concerned about the possibility of immolation. He marveled at the inconceivable statistical improbability of duplicate immolation threats to a theoretical mathematics student within such a short span of time.

He watched Emma bash her way through the door to the master bedroom, and tuck and roll no less than a millisecond before Carmella fired a twelve-gauge shotgun at her head. The deafening *boom* rocked the mobile home, and the glass coffee table beside Oliver exploded into tiny shards.

"Oh! I'm sorry," Carmella cried. "I thought you were one of them!"

"You thought I was a communist accountant?" Emma said. "I'm wearing hundred-dollar yoga pants."

"I don't have my contacts in!"

"We're going," said Bert. He pushed past the women into the living room, and they followed.

Bert had dressed in jeans, deck shoes with no socks, a white golf shirt tucked in at the waist, a leather weave belt, and a lightweight sports coat. How or why he had put together the snappy ensemble was a mystery, but Oliver couldn't help but think the old man looked handsome and dapper.

The bay window overlooking the driveway burst inward, and a man with an unkempt beard, wearing a threadbare, drab olive, three-piece suit forced his way into the living room. He was brandishing a long, weather-worn, wooden-stocked rifle of some kind.

"Communist accountant!" Oliver shouted, pointing.

Teddy jumped over the smoldering loveseat and grabbed the man. He snatched the rifle from the accountant's hands, cracked it in half over his knee, and hurled the pieces back out the window.

"What do you think you're doing, comrade?" the man yelled.

Teddy flipped the communist accountant over his hip, and with one hand full of rumpled suit and the other full of wiry beard hair, threw him full force through the flimsy, burning trailer wall and out onto the lawn.

Oliver caught Teddy's eye and noticed he was grinning.

"I've never been a fan of communism," Teddy said. "Probably because I experienced the Great Leap Forward."

"Speaking of which..." Bert said. The retired cardiologist lifted a potted fern from the corner of the room and chucked it through the window that overlooked the marina. "After you, dear," he said to his wife.

Carmella hopped out the broken window to the footpath below. She was followed by Bert. Oliver was next, and then Teddy and Emma.

"You know," Oliver said, "that's the third potted plant I've seen go through a window in as many days."

They were halfway down the path when a woman called out. "Oliver? Oliver Bell?"

Oliver turned and stopped. It was the police officer—the same attractive police officer he'd met in the burning library in Nova Scotia. Only, she was here, standing on the path behind them. Crazily, she still wore her uniform from the Halifax Police Department, though why she should be in uniform, he couldn't begin to imagine. This was pretty much as far out of her jurisdiction as she could get while still being on land.

His mind flashed to a Humphrey Bogart line from Casablanca. "Of all the gin joints, in all the towns, in all the world..."

"We have to stop meeting this way," Oliver said, impressed by how cool he sounded.

"Where are you going?" she asked.

"Bert has a boat. You should come."

"She isn't real," Bert warned, but Oliver could barely hear him. He liked the way her eyes gleamed in the night. His heart thrilled at the idea of a second chance to get her name, and maybe a phone number. Everything else had become unimportant.

"I was kind of hoping you were going to ask me out," she said.

"I...uh... I wanted to," Oliver began. "But my thesis—"

"She's a glamour," Bert said. The old man had turned around, and now jogged back up the path to Oliver.

Oliver paid no attention. Bert seemed far away. The cacophony of the riot was almost non-existent. The woman was the entire universe.

He was in love. It was something he'd never thought possible.

Slowly, in a stupor, he stumbled back up the path. She held her hands out to him, palms open, beckoning.

"How did you find me?"

"Oh... A trade secret."

"Stop him!" Bert cried.

Oliver reached out to grasp her hands—and paused for the briefest of moments. Somewhere in his reptilian brain an alarm blasted, sounding for his attention. None of this made sense. She couldn't have driven all this way here in riot gear. And why was everything so quiet?

She reached out to take his hands, but Emma sprang up the path and tackled her. For just a nanosecond, Oliver saw that there *was* no beautiful woman. The "woman" was, in fact, another bearded man, this one wearing military fatigues and a fur hat.

A blinding silent flash split the night. He threw his hands up to shield his face. The fog that had so completely wreathed his mind now evaporated just as quickly. But when his eyes adjusted, he was alone. Emma was gone.

"Emma?!" he shouted. "Emma!"

Teddy jogged up the path and stared at the place Emma had just been. "Where is she?" he demanded.

"She's gone," Bert said.

"Gone?"

"It was a glamour. A portal, I think. She touched it."

"A portal? A portal to where?"

"There's no way of knowing," Bert said. "I think they're supposed to lead to a different dimension—the underworld. I've never actually seen one."

"She's in the underworld?" Teddy's face was a distorted mask of sorrow and pain.

"I'm sorry," Bert said.

Oliver stood dumbfounded. What had he done? Had he just killed Emma—the most beautiful human being in existence? How could he be so stupid?

A group of communist accountants charged around the corner and spotted them.

Teddy rolled up his sleeves.

Oliver, suddenly seized by a compulsion, faced the big man. "They didn't take her," he said, calmly. "They're just run-of-the-mill communists. Legion infiltrated them and took her. Legion did this."

Oliver shook his head and cleared his throat. "Man, that's disconcerting. Sorry."

"Don't even try that golden mouth crap on me," Teddy said, placing his gigantic hand on Oliver's face, and pushing him aside.

The big man charged up the path toward the accountants. By the time the rioters realized what was happening, it was too late. Teddy stooped and grabbed the nearest one by the ankles and began to swing him in an impossibly fast whirlwind. Round and round the screaming man went. His wire-framed glasses and Chairman Mao cap flew off into the night. Finally, Teddy released him at just the right moment, and he crashed into his equally dingily dressed comrades who had been trying to escape into the relative safety of the trailer fire. They lay in a groaning heap of contused limbs, confused ideals and stale pipe tobacco.

"Come on," Bert said, taking Teddy by the arm. "She isn't dead. She's going to need you."

Refusing to make eye contact with Oliver, Teddy allowed himself to be led back toward the fishing boat.

Oliver felt like a supreme jerk. He still wasn't sure what had happened. He only knew that he was responsible for it.

As his companions retreated down the path, he stood facing the burning home, waiting for the next wave of communist accountants. They would find him, and maybe beat him up a little bit. He deserved it.

He had let his friends down. He had screwed them over. Emma was so kind. She deserved better. And now she was in the underworld, thanks to him.

A massive hand grabbed him by the shoulder.

"Come on," Teddy said.

"I... I screwed up."

"We'll figure it out. Let's go!"

Oliver fell against the big man, his legs suddenly wobbly. "I'm so sorry, Teddy. I'm so frigging sorry."

Teddy was about to respond when a whistling crack split the air and the trunk of a nearby palm tree burst into splinters.

"No time for that," Teddy said. "They're shooting."

He hoisted Oliver by the waistband and made double-time for the marina. Bullets fired from surplus Soviet and Chinese military rifles ripped apart the nearby foliage.

"I think we're about to die," Oliver observed as he bounced down the path, suspended by the back of his pants.

"Those garbage rods they're shooting haven't been sighted in at least forty years," Teddy said. "Plus, they're accountants. They have terrible aim."

"Like stormtroopers?"

"Huh?"

"You know," Oliver prodded, "Stormtroopers. In *Star Wars*."

"I have no idea what you're talking about," Teddy said.

"*Star Wars!* Luke Skywalker!? Darth Vader!? Alderaan!?"

"I'm sorry. I don't really listen to much disco."

"What!?"

As they climbed aboard *Code Blue*, a loud *whump* sounded from the direction of the trailer and echoed back to them from the breakwater jetty.

"What was that?" Oliver asked as he tried to sort out his atomic wedgie.

"I could be wrong, but it sounded like the gas tank of a late-model Honda Odyssey going up in flames," Bert said.

Teddy groaned.

Bert fired the engines. *Code Blue* came to life.

As they pulled out of the harbor, Bert slowed and took Carmella's hand. Together, they looked back on the neighborhood that had been their home. Several of the trailers were engulfed in flame as crowds of accountants swarmed between buildings, turning over cars and trampling azaleas. A firing line of shabby accountants in drab uniforms crouched at the edge of the marina and shot a volley of bullets in the general direction of their retreating vessel. A blue heron that had been perched on a starboard buoy, sixty yards aft of them, dropped dead.

"Damnit," Carmella said. "What did the heron ever do to them?"

Bert wrapped an arm over her shoulders. "Communist bastards!" he swore. "They have no respect for the working man." He gunned the engines and they passed the breakwater.

The retreating horizon glowed red, and Oliver watched as the fire light faded and disappeared in their wake.

He looked at Bert and Carmella. The old man's arm was around his wife's waist. They faced forward, seemingly uninterested in what they'd left behind.

Oliver admired them. They'd lost more than he could ever imagine having, and still were managing to cope. He envied their strength of character.

He looked at Teddy, who sat calmly in the stern, jaw jutted forward, eyes fixed on the skyline ahead.

He couldn't help but feel the burden of the unspoken debt he owed these people. Not only had they saved his life just now, but they'd done so even after his colossal blunder that had claimed Emma.

He made a silent vow. *I'm going to save her if it kills me.*

Bert tacked on a northerly course, headlong into the waves.

The sun was just kissing the eastern sky when Bert pulled *Code Blue* into a berth at the Islamorada Marina. They had not spoken much on the journey, but as they waited for their Uber, Teddy broke the silence.

"How did Legion find us?"

"That's a good question," Bert said, turning to Oliver. "You obviously recognized that glamour."

"She was at the riot in Halifax. She saved me. Was she a demon or something?"

"No," Bert said, "but Legion must have seen you together. Does someone out there know who you are? Have you met anyone you suspect was possessed by a demon, maybe? Or a familiar? An incubus or succubus?"

"Incubus? Like the band?"

"They're named after a very nasty demon," Carmella said. "I'd explain it, but it's too vulgar."

"Very rapey," Bert summarized. "Have you come across anyone who fits that bill?"

"I...I don't know. I don't think so," Oliver said. "There was one guy who saw the transfer, but Teddy squashed his head with a baseball bat."

"It's true," Teddy said. "I squashed it well."

"And nobody else at the riot knew who you were?"

"Well," Oliver said, "My home was kind of central, in the thick of it. My apartment, I mean. Before it..."

"You've told us about your apartment burning down a hundred times," Teddy said. "Nobody cares, remember?"

"Right," Oliver said. "Nonetheless, I'm sure some of the rioters would have known me, or at least would have seen me on campus before."

"So people who knew you would have seen you after you took transfer of Mayhem?" Bert asked.

"I'm not sure. I was sort of unconscious for a while. Maybe someone saw Teddy carrying me. But the police officer, I met her way before the whole Host thing."

"Probably the same possessed rioter saw you with the policewoman, and then saw you take transfer of Mayhem," Teddy said.

Bert shook his head. "Maybe..."

His tone suggested that he didn't think this was the case.

Oliver tried to think of how anyone might know his identity.

"His wallet," Teddy said. "It was missing when we, uh, absconded with him."

"That's right," Oliver said, "A guy took my driver's license before throwing my wallet into the embers of my burned-out apartment that nobody cares about. The guy was a real dick, too."

Bert snapped his fingers. "That's probably it. I mean, assuming that Legion wasn't after you for some other reason, before you took transfer of Mayhem. If that guy who took your wallet was hosting Legion, then they know who you are."

"Yeah, but how would they find me here?"

"They have an *enormous* network. They could have seen you at a gas station or a restaurant, or maybe when we were out on the boat. Once Amon knows a human host, it's like an APB goes out. He'll hunt you forever."

"Great," Oliver said. It was not the news he was hoping to hear.

"Your apartment burned down?" Carmella asked. "It must have been quite a riot."

"It was a doozy," Teddy said. "Even bigger than last night."

"Could someone have tracked your phone?" Bert asked.

"I don't know," Oliver said. "I mean, it happens in the movies I guess, so maybe?"

"Let me see your phone," Teddy said.

When Oliver handed it over, Teddy smashed it on the pavement, then ground the fragments to smithereens under his boot heel.

"Hey!" Oliver said, "You could have just taken out the SIM card."

"The what?"

"Never mind. I was just supposed to call my mom, is all."

"You can't," Teddy said. "Not if Legion knows who you are. They might try something."

"Something like what?" Oliver asked, toeing the pieces of the phone into a pile.

"I don't know," Teddy said, "some kind of clever ruse, I guess."

"So, I can't call Mom?"

"No."

Oliver checked the time on his Casio. It was five minutes after six in the morning, and he felt like he could use a very stiff drink.

— *Six* —

The Uber driver wasn't crazy about letting Oliver into the car without a shirt, but after some convincing and the handing over of a gold coin worth seventeen hundred dollars, he changed his mind and drove them to a car rental agency in Key Largo. Bert used a Visa and driver's license under the name "Alfred Sharpton," and at Teddy's insistence rented a minivan. Sadly, the only van they had in stock was a base-model Dodge Caravan, and it lacked many of the creature comforts of the Honda Odyssey.

"You know," Oliver said, "Al Sharpton is a pretty famous guy. He's on the news all the time."

"No kidding," Bert said, getting behind the wheel. "Does he look like me?"

"Not really."

"Well, I guess that's lucky."

"Don't you watch the news?"

"Only when I absolutely have to. Even then, I tune most of it out. Watching the news is bad for your digestion."

"It's true," Teddy said. "It causes constipation."

"It certainly binds me up," Carmella chimed in. "Thank goodness for those bowel buddy cookies. I don't know what I'd do without them."

"Where—*where* are we going?" Oliver blurted out, hoping to alter the direction of the discussion.

"To rescue my common-law spouse!" Teddy said. "I thought that was obvious."

"I realize that, but where? And how? And can we please stop so I can buy a shirt... and toiletries?"

Teddy turned to Bert. "Come to think of it, where *are* we going?"

"Miami," Bert said.

Teddy turned back to Oliver. "He says we're going to Miami."

"I know, Teddy! I can hear him."

"Right," Teddy said, tapping his temple knowingly.

Oliver hoped that the big man wasn't too angry. It was, after all, pretty much his fault that Emma had ended up being annihilated, or sent through a portal to another dimension, or... whatever had happened.

103

He was about to apologize again, but Teddy spoke first.

"Just so you know, I've decided to try not to be angry at you. The Bible says we should forgive one another. More importantly, Emma likes you, and would possibly dissolve our common-law marriage if she discovered that I had gouged your eyes out with my thumbs while you were sleeping."

"That was a very specific description of what she might discover."

"Was it?"

They rented a room in a Best Western using the Alfred Sharpton credit card. Oliver asked Teddy to run across the street to a men's clothing store to get him a shirt.

Teddy returned with a small, stretchy, electric blue, paisley-patterned dress shirt with three-button cuffs and an oversized collar.

Oliver held the shirt up to the light, where the spectrally refractive fabric shone in multicolored swirls, like gasoline in a puddle. "There's a lot going on here."

"It's a shirt," Teddy said, "like you asked."

"Don't you think it's a little bit loud?"

"It will definitely help you get fornicating," Teddy said reassuringly. "Just as soon as we rescue Emma."

"Yeah, about that..." Oliver said, turning to Bert. "I'm not really clear on where Emma is, or the whole glamour thing, or the people disappearing in a flash of light thing—or the rescue thing for that matter. I mean, maybe this stuff is old hat for you guys, but I'm completely lost. What's the plan?"

"Oh right," Bert said. "Let's get some coffee going, and we can discuss it on the balcony."

"Can we get some toast as well?" Carmella asked.

"Sure," Bert said.

"Ask for dry toast for me," Teddy requested.

"Will do."

"Dry all around," Carmella said. "I have to watch my cholesterol."

"Anything for you, dear."

While Bert ordered room service, Oliver squeezed into his new shirt and studied himself in the mirror. He looked like a bedraggled, emaciated survivor of some untold, 1990s-era boyband tragedy.

Staring at his red-rimmed eyes in the reflection, he realized that sometimes you really could judge a book by its cover. He felt just about as terrible as he looked. And his thoughts had gone all fuzzy. Normally, when he was confronted with a problem outside his grasp, he would research it. But here he was, simply accepting his own ignorance.

It wouldn't do.

He straightened himself, gave his unruly mop of hair a few rudimentary swipes, then went to the sink and splashed his face with cold water.

He was going to do some research.

"Can I borrow your phone?" he asked Teddy.

"What's wrong with yours?" Teddy asked.

Oliver made a face, and Teddy said, "Oh, right."

Oliver opened the Incredible Daily Facts app.

Lobsters don't die of natural causes.

He navigated to the guide and searched "Glamour."

Glamour—An apparition or image typically created by a celestial being known as a "caster," which can be used to trick the feeble-minded.

Direct contact with a glamour will reveal the object or person upon which/whom the enchantment has been cast.

A glamour may carry a blessing or a curse, that will be released at the time contact is made. A glamour cast by a particularly clever entity may also contain an interdimensional portal, and can be used to bring non-celestial beings directly into the celestial realm, though it should be noted that this is rarely a good idea, and the experience has been likened to "Swallowing bleach while having your skin sandblasted."

Glamour can also refer to "an exciting quality that lends a person appeal," but since you're reading this passage, in this guide, it seems unlikely that this would be the definition you're after.

"Hey," Oliver said. "This guide says I'm feeble-minded."

"Yes," Teddy said. "It's a very accurate guide."

They ate dry toast and drank coffee, standing clustered in a tight group on the much-too-small balcony. Oliver found the toast crunching and coffee slurping very obnoxious, but since he was the reason they were in this situation, he didn't say anything. Bert and Carmella were likely too deaf to notice, and Teddy seemed to be immune to irritation.

"Why are we standing on the balcony?" Oliver finally asked.

"Fresh air," Bert said, breathing deeply before taking a particularly crunchy bite of toast.

Teddy noticed he'd gotten some crumbs on his shirt and swiped them off with his hand. They landed on Oliver's new shirt. Out of politeness, Oliver chose to let the crumbs stay there.

Bert cleared his voice. "OK," he started, then choked on a toast crumb. He had a brief coughing spell, then continued. "Wow, that's pretty dry. Anyway, here's the deal. I believe that the glamour that tricked our feeble-minded friend here was the portal type. In all likelihood, Emma is now in another dimension. Given that this is the work of Amon, or Legion, we can safely assume she's somewhere in the underworld. Is everyone on board with that?"

Everyone nodded.

"I know about one person to whom this has happened before," Bert continued. "She is, it goes without saying, the key to our chance of achieving interdimensional travel and finding Emma."

"Great," Teddy said.

"It isn't all that great. She's not very pleasant."

"That's irrelevant," Teddy said. "I will be charming to the unpleasant woman as long as she can tell us how to get to the underworld. Emma says I'm very charming. I'm sure it will be adequate."

Bert looked Teddy up and down, and shook his head before continuing.

"I very much doubt she'll be able to explain it directly," Bert said, "and there's a very strong possibility that she won't *want* to help us."

"Why not?" Oliver asked.

"Because she's kind of a bitch," Bert said.

"Oh, Bert, you shouldn't use that word," Carmella complained.

"Bitch? Why not?"

"It's offensive to women."

"Is it?"

"Yes!" Carmella said.

"Were you offended?" Bert asked.

"No, but I'm seventy-five."

"OK. Great. We'll stick with bitch then. Everyone OK with that?"

They all nodded.

"This bitch I'm talking about—I met her in an official capacity a few years back. She was pretty heavy into drugs, and she was supposed to overdose. Well, I watched her hoover up every narcotic you can imagine all afternoon, and when the time came, I popped in to help her move on, as I do. And bang-o—

there she was, wide awake, sober as a judge. She was waiting for me."

"Oh *that* one," Carmella said, "You're right. She *is* a bitch."

"Anyway, she knew exactly who I was, like she'd been tipped off about the whole Grim Reaper thing. I figured maybe she was even one of us, but that turned out not to be the case. She threatened to 'dox' me if I ever came for her again. Dox, you know, give out my address to her fans, and tell them who I am and what I do."

"She has fans?" Oliver asked. "Is she famous?"

"Sort of, in a way. She's a YouTuber."

Oliver nodded.

"At any rate, she went up one side of me and down the other. How dare I invade her personal space? Did I even know who *she* was? You know, that kind of thing. So I just took off. I didn't know what else to do. She wasn't dead or dying, you know. I wasn't going to strangle her."

"Why not?" Teddy asked.

Bert ignored him. "I figured the whole thing was some kind of cosmic glitch, except in all my years of studying the celestial universe I'd never heard of that happening.

"A few months later, the curiosity was killing me. I looked her up. She had a channel dedicated to something called ASMR—which I guess is a thing where physically attractive women sit in front of a camera with a ring light reflecting off their eyeballs, and they whisper into a microphone. Men say it helps them fall asleep, but I think it helps them do something else."

Bert made a whole new obscene gesture, using just one hand.

"So, having established what she did for a living, I scrolled through a few of her videos and found one titled 'A Journey Through Hell: An ASMR Account of the Underworld.' It's about this trip she took to the underworld, after meeting a 'hot older guy,' who turned out to be able to cast a spell that made images you could use to travel between dimensions. I mean, she said all this stuff right out in the open, on the internet. I suppose everyone just assumed it was some fantasy fiction she wrote, but I knew what she was talking about. She was talking about a caster, who could create a portal-type glamour, and then I figured out why she hadn't overdosed."

"Why?" Oliver asked.

"She brought back a demon," Bert said. "A minor one, probably. But it's keeping her alive. She's a permanent host of Legion."

The idea of encountering a demon host gave Oliver pause. "Won't she, like, cause trouble for us?"

"Almost definitely," Bert said.

"Should we expect violence?"

"I don't think so. She's never been violent in the past, at any rate."

"That's a shame," Teddy said. "I'm good at violence."

Oliver had seen Teddy's propensity for violence. He was in no position to argue the big man's point.

"Can we please try to have a peaceful exchange with the demon-lady?" he asked. "The whole 'public murder' thing really freaks me out."

"I'm not willing to commit to that," Teddy said. "But I will make a rudimentary effort."

"Where is she?" Carmella asked.

"At a convention," Bert said.

"A convention?"

"It's called 'Influence-Ah' and it's billed as the world's largest gathering of social media influencers. It's in Miami, and it starts this afternoon."

— *Seven* —

At Oliver's first glance, the crowd around the pool area appeared festive and gregarious. Waiters carrying drink trays wove in and out between the deeply tanned sunbathers and attractive partygoers. Loud hip-hop music filled the air, and everyone appeared to be talking at the same time.

It took a moment for Oliver to realize that everyone really was, in fact, talking at the same time—speaking in running monologues to their mobile devices.

On top of the jarring background clamor there was a digital undercurrent of constant notification beeps.

The world of Influence-Ah was a world of a thousand Narcissi gazing into a thousand reflecting pools.

"Which one is the bitch?" Teddy asked.

"They all look like bitches," Carmella said.

"I thought that was offensive to women."

"I'm allowed to say it. That's how it works."

Teddy nodded. "I understand."

Bert squinted, searching the faces in the crowd. "They all kind of look the same," he said.

Oliver had noticed it, too. The women were mostly tall and thin, with long hair, and for the most part, artificially enhanced breasts. The men's features were universally chiseled, and each displayed a perfectly trimmed three-day beard. The men seemed to otherwise have even less body hair than the average Ken doll.

Bert led the group around the pool, zigzagging between Influence-Ah attendees. Oliver tried to concentrate on each individual face, but they were shielded by their screens.

At the poolside bar, Bert tripped over a bottle of bronzing lotion, and cursed.

"Who brings fake tan lotion to Miami?" he said under his breath.

After a while of walking in a semi-stoop, Bert motioned for the group to stop. He straightened and stretched his back.

"This is going to be more difficult than I'd anticipated," he said.

Oliver snapped his fingers. "If she's live streaming, why don't we just open her channel and see where she's streaming from? Then we can triangulate her location based on the background."

"Good idea," Bert said, pulling out his phone.

He opened the YouTube app and searched for "ASMR Cutie." He clicked on a video titled "Live Streaming from Influence-Ah." Sure enough, their target was seductively whispering into the camera, live from an orange deckchair on the opposite side of the pool. She was filming her fingernails, upon which she had painted bright yellow happy faces.

"Right there," Bert said, pointing to a tanned, slim woman with bottle-blonde hair, wearing a yellow bikini.

"That was quite clever," Teddy said to Oliver, "for a feeble-minded person."

"Thanks."

She didn't seem to notice their approach, and didn't look up when Bert cleared his throat. She also didn't look up when Oliver said, "Excuse me."

Teddy plucked the phone from her hand, and set it on the side table next to a can of White Claw.

"Hey!" she said, glaring at the big man. Her glare softened when she noticed how muscular he was. "Whoa."

"Hello, Cindy," Bert said.

She lowered her sunglasses an inch and peered at the old man over the rims. It took a moment for her to make the connection, and when she did, her features hardened once more. "Not you again."

"It's OK," Bert said, "I'm not here in an official capacity."

She rolled her eyes dismissively. "It wouldn't matter if you were," she sneered.

"That thing won't keep you alive forever, you know," Bert said.

"No," she admitted, "but a few hundred years ought to do."

"Is that the deal?" Carmella asked. "Two hundred years, and then eternity in the underworld?"

Cindy eyed Carmella's outfit and wrinkled her nose. "Honey, you need to go shopping. That outfit makes you look fat, and you smell like a bonfire."

Carmella huffed. "I'll have you know, I don't *look* fat. I *am* fat. And furthermore..."

Sensing things were about to go completely off the rails, and desperate to fulfill his commitment to save Emma, Oliver jumped in. "Cindy, we need to speak privately."

"I don't think so. I'm losing viewers just talking to you losers."

She picked up her phone, and brushed a wayward hair out of her suspiciously long eyelashes. Before she could address her audience, Teddy snatched the device from her fingers and set it down on the adjacent patio table.

"You need to talk with us," he said, his voice an octave lower. "It's important. My common-law spouse's life is on the line."

She sat up. "Listen, beefcake. I sincerely don't care."

This time when she went to take the phone, Carmella grabbed it first. The older woman then hurled it into the swimming pool.

"Get up, bitch," Carmella said.

"Oh my God! You're paying for that!"

Carmella's eyes narrowed, and for a second Oliver thought she might slap the younger woman. The mention of money, however, had jangled something loose in his brain. There was an opportunity here, and Cindy's motivation couldn't be more obvious.

"I'll pay for it," he said, "and I'll pay you for your time. You help us, you get paid. Sound fair?"

Cindy peered at him over her sunglasses. "I'm not cheap, kid."

"I understand that," Oliver said.

She eyed the group, obviously sizing up just *how much* they might be able to cough up.

Things seemed to be getting back on track, until Carmella muttered "Whore," under her breath.

Cindy sneered at her. "Have you ever heard of catching more flies with honey?"

"There's no time for honey," Teddy said. "Only Worcestershire Sauce."

"What?"

"You get more flies with honey than with Worcestershire Sauce."

"Vinegar," Oliver said.

"What?"

"More flies with honey than with vinegar."

"That's stupid," Teddy said, "You can catch tons of flies with balsamic vinegar. Fruit flies love it. In fact, you can make a trap for them with balsamic vinegar and cling wrap."

"I think the saying is in reference to house flies, not fruit flies," Oliver said.

Teddy shook his head. "Agree to disagree."

"Look, it's been nice meeting all you whack jobs," Cindy said, "but I'm not helping you. Get out of here before I get hotel security."

"Come on, Cindy," Bert said. "We only need a second."

"And we'll pay you. Like I said," Oliver added.

She shook her head, groaning in exasperation.

"We'll pay you a lot!"

She studied him the way a rattlesnake might study a field mouse. Oliver felt her eyes linger over his paisley shirt. "I'm pretty sure you can't afford me, buck-o," she said.

"I have money," Oliver countered. "If you help us, it's yours."

"And if you help us, I won't rip your arms and legs off," Teddy said.

"You don't want to spend the next two hundred years as a quadruple amputee," Carmella said. "You wouldn't be able to take selfies."

Cindy smirked. "You wouldn't hurt me! Not with all these people here."

Teddy laughed. It was a genuine, heartfelt, terrifying belly laugh, and Cindy's smirk disappeared. The first furrow of concern appeared on her otherwise inorganically smooth forehead.

"Witnesses don't bother him," Oliver explained. "He caved a guy's head in the other night. It was totally disgusting. There were something like forty people there."

Cindy looked like she was going to say something, then decided not to.

"We only need five minutes," Bert pleaded.

"Five minutes," she said, getting up. "Then you weirdos are out of here."

They borrowed the conference center off the hotel lobby. The hotelier at the desk recognized Cindy and made a big deal of offering her coffee or tea for their "meeting." She waved him away.

Everyone sat down on faux-leather office chairs around a short boardroom table. As the hotelier was leaving, he paused next to Teddy and gave the big man an appraising look.

"I'm sorry to ask, sir, but..." he hesitated.

"What?"

"Well... are you Dwayne 'The Rock' Johnson?"

Teddy hiked an eyebrow in exactly the way Dwayne "The Rock" Johnson would.

The hotelier seemed to take this as confirmation, and gushed. "I'm a huge fan."

"No," Teddy said, "I'd say you're just regular-sized."

The hotelier cocked his head slightly to the left, seemingly unsure if Teddy was joking.

"What are you, one-sixty? One-sixty-five? That's about average," Teddy explained.

"Yes... yes, sir." The hotelier smiled politely, and nodded, before backing out of the room and closing the door.

Cindy sighed. "OK. You have me. What do you want?"

Oliver was still unclear on the appropriate phraseology for the information they needed. He turned to Teddy. Teddy shrugged, and turned to Bert. Thus they arrived at the silent consensus that Bert should run the show.

Carmella, for her part, produced a pad and pencil to take notes.

Bert bit his lip and looked Cindy in the eye. "We need the caster."

"From the chair?" She looked genuinely confused and made to stand up.

"What? No! The caster. The person who created the glamour that sent you to the underworld."

"Oh."

"Where is he?" Teddy asked. "Where is the handsome, older guy?"

She cocked an eyebrow of her own.

"You talked about it in one of your videos," Bert said.

"Bob?" she asked. "You're trying to find Bob?"

"We're trying to find Bob," Bert confirmed.

"Are you trying to go to the underworld too?"

"Yes."

"Because it isn't very nice. You won't like it."

"We know."

"You might not even survive the trip. It sucks. It's like swallowing bleach and having your skin sandblasted at the same time. It's also physically demanding. No offense but you and the old lady don't look like you've been going to cross fit. You're both kind of flabby."

"You're right, we don't agonize about our appearance," Carmella said. "We choose to contribute to society in a meaningful way instead."

"Gross," Cindy said.

Sensing that the conversation was once again meandering away from a helpful direction, Oliver interjected. "So, Cindy, this Bob guy... Where do we find him?"

"I'm afraid I can't give you that information," she said.

Teddy stood, cracked his knuckles and made a face that Oliver could only think of as "The face a person makes moments before dismembering another person."

"Hold on," Cindy said, pushing her chair back from the huge man. "I said I can't *give* you the information. I didn't say I couldn't *sell* you the information. You mentioned you had some money..." She turned to Oliver with an upturned palm.

"How much?" Oliver asked.

"Fifty thousand. That's only fair. That's how much I'm losing in ad revenue thanks to you guys throwing my phone in the pool."

"You make fifty thousand dollars a day in ad revenue for whispering into a microphone in front of a ring light?" Oliver asked.

"There's so much more to it than that," Cindy said. "You also have to be very attractive."

Bert snorted.

"It's not just that," Cindy protested. "You have to post to all the socials."

"Post about what?" Oliver asked.

"Just pictures really. Mostly of either your own legs on a beach chair, or something with cleavage. I know how it sounds, but it's quite a lot of work. You have to consider the exposure, and angles, and background. You have to scout out unique locations and remember to shave your legs. I doubt you folks could handle it." She glanced over at Carmella. "Even if you were physically attractive."

"Hey! I was a cardiologist," Bert said. "That was quite a lot of *actual* work."

"Big deal. How many cardiologists do you know with nine million followers on Twitter?"

"It's X. And never mind," Bert said.

Oliver, upon hearing her price, once again felt the situation slipping away. He was like a fisherman who had hooked into a fish that was too heavy for his tackle. At the other end of the strained line was Emma. He was desperate to save her, and it was going to take all the finesse he could muster to pull it off. Unfortunately, he was quite inexperienced at finessing.

He willed a compulsion to take over, so Mayhem could speak through him, but the celestial Host was maddeningly silent.

He supposed he could try to find a metal detector, and maybe hit a nearby beach, but by the time he managed to procure enough money he was sure Cindy would be long gone.

"We don't, exactly, currently *have* fifty thousand dollars," he said.

"Between all of you?" Cindy said. "That's so sad."

She stood, but Oliver jumped from his chair and blocked the exit. He fumbled around in his pocket for a second and produced his nine remaining gold coins.

"Here," he said. "These are worth seventeen thousand dollars."

Cindy took the coins in her hand and felt their weight.

"Are these real?" she asked.

"Yes. And it's all we have. Now can you please help us?"

She stared at them a moment. "Fine," she said, folding the coins in her palm.

Just then, a man in a sportscoat and tan slacks opened the door. He was carrying a manila envelope.

"Oh. I'm sorry folks," he said. "I just need to use the fax machine."

He made his way to the combination printer and fax machine at the far end of the room and began organizing his papers. As he did, he hummed the 1812 Overture, emulating the cannon sounds by softly saying *Ker pow!*

When he finally got his papers in order, he turned to address the group. He smiled. "Beautiful day out there, huh?"

For a moment nobody said anything. Then Bert broke the silence. "Sure is."

"We don't tend to get weather like this at home," the man said. "That's Wisconsin, I mean. It's warm in the summer, sure, but this humidity! Oh boy!"

"Right," said Bert.

The man loaded the papers in the top tray of the machine and hunted for the instructions on how to use it.

"Gee, I guess it's been a while since I sent a fax. I'm not entirely sure—"

"You need a cover page," said Carmella.

"A what now?"

"A cover page," she said. "With the number you're sending it to, and courtesy of whom, and the number you're sending it from, et cetera."

"Oh. Do any of you folks have a pen I could borrow?"

Carmella handed her pencil to the man.

He tried to slide open the paper tray for the printer, but pulled too hard. The tray came out in his hand and dumped the contents on the floor.

"Oh boy," the man said.

Oliver, desperately wanting the man to leave so they could finish their business with Cindy, made his way around the table.

"Here," he said, taking the tray, which the man from Wisconsin had been holding upside down.

He stacked and inserted the blank paper, then loaded it back into the machine.

The stranger proceeded to wrestle with the feed tray.

"Face down!" Bert called from across the room.

"Oh, right," the man said, flipping the stack of papers.

He mashed the numbers on the keypad.

"You have to dial nine," Bert said.

Oliver helped him reset the number.

Finally, the machine whirred to life with a series of beeps and dings that nobody in the room had heard in at least a decade.

"Well, thanks folks!" the man from Wisconsin said. "Sorry to have interrupted your..." It was then that he noticed Cindy. "Hey, I know you! You're on YouTube. ASMR Cutie! That stuff really helps me, uh..." he glanced around at the faces in the room, "get to sleep at night!"

Closing his eyes, Bert brought a palm to his forehead and sighed.

"It's a real pleasure to meet you!" the man said, wanting to shake her hand.

Cindy pulled back.

"Oh, I'm sorry. Are you a germaphobe? I know since Coronavirus a lot of people are. You know, my sister-in-law had it. It was awful. She almost—"

"Five hundred dollars," Cindy said.

"I'm sorry?"

"It's five hundred dollars if you want to touch me."

"Oh. Well."

Oliver assumed the man from Wisconsin would be put off by this and leave, but he slowly reached into his back pocket and produced his wallet. "Let's see," he said.

He counted out five one hundred-dollar bills, and handed them to Cindy. "That should be five hundred," he said.

She took the money and it disappeared into her fist with the coins. Her deadpan face erupted into a wide smile, and she grasped his hand and shook it, before pulling him into an embrace.

"Now, aren't you just the sweetest man," she said in a sultry voice.

"I am, aren't I," said the man from Wisconsin.

With one arm around the man from Wisconsin's waist, Cindy led him to the exit, but Teddy stood in the way.

"Ahem," Teddy said. "Where's Bob?"

"Vista Lane, in Indian Rocks," she said. "I don't remember the number. He calls it 'The Art House' because it's covered in weird metal sculptures. It's purple. You'll know it when you see it."

She took the man from Wisconsin by the arm and led him through the door, then turned. "Don't try to drink with him," she said over her shoulder.

The door shut behind her.

"Indian Rocks," Bert said. "Nice area. There's a great restaurant out that way. Salt Rock, I think it's called. Best tuna steak I've ever had. You remember that place, Carm?"

"I think so. Was that the one with the stuffed chicken, and the floor that looked like teakwood?"

"No—you're thinking of Seaweed Grill, in Belaire Bluffs. Salt Rock had the Perspex floor with the wine cellar underneath, and you had the filet mignon. That was April 2008 when I was still driving the Mercedes."

"The white one?"

"No, the blue one. With the round headlights."

"Oh. That's right. That was a good restaurant! I remember..."

"We should go," Teddy interrupted. "We can talk about restaurants in the car."

Bert checked his watch. "Good idea."

Just as they were about to leave, the fax machine began whirring and beeping again. The printer engaged, and paper began spitting out. Oliver examined the first sheet.

"He sent it back to himself," he announced.

Oliver drove. Traffic was light.

An hour outside of Miami, the van flashed a tire-pressure warning. He pulled into a Chevron outside Andytown to air up and to give Bert and Carmella a bathroom break. He figured he may as well top up the tank.

It occurred to him, as he pumped gas, that he was once again completely broke, and that he no longer had a metal detector, since they'd left it behind in the Honda.

He was going to ask Teddy what to do, when out of the corner of his eye he noticed a leather money-clip, half-hidden under the vehicle. He stooped to retrieve it. There was no identification attached. Folded in the clip were a dozen hundred-dollar bills.

"This is so weird," he said to himself.

Teddy jogged out of the station. "Hey, have you found any money yet, by chance?"

"Yeah... I jus—"

"I need a hundred bucks."

"OK." Oliver peeled a hundred off the money fold and handed it to Teddy, who thanked him and jogged back into the store.

Oliver took the wheel as they drove across the Everglades along Interstate 75, while Bert and Carmella slept. Teddy sat in the passenger seat, and chowed down on a giant bag of gas-station food.

The big man reached into his bag of snacks and produced something called "Big John's Pickled Eggs." The eggs were individually packaged, and inexplicably bright red.

"You know," Oliver said, "this section of I-75 is kind of a mathematical anomaly."

"How so?" Teddy asked before tearing the pickled egg package open with his teeth.

"The American Interstate system is designed and named in a very basic East-West, North-South grid. North-South highways have an odd-number designation, and West-East highways get an even-number designation. This is quite a long leg of West-East highway, but carries an odd-number designation."

"Pickled egg?" Teddy asked, holding the crimson, cured ovum under Oliver's nose so he could get a sniff of vinegar and sulphur.

"No thanks." Oliver continued, undeterred. "This section of the highway is referred to as Alligator Alley. When it was initially built it was considered to be the most controversial highway in America. It was poorly constructed, with essentially no environmental planning, and as a two-lane highway it was the site of numerous head-on collisions. Eventually, the powers that be decided to replace the original Alligator Alley with an extension of I-75. They built in culverts and bridges to let water and wildlife pass underneath. That was one of the first major projects done to protect the Florida panther. I-75 now runs all the way from Miami to Sault Ste. Marie."

"Why do you know all this?" Teddy asked through a mouthful of beef jerky and pickled egg.

"I studied interstate system anomalies when I started getting interested in number theory. I questioned whether there could be a better nomenclature system for developing countries, that could predict anomalies and make routing more intuitive to the public."

"Wow," Teddy said. "That's really boring."

Oliver smiled. "I know."

They drove in relative silence for a while, the only sounds being the roar of the tires across the hot tarmac, the snores of Bert and Carmella from the rear seats, and the smacking, chewing and slurping of Teddy as he worked his way boldly through twenty thousand milligrams of sodium.

Oliver imagined what Emma might be going through. Was Hell the way it was depicted in Dante's *Inferno*? Would she be suspended in a flaming pool of blood, or fighting tooth and nail with the damned on the surface of the River Styx? Or was hell more what his mother had taught him—a total separation from joy?

He turned to Teddy, now drinking the brine from a bag that held a Van Holten's Hot Pickle. "Are you worried, Teddy?"

Teddy examined the bag. "No. I've had one before. They're not that hot."

"I mean about Emma."

Teddy took a second, obviously thinking about it. "She'll be OK," he said. "She's the tough one."

"Really," Oliver said. "I would have guessed you were the tough one."

"Oh no," Teddy grinned, "not even close."

"You aren't worried then?"

Teddy's brow furrowed. "I love Emma, and I miss her. But I have a lot of faith in her. She can handle herself. She understands her limits better than anyone. When she saw you approaching the glamour, which was, in your defense, very sexually attractive before it turned into a bearded communist accountant, she knew that whatever it would lead to, she could handle it better than any of us. She didn't grab it just to prevent *you* from touching it. She did it to prevent *any of us* from doing it."

Embarrassed again by his stupidity, Oliver flushed. In his short, voluntary relationship with Teddy and Emma, he had allowed himself to imagine their group as a kind of celestial-crime-fighting trio. Teddy was the bad cop character—the tough guy. Emma was of course the good cop. And Oliver saw himself as a sort of forensics expert—the smart, nerdy guy who could use his wits to help win the day. The fact that within twenty-four hours of joining the team he'd gotten the good cop banished to the underworld shattered any illusions he had of being "The clever one."

"I'm sorry, Teddy. I feel terrible. I'd do anything to go back and fix it."

Teddy made a gesture that was probably intended to be a comforting pat on the shoulder, but in practice slammed Oliver hard enough into his seatbelt to leave a bruise.

"Don't beat yourself up. You're new at this. It's a lot to take in."

"So how do we find her? I mean, assuming we can even get to the other dimension?"

"No idea," Teddy said. "I suppose we'll play it by year."

"Did you say 'by year?'" Oliver asked.

"Yes, it's a saying," Teddy said. "Because every year is different, so you have to improvise how you play to accommodate for the variability."

"It's ear," Oliver said.

"Excuse me?"

"Play it by ear. As in, you want to play a song on the piano, but you don't have any sheet music. So you use your memory of what the song sounds like to figure out how to play it."

"I don't think so," Teddy said. "That explanation is too complicated. And it only works for pianists."

"No," Oliver said, "you're supposed to extrapolate the message to apply to other situations where you have to act without a blueprint or a formal plan."

"Are you gas-lighting me about this?" Teddy asked.

"Uh...no," Oliver said. "Look it up on your phone."

Teddy typed at his phone for a second, then studied it, turning the screen slightly, so Oliver couldn't see.

"What does it say?" Oliver asked.

"It says you can use either," Teddy said, quickly slipping the phone into his pocket. He then opened a can of Pringles and stuffed a three-inch stack of chips into his mouth. Oliver decided to let it go.

"How do you stay so calm?"

"I suppose you just get used to the crises," Teddy said. "Keep in mind, I've been doing this for almost a thousand years. Things usually tend to work out. Well, that, plus, of course, frequent intercourse with my life partner."

"Right," Oliver said, then quickly, "Hey... uh, what's your charm?"

Teddy removed the thin silver chain from his neck and handed it over.

"Go ahead," he said, "try to break it."

Oliver gave a half-hearted tug on both ends.

"No, like this," Teddy said.

He looped the necklace through the handgrip in the steering wheel and pulled hard. The chain dug deep through the leatherette wrap and into the rubberized plastic underneath.

"Whoa," Oliver said.

Teddy inspected the damage to the steering wheel as he clipped the thin chain back around his muscle-bound neck. "You have to love rental cars."

— *Eight* —

The Comprehensive Guide to Hosting a Celestial Entity describes interdimensional travel as follows:

> *Interdimensional travel has been exclusively mastered by certain beings of the celestial dimension. Host, while widely considered to be beings of celestial origin, appear to naturally inhabit both the secular and celestial planes simultaneously. It is widely believed that Host may only physically manifest in the secular plane through the actions of their human host vehicle. The composition of their celestial existence is unclear, and likewise, once paired with a human host, it is unclear whether they continue to exist on the celestial plane, or simply receive messages or compulsions from it.*
>
> *It is storied that Don Juliano, a thirteenth-century human host, was once transported to the celestial dimension, where he described his Celestial Host as a separate physical being, who followed him through the underworld. Upon his return, the natural relationship between human host and Celestial Host resumed.*
>
> *More recently, Mavis Allaby, an Arizona homemaker, was accidentally transported to the celestial plane when she came into contact with a transport glamour in the form of a decorative wicker sandpiper, which had been cast when a transient shaman named Marvin Halloway suffered an alcoholic seizure on the sidewalk outside her bungalow. She described the experience of interdimensional travel as "Being gradually turned inside out while an intoxicated conga player hammers out a solo on your eyeballs."*
>
> *As such, with the exception of a one-way post-mortem journey, interdimensional travel is not recommended for readers who value comfort or safety. If travel is absolutely necessary, conventional wisdom dictates that a few drinks beforehand wouldn't hurt.*

The Art House was a ramshackle, purple, beach-style bungalow on a small lot. Galvanized metal sculptures of sea turtles, tropical fish and egrets had been nailed haphazardly to the stucco. The lot backed onto the intercoastal waterway. In the near distance, the luxury condo complex of Vista Villas towered over the neighborhood, while the houses on this end of the road appeared weather-worn and slightly dilapidated. Oliver figured this end of the street must belong to the hold-outs—locals who chose not to sell to developers in the face of sky-rocketing real estate values and booming tourism. He imagined this end of the street belonging to a community of Carl Hiaasen characters.

He pulled the van to the curb, then stepped out of the air conditioning into the sweltering Floridian evening. Inhaling atmosphere rich in frangipani and ocean salt, he mentally prepared himself for whatever absurdity and discomfort lay ahead.

"This must be it," Teddy said, stretching. "Let's go to the underworld."

"Whoa, whoa," Oliver said. "Shouldn't we ease into this?"

"No."

Teddy strode, briskly, to the front door. He raised a fist to pound on it, but before he could make contact the door swung outward and a very pretty brunette in a sundress walked into him.

"Oh!" she exclaimed.

Oliver saw right away that the woman was achingly beautiful. Her shoulder-length hair had been pulled half-heartedly into a messy ponytail. Her glowing skin spoke of Florida sunshine and a lifetime of healthy habits. Her impossibly light-brown eyes twinkled with humor and no small measure of intelligence.

She also happened to be carrying a dog-eared single-volume copy of Tolstoy's *Anna Karenina*. The pages were riddled with various bookmarks and index cards. Oliver surmised that she must be some kind of English or Russian major. Who else would read such a dense novel in such a non-linear fashion?

"I'm sorry," she said. "I wasn't paying attention."

Her gaze shifted to Oliver, and he swallowed hard. "Uh... hi," she said, giving him a half-wave.

"Hello."

Even the way his voice sounded, just saying "Hello" made him feel like a dork.

Teddy stooped to insert his face between them, and regain her attention. "Is the caster home?"

"The what now?"

"The caster of glamours?"

"Bob?"

"Yes. Is Bob home?"

"Bob!" the young woman called into the house, "Are you casting some kind of movie?"

"What?" a man shouted from inside the house.

"A movie? There's a guy here who says you're casting."

There was a brief pause then, "I don't think so. Who wants to know?"

"Some big guy," the woman shouted back, smiling at Teddy. "I think it's Dwayne 'The Rock' Johnson."

"Is he here to repossess something?"

She turned back to Teddy. "Are you here to repossess something?"

"No," Teddy said.

"No," she shouted.

"Send him in, honey."

The woman stepped out of the threshold and motioned Teddy into the bungalow. Her eyes met Oliver's as he brushed past.

"Hello... uh—again," Oliver said. Ever since failing to ask the lovely police officer at the library riot for a date, and after being criticized relentlessly about his lack of a love life, he was determined to be more proactive.

"Hi," she said, smiling, "I'm Jessica."

"I'm Oliver. But my friends call me Olly."

"No we don't," Bert said from the path.

Oliver ignored him.

He tried to offer his hand, only to stick it directly into Jessica's abdomen as she made her way past. He felt his face turn a deep crimson. "I'm—so sorry!"

She waved him off, smiling.

Oliver held the door for Carmella and Bert, and watched Jessica climb into an open-top Jeep. Her hair bounced. Her sundress fluttered in the gentle breeze.

Bert waggled his eyebrows knowingly as he made his way past Oliver. "Smooth move, *Olly*."

"Oh, shut up," Oliver said.

Jessica backed the Jeep around and drove off the way they'd come in, waving to him again on her way by.

Aside from essentially punching her in the gut when trying for a handshake, Oliver decided to consider the experience his first successful interaction with a female of his own generation. He had, after all, gotten her name.

The interior of the bungalow was excruciatingly hot. Threadbare cushions on wicker chairs made for rudimentary living room furniture. A disheveled grey-haired man sat at a makeshift desk that was actually a coffee table propped up with dozens of hardcover books under each leg. An old-fashioned typewriter sat before him and a thick pile of typewritten pages was stacked beside it.

The man, who wore a faded purple moth-eaten bathrobe over a pair of board shorts, peered at them with intensely intelligent, and even more intensely bloodshot eyes, over the soft-pink frames of a woman's set of drugstore reading glasses. Nothing moved but his eyes, as the unexpected guests piled into his living room. At the end of his long, thin fingers, a pair of tweezers held the smoldering end of a joint.

"Bob?" Oliver asked.

"Yeah?" the man said.

"This is a little awkward…"

"Hey wait," Carmella said. "Are you Robert Quinn?"

"I'm afraid so," Bob said.

"The writer?"

"Uh huh."

"Holy cow!" she exclaimed.

"I'm sorry… Who's Robert Quinn?" Bert asked.

"He wrote *King of the Docks*," she said. "It won a PEN award!"

"That was a long time ago," Bob said.

"I read it three times," Carmella said. "It was lovely."

"Thanks." Bob offered what Oliver thought of as a polite, academic smile.

"Bob," Bert said, "I'm going to be blunt. We need to travel to the celestial dimension."

"Do you?" Bob asked.

"Yes."

"I only have a little grass left, but I can probably hook you up if you want to leave your number. There's a pen and a post-it pad on the—"

Teddy cut him off. "That isn't what we mean."

Bob sighed, and his gaze shifted around the room. "Let me guess…" Bob pointed at Teddy, "Goodness," then Bert, "Death," and finally at Oliver, "Ooh! Mayhem! Haven't met one of those before." Finally, he leveled his finger at Carmella and squinted. "Uh… I'm not sure. Sorry, dear."

"I'm a retired administrative assistant."

"Oh."

"What *are* you?" Teddy asked.

"I'm just a writer," Bob said, "but I know some things."

"How do you know what we're hosting? How could you tell about Bert?"

"I'm *all-seeing*," Bob said in a magician's voice, waggling his fingers.

He noticed the remnant of the spliff in his hand, and held a lighter to it. He formed his lips into a greedy "O" and inhaled. The small ember flew out of the tweezers and down his throat. He doubled over coughing for a moment. When the paroxysms passed, he stood and scratched at the stubble on his cheek. His eyes were notably even more bloodshot than before.

"So you're not one of us, then?" Oliver asked.

"Kid, I don't know what the hell I am."

"How—how can you not know?" Oliver asked. "You're a caster, aren't you?"

"I'll give you the short version, if you're interested."

Oliver nodded.

"When I was writing 'King' I was pushing myself pretty hard. I'd stay up late, drinking bourbon, clicking away at the typewriter, every night. I'd wake up early every morning to drink more bourbon and watch the boats go out and talk to the guys on the dock. You know how it is when you're on a creative streak: you're drinking and fornicating, and making merry."

"I don't, sir," Oliver said. "I'm a mathematician."

"I'm sorry to hear that. Every young person should write a book. Keeps your brain regular. At any rate, after a month or two on that schedule, I started seeing things. Not hallucinations, exactly. More like an aura around certain people. And the harder I went at the writing, the more intense that aura would become. It's difficult to describe other than it's like a ripple in the space around a person.

"Like any writer experiencing an existential crisis, I figured I was simply drinking myself to death, but that turned out not to be the case. I finally worked up the courage to ask one of those people what it was I was seeing, a lovely young lady named Melody Walker.

"At first, she wouldn't say, but she sat down with me for a coffee anyway. After a while, I suppose she started to believe me, and she had me point out the next person I saw. She got up from the table, approached this guy, and asked to see his charm. Sure enough, he had one. I did the same thing a few more times, and she decided to take me under her wing.

"Melody introduced me to your world—the Host and Legion and Reapers and what have you. We grew intimate."

At this, Bert elbowed Oliver and gave a salacious wink. Oliver shoved the elbow away. He wanted to hear this.

"We fell in love. It was Melody who discovered I could write things into existence. Glamours, as you know them. I'm actually a contributor to that chapter in the guide."

"I read it," Oliver said. "It's very concise."

"Thanks. I really don't think you should go to the underworld."

"Why not?"

"Because it sucks."

"Right," Bert said. "The thing is, Bob, we really don't have a choice."

Teddy raised a hand as if to interject, but instead he burped loudly. The belch, which started as the gurgling growl of water in a boiler, grew in intensity until it sounded like a blasting train horn competing to be heard over a roaring, alpha-male, Barbary lion. Oliver smelled pickled eggs and beef jerky.

The big man thumped himself on the chest, before burping again, even louder. He turned his head toward Oliver as he did, and Oliver's glasses fogged over.

"Whoa," Bob said.

"It looked like you had something to say," Bert prodded.

"My common-law spouse is there," Teddy said, "In the underworld. She touched a glamour."

"My wife is there, too," Bob said. "Same reason."

"You sent your wife to the underworld?" Carmella asked. "That's terrible!"

"It was an accident. I'd been writing."

"You mean you can't control it?"

"Not then I couldn't."

"But now you can?"

"Yes," Bob sighed, "now I can."

"So what happened to Melody?" Bert asked.

"I'd been writing about a tennis player. It was supposed to be a follow-up to 'King.' I was in the middle of a really good session, and got myself engrossed in the story. I didn't notice someone knocking on the door. It was the delivery guy. Melody answered. I glanced up only to see the protagonist of my novel. He was standing right there."

He pointed to the entryway.

"He was wearing the John McEnroe getup—tight white shorts, white shirt, red headband. Everything! My protagonist was delivering a package to my house. It was very unsettling. I realized what had happened, but before I could say anything Melody must have tried to sign for the parcel. There was a bright flash, and they were both gone."

"What was it?" Teddy asked.

"I think it's some kind of plasma that gets released when you break through the space-time continuum. Or the fabric of the universe. Or something. We perceive it as light, only I'm not sure it's technically light—it's more like, anti-darkness. I read up on antimatter annihilation, and all that, and it sounds very similar."

"I meant the package," Teddy said. "What was in it?"

"The package?"

"The package the delivery guy brought."

"Oh. A cardigan."

"What color?"

"Seriously?"

"Yeah."

"Green."

"Great story," Teddy said.

Bob rubbed his face, as though trying to massage away the memory.

"Did you try to find her? Melody?" Oliver asked.

"Yeah," Bob said. "I tried. It took me a while though. I practiced conjuring up a glamour like the one that had sent her. After about six months I finally made one—and I touched it, and sure enough it sent me through to the other dimension. The underworld, I guess you call it."

"But she wasn't there?" Oliver asked.

"Oh, she was there."

"Was she, like, dead or something?"

"No, she was seeing someone," Bob said. "An actuary."

"An actuary? There are actuaries in the underworld?" Oliver was having difficulty processing this. It did not jibe with his preconception of fire and brimstone, vile slush, people turned into trees and the like.

"His name is Phil. He's an asshole."

"Phil?"

"He has a mid-level position at some big firm and thinks he's God's gift. A real piece of work."

"Sorry, I'm still a little hung up on this actuary thing," Oliver said.

"She told me she was tired of dating a creative man. That living with me was like living with a teenager."

"What happened to the delivery man?" Teddy asked.

"I'm glad you brought that up. He was transformed into a quivering gelatinous mass."

"Oh dear," Carmella said.

Oliver tried to imagine eternal existence as a quivering gelatinous mass, in an unknown hellscape populated by actuaries. Then he remembered that Emma, knowingly or not, had taken that risk on his behalf, and he knew he would just have to do the same.

He hoped she had not been turned into a quivering gelatinous mass, and decided to push the thought away. If Melody, Bob's ex, could survive the journey, he was certain Emma could too. He was less certain about his own ability to maintain some semblance of organic integrity, but he would have to cross that bridge when he came to it.

"I think I know what happened," Bob said.

"What?" Bert asked.

"He was stone-cold sober. You shouldn't be sober when you cross. Especially the first time. You might be tempted to resist, and it won't end well. You have to be very relaxed. Ethanol is key."

"Like, how relaxed?" Oliver asked. "Fall down giggling relaxed, or sleep with your face in a public urinal relaxed?"

"You're in the ballpark, but think still a little more relaxed than the urinal option," Bob said.

"Oh God."

"How did you get back?" Bert asked.

"I made another glamour and came through. It works the same on both sides."

Oliver remembered a theoretical physics lecture he'd attended in his undergraduate studies. The lecturer described the Nathan Rosen and Albert Einstein models of wormholes—gravitational anomalies that caused infinite tears in the space-time continuum, punching through the vast unknowable multiverse. He briefly considered how Bob's ability would be of great interest to the theoretical physics community, but more importantly, he calculated just how important Bob had become to their mission.

"So that means we need you to come with us," Oliver said.

"I'm really not keen on bringing people, if I'm being honest," Bob said. "The last time didn't go so well."

"You mean with Cindy?" Oliver asked.

"You know about Cindy?"

"Oh yes," Teddy said. "She's quite a bitch."

"Is she ever," Bob said.

"This won't go like that," Bert promised. "This is a rescue mission."

Bob furrowed his brow.

"I was kind of hoping to finish this manuscript," he said, hesitantly. "I was indefinitely suspended by the university a few weeks ago, and I've sort of burned through a lot of my advance..."

"Would your getting fired have anything to do with the lovely young brunette woman we passed on our way in?" Bert asked.

"I believe it would, yes."

"Did she happen to be married to another member of the faculty?"

"She's a graduate student. She was engaged to the dean, if you must know. I'm kind of helping her through things."

"Writers," Bert said.

"You have a weakness," Teddy said. "For fornication," he added, to clarify.

"I suppose we do," Bob said.

Oliver was desperate to get Bob on board. He felt every minute they spent not finding Emma was a minute closer to never seeing her again. And dammit, he owed her a rescue mission.

He produced the money clip from his pocket. "If you take us, I can give you..." he glanced at the bills, "Just over a thousand dollars."

"Hey!" Bob said, "I'm not Cindy for God's sake."

"Please," Teddy said. "I can't leave Emma there in the underworld. What if she meets an actuary?"

"I'm supposed to have a dinner tonight," Bob said. "With Stephen King."

"Whoa," Bert said. "Stephen King! What's he like?"

"He's an OK guy, but he can be kind of judgmental. I think it annoys him that I still drink and do drugs. He's also very political. Hates Republicans. He says they're all bigots, and he can't see the irony in that."

"Great writer though," Bert said. "I love all his stuff."

"Me too," Bob admitted. "Except for *The Gunslinger*. Remember when Roland summons a demon to fornicate with him. That was so ridiculous and contrived. You can practically taste the cocaine binge coming off the page."

Bob frowned and shook his head.

"Isn't that sort of what's happening to us in real life, though?" Oliver asked. "With the demons, and the Host, and all that crazy stuff? I mean— minus the fornication, for the most part?"

"I suppose," Bob said. "Only we don't take it so seriously."

"So what do you say?" Teddy asked. "Want to skip the judgmental dinner with Stephen King and get drunk with us instead, before traveling through a wormhole in the space-time continuum to rescue my common-law spouse?"

"Yes," Bob sighed, "I guess I do."

Oliver felt a wave of relief, followed by a second, stronger wave of absolute terror. His entire existence had become an emotionally jarring rollercoaster. He was scared to death of traveling to a different existential plane and potentially being turned into a gelatinous mass. Strangely though, his own sense of comfort, for the first time in his life, seemed unimportant. He owed a debt to Emma. He was going to repay it.

They escaped the heat of the living room and stepped outside. A small patio overlooked the waterway. Running alongside the patio stones was a bar with a thatched roof that belonged in a Jimmy Buffet song.

Oliver eyed the multitude of bottles on the back shelves and shuddered. He didn't particularly enjoy the sensation of being drunk, and he hoped he wouldn't get sick.

"Cindy warned us not to drink with you," he said.

"Quivering gelatinous mass," Bob reminded him.

"What are we drinking?"

"Daiquiris."

From under the bar, Bob produced an industrial-sized red blender. He rummaged through the bar fridge until he found a pitcher of homemade daiquiri mix. He poured this into the blender jar until the liquid reached the quarter-way mark, then added ice cubes to bring it to half. He then opened a large bottle of Lamb's 151 Proof rum and topped up the jar.

"Oh good Lord," Bert said.

"Yes," Bob agreed, "we're going to be quite intoxicated."

"I enjoy drinking," Teddy said to Oliver. "This should be fun for me."

Bob blended the concoction, then divided it out into glasses and garnished each with a small paper umbrella.

Carmella had a taste, then made a face and set her drink on the bar. "I think I'll hold down the fort here if it's all the same to you," she said.

"Good idea," Bert said, sniffing his.

Teddy, Bert, Oliver and Bob clinked glasses.

"Bottoms up, fellas," Bob said.

The slushy drink didn't taste bad, per se, but it was more like something produced for hummingbirds, as opposed to human consumption. The rum was sweet, and the mix was sweet, and after a few swallows Oliver wondered if he would get drunk or go into a diabetic coma first.

"These are a little sweet," Teddy observed.

"Here," Bob said, and topped each of their glasses off with cheap Vodka.

Teddy tasted his. "Much better."

"I'm not sure I can drink all this," Oliver said.

Bob reached over and smacked him in the crotch. "Sack up, and drive that tropical daiquiri into you," he said. "It's for your health and safety."

"And for Emma," Teddy added.

"For Emma," Oliver said, holding his nose and taking a big slushy swallow. He involuntarily wretched, but managed to keep the liquid down. His eyes watered.

"There you go," Bob said. "That'll put some hair on your chest."

Teddy laughed. "Appeals to his manhood don't work," he said. "He doesn't fornicate often."

"Why not? Handsome young guy like you?" Bob asked.

"I...uh..." Oliver could feel his tongue thickening in his mouth, which was especially alarming, as he'd only had a few swallows of his daiquiri. Teddy and Bob were already refilling their glasses.

"He puts the vagina on a pedestal," Carmella said.

"What?" Oliver was taken aback.

"It's true," Bert said. "You don't need to worship it, you know."

Oliver was slightly horrified that Carmella had decided to join the fray. He'd come to think of her as an ally—a buffer that would protect him from Bert and Teddy's keen interest in his lack of a sex life. Now he felt somewhat betrayed. "I think we're getting a little sidetracked here," he said, before taking another long swallow of his daiquiri, which burned his esophagus. "Let's get this over with so we can get Emma."

"You can't rush a daiquiri," Carmella said; "you'll get an ice cream headache."

"We also want to make sure we keep these down," Bert said. "No point in going to all this work just to spew."

"He's right," Bob added. "Patience is key. Slow is smooth, and smooth is fast. You know. Like the Navy Seals say?"

Now that a chance to retrieve Emma was within grasp, Oliver was eager to get going. He felt impatient and anxious. He contemplated Teddy, who was calmly guzzling the pink slush from his glass. He had to admit, he admired the heck out of the big man's demeanor.

Oliver had just taken his third sip when an alarming idea occurred to him.

"What if there's more than one underworld?"

"Huh?" Teddy said as he refilled his glass.

Oliver remembered something he'd heard during a lecture about the physics of black holes and existential planes. "What if there's more than one underworld? If it isn't just heaven, hell, and Earth, but, like, an endless multiverse. And what if Emma is in a different layer of this multiverse than Bob takes us?"

"We'll just have to hope for the best," Teddy said.

"Hope for the best?! If there really is a multiverse, the probability of us going to the same place as Emma is essentially infinity-to-one against!"

"Yeah," Teddy said. "We get it. We aren't idiots. So let's hope for the best."

The possibilities weighed heavily on Oliver. God knew he wanted to get Emma, but he certainly didn't want to end up lost in a tiered, multidimensional universe.

"I think we really need to..."

Bob put an arm around Oliver's shoulders, and with his free hand raised Oliver's arm, lifting the alcohol to his mouth. "Here you go, son, have another swallow. Stop thinking. Just do."

Oliver necked down another frozen gulp.

"If it makes you feel any better, every time I've ever gone I end up in the exact same place."

"Really?"

"Sure."

"You've gone what...two or three times?"

Bob looked a little uncomfortable and scratched at his stubble. "No... more than that, I'd say."

"Why? I thought you said it sucked?"

The writer looked over his shoulder toward the living room, and it was obvious that he was having reservations about the discussion.

"Well, there are some reasons I have for going there. We'll just leave it at that. And the important thing is, it's always the same location."

This reassurance made Oliver feel somewhat better.

"I need food," Teddy announced. "I can't drink this much without eating. Do you have any pickled eggs?"

"I'm afraid I don't," Bob said. "I can, however, offer you some of Jessica's protein powder to mix with your daiquiri, if you like."

Teddy nodded. Bob disappeared into the house and reemerged a moment later with a Costco-sized plastic tub of Vanilla-flavored whey protein. The big man spun off the lid and cast it aside, before scooping a huge quantity of powder directly into his mouth.

"Oh, hey!" Bert said, "That'll bind you up! That stuff is like concrete!"

Teddy smiled, his teeth coated in gooey pink slurry. "I'll be fine."

He ladled another scoop into his mouth and then washed it down with a half-glass of daiquiri.

"I think we're getting there, team," Bob announced before running another batch of daiquiris through the blender and topping everyone up.

Oliver took another sip and closed his eyes, trying to imagine what they were about to experience, traveling to the underworld. He pictured Emma, and wondered where she was, and whether she was safe. He must have drifted off, because a moment later his forehead hit the bar and made a thud.

He was acutely aware that he was paralytically drunk.

"How many have you had?" Teddy asked him.

"This is still my first," Oliver said, indicating his nearly full glass. "But he did just top it up."

"Wow!" Teddy said.

They kept at it for a while.

By the time Oliver had finished his drink, he could no longer confidently ascertain which direction was up. He had abandoned his reservations about traveling to the underworld and had substituted, in their stead, reservations about the colossal hangover that awaited him. He was keen to get moving. Emma was, after all, depending on them. He intended to rouse the troops, but when he tried to speak he only managed a wet burp. Then he fell off his bar stool.

Oliver had watched Bert make a valiant effort to consume a copious helping of ethanol while maintaining his dignity, but in the end the old man had succumbed, and now snored softly in his lounge chair, his chin to his chest. A thin strand of bright pink drool hung from his lower lip.

Astonishingly, Bob was no worse for wear. He'd spent the evening regaling Carmella with stories about life as an author. He was in the middle of recounting a trip to New York during which he'd gotten into a three-way fistfight with Noam Chomsky and Salman Rushdie when his phone rang.

"You'll have to excuse me a moment," he said politely.

"Hello? Oh, hi, Steve. Right. I'm sorry, it slipped my mind. Yeah, I'm mostly just lounging around—haven't written anything in a while. You? Nice! Well, I'm glad to hear it. What—no, I just figured it would be about, you know, an alcoholic writer, a magical retarded person, some kind of monster, and I don't know, ichor I guess—Stephen? Steve?"

Bob looked at his phone. "He hung up."

"Why did you tell him you aren't writing?" Carmella asked. "There's a massive book growing on your coffee table."

"You know the story about Tantalus, how he could never grab the fruit from the tree no matter how close it looked?"

"Sure."

"My fruit is the end of that book."

"But it must be nearly done. It's huge!"

"That's the first draft of the first chapter," Bob explained.

"Hmmm," Carmella said. "What's it about?"

"You know, I'm not sure yet."

Teddy stood so suddenly that Oliver startled and fell off his barstool again.

"As soon as we get Emma, I'm going to Tampa to arm-wrestle the fishermen!" the big man announced.

He took two steps, and collapsed face-first on the patio stones.

"Hey," Oliver slurred, "he dan get crunk after all!"

"OK," Bob said, "I think we're just about ready."

He walked into the house and came back with the typewriter. He lined up four of the empty rum bottles on the bar.

"You awake, kid?" he asked Oliver, who was sitting on the ground, his cheek against the leg of one of the stools.

"Uh huh," Oliver managed. "Just getting my bearings."

The bar felt cool against his face. He hoped hell would be less humid.

"Think of something happy, and tell me what it is."

Oliver closed his eyes. He hunted through the recesses of his memory for the perfect item that would be untainted by the ravages of time. He settled on something from elementary school. He pictured his Grade Three teacher Mrs. Hanson. She was smiling, and handing him back a test-paper with a scratch and sniff sticker on the corner. "My math textbook from Grade Three," he said dreamily. "It had a picture of a snail shell on the cover."

Bob tapped away at the keys of the typewriter. There was no paper in the device. When Oliver turned again to look at the rum bottles, there were now three bottles and his grade-three math book. The glamour was a perfect likeness. The book looked weighty, and inviting, and extremely real.

"Whoa," Oliver said. "That's... amazing."

Bob appeared to study Teddy for a moment, and then began typing again. Now there were two bottles, a math textbook, and a jar of pickled eggs.

"Good choice," Oliver said, giving a very clumsy thumbs up.

"What does Bert like?" Bob asked Carmella.

"Orthopedic insoles," she said without hesitation.

Bob typed away, and in place of the third bottle was a cardboard box containing a pair of top-of-the-line Aetrex Orthopedic insoles, which the box claimed would help with arch support and ball-of-foot pain.

Without typing, Bob stared at the last bottle, and it winked out of existence, replaced by a dog-eared copy of *The Catcher in the Rye*.

"I guess we're both book guys," he said to Oliver before helping him to his feet.

Bob came around the bar and crouched beside Teddy. "Wake up, big fella."

Teddy groaned.

"There's pickled eggs," Bob offered.

Slowly, Teddy got to his feet. He ambled to the bar on wobbly legs, looking to Oliver like a gigantic baby deer with a human growth hormone addiction. He reached out for the eggs. There was a bright, soundless flash, and he was gone.

Carmella woke Bert and roused him from the lounge chair. "Oh Lord," Bert said, "I'm hammered."

She kissed him tenderly on the forehead, then led him to the bar.

"I love you, dear," she said. "These are for you."

He noticed the insoles, and reached for them. He was about to respond to her when he, too, disappeared in a flash of light.

"You sure you're up for this, kid?" Bob asked, turning to Oliver.

Oliver, to his great surprise, realized that he was, indeed, up for this. The time had come for him to perform his duty.

He would have loved nothing better than to articulate his newfound enthusiasm for the mission, but unfortunately he was absolutely, staggeringly drunk, so instead he mumbled, "In for a peony, et cetera."

He reached forward and grabbed the textbook. For the briefest of moments, he perceived that it was still nothing more than an empty rum bottle, and then the world blinked out of existence.

— *Nine* —

Celestial Being 472-19a

Danger Level 2

When matter and antimatter collide, particle physicists describe the subsequent reaction as "annihilation."

While these particle physicists would be quick to explain that the laws of thermodynamics must still apply to such exotic interactions, rendering them entirely predictable, they will also admit that the idea of turning a human being into an explosive flash of light and a fine, interdimensional mist of bosons, antineutrinos and baryons would make for an outstandingly cool party trick.

Oliver Bell, however, would argue that the experience was not particularly fun, and should be reserved for only the most dire of occasions, when no conceivable alternative options exist.

The first thing he felt, after his annihilation, was a sense of extreme depersonalization. Had he taken the time to experiment with psychedelic, mind-altering drugs, he might have been better prepared for the experience. But as an interdimensional cloud of high-energy photons and exotic particles, he was maddened by the sensation of having an itchy nose and yet having no nose to scratch, or indeed appendages with which to scratch it.

He was nonetheless dazzled by the thought that he was somehow able to maintain a stream of consciousness at all, with no brain, organs or cellular structure to speak of.

He also had a very distinct sensation of motion. Though it was difficult to reconcile with his existence up until that point, he intuited that he was gliding between the physical layers of a tiered multiverse. One moment he would sense that he was in space, and the next moment he would sense that he was in, for lack of a better term, not-space.

For a while he believed he was heading to a very specific destination, but just as he was sure he was about to arrive, the bearing of whatever it was that constituted his sense of self changed drastically, and reversed course. He was drawn backwards, and the sensation was much like what he imagined a glass of Pepsi might experience when being siphoned up a drinking straw.

As he plowed through the folds of the multiverse, now in reverse, he accelerated until he became convinced that he had somehow exceeded the speed of light and that time was bending around him. He briefly became a black hole.

"Do not turn into a quivering gelatinous mass," he reminded himself, now understanding exactly how that could happen.

As space and time wrapped around him, the waves and particles that made up his being began to organize. He then had a mathematically astute thought: "The human body has roughly 7x10^27 atoms in it. That is enough to run a nuclear power plant for thirty years. Therefore, if my essence is truly annihilated, wouldn't it cause a massive explosion?"

Everything stopped moving.

Bright sunlight penetrated his eyelids and speared directly into his brain. He groaned. The fact that he now had eyelids and the fact that he could groan again was not lost on him.

Gentle surf crashed on a nearby beach, the rhythm of the waves like music. Something licked his face.

Oliver opened his eyes.

He lay his back on the worn wooden planking of an old fishing pier. He gripped an empty Lamb's rum bottle. He remembered his heroic effort to chemically relax himself on Bob's back patio, and pressed his fingers against his forehead, probing for signs of a hangover. He detected none.

A scraggly yellow animal that resembled a terrier, but was, in some unnamable way, not *exactly* a terrier, pawed at his shoulder and licked him.

"Hey," he said.

The dog, for lack of a better term, nuzzled its cold nose into his neck, and he sat up.

"What gives?"

The dog cocked its head, perked its ears. It wore a red collar with a blue anodized aluminum tag. Oliver squinted. It read:

Name Unknown—Subtype Mayhem
Nonverbal
Celestial Being 472-19a
Danger Level 2

"Mayhem?"

The dog panted, and sat on its haunches.

He was looking at his Host—an honest-to-God celestial being. He didn't know what he'd been expecting his Host to look like, but whatever it was, he hadn't been expecting a dog.

Oliver scratched it behind the ear. Mayhem leaned into his hand.

"Where am I?" he asked.

Mayhem didn't answer.

"Nonverbal. Got it."

Oliver got to his feet and tried to take in his surroundings.

He turned around, looking for Teddy, Bert and Bob.

"Guys?" he called out. There was no response. The pier was empty. The first tendrils of panic began to wrap around him.

"Bob? Teddy?" he called out again. The only answer was the gentle sound of light surf against the pilings of the pier.

He checked the water on either side, to make sure his friends hadn't missed their marks, but he saw only turquoise waves.

He wracked his brain, trying to remember what Bob had told him. He'd said he always ended up in the same place whenever he went to the underworld. He didn't mention anything about a fishing pier!

Had he become separated from them, somewhere along the way? Was he lost in the multiverse?

Mayhem, whimpering, pawed at his leg.

"What?"

The dog turned toward the far end of the wharf, and whined.

Oliver followed the dog's gaze. There was something about the pier— something familiar. The broad, creosote-stained planks and handrails were weathered and splintered. Small shelters set at even intervals, offered shade to any potential fishermen—men who would spend their days trying their luck in what he now recognized as the Gulf of Mexico. Seagulls and pelicans perched on the ancient red shingles of the shelter roofs. The sun flashed off gentle waves that stretched out to the horizon.

A row of condominiums lined the endless beach. Palm trees swayed lazily between the unnaturally clean buildings.

A small blue and white dory dangled from ropes over the distant leeward rail. It was suspended by an ancient block and tackle, and swung back and forth in a soundless arc, propelled by the warm wind.

He had been here before! This was the Redington Long Pier! He was in Redington Shores, literally a twenty-minute drive from Bob's tiki bar.

Had he accidentally teleported through space instead of traveling to the underworld? Had Bob tricked him?

No. Mayhem was a separate physical being. He was definitely somewhere dimensionally different.

"What are we doing here?" he asked the dog, who of course offered no answer.

When Oliver was in Grade Eleven, his parents, Jack and Mavis, had rented a condominium at the base of the Long Pier for his March Break. At Mavis's insistence, they rented a car and explored the outlet malls and sightseeing stops along the Gulf Coast. But for three days, Jack Bell took his son fishing off the pier, where they caught mackerel, sea trout and amberjack from morning to midnight.

Years later, the structure partially collapsed during Hurricane Harvey. The remnants were torn down sometime in 2019.

And yet, here he was. There was no mistaking it. This was the Redington Long Pier.

He followed Mayhem's gaze, and adjusted his glasses. A lone figure sat on a bench beside the swinging dory.

With no idea what else to do, Oliver walked toward the stranger. The planks creaked under his shoes. Mayhem followed, panting at his heels.

Walking the length of the wharf was like strolling through history. Oliver tasted the salt air, and smelled the faint, sweet aroma of tropical flowers. He inhaled deeply, overwhelmed with nostalgia. God, how he had loved this place!

As he drew closer, the man at the end came into sharper focus. He wore khaki shorts and a seventies-style button-up green shirt with epaulets on the shoulders. The brim of a Tilley hat shaded the stranger's face, but there was something shockingly familiar about his posture.

The man sniffed loudly—and very distinctly—to clear his sinuses, and clarity dawned. Oliver knew that sniff!

It was the very distinctive double-sniff of Jack Bell. Oliver was looking at his father.

His heart trip-hammered in his chest. He leaned closer and stared, thinking he must be mistaken, that there was no way on earth the man on the pier could really be his dad. But it was no illusion. His father scratched absently at his mustache and eyed the far horizon, still apparently unaware of Oliver's presence.

This latest development in what had, without any doubt, been the strangest day of Oliver's life, was particularly shocking on account of the fact that his dad had been dead for nearly five years.

Tears blurred his vision, and for a moment his father and the landscape shimmered like oil droplets in water. He blinked furiously, worried that when his vision cleared the specter would be gone.

For some reason, Oliver flashed back to his prom night. He hadn't thought about that night in ages, and now he remembered it with seemingly unnatural clarity.

The day had not gone to plan. Oliver's date ditched him for another boy at the last minute.

He was ever-so-slightly heartbroken by the gesture.

He and Heather Laidlaw had been friends since middle school, and during the course of their friendship, while he had maintained the image of the quintessential scrawny nerd, she had blossomed into a beautiful, confident woman. While he held no illusions of romance, he'd still been looking forward to accompanying her to the dance. Without meaning to objectify his friend, in his heart of hearts, he thought it might give him a small sense of satisfaction to be seen as something other than a math nerd by his classmates when he showed up with such a gorgeous, well-liked woman.

Unfortunately, a much more handsome, much more muscular, and much more popular boy named Rick Moriarty had made a move on the day of the prom, and Heather had apparently been swept off her feet. She broke their prom plans via text message, just two hours before they were due to meet. Oliver was deeply embarrassed by the whole ordeal.

His father knocked on his bedroom door and allowed himself in, before taking a seat on the edge of his bed next to Oliver.

"Put on your tux."

"No way, Dad. I'm not going."

"I paid to rent it. Put it on. I'll get dressed up. We'll get some pictures in the backyard for your mother. She wants prom pictures. Since I paid to rent the thing, that makes me the boss. Get dressed."

"What!?"

"You heard me," Jack said calmly. "Suit up, Romeo. I'm your date tonight."

With that, Jack left the room.

Oliver was too flabbergasted to object further. When he thought about it, though, since he'd already suffered a catastrophic humiliation, he figured he might as well do what his parents wanted if it would make them happy.

Jack didn't have a tuxedo, but when Oliver emerged from his bedroom, his dad wore a dark charcoal suit with a vibrant yellow tie.

"You look very handsome," Jack said, fixing a short-stemmed red rose through the lapel button-hole of his suit.

"Ah... thanks. You too."

"Heather has your actual boutonniere, so this will have to do," Jack explained.

"Don't remind me."

"Fifteen bucks I paid for that thing. What a waste. Hopefully Randy will wear it."

"Ricky."

"Oh right. Well you know—Ricky... Randy... it's all the same."

"I hope it gives him allergies," Oliver mumbled.

"Yeah. It probably won't though. He'll probably end up screwing your friend all night and having a terrific time."

"Dad!"

"I'm just saying. The sooner you get your head around this one, the better it'll be for you. Get the whole grieving process out of the way as quickly as possible, you know?"

"Oh God." Oliver was severely regretting his decision to go along with the tuxedo plan.

"Well, I mean, it's for the best, when you think about it. Kind of shows you who your friends are."

"I don't have any friends."

"You have me. We're friends."

"I guess so," Oliver said. "God... that's so sad."

Jack smiled. "I'm the best kind of friend, kid. I'm the kind that sacrifices his own pursuit of happiness to put money in an RESP for eighteen years so you can buy pizza and beer when you move out. Now come on. Your mother's waiting for us."

After a backyard photoshoot that Oliver could only pray would never find its way onto the internet, he and his father sat together at the picnic table. Oliver tugged awkwardly at the collar of his dress shirt. He felt rather juvenile, dressed in what felt like a child's James Bond costume, hanging out with his dad amongst the buzzing bees and singing birds and blooming flowers, and the gentle June evening warmth. He was unable to hide his misery.

Jack didn't acknowledge this at first, and instead jogged into the kitchen, returning with two cold bottles of beer. He opened both, setting one in front of Oliver.

"Do you think I'm a loser, Olly?" he asked.

"Of course not!"

"Did you know my prom date dumped me at the last minute?"

Oliver shook his head. He'd never thought to ask about it.

"You never really think of your parents' prom, do you? You ever wonder why that is?"

"I... I guess I don't know."

"It's because they're insignificant. I mean, it's a big deal to a few people who organize it and it's probably a big deal for the folks who aren't going to have any more education beyond high school because it's their last school party, and what have you, but at the end of the day, to me at least, it was always like somebody else's wedding. It wasn't my thing. And I'd be shocked if you told me that you'd been genuinely looking forward to it."

Oliver, despite his burning cheeks, smiled. "I'd been kind of dreading it, to be honest. I mean, I wanted to go... you know... with Heather. But once we got there it was bound to be awkward."

Jack lifted his beer and they clinked bottles.

"So, if you're like me, what you're feeling is that maybe you've come up short somehow."

"I guess. Like, it's supposed to be some kind of rite of passage or something? I'm a little humiliated about how it turned out."

Jack put an arm around his son's shoulders, pulling him close. "You're a marathon runner who didn't win the fifty-yard dash. This isn't your race, pal. You're made for something else."

They drank in silence for a while, before Jack rubbed at his face and sighed. "You have a special mind, Olly. I think you know that. You're a good person... with a kind heart... but that brain of yours—I don't know son. It's one in a million. One in a billion, maybe. And your life is going to hurt a lot, because people aren't going to understand you, and that will feel like rejection. But that pain—well—it will build character. Then, eventually, someone will get you. You have to have faith. You're here for a reason, and somebody else will see that. You won't be alone forever. I promise."

Oliver had never heard his father sound so earnest. He just nodded.

"Life is funny, that way," Jack said, tracking a robin that hopped along the grass at the edge of the lawn; "you think it's breaking your heart, only to realize years later that it's saving your soul."

It had been their last heart-to-heart.

A few months after that day, his dad was diagnosed with metastatic colon cancer just as Oliver was preparing to leave for his freshman year in Halifax.

Jack tried an aggressive regimen of chemotherapy to shrink the tumors and buy some time. He insisted that Oliver go to school.

"I'll be fine," he'd said. "I'm tough as nails. You go finish up the semester, and when you come home for Christmas, this will all just be routine."

Luck hadn't been on his side, though. The day Oliver wrote his last final, his father was readmitted to the hospital, this time with pneumonia. His immune system had been ravaged by the chemotherapy, and by the time they caught the infection he was already in septic shock.

Oliver, driving through the winter's first storm, wept the entire four-hour trip home.

He went directly to the hospital, where he caught Jack's last brief period of lucidity. His father promised to watch out for him in the afterlife, assuming he was able. They hugged, and Jack felt like no more than a bag of bones in Oliver's arms.

He slipped into a delirium that night, then three days later he was gone.

His passing had thrown Oliver into a painful spiral of grief.

In the months after his death, Oliver would lock himself in the dormitory bathroom with the shower on, just to cry privately. It was a daily ritual. The painful, necessary routine had, in fact, been the impetus for him to move out of shared accommodations and into the apartment above the Old Dairy Deli and Donair.

He still struggled with his dad's death—with the way it was so *permanent*.

But now, against all reason, that permanence was in question.

As improbable as it was, a very much alive Jack Bell was sitting on a bench, on a pier that wasn't supposed to exist, not ten feet away.

"Dad?" Oliver said.

Jack turned and smiled. He was a young man, no older than thirty-five.

The puffy steroid cheeks and hollowed-out chemotherapy eyes were gone. His mustache was as black as coal. Waves of dark hair tumbled over his forehead and around his ears from under the hat.

"Hey, Olly!" Jack stood. "You're finally here!"

"Dad!"

They grabbed one another in a tight embrace, but in doing so Oliver accidentally clunked his father in the back of the head with the rum bottle. He'd forgotten he was carrying it.

"Yowch!"

"Oh! I'm sorry."

Jack rubbed the back of his head, still smiling. "I guess it worked!"

"What worked?"

"This!" Jack patted him on the shoulder. "You're here!"

Oliver considered things. He was standing on what he realized was the sacred ground of his personal happy place, embracing a deceased man he had loved dearly.

"I'm dead, aren't I?"

Jack laughed. "No, no! You're alive. We intercepted you when you set off for the underworld."

"Intercepted!? How!?"

Jack laughed again. "It's probably a bit disorienting. Remember how I promised I would be keeping a close eye on you?"

The idea that his father had somehow managed to keep up that seemingly impossible dying promise made Oliver's heart skip a beat.

"You were watching out for me?"

"Of course!"

For the first time since Jack's passing, Oliver was comforted. He blinked hard, swallowed, and managed to nod.

"We were tracking you when you set off to dimensions-unknown, and, well, we managed to bring you here."

"What about my friends?" Oliver asked.

Jack shifted his gaze. "They're more or less safe... for the time being, anyway."

Oliver allowed himself to relax a little. Jack Bell had never let him down, and there was no reason to think he would start now. He trusted his father, even if he still couldn't exactly trust what he was seeing.

"Is this real?"

He desperately hoped it was.

"You mean, are you dreaming?"

Oliver nodded.

"Well, that sort of depends."

Jack reached into the pocket of his shorts and produced a set of old nineties-style cellular phones, one blue, the other red. He inspected the phones carefully.

"These are called Advanced Transport Integration Units—ATIUs for short. They're tricky little things. The amount of R and D behind them is staggering, especially when you consider that they're basically a single-use product."

Jack placed the phones gently down on the railing.

Oliver studied them carefully. They looked like regular Nokia handsets. There was nothing particularly "advanced" about their appearance. In fact, if anything, they appeared to have been left in a forgotten junk drawer for a couple of decades. There was even a fine patina of swirl marks on the screen of the red phone, where presumably it had been placed in someone's pocket along with their keys.

Jack took a step back. "In a few minutes the phones are going to ring. At the other end of the line will be a code, written in the language of reality. We call it 'Creation Code.' Maybe you've heard of the theory that postulates reality as being a type of computer program? This code is the actual backbone of what you and I think of as the universe."

Oliver gasped. He leaned closer, staring in newfound awe at the gadgets.

In advanced mathematics circles, there was a long-running, ever-evolving idea that the physical universe followed a type of mathematical instruction code. If the code could be correctly interpreted, it would solve the mysteries of science.

The clues that such a code existed were said to be the number pi, the arborization pattern of plants, and the repetitive existence of natural fractals in everything from the crystalline pattern of ice to the shape of a periwinkle shell. The fact that Oliver's father had just so nonchalantly confirmed that not only was the Creation Code Theory correct, but that it could be manipulated, put Oliver in the uncomfortable position of holding a piece of knowledge that no other human could possibly hope to know. How, he wondered, could he ever explain what he'd just learned? He knew, without a doubt, that he simply couldn't.

"Should I..." he paused, still struggling with the enormity of the information. "Should I know this stuff?"

"Knowledge is power," his father said. "You might as well know what you're up against."

"What am I up against?"

"Right now... You have a choice to make. It's a real doozy, too."

Jack picked up the blue phone. "The blue phone takes you to Halifax—"

"Halifax?"

"Just... hang on. This'll all make sense in a second. Like I was saying. If you answer the call on this handset, you get your life back, or, that is to say, a *version* of your life. One that you'll be comfortable with. We can't change the past, but we can help you hit the reset button—reintegrate you into the secular world.

"You'll be found, confused, on the university campus. You'll have some memory issues. They'll check you out and decide you had a concussion during the riot. If you remember anything about the Host, glamours, your trip here, or the nature of the afterlife, it will sort of be like a dream. You'll carry on in your academic career, though on a slightly different trajectory. You'll probably get a job in the private sector after that. You'll most likely live to be an old man with a largely peaceful life—but of course, the future isn't guaranteed. But that's the blue-phone program. It's the road you were traveling until now."

"That's quite the program," Oliver said, trying to take it all in.

"No kidding! It took a team of hundreds of engineers and programmers to design and build it. We're talking about tens of millions of dollars worth of resources invested. You have to understand, intervening in the secular world consumes an enormous amount of manpower and energy. They built this as a thank you gift to you, for working with Mayhem here. Not an easy job, from what I understand."

Jack bent down to pat the scruffy yellow terrier.

Oliver's mind reeled. It had never occurred to him that there might be a do-over option. "I... I can just go back?"

"Yes. And there's no shame in that. You played your part! You carried the torch, and you did it very well, for days. A lot of people... In fact—most people—couldn't handle what you've been through. You conducted yourself with grace and bravery, and you deserve a good, long, happy life. That's what the blue phone offers."

"Mayhem would get reassigned, and you would carry on as though none of this," Jack swept his arm back toward the shore, "had ever happened. In fact, you would probably forget about it entirely."

"What happens to my friends? Emma and Teddy? And Bert and Carmella?"

"Their fate would be out of your hands," Jack said. "Though in fairness, you should know that their fate is pretty much out of your hands anyway. You might intertwine your destinies, but you can't necessarily control them."

Oliver considered the implications of going back. He imagined returning to the advantages and comforts of a normal life. But what was the cost? His friends? His recent illumination? His newfound sense of purpose? His reunion with his father? Everything he had recently gained was on the line.

"What does the red phone do?"

"You mean the vermillion phone?" Jack asked.

"Vermillion?"

"You can call it red if you like," Jack said, "but Nokia describes the color as vermillion."

"Let's stick with red," Oliver said.

"Fair enough."

Jack smiled. "The red phone is kind of like a promise."

"A promise?"

"A hazardous journey, small wages, constant danger, negligible chance of success, and a guarantee of anonymity in the event of such, etcetera, etcetera. In other words, you continue on the path you're on, and in all likelihood experience a brief, violent thrill ride of a life before dying young and breaking your mother's heart."

Oliver bit his lip. He imagined his mother grieving not only her husband, but now her son. He felt ashamed that he hadn't been considering how all this would affect her. And here he had the chance to go back, and to be a better son, and to spare her the consequences of this chaotic existence.

He looked down at Mayhem, who met his gaze. He tried to remember what his life had been like before. It hadn't been bad. But it hadn't exactly been great, either. He'd been safe, sure, but he'd also been trapped by the invisible cages of inevitability and comfort. If he could go back in time and meet his former self, would he like that person? Could he be that person again?

The phones on the railing rang in tandem, playing the classic Nokia ringtone. It was the ringtone that had formed the ubiquitous soundtrack of irritation in the movie theaters and libraries of 1990s North America.

The screens illuminated yellow, reading, "Incoming Call."

"You say if I choose the blue phone, I'll what? Forget about my friends? Forget about meeting you?"

"Pretty much."

"Will I ever see you again?"

"Maybe. In sixty years, give or take."

Jack looked at him expectantly, a boyish grin on his face. "So, what's it going to be?"

Oliver looked at the blue phone. He knew that world. It was safe. It was common. It was *understood.*

He remembered Robert Frost. *Two roads diverged in a yellow wood...*

Oliver picked up the red phone and answered it. "Hello?"

There was no answer. Oliver waited, listening. He'd been expecting something—some meaningful event to occur. He thought, perhaps, he was about to hear the actual voice of God. Instead, he was met with complete silence. He frowned at his father, and shrugged.

"Congratulations," Jack said, clapping him on the shoulder.

"For what?"

Jack beamed. "You're about to be the first transdimensional, living human being to walk the shores of the nineteenth tier of the divine multiverse."

Oliver tried to wrap his head around what his father had just said. *The nineteenth tier.* The multiverse was real! And it was numbered!

That meant it could be measured!

That revelation alone would be a Nobel Prize-worthy discovery! And here he was, physically standing in it—in a new dimension, where no living human had been before. He was momentarily overwhelmed.

He felt like Neil Armstrong might have felt if, instead of spending years training in the space program, Neil had simply shown up for work one morning and had been abruptly deposited on the surface of the moon without fanfare.

Oliver didn't think he'd personally done anything to deserve such a monumental achievement. He was more like an imposter—like he'd cheated his way here. Walking around carrying an empty rum bottle only enforced this perception.

But his father's big, proud smile suggested otherwise.

"Is this a good thing?" Oliver asked.

"Well, it's certainly a thing. Whether it's good or not has yet to be determined. But it's definitely a big deal in my books."

"I didn't feel anything when I answered the phone just now."

"Well, you wouldn't. You picked the red phone."

"But you said the creation code—"

"Oh, I should have clarified. That was *only* in the blue phone. The red phone was the par-for-the-course option. It's literally just a phone."

"But why have a red phone at all? It doesn't make any sense!"

Jack stared at the phones, as if considering them for the first time. "Hmm, I don't actually know. I think it was just a cooler way to present your options, like in *The Matrix*."

Oliver shook his head. Whatever preconceptions he might have held concerning the afterlife, they had been off by miles.

The blue phone stopped ringing.

"Well," Jack said, "that's that, I guess."

He grabbed both phones and unceremoniously dumped them into a nearby garbage can.

"Welcome to heaven, son."

— *Ten* —

With a bounce in his step, Jack led the way down the pier toward the beach.

So brisk was his father's pace, that Oliver, wanting to look in all directions at once in order to take everything in, fell behind. Mayhem nudged his calf, and Oliver jogged to catch up.

"You probably have questions," Jack said.

"So many questions."

"Fire away."

"Where are my friends?"

"I'm going to answer that for you, but I have quite a nifty visual aide that I think will help. It's in my office."

"But they're safe, right?"

"They're safe," Jack agreed. "Well...they're safe-ish. They aren't dead, if that helps."

"Do they need me?"

"Maybe. It's hard to say."

A knot of concern formed in Oliver's stomach. Until this point, his relationship with Bert, Teddy, and Emma had been fairly one-sided. He needed them to coach him through his introduction to this strange new world. They had collectively been his rock—voices of experience. He was so new at being a player in the cosmic universe that he wasn't sure he even qualified as a rookie.

"How am I supposed to help them?"

"We'll tackle the details shortly... with some assistance from a friend of mine."

His father turned to look him in the eye. "I have every confidence in you, Olly."

Warm blood rushed to his face, and he tried to suppress a smile. He felt the same silly pride he remembered from when he was a boy, showing his father a perfect report card, or scoring a three-pointer in front of his dad at a junior-high basketball game. He didn't really care if it was childish. He didn't care if a psychologist might suggest he was putting too much weight in his father's approval. It was a feeling he had needed for years, and he was grateful for it. "Thanks, Dad."

His father winked and walked on. "Like I said, we'll tackle the rescue details in due time. But surely you must be wondering what all this means. How you got here... where, exactly, *here* is?"

"The multiverse is real, obviously," Oliver began.

"Yeah. It's real."

"How many levels are there?"

Jack seemed to ponder how to answer the question. "There's a pretty good theory that the levels are infinite, or nearly infinite. And that doesn't account for the even more important question of 'How many level nineteens are there?' Which we also have come to suspect are infinite.

"We've only been able to prove the existence of a few hundred tiers, all in the divine to anti-divine direction. We call that the 'Near-field multiverse,' since we can observe it and measure it. We have yet to prove the existence of lateral universes—by that I mean the universes that branch because in one you bought a Coke, and in another you bought a Pepsi—that sort of thing. But that's a topic for a different day; the main takeaway here is that there's a tiered multiverse, and you are currently on divine tier nineteen."

"What's the difference? Between the levels, I mean."

"When you go up in number, in our nomenclature system, you come closer to oneness with eternity. God, if you will. When you go the other way, you become more separated from it. Basically, it boils down to structure versus entropy. Secular earth—the universe you came from, is level zero. It's the only level inhabited by the CL, which stands for 'currently living.'"

Oliver remembered Bob's story about Melody and the actuary. "Are you still an engineer here, in the afterlife?"

"Of course."

"Are things good? Are you good?" Oliver asked.

What he meant to ask was whether or not his father still had any lingering effects from his illness, but he couldn't bring himself to ask it—the idea that there was cancer in the afterlife was absolutely horrifying.

"Very good," his father said. "This place is beautiful. The weather's great. The food is terrific. Everyone's health is excellent. My hair isn't grey anymore. Technology is way more advanced. Everything just works. It's pretty amazing."

"So no Hurricane Harvey to wreck the fishing pier?"

"Exactly."

"Do you live forever here?"

"You can," Jack explained, "but most people move on after a while. As you achieve a certain level of wisdom, you have the option of graduating to the next tier. Those who hang on take on important positions and become the main decision-makers for this tier, but eventually most people move along. There's very little sadness here, because you inherently understand that time is no longer your master. In an infinite existence everything is eventual. You know that Vera Lynn song? 'We'll Meet Again?'"

"Where are Teddy and Bert and Bob?"

"We'll get to them," Jack said. "Suffice to say, we're lucky enough to have a bead on their location." He put his arm around his son and led him back toward the beach.

A pelican landed on the planks in front of them and before Jack could shoo it away, Mayhem charged at it, barking. The pelican startled and took flight.

"That's some beast you have there," Jack said.

Oliver saw a twinkle in his father's eye. "What are you smiling about?"

"Mayhem here was due to be transferred, and I may have pulled some strings. Lately, Host like Mayhem have been disappearing when they transfer. You saved us from losing him, and he's a pretty important little guy. Which technically makes *you* a pretty important little guy as well."

Oliver stopped walking. The idea that his father had somehow been behind all the drama of the last week was weirdly unsettling. His father was not, to Oliver's knowledge, in any way a violent man. And yet, violence had been the hallmark of life with Mayhem.

"You...you killed that cop? Detective Jenkins?"

Jack laughed. "No, no! Nothing like that. I just helped nudge you into being in the right place at the right time. And look! It worked! If it wasn't for you, Mayhem... well... I think that's a topic we'll be covering shortly. The visual aide will help you digest it."

"You say you nudged me? How did you nudge me, exactly?"

His father picked up the pace, and Oliver hurried to keep up.

Jack frowned, as if contemplating how to explain things in terms Oliver could understand. "On secular earth, you have free will, right?"

"I used to."

Jack nodded. "Good point. But you know that term 'Fishers of men'?"

"Sure. From the Bible. I think it was what Jesus said to one of the disciples. There was a Sunday School song."

"Well, here, it's sort of how we use the Host. We can't make decisions for you, on secular earth. But we can manipulate things such that options are presented to you that might alter your course. Keeping with the fishing analogy, it's up to you to take the bait."

"So that's what you do here? You manipulate things on secular earth?"

Jack shook his head. "No, not usually. But I was lucky in the sense that I have the ear of another engineer. A really bright guy. He's on the secular earth planning committee. I'd caught wind that you might be in a bit of trouble, and we came up with a series of events, acted out by the Host, and with the blessing, of course, of some of the higher-ups, in which you would be allowed to survive."

Oliver startled. "Allowed to survive!?"

"It was a pretty near thing. They had to get rid of that thesis of yours somehow. I am sorry about that, by the way. It was brilliant. I was really proud."

Oliver felt his face flush again. "Then why did they have to get rid of it?"

"Well, frankly, it was going to kick off a nuclear apocalypse."

Oliver stopped. All the oxygen seemed to have been sucked out of the atmosphere. He struggled to breathe, and his throat made an odd *gurk* sound.

With Jack patting him on the back in encouragement, he got a few deep breaths, but only for a second before he went the other way and completely hyperventilated.

Finally, he managed to calm himself with hope. Specifically, he hoped he simply hadn't heard correctly. "I'm sorry, Dad. I thought you just said nuclear apocalypse."

"Yeah... I probably shouldn't have been so cavalier about breaking it to you, but there it is. Since we serve the Great Balance, and all that, we had to intervene."

"How—how was my thesis going to start a nuclear war?"

Jack scratched thoughtfully at his chin. "You may have failed to consider the ramifications of a universal coding software as it would pertain to national defense codes. Specifically, launch codes."

Oliver pictured all the 1950s-era films he's ever seen of nuclear explosions, playing out simultaneously. Los Alamos. Bikini Atoll. Tsar Bomba.

"Oh God!"

"Yeah," his father said. "Not your fault. You had the best intentions."

"I was imagining video games."

"I know. Everyone felt pretty bad for you. In the original plan, you would...um...succumb in the library fire. Fortunately, my friend Peter—he's the guy I mentioned who sits on the planning committee—he gave me the details, and we were able to convince the Host to intervene on your behalf.

"We had to write an appeal to one of the archangels. It was quite a thing, but we managed to pull it off.

"Pull it off—?"

"We knew we really needed to do something special for you, or else a year later you'd be back with the same computer code. Mayhem was going to be transferred, and I had this idea that maybe he could go to you. So, the Host intervened and you got out of the library alive."

"But Teddy and Emma—they weren't in the library."

"No, you're right. They weren't," Jack said, waiting.

"The police officer?"

"Heather Long," Jack said. "Serenity."

Oliver reeled at the news. "Does she know? Does she know she's a human host?"

"Probably. Assuming she recognizes compulsions for what they are, she would have known, though it's anyone's guess to what extent she understands her...uh...condition."

"I was going to ask her on a date."

Oliver felt especially stupid for not asking her, since they now had a shared experience that would have made for a great icebreaker. Of course, he'd been a bit busy since they'd parted ways.

Jack bent to pet Mayhem again. The dog-like entity leaned into the man's stroking hand and wagged its tail. Mayhem, apparently, liked having his head scratched.

The bait and tackle store at the base of the pier was open, but nobody worked the counter. They passed through, sauntered down the approach toward Gulf Boulevard. A sign Oliver remembered from his youth hung over the stanchions. It read, "If there's no fishing in heaven, I'm not going."

"Coffee?" Jack asked. "It's really good here."

"Do we have time?"

"Of course. You have to understand, things aren't going to happen instantly. If I were you, I would consider this experience as a brief respite. Make the most of it."

"Sure," Oliver said.

"Sure what?"

"Sure, coffee."

"Oh. Good. This way, then!"

Jack jogged across the street, and Oliver stooped to pick up Mayhem, awkwardly cradling the dog-like entity and the empty rum bottle in his arms before following.

When Oliver caught up, Jack hiked an eyebrow. "You know you don't have to carry him. He's nonverbal, but he's infinitely more intelligent than either of us."

"I get that, but I was thinking of Arthur Dent," Oliver said, referring to his childhood poodle who had been squashed by a passing station wagon when he wandered into traffic. Oliver had always felt guilty about Arthur Dent. He should have put the time into training some street smarts into the dog. Arthur Dent, in his opinion, hadn't been given a fair shake at life.

Setting Mayhem on the sidewalk, he looked around, trying to memorize every detail of his environment. Things were remarkable in their familiarity. Cars whizzed past. Toyotas, Fords, Chevrolets—recognizable, yet subtly different than the models he knew back in the secular dimension. None of them would seem out of place, however, parked up on a campus street.

"There are Toyotas in heaven," he said, in wonder. "I can't believe it!"

"What's missing?" his father asked.

Oliver looked closer. "Exhaust? Everything's electric?"

"Electric, Hydrogen or nuclear. There's still internal combustion, but those are mostly owned by collectors these days. Like I said, the tech here is way ahead."

Jack paused on the sidewalk across from the pier. "Are you hungry?"

Oliver was, but he also felt pressed for time. "I'm worried about my friends, Dad."

"I know, and I'm going to help you find them, but this is going to take a bit of time. There are things you need to see. Things I need to show you. For instance, how do you plan on sending yourself into the ether? And how do you intend to locate them once you're there?"

Oliver hung his head, feeling a bit stupid. He'd assumed that if his father could retrieve him out of the multiverse, he must also be able to send him back out into it. "I guess I don't know."

"Right—and we have the foundations of a plan. But it's going to take some effort. So why don't we grab something to go? It'll make you feel better. Trust me. Consider this the equivalent of that time when Luke Skywalker had to train in the swamp with Yoda in order to learn the force."

"Will there be physical activity? Because I didn't bring any gym clothes."

"No. That was just an analogy. You'll mostly just have to learn how things work."

"Lecture format?"

"More like an informal seminar. You'll be fine."

"Well, OK then."

Jack nodded.

Oliver thought about Teddy, Emma and Bert. He realized that if he was ever going to see them again, his father was his only hope of doing so. He trusted Jack. Jack was the most trustworthy person he had ever known. Once again, it was probably best to resist nothing.

Opening the door to a coffee shop called Gypsy Souls, Jack motioned Oliver inside.

The aroma in the cool, dark café was overwhelmingly pleasant. The sweet scent of a bakery perfectly complemented the perfume of strong, percolating coffee.

A young woman in a black T-shirt with a name tag that read "Becky" worked the counter. Jack ordered coffee and muffins, while Oliver puzzled over band posters that had been tacked to the bulletin board. *The Grantrepreneurs*, featured prominently, as did *Cary and The Girls from Alcyone*. He'd never heard of either.

When his father joined him, he asked, "So are all these people dead?"

"Sort of," Jack said. "We've all died on the secular world, if that's what you mean."

Becky, the woman working the counter, fussed over a milk-frother. She did not appear to be particularly concerned with the concept that she was dead. "Do they know?"

"That they're dead?"

"Yeah."

"Of course."

"So, in an infinite afterlife, this woman has chosen to work at a coffee shop?"

"Uh huh."

"Why?"

"Because she wants to make money and to have a sense of purpose, and it's easy. She was a gastroenterologist in Pittsburgh. Imagine how relaxing it would be to go from that, to making cappuccinos. We can assume she also gets an employee discount on the muffins and scones."

Becky called out, "All set, Jack."

Jack thanked her before leading Oliver out to the sidewalk.

"I feel a little awkward, walking around with this empty rum bottle," Oliver said.

"Nobody will give it a passing thought," Jack said. "Hold onto it. We might be able to use it for something."

Oliver nodded, and tried, with some difficulty, to stuff the bottle into the waistband of his jeans.

As he did this, he looked out the window toward the sidewalk where a group of young people passed by, talking and laughing.

An odd thought occurred. "Do people get old here?"

"I don't think so," Jack said. "You never see anyone who looks older than forty. I think it has something to do with biology—cellular apoptosis, or cell death, if you will. But it's outside my wheelhouse. People just seem to stay young."

Oliver marveled at this new piece of information. An eternity without aging, in a world without time. He thought of Emma and Teddy, and Bert and Carmella, and he wished they could see it. The idea that it was all real—that there was this wonderful place where you physically materialize after you die, was unspeakably comforting, but almost horribly so. He realized that he was going to have to spend the rest of his existence in a state of untestable faith. The afterlife was real. He'd been there. He'd bought coffee and muffins!

"You know, Dad, I'm concerned this experience is going to screw me up in some profound way."

"You'll be fine," his father said, bluntly. "But it would definitely be best if you didn't tell too many people about all this. If you have to talk about it, try to be vague."

Unable to imagine that he would be "fine," the pragmatic part of Oliver's mind inherently understood he was just going to have to get on with it, regardless of how it affected him.

Jack set the pace, and Oliver hustled, once again, to keep up. His father's tendency toward long strides was an obvious carryover from the man's earthly existence.

"Where are we going?"

Jack pointed at the towering yellow Angler's Cove condominium complex across the street.

"Do you live there?"

"For now, it's where I work."

"I thought you were an engineer."

Jack smiled. "You'll see."

Oliver bent down to pick up the dog again, and Jack stopped him.

"I know I don't have to remind you, but just in case, like I said earlier—

that isn't a dog. It's a hyper-intelligent sentient being that can predict the future. It's not going to run in front of a car."

"It licked my face," Oliver said.

"Well, I suppose it's *kind* of a dog."

"Why can't it talk?"

"I don't know. Ask it."

"Hey, Mayhem, why can't you talk?"

Mayhem sat down on the sidewalk and used his hind foot to scratch himself behind the ear.

Jack laughed.

Just as Oliver began to adjust to the striking familiarity of everything in the afterlife, an animal resembling a wagon wheel made of human skin turned the corner and rolled up next to them on the sidewalk.

He jumped back and gasped.

The inner circumference of the wheel was lined with some kind of gills, puffing open and closed. A slit in the skin opened, revealing a dazzling blue eyeball. A second slit opened, revealing gleaming white teeth.

"Pardon me," the wheel said in a deep voice as it wove a path around Oliver and his father and continued down the sidewalk.

It was the single weirdest thing Oliver had ever experienced.

Jack intuitively patted his son on the back, preventing the onset of another anxiety attack. "Orphanim," Jack explained, "A subtype of biblical angel. You get used to them."

"You—you get used to them?"

"Sure. They're harmless. A little weird at first, mind you."

Oliver had a million questions. He knew almost nothing about biblical angels, other than the fact that they were obviously pure nightmare fuel.

"How do they eat?" he asked, then after a moment's consideration, "*What* do they eat?"

"You know, I'm not sure," Jack said. "They kind of keep to themselves. Between you and me, and not to be rude, they sort of freak me out."

"No kidding..."

Jack led the way to a crosswalk, and they jogged through traffic once again. Mayhem stayed at heel.

At the door, Jack handed Oliver the coffee tray while he fished in his pocket for a key.

Oliver freed his cup from the tray, and took a tentative sip. It was like velvet. The flavor was strong but complex and delicate, with distinct floral and chocolate notes. The caffeine gave him an instant rush of euphoria and energy. "Oh my gosh—that's insane!"

"Right?" his father smiled, before leading the way up a flight of stairs to the second floor, and then along an outdoor walkway to apartment 203.

Upon entering, Oliver was immediately overwhelmed with nostalgia. The door opened to a hallway that had been decorated with beach-themed paintings. To the right was an open kitchen and living room. A large plastic marlin hung on the wall over the couch.

"We've been here before," he said.

"We were here for your Grade Eleven spring break. In fact, I should give you the scoop. This building is what we call 'a vestigial place.' It basically means it's the same in the secular world as it is throughout the multiverse. About half of all the structures on the secular plane are also present here, but this particular building is considered 'vestigial' because it's present on all known planes of the multiverse. I guess you'd consider it..."

"A node," Oliver finished Jack's sentence.

"Yeah. Exactly."

Taking a seat at the kitchen table, Jack continued. "Coincidentally, that family trip was the best vacation of my life. It's what convinced me to set up shop in Florida. It just so happens that the building is vestigial, so I can work out of it. I requested this apartment."

"I still don't really understand what you do."

"Remember when I said I would look out for you?"

"Sure."

"That's a part of it. I'm still fairly low on the totem pole. I work on the technology R and D side of things, but it means I have access to what's happening on secular earth."

Standing, Jack moved to the kitchen where he rummaged through a drawer.

"As luck would have it, that visual aide I talked about is actually one of the projects I've been working on. Here, let's have a look."

He produced a white rectangular device, and brought it back to the table, where he set it gently down. He thumbed a switch, and a holographic image appeared and hovered in the air under the chandelier.

The floating, semitransparent hologram was cuboidal in shape. Lines formed a complex, multidimensional grid through the cube, and various data points in the grid were marked with colored numbers.

Puzzled, Oliver stepped around the hologram, examining its design.

"Take a guess," Jack said.

He examined one of the numbers.

717-21b

He thought of Mayhem's tag. "Are these the Host?"

"Very good!" Jack's voice was bright with delight. "Yes! Some of them are Host. Each data point represents a celestial entity that we track as they navigate the near-field multiverse. The Host itself—or themselves… I still get tripped up on the pronouns—they don't tend to travel between planes. But other celestial spirits and entities do it all the time. And we try to keep track of them."

Oliver set the rum bottle on the kitchen countertop and approached the hologram. "What are the axes?"

"The x and y axes are geographical location. We have the center point on ourselves right now. We can set that however we want, sort of like a GPS display. The range is set for five kilometers, see?"

He pointed to a key at the edge of the display.

"Z axis is the multiverse. Up is divine, and down is anti-divine."

Oliver gulped. Had they really been able to penetrate other dimensions to this extent, where they could create a real-time map?

"This is incredible!"

Jack reached into the hologram and made a motion, sliding his index finger and thumb apart. The display zoomed, elongating the inner cubes and changing them into rectangular prisms. The layers of the multiverse widened and then disappeared until the display showed only a single box. Red lettering designated the box "*472-19a.*"

"That's Mayhem," Oliver said.

Jack crossed the room to the sofa and called the dog. "Here, Mayhem! Come over to me."

The sentient, future-predicting dog-like celestial being trotted over to the sofa, and Oliver watched the screen and saw the designated number slide along the x and y axes.

The display then changed, showing a complex rectangular prism that Oliver recognized as a Schlegel diagram, a five-dimensional graph.

"Whoa," he said. "The amount of computational power you would need to do this is staggering."

Oliver walked around the diagram, seeing it from another angle. He noted that Mayhem's position appeared to change as he rounded the complex geometric display, even though the dog was staying in place. "What does the extra facet represent here?" he asked, pointing.

"Time," Jack said. "And that one, as you can guess, is pretty complicated."

"They travel through time?"

Before his father could explain, a realization struck home. "My friends! We could find them on this map!"

Jack grinned. "I always said you were a smart kid."

"Can we use this to make sure they haven't been turned into quivering mounds of gelatinous goo?"

"Huh?"

"Apparently it's a thing."

"Oh."

Jack pulled up a chair, and sat down in front of the hologram. Playing with the controls he swept through the strange map like it was second nature, taking the image down to level negative twenty-seven.

Pausing, he rubbed his chin. "I don't know about 'gelatinous goo,' but there is something weird happening. I noticed it before I walked down to the pier.

"Bert and Teddy were separated from Robert Quinn somewhere in the ether. They sort of fell off the map, for lack of a better term. Since we intercepted you, I'm wondering if someone, or I suppose some*thing*, did the same to them. So now they're out in the anti-divine multiverse, presumably in the ether between structured layers, and they're separated from Bob. Without anyone able to cast a glamour that can take them home, they're kind of in a pickle."

"Who would intercept them?" Oliver asked. "Who else would have the technology?"

Jack, who was pre-occupied, operating the map, pointed absently at Oliver and raised his eyebrows. "That's where this all gets a little more complicated."

Oliver was wondering how much more complicated things could possibly be, when a knock at the door made him jump.

"There he is!" Jack quick-stepped to the entryway, opened the door, and a slim man with a bald head and dark skin, wearing a smart, navy blue suit and yellow tie strode into the apartment.

He extended his hand to Oliver and they shook.

"Oliver. I'm Peter Lalonde. I'm a friend of your father's."

Peter then turned to Mayhem. "Hello, Mayhem."

Mayhem, busy licking his tail, looked up momentarily.

Peter faced Oliver again. "That was very brave of you, choosing the vermillion phone. Congratulations, son."

"Yeah, I'm still having a little trouble with the whole red-phone thing—"

"Vermillion, son. Vermillion."

Jack interrupted. "Olly, Peter is an engineer-physicist who works with me at the Department of Interdimensional Transportation."

"For heaven's sake! The what now?"

"The D.I.T.," Peter said. "We track the movement of celestial beings through the near-field multiverse. Here, look."

Peter pointed at the hologram to the space where Jack had zoomed in on anti-divine level twenty-seven.

"Your friends entered reality here."

Peter zoomed into a spot on the line between levels -26 and -27. In faint, flashing orange font, Oliver could make out two alpha-numeric designations. A third, pink designation flashed in the same location, but it was only marked as "xxx." A white question mark hovered underneath the line, in the box labeled "Level-27."

"What's that?" Oliver asked, pointing at the row of pink Xs.

"Death," Peter said. "You know him as Bert."

"And the question mark?"

"We think it's the caster."

"Bob?"

"Mr. Quinn, yes. He's the one all the way on level negative twenty-seven."

"Why is he a question mark on this map?"

"Truth be told, we aren't exactly sure how to classify him. He isn't human, at least, not entirely human. He must be some kind of celestial being/human hybrid, though I'm pretty sure that would have been a surprise to his father."

"So how are you tracking him?"

"Temporal radiation," Peter said. "All celestial entities emit trace temporal radiation—tau leptons, to be specific. Leptons decay backward and forward in time. That temporal radiation ripples through the multiverse. In this universe we use satellite imaging to detect those traces. By determining the wavelength of radiation and the amplitude, we can determine the depth and direction of a celestial being in the multiverse."

"Unreal!"

Peter shrugged. "We've had a long time to develop the technology."

"OK. Check out the location of your friends," Jack said. "Notice how, other than Bob, they're not in the box? They're tracking along the line. See?"

"Sure," Oliver said.

"We call those lines *the ether*. Essentially the lines represent the spaces in between space, the fabric that separates planes of the multiverse. And even though the ether is represented this way, it actually makes up the bulk of material in the multiverse. We estimate 99% or more. We just can't see it. It has no obvious practical function. So, to us, it's sort of a black box."

"And that's where my friends are?"

"We believe so. It's where their Host are, at any rate. We think their transport was deliberately intercepted, the same way we intercepted you. The caster... um... Bob... probably doesn't have any real idea regarding what he's doing. He almost certainly has no idea of the power he's meddling with. He can conjure a glamour that takes him to a very specific level of the underworld, but all this stuff..." Peter gestured to the holographic display... "he wouldn't know anything about it. I suspect he's probably willfully ignorant."

Oliver nodded. He hadn't known Bob for long, but Peter had the man pegged.

Peter continued. "You understand about the Host, and how they're able to intuit the future and act to change it, yes?"

"I've been reading up."

"Well, there are...other beings with that particular talent."

Other beings? Oliver thought of Amon. He thought of the man who had pointed the pistol at him beside the downed George Orwell statue. "You're talking about Legion."

Jack and Peter exchanged glances. "Yes. Legion," Jack said. "You *have* been reading up."

"We think Legion knew exactly where your friends were headed," Peter said. "We think they somehow nudged them off course—quite possibly with similar technology that we used to bring you here, when we found you transitioning between material layers of the multiverse in your immaterial state."

Oliver flashed back to his existence as a cloud of subatomic particles. Remembering the maddening itch, he scratched at his nose. "Why?"

"Our guess? They want to trap the Host. Host are finite in number. In theory, by removing enough of them from secular earth, they could offset the balance that allows the human race to thrive.

"They attack the Host when they're most vulnerable, during transference, or, obviously in this case, by using a glamour and capturing them when they dematerialize. They must have caught wind of your plan."

Oliver tried to imagine how Legion could possibly know they were planning to go to the underworld, when he remembered Cindy. Hadn't Bert told them she was hosting a demon?

He brought his palm to his forehead. "Oh God."

"Your father and I believe that they are using the ether—the layers between the layers of the multiverse—as some kind of prison. This, in my opinion," he waved toward the map, "confirms our suspicions."

Peter manipulated the display until it showed a map of the earth. He zoomed in over Europe, and then to an island off the Italian coast. He manipulated the image down through the anti-divine tiers of the multiverse until he found the Host ID 8115-14X situated on the line between level negative twenty-six and negative twenty-seven.

"We happened to catch this guy entering the ether last year. He's a roamer—a type of celestial being that floats constantly through the multiverse. That was the first time we ever witnessed anything materialize in the ether. We've never seen him exit."

"And now your friends are stuck on the same level," Jack said. "It can't be a coincidence."

"But I can...um...unstick them, right?"

"We're dealing with a lot of theoreticals, but we believe it's possible. We'll get to that."

Oliver had a million questions, not the least of which was how he was supposed to travel the multiverse without Bob's help. He was going to ask, but Peter held up his hand.

"There's another problem—a bigger one. Legion has been getting quite aggressive on the secular world. There's a pattern to it. I need to show you."

He took control of the hologram again, this time focusing on the Redington shores region on the secular plane. As he zoomed in, a map of the area once again appeared on the x-y plane. As he enhanced the image a grey roadway resolved, until dozens of black question marks and exclamation marks appeared. They seemed to be slowly filing along Gulf Boulevard, gradually moving northward past the Angler's Cove condominium complex.

"What am I looking at?" Oliver asked.

"Legion," Peter said. "In the secular plane—all organized together, presumably infiltrating some kind of march or protest."

"Which can't be good," Jack said. "We saw the same thing at the riot in Halifax. And then again with the communist accountants."

"These protests provide the perfect cover," Peter said. "When violence breaks out, nobody questions it. Legion can infiltrate, create havoc if they're lucky, send a Host being to the ether, and leave. Half the time the people they possess won't even know what happened. They'll chalk their actions up to mob mentality."

Peter picked up a remote control and turned on a dusty, flat-screen television, the type that would not have been out of place on the discount shelf of any secular Best Buy. The TV sat on a cheap-looking stand in the corner of the living room. The picture came to life, showing a street reporter gesticulating wildly, speaking animatedly into a microphone bearing a Bay News 9 flag. Protestors marched past, but the volume was muted and Oliver couldn't tell what, exactly, they were protesting. A crowd paraded up Gulf Boulevard, carrying signs that read "No Censorship!" and "End Government Control!" and "Newman's Own Salad Dressing Freedom Rally!"

A competing protest marched in the other direction across the street. These protestors held signs that read "More Mandates!" and "Independence = Dog-whistle!" and "The Shake Shack Protest for Public Sector Dominance."

Members of the competing groups eyed one another angrily. Chaos threatened to erupt.

"More corporate-sponsored protests," Oliver said glumly. "Terrific. Can I assume that this is not happening in heaven, and that we are somehow watching the news on secular earth?"

Peter nodded. "Indeed."

Before the library fire in Halifax, he had never really given much thought to the dangers of social media. He had worried a little, of course, as most scientists did, that social media could be perceived as a threat to scientific progress. After all, if one's predictions were nullified by an experiment, one could simply turn to social media to have their beliefs enforced by like-minded individuals. But that was a more nebulous concern. What was now becoming clear, however, was a more immediate social problem. The constant positive reinforcement of one's views from one's social-media echo chamber was creating a new form of malignant narcissism based entirely on ideological entrenchment. It shouldn't have been a surprise that corporate America would glom onto the phenomenon in an effort to tie their brand to entrenched politics. After all, it guaranteed a loyal customer base. But the result of their interference, from what Oliver could tell, was a turbocharging of the anger and resentment between the hyperpolarized extremes of the spectrum.

They watched the protest unfold. When the first punch was thrown, Peter shook his head and turned off the screen.

"The human race is doomed by the human condition," Oliver said to himself.

"That isn't entirely true," Peter said.

"We thought Legion was drawn to these things because they're energized by anger, or somehow feed off it. And while that might have made sense in the past, these episodes are happening too frequently. There's too much infiltration. And there's too strong a geographic pattern. The common denominator is *you*..."

"Me?!"

"Of course. Your father and I suspect there's some kind of connection between Legion, your friends and yourself, or, if not you, then your Host entities.

"I mean, this is literally just across the street from us, albeit on another plane of existence. There are more Gulf Boulevard protests scheduled over the next three days. Then when you consider the senior's trailer park riot, and the Halifax riot before that. It's like Legion is weaponizing social unrest, and using it against you.

"If you were to go back to the secular world, right now, to Mr. Quinn's house, where you're supposed to be on secular earth, you would be in imminent danger. That house is situated smack-dab in the middle of these protest routes."

"I guess it makes sense," Oliver said. "Even taking into consideration the current shift toward civil discord, there have kind of been a lot of recent... uh... *personal* incidents."

Peter nodded. "You're lucky in a way. Legion can't come into the divine multiverse. But just so we're clear, you have to assume they're looking for you."

Oliver felt, not for the first time, that he'd haplessly bumbled his way into something much bigger and much more dangerous than he was capable of comprehending.

"You're saying the forces of hell are, what, hunting me?"

"Quite possibly," his father said. "But we've got more questions than answers at this point. Can you think of anything you might have done to get their attention?"

Oliver sat down hard.

"There might be something, but I'm not sure. Teddy is dead set on killing this Amon guy. It's how we met. They thought Amon had possessed me, so they kidnapped me and took me to see Bert. Teddy was actually planning to kill me with a baseball bat, but we got it all straightened out."

Peter and Jack shared an ominous look that Oliver didn't care for in the least.

"I told you," Peter said.

Jack nodded, frowning.

"What?" Oliver sputtered. "What did I say?"

"Amon is a big problem," Jack said. "He's powerful. He's incredibly destructive, and he's dead set on the extinction of the human race. Amon is the one we think is behind the disappearing Host."

"He's also basically indestructible," Peter added. "At least when it comes to conventional, secular technology. Teddy probably isn't aware of that. But a baseball bat is going to come up a little short."

Jack snapped his fingers. "Actually, this kind of makes sense. What if Amon knew about Oliver's thesis? What if he saw it as an opportunity? The first big Legion infiltration was Halifax, right? Would it not stand to reason that he was after the thesis—the code that could trigger Armageddon? If Teddy was tracking Amon, maybe Teddy and Emma are coincidental variables. Maybe it's just about Oliver."

Sensing another anxiety attack, Oliver stood and paced, trying to remember to breathe.

Something nagged at him. "No wait! If Amon is behind the disappearance of the Host, and the Host disappearing is why Teddy has such a hate-on for the guy, maybe Amon was only after my friends all along. After all—it seems like he's probably now trapped them in the underworld, and yet I'm here with you guys."

"Maybe," Peter said, his face grim, "But it doesn't feel right. Secular intervention is very resource-intensive. I can't imagine a demon as powerful as Amon would bother hunting down Host beings like Goodness or Forbearance. They're just pawns in a much bigger game. He would more likely only take Host targets of convenience. But to get his hands on a doomsday code? I think we have to assume he knows about the thesis."

"Then that means he knew about me before—before Mayhem. Before Teddy and Emma! Before I had anything to do with this!" Oliver felt his pulse quicken. He couldn't quite move enough air. Colorful flashing sparkles crowded his vision.

The idea that he'd been personally targeted for demonic interference in his previous life, during what now seemed like a distant period of extreme innocence and naïveté, gave him a terrible sense of existential vertigo.

"Just breathe, buddy. This is all speculation," Jack said.

Oliver tried to get a deep breath.

"It makes sense, though." Peter put a hand on his shoulder, and looked him in the eye. "Amon is after you."

Oliver dropped to his knees and made inadvertent history, suffering the first full-blown panic attack ever experienced on the nineteenth divine tier of the multiverse.

Eleven

"Just drink it, buddy," Jack coaxed.

Oliver took a tentative sip of water. He tried to swallow, but half of it went down his windpipe. He choked, and Jack and Peter slapped him on the back until he got his breathing under control.

"OK," Oliver said. "I think I'm OK."

He wasn't OK. But he felt foolish and wimpy, still gripped by primal fear. *An infernal demon was hunting him.* It was the stuff of horror films—the cheesy ones that went straight to Netflix.

He grabbed the edge of the table, convinced that if he didn't ground himself his tenuous grip on reality would simply let go, and he would become, for lack of a better term, a nut-case. At the same time, his throat felt as narrow as the barrel of a pen. His diaphragm still hadn't fully unlocked. "This—this is crazy," he managed to squeak. "I'm nobody!"

Jack continued patting him on the back, gentler now. His father knew how these episodes went. Even after almost a decade, he could coach Oliver through them.

Oliver nodded his thanks.

After a minute, the constriction around his airway loosened.

"You OK for real?" Jack asked.

"Yeah. Yeah. I'm good."

Peter, who seemed not at all able to sense that Oliver was lying through his teeth, cleared his throat. "Good. Let's get back to business. Amon wants that code. We know that every physical copy was destroyed. But, of course, there's one copy that can't be."

Oliver hiked an eyebrow, and Peter reached out with his index finger and tapped him on the forehead.

"But he can manipulate the multiverse!" Oliver exclaimed. "Surely he can write a simple computer code!"

"It doesn't work like that," Jack said. "Amon is generally relegated to the underworld. The underworld is ruled by chaos. In fact, his name is synonymous with it.

"His ability to travel through dimensions relies on a mystical approach to science. He can intuitively intervene in the multiverse. He can intuitively contribute to chaos on the secular plane. But it's unlikely that someone who thrives on chaos would intuitively be able to write a complex computer code, and more unlikely still that he could deliver such a code to the secular earth and apply it. He would still need someone who understands programming to write it. He needs someone to do his bidding."

"Anyone could write it," Oliver said. "It wasn't rocket science!"

"That isn't true," Jack said. "If anyone could write it, they would have. *You* wrote it. And that makes you a person of interest to him. It certainly made you a person of interest to *us*."

"Why didn't they just...you know...possess me and make me hand it over?"

"In all likelihood they tried. Possession by Legion is generally temporary and can be a very subtle experience. It isn't like in the movies. Your head doesn't spin around. You don't tell a priest how his mother passes time in the underworld. Can you think of a moment of weakness you might have experienced, where you thought about doing something entirely out of character?"

It came to him in an instant. About a month and a half before the Halifax riot, there had been a coronavirus exposure in the computer science building on campus. Oliver had to isolate in his apartment for five days. Though he hadn't been particularly concerned about getting sick, he'd been unable to stop himself from obsessing over the idea of sending a nearly complete copy of the code to his supervisor, Gerald. He was generally secretive about his thesis, yet for three days he wrestled with every fiber of his being against what he could now only think of as a *compulsion* to pass his work on. For those three days, he had been convinced that he would end up in a vegetative state, and that the work would be lost.

Had he sent his nearly complete thesis along, he was now certain that Gerald would have disseminated it. His supervisor might have even taken credit for it in an attempt to advance his own career. Oliver understood this with the kind of impersonal detachment that could only be experienced by a man who had very nearly accidentally triggered a nuclear apocalypse.

He turned and walked across the room to the sliding patio door. Opening it, he stepped onto the balcony and felt the gentle breeze on his face once more.

"What's wrong?" Jack asked.

"I just need a little air." The existential vertigo, that sense of a major uprooting of everything he'd ever known, came in waves, and Oliver felt as though he were on a rudderless boat, being wrenched this way and that by titanic, cosmic tides.

"Just keep breathing," Jack said, joining his son at the railing, overlooking the gulf. "Don't fight it. Just accept things. We're going to sort it out."

"I don't know if I can sort it out," Oliver said, his eyes brimming with tears. "This is a real mess. I don't know what I'm doing! I can't fight Amon! I can barely talk to girls! I'm not Teddy, or Emma, Dad."

"No," Jack agreed. "You aren't Teddy or Emma. You're Oliver Bell. You're the unsuspecting genius who accidentally wrote the doomsday code. You're the first living human being to visit the nineteenth tier of the divine multiverse. You're the human host of celestial Mayhem!"

"You mean, you think I *can* take on Amon?"

"Oh. No," Jack said. "No, you definitely can't. Sorry for the confusion. What I meant is that you should try talking to girls more. Assuming you survive this ordeal, of course."

Oliver, who had allowed his dad's pep talk to inflate his self-esteem, imagined the farting sound a balloon makes when you let go of the end and let it fly around a room.

Peter joined them on the balcony. "If it makes you feel any better, Oliver, it's extremely unlikely that you would have to physically confront Amon, himself. He generally doesn't manifest on the secular plane.

"In order to do so, he would have to create a very particular set of circumstances to escape the underworld. Even then, he can only do that by building a wormhole, where an underworld tier of the multiverse is manifest on secular earth. Along with a perfect storm of pestilence and civil unrest, there's a human sacrifice involved, and it has to be someone possessed by a very particular subtype of demon from the underworld. It would take an enormous amount of manipulation and energy. To the best of our knowledge, there are only a few prior incidents over the last millennia."

"Pestilence, you say?" Oliver asked.

"Yes," Peter continued, apparently not noticing the growing concern on Oliver and Jack's faces. "Pestilence is generally a harbinger of his arrival. The Japanese Smallpox Epidemic in 735AD, the second Black Death in 1346, the Cocolitzli epidemic in 1576. Historical records suggest that Amon was able to manifest briefly on earth during those times. We believe his attempts to establish a permanent presence or dominance were previously thwarted by the Host, but the cost in human lives is said to be tremendous. It's quite lucky, in a way, that our current timeline is..." Peter stopped when he apparently noticed the look on Oliver and Jack's faces.

"What? What did I say?"

"What about the COVID pandemic?" Oliver asked.

Peter seemed to consider this and frowned. "I suppose. One could argue that the conditions are *suggestive* of another upcoming attempt. I guess, when you think about it, between widespread, social-media-fueled, corporate-sponsored outrage and the coronavirus..."

He trailed off, and his brow furrowed deeper.

Understanding seemed to blossom.

"Oh dear."

"Oh dear?"

"Yes," Peter said. "I suppose it's... concerning."

"So, what happens if he decides to visit the secular earth?"

"From my understanding, he essentially creates a portal to the underworld through which he can directly communicate with Legion. He becomes something analogous to a military general—think Napoleon at Waterloo. Legion will possess people in droves, and these people will do his secular bidding for him. You know how it goes from there. Conquest. Famine. Pestilence. Death."

Jack chimed in, "Human sacrifice! Dogs and cats living together! Mass Hysteria!"

Oliver frowned. "The Host can stop it from happening somehow?"

"If history is going to repeat itself," Peter said. "To be honest, Oliver, we're sort of at the limits of my research on the subject. I don't really know how to stop it. Mayhem, here, probably has some idea."

They all turned to Mayhem, who was busy chewing on the back of his hind leg.

Oliver tried to imagine what an open portal to hell might look like. He'd seen a movie once where a crew of astronauts accidentally opened a portal to hell on a spaceship. It was terrifying.

"Would it be like in that Sam Neill movie?" he asked, hoping very much that it would not.

"*Jurassic Park*?" Peter cocked an eyebrow. "No, it would be nothing like that. Dinosaurs have nothing to do with this."

"What? No. You know... the one with the spaceship, and the portal to hell?"

"Are you thinking of *Alien*?"

"No."

"I think he's talking about *Armageddon*, starring Bruce Willis," Jack said.

"*Armageddon*!? No... it was Sam Neill. They were in space."

"Oh," Peter said, "*Interstellar*. No, it wouldn't be like that either."

"Never mind."

Oliver shook off the memory of the movie, but realized there was something bothering him about Peter's explanation of Amon.

"You're saying Amon can create a portal through the multiverse, but he can't possess people—or like, Legion does it for him? I don't get it. If he's so powerful, why doesn't he just take me over and make me give him what he wants?" Oliver asked.

"A few reasons. First of all, Amon isn't like the rest of Legion. He's an eternal being who's been cast down. He isn't Lucifer, but he was, I suppose, a sympathizer. He also wasn't Host. He was more like upper management for the Host, and so he's assumed a similar role in the underworld. But just like a bird fancier can't fly, Amon can't necessarily do the same thing his charge does. So normally, when there's dirty work he wants done on secular earth, he dispatches Legion to do his bidding. The Host, on the other hand, are a little more autonomous. They don't necessarily take orders from higher up, where they work toward a common purpose. Because Legion is inherently chaotic, they need structure to accomplish any given directive, and Amon provides that structure."

"So why did Teddy and Emma think he possessed me?"

"Excellent question. In all likelihood, they simply don't know how Amon functions. We have the benefit of celestial knowledge here. They're working from what they've gleaned from thousand-year-old obscure demonology guides, many of which were written by medieval monks after the consumption of more than a few alcoholic beverages. But while Teddy might think he's doing one thing, his Host might be working through him to accomplish something else entirely, and his Host almost certainly knows the fundamental nature of Amon. The fact that Teddy is attuned to Amon's work speaks volumes. His Host is obviously on some kind of mission.

"Host pairs like Teddy and Goodness 417-5D work entirely by symbiotic intuition. They act on the human's instinct, which is affected by the celestial being's motivation. While Teddy might not appreciate the mechanics of the multiverse, he's able to thrive because he lives almost entirely in commitment to the Great Balance—that means he's in the hands of his Host. He might have thought he was striking a blow against Amon by kidnapping you, but 417-5D was likely acting through him to protect you from falling into the wrong hands. Notice—you're still alive. The world hasn't ended. All is as it should be, in that sense. Whether rescuing you was the means or the ends, only the Host can know."

Oliver thought about what this meant. Assuming he was able to reunite with his friends, he would now be in the unique position of possessing knowledge about Amon that far exceeded theirs. That meant he might actually be useful for the first time in their relationship. The idea had some appeal.

He had another lingering question. "How did you get me here?"

"We used Mayhem," Jack said. "There's been a good deal of attention on you, including the attention of some of the more...er...*predictive* celestial beings. By pairing you with Mayhem, it made it simpler for us regular folk to track you."

Predictive celestial beings. Oliver pictured the human-skin-wheel thing he'd seen outside the coffee shop and felt the vertigo resurge. He fought it and the sensation worsened. Then he remembered his father instructing him to accept it, so he tried that. It didn't go away, exactly, but it became livable.

"An interception device was purpose-built in the Department of Ethereal Analytics," Peter continued. "Don't ask us how it works, because it's the type of thing that takes a real Einstein to develop. In fact, Albert Einstein *himself* is one of the project leads."

That gave Oliver a start. "What!?"

Jack smiled. "Yeah, he was very interested in helping you. As you can imagine, he had some particularly keen sympathies regarding the situation with your thesis and its potential to inadvertently end the world. As the architect of the science behind the atom bomb, I think he saw this as a shot at redemption."

Peter picked up where Jack left off. "The device was activated at nine o'clock last evening, just about the time you entered the multiverse, and then Jack was instructed to walk out on the pier at eight this morning and to wait for you."

"And it was only programmed for me. Not for my friends?"

"An oversight," Peter said, "but in a way, a lucky one. When it became clear that you had all entered the multiverse together, we were able to track everyone. It gave us our best evidence yet, in terms of what Amon is doing with the Host. You have to imagine how complicated it would have been to find them if we hadn't been tracking you. It would literally be like a needle in an infinite haystack. Even on this relatively advanced plane of existence there isn't enough computational power to search through infinity. It's possible... some might even say probable... that this entire scenario was manipulated by upper-echelon celestial beings in order to lead us to this evidence."

Oliver sighed in resignation.

It was high time to let go of his anxiety. There were forces at play that were simply way beyond his ability to understand. Worrying himself about it all would be about as useful as worrying about when the next asteroid was going to hit the earth. There was no intervention he could take that would significantly alter the cosmic landscape. If he was to be a pawn in a celestial game, he would just have to be a pawn.

He had to focus his energy on his own role, instead of the bigger picture. Whatever came next, he was going to have to deal with it. He would do his best to be a small, effective cog in the giant, multidimensional machine.

That's what Teddy did, and it seemed to work. Teddy rolled with things. Teddy had faith in the process.

To do less would make Oliver a doubting Thomas, and since great effort had obviously been employed on his behalf, the least he could do was show some faith.

Thinking of Teddy brought him back to his original concern. "So how do I rescue my friends? I'm guessing there's a plan of some kind. I suspect I'll need them."

Peter smiled and motioned for them to follow him to the kitchen. He pointed at the holographic map. "We know your friends are alive but we can't conceptualize what happens in the ether. We don't know if there's oxygen, for example."

"Or gravity," Jack added.

"But you said they were safe."

"*Safe-ish*," Jack corrected him. "Obviously they aren't dead, or we would know—they're good people. They would enter the divine multiverse. We track that kind of thing. And the Host—they're eternal beings. They can be trapped, but it would be almost impossible to destroy one."

"You said Amon is the same way. I think you used the word 'indestructible.'"

"He certainly can't be killed with secular technology. But if we had some sort of interdimensional weapon—"

"Then let's get that!"

"A weapon?" Jack asked, surprised.

"Yeah!"

"No!"

"Why not?"

"A: because nothing like that exists. Believe it or not, heaven doesn't have much use for advanced weapons systems. And B: because we don't want you setting off after a lord of the underworld, under the probably false impression that some sort of heavenly BB gun is going to take him down. The best-case scenario would be putting him into some sort of somnolent state. And if he *does* manifest on earth, I very much hope that you'll recognize that taking him down is the job of *other* Host pairs, and you will stay the heck out of it! We can't risk him getting to you. Capiche?"

Oliver was disappointed. He'd hoped for some incredibly convenient device he could use to put an end to the demon lord. Now he felt kind of childish.

"Why bring me here at all, then?"

"Because we wanted to offer you the mulligan," Jack said, "which you turned down, of course. But also, because we wanted to arm you with some enlightenment, which you could then share with other human hosts. We thought an exchange of information would be to everyone's benefit, should you choose to continue on your mission. Our big concern was the disappearing Host, and we wanted to warn you about that. In context of what we've discussed, however, that may be the lesser of our troubles at the moment."

While he processed this, Oliver stared at the faint icons on the multiverse map, and it occurred to him that one was missing.

"Where's Emma? She was transported earlier, from the riot with the communist accountants."

Peter frowned. "I assume you've noticed by now that the icons in the ether haven't moved at all."

Oliver hadn't, but he nodded, seeing that while Bob's question mark seemed to be hovering around, with a new question mark on level negative twenty-seven, the icons representing Teddy's Host and Bert were fixed in place.

"We're looking at the location where they materialized in the ether. We can't track them through it. Time—lepton decay—none of the rules of physics apply in those in-between layers. The only reason we have any bearing on where your friends went is because of you. We can assume that the ether between layers negative twenty-six and twenty-seven has some meaning to Amon, since he's the one who probably intercepted your companions. But that doesn't necessarily mean that's where Emma ended up."

"In other words, you have no idea."

Oliver returned to the railing and stared out over the Gulf of Mexico. He tried to picture her beautiful face.

"Dare to hope?" his father suggested, joining him. "If she and her Host are on the same ethereal plane as Teddy and his Host, there's a chance they can find one another."

"Which also means there's a chance they won't. I mean, the multiverse is infinite! She could be anywhere!"

"I don't think so," Peter said. "Some levels are more active than others. Level negative twenty-seven is a relatively active level. Remember, Amon uses mysticism—not hard science. He works on intuition, kind of like Mr. Quinn. He probably doesn't have infinite access to every tier of the underworld. He'd be most at home fairly close to the secular world. He might manipulate the nearfield, but I can't imagine he would involve himself in affairs a few hundred layers further down in the anti-divine. He sent your friends to the ether between negative twenty-six and twenty-seven. There's that other celestial being trapped in that same layer that we just happened to catch. That's probably the only layer of the ether Amon has any access to. He presumably understands the structure of the multiverse, since he was a celestial being, but that doesn't mean he can manipulate it."

Oliver would just have to hope that Peter was right. He considered his known problems, ticking them off on his fingers.

His friends were trapped in the ethereal substrate of the multiverse, the unknown fabric between physical universes, that might or might not represent an actual place.

He was being hunted by an indestructible, supernatural demon.

He was connected, by cosmic power, to a dog.

He had no idea how to fathom the task at hand.

And to complete the picture, he was having a chat with his dead father and another dead engineer named Peter.

He remembered a verse his mother used to share with him when he would get overwhelmed by exams and school projects. "Sufficient onto the day are the troubles thereof."

He couldn't control where Emma was, so as Jack suggested, he would just have to hope. And while he might not be able to perceive the big picture, he remembered that he was just a little cog in the big machine. He would tackle the things he could tackle. He would accept those things he could not.

So then, what would be the most common-sense approach?

When you broke it down, there were really two problems to consider: his trapped companions, and the fact that Amon wanted to manipulate him into revealing the code that would cause a nuclear apocalypse.

It went without saying that he would have to save his friends first. If Amon were to get the better of him, the thought of leaving them eternally stuck in the space in-between space was horrifying. That meant he had to find a way to travel to the ether and come back with them.

He didn't know if the theory of competitive substitution that dictated the march of technological progress on earth would apply in an eternal plane of existence, but he did know that a society advanced enough to scour the planes of the multiverse for trace lepton decay, which could then pluck an ethereal interloper out of space-time and materialize him on a fishing pier, would surely be capable of a technological solution that could send him to the underworld.

Accepting this, he focused on the rescue itself. If Bob was in a known location, maybe it made sense to find *him* first. That way, if the technological solution, which would undoubtedly have never been tested in the ether, were to fail, Bob might still be able to cast a glamour to bring them back to the secular world. Bob could be the backup plan.

"OK," Oliver said. "I know you wouldn't have brought me here without a plan to send me back. So how do we get to the underworld?"

Jack gave his son's shoulder a gentle squeeze. "You might have to accept a difficult reality," he said. "If Amon knows about you, and it looks like he does, that complicates things."

"Yeah. I realize that. But I don't have a choice."

Peter took a place at the railing on Oliver's other side. "Amon is probably setting a trap for you. Since he obviously failed to intercept you when you first entered the multiverse, he may very well be expecting you to return for your friends. It's impossible to say how much of our technology he can fathom, but if he knows we have you..."

"If I try to rescue them, what happens?"

"Well," Peter said, "if he knows you're paired with Mayhem, and he senses your transporting to the underworld, he'll stop at nothing. You're the key to the end-times. It would be awfully convenient for him to get his hands on you. If he does, God only knows what he'll do to get the information he needs."

Oliver imagined himself being waterboarded. He pictured photographs of nude Abu Ghraib prisoners, stacked in pyramids. He studied his fingernails and could almost visualize what it would be like having them pried off.

He wasn't built for enhanced interrogation. "OK, so why don't you guys go?"

"We can't," Peter said.

"Why not?"

Oliver was slightly ashamed of the tremble he heard in his own voice.

"Well..." Jack looked uncomfortable, "we're dead. We can't travel backward through the multiverse. We're on an upward-only trajectory. We're fundamentally different than you. We have no secular body."

"What about those roaming entities you talked about? Or biblical angels?"

"They don't answer to us," Peter said. "They're on an entirely different wavelength, and won't concern themselves at all about events on secular earth."

"But what about the Great Balance?"

"That's our business. Not theirs. Their purpose is larger, and beyond our comprehension."

Peter met his gaze. "It puts you in a bind. You, alone, could rescue your friends. And yet you are also in the precarious position of knowing that to do so would mean deliberately walking into a trap, and potentially giving Amon the key to render the human race extinct."

Oliver scratched his head in thought. Returning to the kitchen table, he took a seat and stared at the hologram.

He knew there had to be a solution, but for the life of him he couldn't imagine it.

Mayhem padded across the room, sat on the floor and rested his chin on Oliver's knee. Oliver absently patted the not-exactly-terrier.

Somewhere in the recesses of his mind, a puzzle piece fell into place.

"What about Mayhem?" he asked.

"Where you go, he goes," Peter said. "We aren't going to experiment with forcefully breaking that bond."

"But, I mean, he can predict the future, right?"

Mayhem perked his ears.

"Yes..." Jack said, hesitantly.

"What if we let Mayhem time things? We let him choose when to go? If he leads the way, we could time it so I get in and out before Amon finds me."

"I don't know..." Jack began.

"You said it yourself, Dad. He's vastly more intelligent than we are. Clairvoyant and all that."

Mayhem whined.

"You think you can do it?" Oliver asked.

The not-precisely-a-dog blinked. It was a very purposeful-looking blink. It was a blink that seemed so purposeful, Oliver considered it an affirmative communication.

"I'm pretty sure he can!"

"Wait. Because he blinked at you? You're going to risk an extinction-level event based on a blink?"

"Well, when you word it that way..."

Mayhem padded over to Jack. They locked eyes. Mayhem blinked again. "Well dang," Jack said. "I guess he probably can."

— *Twelve* —

Oliver felt better.

He shared his blueberry muffin with Mayhem as the two stood on the balcony, overlooking the gulf.

He thought of Bert, and remembered the old man insisting they have their breakfast on the balcony. He had taken quite a liking to the not-so-grim reaper. Bert and Carmella offered him something he was in desperate want of—namely, non-academic role models. He wished his dad could meet them.

Brushing crumbs off his tight paisley shirt, Oliver mused that he had now experienced the absolute pinnacle of the muffin. It was like eating a cloud inside a cookie. The textural perfection was pure culinary wizardry.

This didn't take away from his sea of troubles, necessarily, but it did help him relax. For example, while certainly flavorful, the blueberry muffin could give almost no help whatsoever in confronting an ancient demon. And while the muffin was indeed exquisitely moist and bursting with fruitiness, it could offer little in the way of interdimensional transportation.

Oliver squatted low and stroked Mayhem. "You can help me with all this stuff, right? I'm counting on you."

The not-entirely-a-canine licked his arm. Oliver wasn't sure if this was a sign of affection, or an indication of wayward muffin crumbs.

"I assume there's some kind of technological solution for interdimensional travel?" he asked over his shoulder.

"There is," Peter confirmed. "It's still experimental, but we have no reason to believe it won't work. It's based on the same scientific principles we used to intercept you."

"We've been given authorization by one of the higher-ups to let you use it," Jack said. "But it has to be done in secret."

"Why?"

"Because sometimes it's best if the left hand doesn't know what the right hand is doing."

"Even in heaven?"

"Especially in heaven," Jack said. "Did you ever read the Old Testament?"

"We covered it in Sunday school."

"Did they go into all the eye gouging, and angels of death and pillars of salt and what have you?"

"Not, maybe, to the full extent of the text, but I mean—come on!" Oliver gestured at the pristine beach that stretched miles in either direction. "This is paradise! There are people out there having a picnic!" He pointed.

"We just don't want to attract too much attention," his father said. "Some might interpret what we're doing as... well... an offense against God."

"What!?"

"Yeah, some of the more old-school entities can be pretty touchy," Peter confirmed. "Probably best not to be too shouty about any of this."

"What would they do to us?" Oliver fought back a new tide of cosmic dread.

"Maybe nothing," Jack said, his voice cheerful. "Maybe cast us down into a pit of eternal hellfire. It's hard to know."

"Keep it a secret," Oliver said. "Got it." He took a deep breath and inhaled the fresh scent of the sea. He pushed thoughts of pitchforks and brimstone out of his mind.

Bert was right about one thing—the fresh air was good for the mind.

"So where is this device?"

Oliver pictured a gigantic computational super-center roughly the size of a skyscraper, designed to run an above-ground super-conducting super-collider that sprawled over the landscape in a vast, thousand-mile arc. He imagined arrays of highly advanced processing units, stacked story upon story between cooling racks and gargantuan memory banks, the likes of which no human had ever dared to imagine.

"It's in the top drawer of the AV cabinet in the conference room at the office," Peter said.

Oliver nodded. "Oh."

"We're going to have to abscond with it," Peter said. "Only I'm not entirely sure how."

"I actually have an idea," Jack said, "but it won't be without risk."

Entwined in heavenly traffic, Oliver stared in wonder as the self-driving van wound its way through the divine streets of heavenly Florida. Men and women talked and laughed outside shops and cafés. People walked dogs, and rode bicycles, and jogged along the sidewalk in workout gear. Other than it being a rather pleasant day, suggestive of an alternate timeline wherein Norman Rockwell centered his work on the Gulf Coast, nothing Oliver saw screamed "You are in an alternate dimension!"

Then they passed a church where two spherical creatures appeared to be locked in deep conversation on the stairs to the entrance. The distinctly unearthly beings had glowing, orb-like bodies, covered in what looked like dozens of flapping birdwings, and both otherworldly entities had multiple sets of eyes that peaked out from under the helter-skelter arrangement of bone-white feathers.

"What in the world?"

"Seraphim," Jack said.

"Let me guess. You get used to them?"

"No," Peter sighed, "they're still pretty weird to me."

The van turned east, away from the beaches, and soon they were in a bright, clean industrial park with gleaming two- and three-story office buildings. Each office complex was fronted by palm trees or fountains, and maintenance people busied themselves with lawnmowers and leaf blowers in just about every green space.

The self-driving van pulled to the curb at the front entrance of a nondescript office building. A few vehicles were parked in the adjacent lot, but overall the place appeared to be fairly quiet.

Peter and Jack had gone back and forth, nitpicking details of the plan, and now Peter snapped his fingers.

"What we really need is a distraction," he said. "That should be my job, I think. I've always suspected that I could be quite devious, if a situation called for it. So how about I take care of the distraction, and you guys head to the conference room on the second floor. You really don't need me for that part. Get it, and get out. We'll reconvene at the van. If either party doesn't return, assume they've been caught and proceed from there. If capture is imminent, Jack, you give Oliver the device and send him to the underworld. This isn't a vestigial building, so try to use the ground floor so he doesn't break his neck. Everyone clear?"

Jack and Oliver both nodded. Mayhem, for his part, appeared to have fallen asleep.

The van pulled into the parking lot of a white stucco office building and came to a stop in the shade of an orange tree. A man in a yellow, high-visibility vest waved to Peter, and Peter waved back.

"Who's that?" Oliver asked.

"Luke. Good dude."

"Will he—like—try to stop us?"

Jack smiled. "Only if we litter."

"Ready?" Peter asked.

A knot formed in the pit of Oliver's stomach. He felt like he'd been thrust into the role of a Navy Seal. Adrenaline coursed through his bloodstream. "Ready."

"OK, let's go."

They walked through the front entryway of the building, Mayhem trotting a few feet behind. They were immediately confronted by a smiling man at a desk. The man's name tag read, "Hi. My name is Paul."

"Gentlemen," Paul said, getting to his feet, "and...er...celestial beings," he eyed Mayhem. "What can I do for you?"

"I'm going to be honest with you, Paul," Peter said. "I need you to stay here and chat with me while my friends abscond with an experimental device."

Oliver felt his jaw physically drop. Until that moment, he'd always assumed it was just a figure of speech; but no, his mouth hung wide open.

"Is your mouth OK, son?" Paul asked. "It looks like you're trying to catch flies."

Oliver raised a hand, and pretended to stifle a yawn. "Sorry. A little tired, is all."

Paul smiled. "We've all had *those* days."

"Would it be alright if I start distracting you now?" Peter asked.

"Sure," Paul said. "Whatever you need, Pete."

Peter made a swiping gesture, and gave a meaningful look to Jack and Oliver. Under his breath, but still much too loudly and urgently, he whispered, "Go!"

Peter then turned to face Paul. "Great weather we're having this week," he said.

Jack led Oliver and Mayhem around a corner, up a flight of stairs, past a row of empty cubicles, to a conference room with windows that overlooked Seminole Boulevard.

"The cabinet," Jack pointed. "I'll stand watch."

Oliver jogged over to the computer cabinet and opened the drawer. His breath caught in his throat. There was nothing inside but a pen.

He was about to inform his father that the mission had failed, when he inspected the silver instrument more closely. It was not, in fact, a pen. A series of plastic dials had been set in the barrel, and a label in four-point Helvetica font read:

Ethereal Analytics Leptometry Division: Hepta-Polar Trans-Substantive Interdimensional Illusionary Experimental Device 62-A58—Cast Master 4000 v3.1 (skunk)

"Got it," he whispered.

Jack led the way back, past the cubicles, down the flight of stairs. They turned the corner and saw Peter and Paul, who were watching, on the television monitor at the greeting desk, some kind of ball-sport that Oliver didn't exactly recognize but thought might possibly be what the Australians referred to as "footy." Paul was making small talk about the game.

Peter saw Jack, Oliver and Mayhem, and his eyes widened.

"Paul, I have to go! Great seeing you!"

"You too!" Paul said, enthusiastically. "See you tomorrow!"

In the safety of the minivan, Oliver turned to Peter. "That was the absolute worst example of subterfuge I have ever seen in my life!"

"I admit, I'm a little out of practice. I mean I've been here for almost two hundred years. We don't get a lot of opportunity for skullduggery in heaven. But it did work, didn't it?"

"Why did Paul just let us go like that?"

"Paul's been here for four hundred years," Jack explained, a devilish grin on his face. "He was even more out of practice than us!"

"That was exhilarating!" Peter pumped his biceps. "Whoo-hoo!"

He held his hand up, and it took a second before Oliver realized he was asking for a high five. Oliver gave him one.

As the van pulled away from the Department of Interdimensional Transportation, Peter gave Jack and Oliver a brief demonstration, talking them through the functions of the device, which he simply called the Cast Master 4000.

A dial at the base could be turned to a number between negative 60 and 60, and this indicated the depth of the excursion through the near-field multiverse. Two sub-dials were labeled "N-S," and "E-W," and were for target acquisition in space, measured in units that approximated ten meters. A fourth dial was labeled "alt," which Peter explained was "altitude." He further explained, "Don't touch that."

A yellow switch, when deployed, opened a small side panel in the device that was labeled "T."

"The T stands for 'Time,'" Peter explained. "Whatever you do, don't fiddle with that one."

"Time as in—time travel?" Oliver thought he must have misheard.

"Yes, yes time travel. Please don't touch it."

"Why not?"

"It's theorized that it would end the universe, and quite possibly the entire multiverse."

"Theorized like the theory that the first atom bomb would cause atmospheric ignition?"

"No—more like theorized the way Schrodinger's cat was theorized to be in a state of both life and death until the box is opened."

"It sounds like you're saying there's a fifty percent chance that this little switch on this pen-sized device can destroy the entire multiverse?"

"That's one way to look at it. Just so long as nobody messes with it, though, there's a zero percent chance of that happening."

Oliver scratched his temple. "Why in God's name would you put it on there?"

"Because in heaven, nobody would intentionally end the universe. And because, frankly, we were curious if it could be built."

"Does it work?"

"Now how could we possibly know the answer to that?"

Oliver gave up, determined not to fiddle with the time function. Peter continued the demonstration.

By pressing a red button on the side of the barrel, the laser-pointer-like instrument would cast small transport glamour on an object, which could then be used to transport the user or a test subject through the multiverse.

"Until now, all we've ever transported are inanimate sensors. We send them out on a timer, measure temperature, air quality, radiation levels and what-have-you, and then have them return to us with that data. We use lepton emitters on the sensors, and then we can QA our Host tracking software by tuning it to them. You kind of get a double whammy of data for each experiment."

"The public service here is really a step up," Oliver said.

"We try," Peter smiled.

Oliver had assumed the van was taking them to the Tier-19 version of Bob's bungalow, so he was surprised when, instead, it pulled off Gulf Boulevard and the doors slid open back at the Angler's Cove condominium complex.

He was about to protest when Peter held up a palm.

Oliver, confused, slapped it.

"What was that?" Peter said.

"I thought you wanted another high five," Oliver explained.

"No, I was trying to cut off your query as to what we're doing back here."

"Oh."

Peter held the silver device so it flashed in the sunlight. "I need to calibrate this. Remember what we were saying about vestigial places? The thing is, this is the only one I've ever worked from."

"Right," Oliver said. "But Bob's tiki bar is obviously..."

"An unknown entity, as far as I'm concerned," Peter said. "I'm sure it's fine, but I'm a lot more comfortable testing one variable at a time. I don't want to blow you up, or have you suddenly materialize inside a concrete wall, or ten thousand feet above the ground."

Pooching his lower lip, Oliver somberly nodded. He had already considered this possibility, but had decided that his only defense against such mishap was to stick to known vestigial places (essentially the condominium complex and Bob's backyard), follow instructions, and then, beyond that, hope for the best.

He remembered the look on Teddy's face when Emma flashed out of existence after saving him from the glamour. He knew that, whatever the risk, he had no choice in the matter. He owed them his best effort.

Still, he wanted Peter to know he could comprehend the danger, should anything go wrong. "I understand, and I appreciate your concern for my safety."

"This thing isn't designed to deposit, uh, things into the ether, you know."

"Right. But you have a potential solution?"

"I think so."

"OK..."

"The history of scientific achievement is practically dripping in blood. You will essentially be a test subject in an interdimensional..."

Now it was Oliver's turn to interrupt. He held up both hands in surrender. "I hereby waive you of any responsibility. I, Oliver Bell, being of sound mind..."

"Are you mocking me?"

"A little."

"Is it at least in the fun way? Like how friends on secular earth will mock one another in good-natured jest? That wasn't a thing, in my day, you understand. I think they call it 'Busting a cap.'"

"Yeah. I mean, no, it's not 'Busting a cap.' That's something else. The saying is 'Busting your balls.' But yes, I was just busting your balls a little."

"Is it a sports thing? The balls part, I mean?"

"I don't know. I always assumed it was a testicle thing."

"Ah," Peter smiled. "Well, it seems I've finally had my balls busted. How modern!"

He grinned, but when he looked back to the Angler's Cove condominium complex, the smile faded. "In all seriousness, you know this is dangerous, right?"

It seemed like ages since safety had been a primary concern. In reality, it had only been about four days. "Yeah, I know."

"OK."

Jack cleared his throat. "With Peter having said all that, if I understand correctly, there's no reason it shouldn't work."

"That's reassuring, Dad. Thanks."

They made their way to apartment 203, and with the door closed and locked behind them, Jack took the device from Peter and studied it. "Let's do a preliminary experiment."

He fiddled with the controls while Peter worked the holographic computer. Jack showed Oliver what he was doing, and he set the Cast Master 4000 to negative level 1, then passed it to his son.

"Just aim at the rum bottle, and press the button." He set the rum bottle on the table next to the hologram, then crouched down to watch the action, looking very much like a first-base coach.

Oliver aimed the device at the bottle and pressed the red button. Instantly, soundlessly, the rum bottle was replaced with a rotting skunk carcass.

"Ew. Why is it a dead skunk?"

Even as he said it, he realized he could smell the thing.

"We don't want someone in another level of the multiverse accidentally touching the glamour," Peter explained. "Even animals tend to avoid the carcass. And insects generally aren't big enough to trigger it."

"It stinks to high heaven! No pun intended."

"Yes, we're quite proud of it," Peter said.

Oliver's father approached the glamour. He reached out and poked it. The deceased animal shifted slightly under the pressure of his finger. Oliver was impressed by the distinct lack of anything happening.

"Won't work for us, see," Jack said, poking the skunk again. "Looks like you're up, kiddo."

Oliver approached the carcass while Peter and Jack watched in genuine fascination. He gingerly extended his hand, as though expecting a static shock, when Peter shouted, "Wait!"

Oliver yanked his hand back.

"Take Mayhem!"

"Oh," Oliver said. "Right."

Tucking the Cast Master 4000 into his pocket, he called the not-exactly-a-dog, who plodded over and sat on the floor at his feet. Oliver stooped and picked him up, then reached out with his free hand and grabbed the skunk.

There was a flash of light, followed by a sensation of becoming unstuck from the universe that Oliver thought would be quite akin to the feeling a champagne cork might experience when popping out of the top of a bottle. This was followed by the more difficult-to-describe sensation of becoming re-stuck in a slightly different version of the universe. Overall, the journey wasn't particularly unpleasant, and, unlike his previous experience, it seemed to carry no risk, whatsoever, of turning him into a quivering gelatinous mass.

Just like when he arrived on the fishing pier, Oliver realized he was lying flat on his back, gripping a Lamb's rum bottle. The celestial terrier panted at his side. He opened his eyes and noted he was on the floor of the apartment he had just left.

"Wait," he said. "Did it work?"

"Did what work?" a woman asked.

He sat bolt upright. A woman in her thirties with curly hair and a pair of sunglasses clipped to the front of her polo shirt stood in the kitchen staring at him. She was holding a bag of snap peas and appeared to be putting away the groceries. Oliver's sudden materialization in her living room seemed to have caused her some mild surprise.

"Oh. Hello," Oliver said.

"Hi."

"Sorry for the interruption."

Oliver got to his feet.

"No problem," the woman said.

"Are those snap peas?"

She examined the bag of snap peas in her hand. "Yes."

"How are they?" Oliver asked, fiddling with the dial on the Cast Master 4000.

"I haven't tried them yet."

He set the Lamb's bottle on the table, pointed at it, and cast the skunk glamour on it.

"Ew," the woman said.

"I'll just be going. Nice to meet you."

"OK."

He scooped Mayhem under his arm, then grabbed the skunk. Almost immediately, he found himself lying supine on the floor once again. Mayhem sniffed at him, then licked his ear.

"You alive?" his father asked.

Oliver sat up. "I think so."

"He's alive," Peter confirmed, manipulating the hologram. "Otherwise, I'd be able to see it here."

Jack helped him to his feet. "How was it?"

"It was OK," Oliver said. "There was a woman putting groceries away, though. She saw me. She had a bag of snap peas in her hand. Have I like, broken the space-time continuum or anything like that?"

"Probably not."

"Why didn't it hurt? When I came here, it was exquisitely uncomfortable."

"We're a little more refined with our glamour technology than Bob," Peter explained. "It would be like the difference between drinking twenty-five-year-old single malt scotch versus pruno made in a prison toilet."

"No kidding."

Peter produced what appeared to be a very compact 3D printer from his briefcase. When he turned the device on, it interfaced with the holographic computer. Using an extremely intuitive CAD program that would have been worth roughly one hundred billion dollars on secular earth, he designed a small gear for the Cast Master 4000, and in seconds printed the object.

He then used a tiny screwdriver to disassemble the device, exchanging the gear attached to the level-dial for the new one.

"Here," he said, "have a look at this."

He handed the device to Oliver. The level dial could click into gear both on the correct level and between each level.

"Seriously?" Oliver asked.

"Yup," Peter said.

"But doesn't it, like, need to be calibrated to account for the infinite probabilities of ethereal spaces between space?" Oliver asked. "After all, from a mathematical perspective, there are technically more numbers between zero and one, than there are total numbers."

"Let's hope not," Peter said. "If so, you're screwed."

"Should I try it?"

"Oh no! It's far too dangerous."

"What?!"

"We have no idea what happens in the ether," Peter reminded him. "We know that in the particular level where your friends are being held, they seem to be in a survivable state. Beyond that, we're at a loss."

Jack cleared his throat. "The best thing we can do, I think, is get you to Bob. Bob is your backup. If the device fails in the ether, Bob can probably get you home."

"The Cast Master 4000 is yours," Peter said. "You can use it whenever you absolutely need it on any celestial plane of the multiverse. It won't work on secular earth, but as long as you're in the underworld it should continue to function normally. To travel with a companion, just keep physical contact when you touch the glamour.

"Try to use it only in vestigial places. I'll arrange to have a list of the ones we know around here uploaded to the Incredible Daily Facts app for convenience, though you'll obviously need a phone connected to the internet for that to work, and we have no idea what the carrier system is like in the underworld. A point for further study, I guess. You can, we assume, use the Cast Master 4000 in Bob's tiki bar, which is going to be your departure point. Once you return to secular earth, the device will essentially be rendered ineffective, though you may feel free to have it as a keepsake, memorializing your historic journey through the multiverse."

Oliver considered the implications of what he'd just learned.

"But Dad, once I find Teddy and Emma and Bert, can we come back here? Can I spend more time with you? I'd love for you to show us tier nineteen. You could meet my friends. Teddy's great. You'd really like him. And he'd be thrilled to learn all this stuff..."

His father sighed, cutting him off. "No, Olly, I'm afraid not. Once you rescue your friends, go straight to the secular world. It's where you all belong. It would be dangerous to bring anyone else here. Remember what we were saying about the Old Testament beings?"

Oliver nodded.

"We need to stay on their good side. Plus—getting you here without blowing you up was incredibly complicated. I'm not sure many people in the engineering department would be on board with bringing more people here for a casual visit. They all have people too, you know. It would raise a lot of questions. It would bring all the wrong kinds of attention."

Oliver had been under the impression that his father would now, once again, play an integral role in his life. Realizing this wasn't the case, his eyes welled up. He jutted his jaw and tried to fight back the tears, but they spilled down his cheeks regardless.

"Oh, buddy," Jack said before kissing his son on the forehead. "You know I'm keeping an eye on you. And if you're absolutely stuck, I'm here, OK? I'll figure something out. Look—we did it once."

Oliver swallowed. "Right."

"You OK?"

"Yeah." His voice was high and choked. The lump in his throat wouldn't go away.

Jack tousled his hair. "I know it's hard."

"Will I get a choice? When I die, I mean? Can I come back here?"

"I did," Jack said. "To be with my dad. They let me choose my level within a range. I chose here."

That made him feel better. "Will you wait for me here, before you—you know—move on?"

"Of course! As long as it takes!"

"Promise?"

Oliver couldn't believe how childlike he sounded, but he was dead serious. "Promise."

He wiped his eyes and sniffed. "Sorry."

"You Canadians always say sorry," Peter said. "It's uncalled for."

"I just—I was having a moment. That's all."

Jack sighed. "Well, if you're OK, we should get to Bob's. I'll take you. There's some stuff I want to go over.

"I think this is goodbye for us," Peter said; "for now, at any rate."

Oliver reached to shake his hand, and searched the man's kind face, finally locking eyes. "I can't thank you enough for everything."

Peter grasped Oliver's hand between his own and gave a firm, single shake. "Best of luck, kid. There are a lot of folks up here cheering for you."

Outside the elevator, a silver minivan rolled silently up to greet them, and Oliver was suddenly overcome by a profound feeling of missed opportunity. There was so much here to explore—an entire muliverse, in fact—and here he was leaving without even spending a night.

His heart lurched in his chest. Doubt clouded his mind. For the first time since materializing on the fishing pier, he was uncertain about what he should do. There was so much to learn. And wasn't life about learning?

But then he remembered Emma. He thought of the way she had wiped dirt from his eyes. He thought of Teddy and of Bert, and how they had taken him in and helped him—befriended him, even. Teddy had gone so far as to forgive him. He owed them.

He climbed into the van.

Mayhem rode on Oliver's lap in the front seat. Jack programmed Bob's address into the navigation system.

As the van rolled into traffic, Jack turned to his son. "Now that we're alone, there are a couple of things I need to tell you."

Oliver nodded. He'd been expecting something like this.

"First, your mother. Once you rescue Teddy and Emma, and this mess gets sorted out, try to check in on her. If Amon is still onto you, at least try to send her an email or something. She worries."

"I will, Dad."

"Next, finances. I know you've had to borrow a lot for school—"

"It's OK—"

"No, hear me out. I'm sorry about that. We thought I'd still be working. I would have bought more life insurance if I'd known. So, if you need to sell some stuff of mine, go ahead and do it. There isn't a lot, but there was your grandmother's house. It might be worth fifty thousand or so. And I had those first editions in my office—they're worth something. Consider them yours, OK?"

"I don't need money," Oliver said; "human hosts can find it. We use a metal detector. It's this whole thing where you can always find what you need."

"Really?"

"Yeah."

"Well, that's cool."

"So, what do you want me to do with your first editions? Do you still want me to sell them? I mean, are earthly possessions now meaningless due to your newfound eternal wisdom?"

"No! What are you, crazy? I worked my butt off for that collection! Keep it intact!"

"Right."

His father reached over and squeezed his hand. "You know, we weren't sure it was going to work—grabbing you out of the multiverse like we did. I wish we could have caught your friends as well. I'm sorry I hadn't accounted for them."

"It's OK," Oliver said. "They'll understand. Plus," he hesitated, not wanting to sound corny, "it was good seeing you again."

"It was," Jack smiled.

The older man shifted in his seat. He opened the center console and produced three envelopes. Two were white, and the third was silver. He passed them to Oliver.

"The silver one is from the higher-up guy who helped us," he explained. "I'm guessing it's a set of instructions for you, but it's above my pay grade. Open it when you get back to secular earth."

"When you say 'higher-up—?'"

"He's the one who approved our intercepting you. Nice guy. He collects guitars. You'd like him."

Oliver tried to imagine a white-robed, grey-bearded God perusing the aisle of a pawn store looking for a Les Paul.

"What about the other two?"

"The other two are letters for you and your mom. They're, uh, personal. And it would be very much frowned upon if anyone knew I gave you these."

Oliver heard the hesitation in his father's voice and looked up to see tears tracking down his face. "Dad?"

Jack cleared his voice. "Listen... you know, it's OK here. It's wonderful, in fact. You know I'm fine, now, right? Not sick. Feel great every day. All that."

"Yeah..."

"But Olly, I'd be lying if I told you I wasn't a little bit lonely. I miss you and Mom. I miss watching movies with you. I miss going on vacations with you. I miss my family."

"I miss you too, Dad," Oliver said. "So does Mom."

As the van turned itself off Gulf Boulevard and into the side street that led to Bob's house—at least, what was Bob's house in the secular world—Jack and Oliver leaned across the center console and embraced. Mayhem, trapped between the two men, struggled briefly before extricating himself to the back seat.

Oliver felt like a small boy in his father's arms, and he marveled that the man he had watched wither away could be so young and strong once more.

When the van pulled to the curb, they broke their hold and wiped their eyes.

"I guess renowned English musician Eric Clapton was full of it," Jack sniffed.

"Huh?"

"There are plenty of tears in heaven."

"That was a groaner, Dad."

"Hey. Just because I'm dead, doesn't mean I'm above the occasional dad joke. I'm still your father, after all."

They walked up the driveway to Bob's bungalow, which in this layer of the multiverse had been painted a very pleasant light blue. Jack knocked on the door.

A young man answered with a smile.

"Hello," Jack introduced himself, "I'm Jack Bell with the Department of Interdimensional Transportation. We need to use your tiki bar."

"Be my guest," the man said.

Jack and Oliver made their way through the exceptionally clean house to the small back patio. The tiki bar, while structurally similar to the one in the secular world, was devoid of liquor bottles. The blender was there, but the shelves held mostly books and magazines, and some kind of odd blue fruit that Oliver didn't recognize.

"I use it as a juice bar slash library," the homeowner explained.

"Does this mean it's vestigial?" Oliver asked his father.

"I don't know. But we do know that your friends left from here, and that Bob is still alive, so it must exist on level negative-27."

Oliver set the dial on the Cast Master 4000, and double-checked his math.

"So I want to go forty-six levels down, right?"

"Right."

"And Bob should be there."

"Right."

"And it will technically be hell?"

"Technically, yes."

He pictured fire raining down from the sky, people buried upside down in sewage, and all the other fantastical scenes depicted in Dante's *Inferno*. He shivered.

"What should I expect?"

"I have no idea," Jack said, "but it probably isn't going to be great."

"OK."

Oliver had forgotten the Lamb's bottle in the Angler's Cove apartment. Jack bee-lined toward the bowl of fruit on the tiki bar.

"Excuse me," he said to the homeowner, "could we have this banana?"

"No problem."

"Here you go, Olly," he said, propping the banana up on the bar.

As he did so, a prick of red light flickered in the sky. Oliver stared at it for a second, and soon another point of light joined it. Then another.

"Uh…"

Jack looked quizzically at him and then followed his gaze.

"Uh oh," he said. "Biblical angels."

More lights appeared in the sky. Now there were dozens of them.

"What do we do?" Oliver asked.

"You scram," Jack said. "I'll figure this out, whatever it is."

A sound arose. At first it was faint, but it quickly intensified, growing louder and louder until it was deafening. It reminded Oliver of a tornado siren, only it seemed to be coming from some sort of brass instrument.

"Go!" His father yelled over the crescendo. "I'll deal with this!"

"Are you sure?"

"Yup!"

Oliver pointed the Cast Master 4000 at the banana and pressed the button. The fruit was replaced by a rotting skunk carcass.

"Ew," the homeowner yelled, squinting at the dead skunk. "Do you mind if I ask what's going on?" He had to shout to be heard above the racket.

"He's going to the underworld!" Jack shouted, a maniacal grin of extreme paternal pride on his face. "My son is an interdimensional traveler! The first human to do it!"

"I see," shouted the homeowner.

Oliver took Mayhem under his arm. "OK, buddy," he said, "bark or something when it's safe to go."

Mayhem wriggled in Oliver's grasp, and the not-precisely-a-scruffy-dog shut his eyes tight. The eyes moved back and forth under the lids, and Oliver sensed that the creature was hunting for something far, far away.

Mayhem's breathing grew rapid. His heart hammered in his chest and beat like a drum against Oliver's hand. His fur warmed until it was so uncomfortably hot that Oliver could barely hold on.

Oliver had the distinct sense that he was gripping a capacitor on the verge of a powerful electrical discharge.

The lights in the house flickered. A pall of semi-translucent darkness, much like what Oliver had experienced on Bert's boat, settled over the patio. The blaring trumpet chorus sounded momentarily far away.

"Whoa," the homeowner said.

Mayhem opened his eyes. The darkness dissipated. The trumpets grew louder again, and the homeowner covered his ears. The dog barked twice.

Oliver hugged his father one last time. "Love you, Dad."
"Godspeed, Olly," Jack said. "Be good."
Oliver grabbed the skunk.

— *Thirteen* —

Later, when he would consider it, Oliver would conclude that being blasted into quadrillions of subatomic particles, flung through the cosmic ether and then reassembled atom by atom was one of the more relaxing portions of his journey to the underworld. As a cloud of bosons, gluons and other exotic hadrons, he was able to reflect on his visit to the nineteenth divine tier of the multiverse. It had certainly been informative. He looked forward to sharing his new knowledge with Teddy and Emma.

The journey had offered closure, the likes of which no living human had ever experienced, and Oliver saw this as an incredible gift. Just knowing that his father still existed as a productive member of an advanced society was a weight off his shoulders.

He would never again have to wonder what happened to Jack's eternal soul. He'd had coffee and muffins with it!

Faith was great. Faith was important. But for secular mathematicians in a cynical society, faith had its limits. He, alone, was now party to evidence. Did his need for such evidence make him a doubting Thomas? He supposed it did. But better to be a doubting Thomas than a cynical Sandy.

Oliver was also overjoyed to know that the universe was infinitely more complex than human understanding could comprehend.

The idea that humans were somehow a species at the apex of knowledge had always depressed him, and now he could cast the thought aside. When it came to the cosmos, and the reconciliation of spiritual and scientific understanding, humans were idiots. This shouldn't have been a big surprise.

He thought of all the television and YouTube scientists, so certain of their knowledge, and so quick to dismiss the spiritual as antiscientific. It was funny how unbelievably wrong they all were about the nature of things. If the swirl of pico-matter that constituted Oliver's physical-self had been in possession of a face, it would have grinned.

He reflected on his dramatic exit from the divine version of Bob's tiki bar. He could only hope Jack and Peter wouldn't be in too much trouble. The cacophonous fanfare that had marked his departure was unsettling, sure, but in reality, he had no way of interpreting its meaning. Were the angels warning him not to go? Were they wishing him luck on his journey? Were they a bunch of Old Testamentarians, coming to arrest his dad? If so, what would they do to Jack? He couldn't imagine the punishment for his father's indiscretion would be too brutal. Heaven had seemed pretty civilized. But whatever the case, it was completely out of his control. Like an alcoholic at an AA meeting, he reminded himself to focus on the things he could change, and accept the things he couldn't.

He hoped that if he could pull off his own mission, and rescue Emma, Bert, and Teddy without being captured by Amon and triggering a nuclear apocalypse, perhaps even the most stringent of the Old-Testamentarians would cut his dad a break. And the fact that Mayhem was on board with their plan reassured him. Surely, the cosmic not-quite-a-dog wouldn't intentionally lead them into committing a biblical transgression—or at least, he hoped, not a serious one.

As Oliver's essence coalesced, he mentally prepared himself for materialization. For a moment, he had the sensation of being nothing but a floating pancreas, and then the rest of him popped into existence.

He materialized lying on his back in an icy puddle, clutching a banana. A cold, howling wind whipped rain and salt spray across his face. Freezing water pooled in his paisley shirt and in the back of his trousers.

The twenty-seventh tier of hell was going to be unpleasant.

Squinting into the inky blackness of the tempestuous night, he found the dog. Mayhem whimpered, looking absolutely miserable with his ears back and his tail tucked between his hind legs.

"You look like a drowned rat, buddy," Oliver whispered.

Scrambling to his knees, more cold water sluiced down the back of his pants and Oliver fought the instinct to yelp at the shock. If some horrible, hell-spawned beast was waiting for him here, he didn't want to alert it to his presence.

Mayhem whined again, louder this time.

"Hey, it's OK. It's OK."

Oliver picked up the wet, trembling dog-like being and cradled it against his chest. Mayhem shivered so hard, Oliver thought the poor thing would dislocate a hip.

He willed whatever warmth was in him to make its way to the unhappy celestial terrier.

If anything, Oliver had expected oppressive heat, and hadn't mentally prepared for winter Hades, though, now that he thought about it, being cold and wet was a special misery unto itself, so perhaps such an environment was more appropriate for an underworld reserved for the eternally damned.

"This sucks," he whispered.

Finding his bearings, he crossed the patio to the tiki bar, and set the banana on the uneven countertop. The bar stood askew, as though it had been blown loose from its anchor points.

Ducking low, he brought Mayhem inside. There was no escaping the roaring gale, but at least the bar could act as a kind of windbreak. He set the terrier down on the patio stones, out of the worst of the storm.

It had been broad daylight when he departed the nineteenth divine realm, but it was full dark here. Assuming time of day was constant between levels of the multiverse, he must have been in transit for at least a few hours.

Oliver circled the perimeter of the tiki bar, squinted into the dark, curious what the denizens of the underworld might look like.

As he did, the wind picked up, driving rain and sleet painfully against his skin. He held his hands to his face, palms outward and peered through the slits between his fingers. The palm trees, at least the ones he could make out, were bent double in the wind. Whitecaps ripped across the inland waterway.

None of the nearby homes were lit. This might have been due to a storm-related power outage, but then again hell might be without electricity.

The place gave him an overwhelming sense of depressing aloneness. The entire neighborhood could be abandoned, for all he knew. He might be the only person for miles in any direction.

Long ago, on a Sunday, after church, he'd asked his mother about hell. He would have been six or seven years old at the time. She explained that hell just meant separation from God.

The answer had been practically meaningless at the time to a kid who was worried about hot coals, and red devils with swishing tails, but now her words sent prickly shards of ice through his veins.

This was a place without any goodness. It was a place where happiness and joy would simply shrivel and die. It was a place of abandonment. Creation without creator.

He shivered. He hated it here.

He had to find Bob—find Bob, and get the hell out of hell.

He double-checked to make sure there were no nearby demons to over-hear him, and took a calculated risk.

"Bob!" he called cautiously into the wind. "Mr. Quinn?"

His voice disappeared in the storm.

He leaned over the tiki bar.

"OK, Mayhem, you stay here. I'm going to check if he's in the house."

He turned up the considerable stretchy collar of his paisley disco shirt and hustled through the rain to the back door. Unlike the multiverse's other versions of Bob's house, this building was falling apart. It was clad in tired, dirty, weather-beaten siding that had torn off in places, exposing a thin layer of tattered plastic vapor barrier over chipped and eroding cinderblocks. The patio doorframe sat crooked in the wall.

Oliver knocked.

"Hello? Anyone home?"

When he knocked a little harder, the door fell off its rotten frame and crashed into the living room with a wet thud.

So much for stealth.

He bent to examine the ruined doorframe. Pill bugs crawled through channels in the spongy material.

Tiptoeing into the living room, he tried to push away thoughts about the integrity of the structure.

Was the house abandoned? He was sure he'd seen the icon representing Bob in the vicinity of this place, back on his father's holographic map. But then there had been that other icon—that other question mark.

Had Bob been captured by Legion? By Amon? Had they inadvertently sprung the trap intended for Oliver on the pot-smoking writer?

If so, that meant he was now on a rescue mission. Pressing his palms together in a gesture of prayer, he was struck by the softness of his own hands. His was an academic hide. He was woefully ill-equipped for such a transdimensional endeavor.

So how to find and/or rescue a leisurely creative in an unknown dystopian dimension? Oliver remembered the adage about how to eat an elephant. The best strategy, he figured, was to break the task into smaller parts in order to avoid overwhelming despair. The less time he spent considering the impossibility of the job, the more time he could spend attempting it. The first order of business was to search the house. That much, at least, he could surely manage.

"One step at a time," he whispered.

He stepped forward, tripping on the fallen patio door, and sprawled face-first on the damp, stinking carpet.

"Ouch!"

He brought a hand to his nose and felt the bone. It didn't feel broken, but it smarted enough to bring tears to his eyes.

"OK," he whispered, getting to his feet, "let's try that again."

He crouched low. Although just *how*, exactly, crouching was supposed to help him, he couldn't say. Maybe it was something he'd seen in a movie. He felt kind of stupid, and straightened.

It was time to get on with it. If hell-spawn were waiting for him in the house, so be it. He was a mathematician, for God's sake, not a commando.

He ventured a little further inside and was immediately struck by the dank scent of moldy furniture and carpeting. A rogue wave from the inland waterway crashed over the patio, and into the living room. Outside, Mayhem yelped, and for a second Oliver's heart trip hammered, thinking the dog might have been swept out to sea, but he breathed a sigh of relief when, through the nearly opaque veil of rain, he saw the little beast scrambling up onto the tiki bar countertop.

He got back to the task at hand.

"Bob?" Oliver called again, his voice little more than a shaky whisper.

Over the powerful wind and driving rain, a man's cry emanated from deeper in the dark structure. It sounded like a howl of pain.

He wasn't alone. Oliver willed himself not to panic.

"Hello?"

With no response forthcoming, he ventured a little deeper into the room, cognizant of the drip-drip-drip of water from the ceiling.

The place was a God-forsaken mess. A dense carpet of black mold climbed the interior walls. The bay window overlooking the patio had shattered. Every flash of lightning revealed scurrying insects.

He was torn between wishing for a flashlight and being grateful that he didn't have one.

A grungy mattress leaned against the wall where Bob kept his typewriter in the secular world. Random trash was scattered everywhere. In the kitchen, cupboard doors hung askew on their hinges, revealing broken shelves full of smashed dishware and detritus.

Oliver had a weird, seasick sensation. This he attributed to the irreconcilable schism of being in two places at once. Some impenetrable hyper-physical barrier separated this horrible place from Bob's rather comfortable home in the secular world, and he could still somehow sense the presence of that other, better place.

His nerves sang like high-tension wires in a hurricane, screaming at him to run back to the patio, grab Mayhem and use the Cast Master 4000 to escape to some other level of the multiverse.

When creeping panic made a tight knot in his throat, he closed his eyes and imagined his father patting him on the back, coaching him to breathe. In his front pocket he felt the reassuring shape of the heavenly device. He exhaled through pursed lips. He could leave if he needed to.

His breath caught. He turned to see a fat, hairy spider scurry across a rotten windowsill into a dark recess where the drywall had given way. How many of them were in here with him? A dozen? He wasn't crazy about spiders.

On the verge of turning on his heel, he heard another muffled cry.

It was a horrible sound. It was the kind of sound he associated with movies about serial killers. It was the sound he imagined Vincent Van Gogh might have made as he sawed through his own ear.

"Don't panic, Olly," he whispered. "You can do this."

He had no idea if he *could* in fact *do this*, but since nobody else was around to offer him words of encouragement....

Balling his fists in expectation of a fight, he skulked across the living room and down the hallway.

The first door was the washroom.

When he chanced a glance inside, a rat the size of a football leered back at him over the rim of the toilet bowl. The rat clawed its way onto the seat and jumped to the floor before scampering into a hole in the bottom of the vanity.

Oliver's heart pounded double-time.

"You can do this," he whispered again. "It was just a rat. You're not going to run away because of a rat."

The next room was empty, save for peeling wallpaper and warped floorboards.

That left one more, at the end of the hallway. It had to be where the sounds had come from.

He listened.

He'd read an Andy McNab book once, in which the special operator opened his mouth to improve the acuity of his hearing.

Oliver opened his mouth.

A fly flew into it, and zoomed directly past his tonsils into his airway.

He gagged, sputtered, cursed, and spat the buzzing insect onto the moldering carpet.

He crouched again, certain that whoever was in the bedroom would have heard the ruckus. He counted ten seconds, then ten more. He waited. Nothing happened.

A faint, flickering orange light emanated from the crack under the door.

Creeping forward, he pressed his ear against the splintered wood. Something shuffled on the other side. Whatever was making that noise was obviously something much bigger than a rat. Then came another agonized groan—definitely Bob this time.

"Oh... Oh God!" Bob cried.

Oliver couldn't just stand there and leave the writer to be tortured. Steeling his resolve, he took hold of the doorknob and twisted until he felt the latch come free. His pulse quickened.

Praying hinges wouldn't squeak, he pushed. It opened just enough that, with his head against the wall, he could see in.

Dim candlelight illuminated what appeared to be the only dry, and somewhat intact room in the house. Bob lay prone on a bedspread that featured depressing brown cars of the 1980s. Oliver recognized a Dodge Lancer. He had, in fact, owned a brown Dodge Lancer. He learned to see its unreliability as a virtue, since the inevitable breakdowns gave him a perfect excuse to climb out of the terribly depressing brown interior. It was not an automobile he considered to be worthy of celebration on a bedspread.

The writer lay face-down wearing only white boxer shorts and thick wool socks. His clothes lay in a heap beside the blanket, and his pink-framed drugstore glasses and Birkenstock sandals sat atop them.

With the writer's head turned away, Oliver risked opening the door a little further.

Straddling Bob's back was a very red—and very naked... woman. Candlelight flashed off the damp patina of sweat that covered her slim, athletic body. An ebony set of pointy horns rose from her surprisingly luxurious, jet-black hair. A long, thin, forked tail swished back and forth as she clawed at the writer's pale, wrinkled skin.

Bob groaned again.

Oliver blinked. Was Bob being skinned alive by some sort of blood-soaked sex devil? What the hell was happening?

He used his sleeves to wipe his glasses, certain that the raindrops on the lenses were distorting his vision. But no. The woman was bright red, from head to toe. She was not, as he had initially interpreted, covered in blood. She wasn't wearing some kind of kinky red bodysuit. Her skin was just...red! And she had a forked tail! She was a devil, just like the cartoonish demons he might have imagined as a kid!

She raised her arm. Oliver gasped. She gripped some kind of weapon. Though on closer inspection—

She swished the feather duster down against Bob's back in a playful swipe.

"Ooh..." Bob moaned. "That's the spot."

Bob was not, it would seem, being tortured for information. Bob was in the opening stages of getting laid.

"*Oh! Shit!*" Oliver said, and leapt back slamming the door.

Immediately, a commotion kicked off inside the room. The distinct sounds of a juxta-coital couple unentangling and then scrambling to clothe themselves were obvious. After a moment, Bob opened the door to the hallway and peeked out.

"Hi kid."

Bob's glasses sat crooked on his face. His hair was a sweaty mess.

"Hey Bob," Oliver said.

The writer slipped out of the bedroom and closed the door behind him.

"Is the big guy with you? And the old one?"

"No," Oliver said. "Sorry to have barged in like that. I had no idea—I thought you were being, um, tortured or something."

Bob chuckled. "Can't torture the willing, I suppose. I guess we have a classic case of *coitus interruptus*. Reminds me of my college days."

"But you still work at the college."

Bob thoughtfully fingered a part in his grey mop of hair. "That's *true*."

The writer fixed his crooked glasses. "Listen, I'm the one who should apologize. I thought I lost you."

"I was, uh, intercepted."

Bob cocked an eyebrow.

"By my father."

Bob cocked his other eyebrow.

"In heaven."

Bob cocked the space between his eyebrows. "God? You met God?"

"Wait," Oliver said. "What?"

"You just said you were intercepted by your Father in Heaven. I assumed you must be a Mormon or something."

"My *actual* father," Oliver said. "It's complicated. The important thing is, I need your help. Teddy and Bert, they're stuck in the ethereal plane, and..."

Bob removed his glasses, huffed on the lenses, and cleaned them on his bathrobe. He replaced them on his face, once again askew, and leaned against the wall. The moldy wall gave way and he tumbled through the rotten gyprock into the bathroom.

Standing, he brushed himself off, ignoring the gaping hole in the wall before giving Oliver a concerned look. "Are you high, or something? Because it sounds like you're high."

"No!" Oliver was about to launch into an explanation of the multiverse, but they heard a bang from behind the closed door, along with a woman cursing in Russian.

Bob called over his shoulder. "Irena, honey? Everything OK?"

"Yes," came the reply. "I'm almost decent. The window fell out of its frame. This place is not very romantic, Robert."

"Robert?" Oliver asked.

Bob scratched his stubble and peered at something over Oliver's shoulder. He seemed to be struggling to explain the situation. "Listen. This is all going to seem a little weird. Don't freak out, OK?" he said, and made to open the door, but paused. "And maybe don't mention Jessica. Irena can get a little hot about that stuff."

"Wait a minute! You're—you're what?" Oliver hissed, "*Cheating* on Jessica? With the...uh...reddish lady in there?"

Oliver pinched the bridge of his nose, which still stung from his fall. He suddenly wanted nothing to do with the whole Bob situation. He had enough drama to deal with. The writer's bizarre love life was well outside the purview of his mission. It probably would have been wiser just to dive into the ether, and leave the world's oldest adolescent to his own devices.

"Geez. Try not to be so judgy," Bob pleaded. "We're talking about completely separate worlds. Different realities!"

"Look," Oliver said, "I'm sorry if I sounded judgmental, but this is kind of messed up. I mean... you're tangled up in what? Some kind of interdimensional love triangle?"

"No! It's nothing like that!" Bob whispered.

Oliver waited.

Bob nodded. "OK. It is actually pretty much exactly like that. Best not to mention it to Jessica when we go back, either. I mean, it's generally don't ask, don't tell, but let's not rock the boat."

Oliver shook his head. "Fine. But you'll help me, right?"

"Sure kid. Whatever you need."

"Well, good then," Oliver said, not feeling particularly good at all. He'd been in hell for five minutes and already he was cutting deals.

"All set, honey?" Bob called.

"Yes, yes," the woman answered.

Bob opened the door to the bedroom.

Irena, the bright-red, horned woman, stood in the center of the room. She wore jeans and a military-style olive-green shirt. She'd somehow styled her thick, dark hair, and it tumbled gracefully around her obsidian horns. She wore her tail tucked out of sight. Oliver assumed it must fit down the back of one of her pant-legs. Her skin was as smooth as silk, and nearly flawless, save for the fact that it was a perfectly uniform fire-engine red.

He had to admit, she was beautiful in a very weird way. Despite her *condition*, for lack of a better word, she carried herself with confidence, and moved elegantly across the room.

He'd seen her completely nude, only seconds before, but if she was blushing, he couldn't tell. That would be one advantage, he supposed, of being the shade Peter would have undoubtedly described as "Vermillion."

Uncertain what else to do, Oliver offered a hand. "I'm Oliver Bell," he said.

"Irena Klebnova." Her hand was warm to the touch.

"Irena is my... that is to say... *our* captor, in a sense," Bob said, as means of introduction.

"Captor?!"

Oliver turned, hunting for the best exit. He could run down the hallway, jump behind the tiki bar, grab Mayhem, and then maybe he would have time to set the Cast Master 4000 before—

"Sort of," Irena said. "I'm supposed to stop the incursion of Host. It's what the LSF is all about."

"LSF"?"

"Legion Security Force. Think of it as the worst-funded spy agency in history."

Oliver groaned. He'd been captured by a demon after all, though the circumstances were a little unusual. He chastised himself for letting his guard down. But she'd been stark-naked for *Pete's sake*!

He imagined being tortured for information about his computer code. "What are you going to do to us?" he asked.

"I'm pretty sure Legion intends to kill any unauthorized visitors," Bob said. "Fortunately enough, Irena is also my underworld girlfriend. Between that, and the fact that her paycheck is barely minimum wage, she won't turn us in."

"He jokes that I am the girlfriend from hell," she chimed in.

"I see," Oliver said.

"When Bob visits the underworld, he and I spend time together," she explained. "I also happen to work for the security service that detects interdimensional traveling beings. That is how we met."

"It was very romantic," Bob said. "She nearly shot me. Luckily, I'm quite charming."

Irena shook her head. "Well, Prince Charming, you should know that the LSF was very active all day today. They were watching for an unauthorized interdimensional transit somewhere along the Gulf Coast. Specifically, we were told there could be a secular human incursion. You are lucky that I was on shift."

"Wait," Oliver said, holding up a finger. "I need to process this."

If they were on high alert for a secular human, that meant that Legion really *was* setting a trap for him. It was a monumental stroke of luck that Bob happened to be boinking the demon security agent tasked with his capture.

"Are you saying they knew we would be coming?"

Irena eyed him up and down. "I would guess that *you* are the person they are looking for, since Bob has been here a thousand times and nobody cares. Does that make sense?"

"If I say yes, are you going to turn me in?" Oliver asked.

"No," Irena said.

He turned to Bob, who appeared to be hunting through the pockets of his bathrobe for the remainder of a spliff, then back to Irena.

Her face, red though it was, appeared to be kind. Kind and mischievous. He needed Bob's help, and Bob obviously trusted her. He decided he would have to do the same.

"Then yes. I think they're looking for me."

The red woman nodded. "OK then. Hopefully they don't send anyone else."

"Who would they send?"

"Other agents like me. Only, not agents who are having a sexual relationship with Robert."

"That you know of," Bob interjected.

She punched him playfully on the arm.

Oliver's thoughts were on Amon. His instincts had him expecting a confrontation with the all-powerful demon. He'd expected the trap to be a little more elegant. "Has there been—like—a specific warning about me?"

"No, nothing like that. We were just told that a human might attempt to access the area."

"OK," Oliver said. "And LSF is some kind of police force that works for Amon?"

"Who is Amon?" Irena asked.

"They work for the party," Bob explained.

Oliver tilted his head. "'The party?'"

"It's a one-world government sort of thing," Bob explained. "Think George Orwell, only with the eternally damned. Some of them look like farm animals. It's pretty weird. Did you ever read that Canadian book? What was it called—'Pasture' or something. It was about transplanting criminals' brains into livestock?"

"Apastoral?" Oliver had, indeed, read it, when it won a book award.

"That's the one. This place is a lot like that, only the convicts with the LSF have guns, and some of them look like animals, but others are, well, for lack of a better term," at this he gestured at Irena, "pretty hot."

"And LSF works for a one-world government?"

Even as he said it, Oliver realized it made sense in a way, that centralized, unopposed power would be the order of the day in hell.

"Orwell himself could have written the constitution."

"I saw a man crushed by a George Orwell statue, not four days ago."

"Lucky it wasn't a David Foster Wallace statue," Bob said. "Now *he's* heavy."

Irena laughed.

"See?" Bob said. "I'm charming."

"So, Irena," Oliver said hesitantly, unsure how to broach the subject of her appearance, "I don't want to be rude, but are you...like—"

"Ukrainian?" she asked.

"Uh..."

Oliver didn't know what to say.

There was an awkward pause before Irena and Bob burst out laughing again.

"I'm a second-order demon," she said. "Eternally damned, if you will. I'm also Ukrainian, if you were wondering."

"What does that entail?"

"It means I was born in Ukraine."

The demon was a *comedian*.

"You *know* what I mean."

"Well, mostly it means I'm red and have horns and a tail. It's how I arrived here. Everyone here is somehow...should I say...malformed? Third-order demons look more like animals, as Robert said. Nobody looks normal here. I suppose it is part of the punishment."

"But as a demon, don't you, you know, torture the souls of the damned for all eternity?"

"That's sort of... How would you say it, Robert?"

"A stereotype," Bob said.

"Being here is not a very good time," Irena said. "You will probably already have noticed. The weather is terrible. There are bugs and rats everywhere. And the people are jerks."

"Is everywhere like this?" Oliver gestured at the hole in the wall where Bob had fallen through.

"No. Not this bad. This neighborhood was abandoned after a hurricane a few years ago. Everything is just cheap. Think 1970s Russia."

"Hopefully we won't be here too long. Our friends need help, and this was sort of a waypoint," Oliver said.

Bob scratched his chin. "Where, exactly, are the other guys?"

"They've been intentionally intercepted and transported into an uncharted extra-dimensional holding place between layers of the multiverse called the ether, presumably by a lord of the underworld named Amon. There are two schools of thought on why Amon would do this, but it is strongly suspected that this was done to set a trap for me, such that I might attempt to rescue them and end up handing over an intelligent computer algorithm I designed for my thesis, which, unfortunately, contains an instruction code for starting a nuclear apocalypse."

Bob pursed his lips. "Oh..."

Oliver was about to explain the second school of thought, when he was interrupted by a deep, terrifying growl. It came from the darkness of the hallway behind him. Low and rumbling at first, the guttural sound escalated into a feral snarl.

The trio stepped back into the bedroom, which smelled like lilacs and juniper with a faint undertone of burning sulphur.

"That can't be good," Bob said.

Though Oliver had no recollection of withdrawing it from his pocket, the Cast Master 4000 was suddenly in his trembling hand, pointed down the dark hallway toward the source of the sound.

Bob and Oliver simultaneously adjusted their glasses as though the lenses could somehow penetrate darkness if looked through just right.

The snarling intensified. It had to be some kind of predator. A tiger? Or a leopard?

"It sounds like a bear," Bob said.

"Or... maybe it's a bad demon," Irena said.

Oliver did not care for the words "bad demon," whatsoever. "I thought you said that was a stereotype."

She shrugged. "Do I contradict myself? I am large. I contain multitudes."

"Walt Whitman," Bob said. "Nice."

She continued to stare, her full attention on the dark hallway. She looked nervous, which meant that a bad demon was not something Oliver wanted to encounter.

There was a faint scratching of claws on rotten floorboards. Predatory eyes flashed in the dim candlelight.

"Oh my Lord," Bob said.

Mayhem sprinted down the hallway and growled at Irena, his lips curled upward, baring his sharp teeth.

"A puppy!" she cried, squatting to pat the not-exactly-a-puppy.

Mayhem stopped growling and turned to Oliver. Could a celestial, all-knowing being look confused? Oliver decided that yes, it was possible. He shrugged.

Mayhem let the demon stroke his wet fur for a few seconds before retreating to the dry, relatively warm bedroom where he proceeded to fluff a corner of the Boring Cars of the 1980s puff with his snout. He curled into a ball and closed his eyes.

"We never see dogs here," Irena said. "I love dogs!"

"That's Mayhem," Oliver explained, "the celestial Host."

Irena froze.

"This dog is Host?"

"Uh huh," Oliver said.

"We should leave," Irena said. "Right now."

Oliver swore he saw the color drain from her vermillion face.

"They will know he is here. They can track Host movement."

Track host movement... Oliver thought again of that phrase: *Bad demon,* and his heart skipped a beat.

"How?" Bob asked.

"Leptons," she said.

"What?" Bob asked.

"There's no time! Come on, puppy."

Irena hurried into the bedroom and scooped up the wet dog.

As tempting as it was to simply run, hell for leather, Oliver knew for certain that Bob's patio was a safe jumping-off point for interdimensional travel. He checked the dial of the Cast Master 4000. His friends were only half a level up from where he currently stood.

"Hold on," he said, "we have to get Bert and Teddy."

"No time," Irena said.

"It will only take a second!"

In his agitated state he accidentally wheeled the dial too far, and then misadjusted again in the other direction. Finally, he set it for negative twenty-six and a half, but then he remembered that, by the device's logic, whatever level he was currently on was zero, and he actually wanted to set it to zero-point-five.

"Dang it!"

"How?" Bob asked.

"How what?" Oliver asked, irritated, and still squinting at the fiddly dial in the darkness.

"How do we get Bert and Teddy?"

The writer was on a delay circuit.

"We have to find them in the ether," Oliver said. "It's complicated. That's what this thing is for."

"Your friends are in a Schrödinger state," Irena explained. "They both exist and don't exist in two adjacent tiers of the multiverse."

Oliver stopped fiddling with the Cast Master 4000. Irena, the Ukrainian red demon who was on-again, off-again dating lauded author Robert Quinn who happened to live in a different dimension, had just summed up the root of their problem in quantum physical terms.

"You know about the multiverse?" Oliver asked.

"In Ukraine, I was a theoretical physicist. Here in hell, I was on the quantum transfer-interruption build-team before I was demoted to security for insubordination."

"I never knew that about you, Irena," Bob said. "Fascinating."

"Just give me a second," Oliver said. "This is difficult in the dark."

"We should hurry," Irena urged.

He finally got the dial set. "Aha!"

He made to go to the tiki bar, but Irena pushed him in the other direction. "There is no escape from there," she said. "They will find you."

"No... we..." It was too late. Irena and Bob had already darted out the front door.

He ran at their heels to the driveway, where a Sheriff's car bearing a shield with the LSF logo sat parked. He tried to protest—but he could probably trigger the Cast Master 4000 from just about anywhere in the vicinity of Bob's house and it would work. The tiki bar was the ideal location, of course, but he would settle for the driveway.

Before he could explain, Irena wrenched open the back door of the cruiser and shoved him in.

"No wait!"

She slammed the door, and then she and Bob climbed in the front seats. She set mayhem on the center console. The dog whined.

The sulfurous smell of burned matches was stronger in the car, and Oliver wondered if the smell was coming from Irena, or if it was just some trace chemical in the atmosphere of the underworld.

She tried the ignition but the car just clicked. She swore. She tried again, but the engine wouldn't turn over.

"What's wrong?" Bob asked.

Rain hammered down on the roof and Oliver strained to hear.

"In hell, nothing ever works like it's supposed to," she explained.

"It's OK," Oliver said. "If we could just go back to the tiki bar, we can use this thing to—"

A pair of headlights slashed through the storm and illuminated the moldering house.

"Oh no," Irena said.

"Bad demons?" Bob asked, shrugging deeper into his bathrobe.

"Security. This will be a problem. Back inside the house!" she exclaimed. "Hurry!"

Bob turned to Oliver. "Is she running?"

"Yes."

"I'm guessing that means we should probably run too."

Bob snatched Mayhem from the console, scrambled out of the car and ran up the driveway after her.

Oliver tried to do the same, but discovered he was locked in the back and there were no door handles.

The lights grew rapidly closer, and over the storm he could hear the scream of an engine.

He banged on the window.

"Bob! Come back!"

Bob had almost made it to the front door. The writer turned around, and Oliver thought he saw Bob doing the mental calculations of how soon the headlights would arrive versus how long it would take him to free Oliver. Bob flung the dog through the front entrance and raced back to the car, popping

Oliver's door. "Hurry, kid!"

The two men sprinted to the house just as a black-and-white SUV with a flashing light-bar skidded to a stop behind Irena's cruiser.

Bob slammed the door, pressed his back to it. "So, uh, what's the plan?" he wheezed. His glasses had fogged, and his bathrobe was sopping wet. He looked miserable.

Irena produced a set of zip ties from the back pocket of her jeans.

"Hands behind your back," she said. "Both of you."

"What?" Bob said, but Irena roughly yanked his wrists and expertly zip-tied them together.

Oliver wondered what in the world had possessed him to trust her. She was a demon, and one who looked exactly like what he had imagined a demon would look like. He felt like a complete idiot.

He considered shooting her with the Cast Master 4000 and taking his chances with the ethereal realm, but couldn't just leave Mayhem. His father had been very clear about not breaking that bond.

"Mayhem!" he whispered. With or without Bob, he was getting out of here. For one thing, he didn't want to end up in a position where he might be forced to disclose the doomsday code. Perhaps more importantly, Teddy, Bert, and Emma were depending on him.

"Now you," Irena said to Oliver.

"I... I don't think so," he said, raising the device. He figured if he could momentarily cast a glamour on Irena, it would at least buy him and Bob a minute to find Mayhem and escape.

"You have to trust me." Irena continued to approach him. "I am not a bad demon. I would not hurt you."

There was sadness in her eyes. She seemed to fully expect him not to trust her.

Weirdly, he *wanted* to believe her. When he'd heard a podcast about the BTK killer, Oliver had wondered why anyone in their right mind would allow themselves to be restrained by a home invader. Now, he realized, it was because people *wanted* to believe they would be OK—that their captor would keep his word. They acted on what they *hoped* was the truth.

Was he making the same fatal mistake?

"OK," he said. "OK."

He slipped the Cast Master 4000 into his butt pocket, and then turned so she could restrain him.

She zip-tied his wrists together just as the front door crashed open and a portly man with a pig snout instead of a nose barreled into the entryway. The man wore a drenched green uniform that strained at the buttons over his ample belly. He was pointing a pistol this way and that and shouting in a surprisingly high-pitched voice. What he was shouting was anyone's guess, because the man was obviously very excited. When he gulped air after every few lines of shouted, incoherent instructions, his pig snout made a snuffling sound.

"Whoa, whoa, whoa!" Irena exclaimed.

The portly man panicked upon hearing her voice and fired two rounds into the ceiling four inches to Oliver's left.

Deafened by the gunshots in the enclosed space, Oliver hit the deck, which was no easy feat given the position of his hands zip-tied behind his back. He bumped his forehead hard, and the bridge of his nose took another solid whack.

"Did I get him?" the pig-man asked, as if wildly thrilled at the possibility of having just shot someone.

"No!" Oliver said. "I'm OK."

With much awkwardness he got back to his feet.

The pig-man pointed the pistol at Oliver again and squeezed the trigger. A section of damp drywall to his right crumbled and Oliver dropped to the ground once more, hitting his forehead a second time.

Maybe he wasn't going to be interrogated after all. Maybe he would just be murdered. Or maybe it was just hard for Amon to find good help. It was impossible to know why things were taking this particular turn. In either event, he was pretty sure he had a concussion.

"Calm down!" Irena shouted. "I have them in custody!"

"Wh—what?" the man said, eyes darting back and forth between Irena, Oliver and Bob.

"I have them in custody," she said. "Commander Irena Klebnova. I'm with LSF."

"Oh," the pig-man said. He seemed to realize he was outranked, and made to snap to attention. In doing so, he pointed his smoking pistol directly at his own temple. Oliver winced.

"Constable Mike Knudson. Group Six, Enforcement Division."

"At ease, Constable," Irena ordered.

The man relaxed slightly, lowering the pistol and sweeping the entirety of his upper body with the muzzle in the process. Resting his hands on his hips, he jabbed the barrel of the gun into his belly.

"So which of these vermin is the Host?" he asked.

"Vermin?" Bob asked. "What is this, a cartoon?"

Irena cleared her throat, addressing the constable. "I plan to question them."

Constable Mike Knudson looked uncomfortable, shifting back and forth. "My, uh, orders, as I understand them, are to shoot on sight."

"And those orders are from Enforcement Division?" Irena asked.

"Uh, well…" Mike Knudson said.

"Are those *really* your orders?" Irena asked. "I can check. Or were your orders, perhaps, to *capture* them?"

"I believe," Constable Mike Knudson snuffled a snuffle that Oliver thought of as the snuffle one makes when one who has a pig-snout for a nose is embarrassed in front of a senior officer, "there may have been something about capturing them."

Irena shook her head. "Mike—can I call you Mike? These are high-value prisoners. They have information we need."

"What kind of information?" Mike Knudson, the pig-man, asked.

"You know I can't disclose that."

While Irena was huddled with Mike, she waggled fingers behind her back: a clear signal to Oliver and Bob that they should make their escape through the open patio door, toward the tiki bar.

They made short, shuffling steps in that direction.

Bob had almost made it, and Oliver was just behind, when a flash of lightning illuminated them in the doorframe.

"Hey!" Mike said. "They're escaping!"

He raised his pistol and pointed it at Oliver just as Mayhem came bounding into the living room from the hallway. The small yellow not-terrier launched itself in an arc across the living room. The dog had transformed somehow. Impossibly long and serrated canine teeth protruded like the fangs of a sabertoothed tiger. In that moment, Mayhem was the most terrifying animal Oliver had ever seen.

The animal's jaws clamped down on the pig-nosed officer's arm.

"Yowch!" Mike screamed. The gun, with a hand still firmly gripping the butt, fell to the floor. Arterial blood fountained from the stump of his wrist.

Oliver stared at the pumping stump in shocked disgust. *Danger Level Two* was all he could think. It echoed around and around in his brain as he watched Constable Mike Knudson exsanguinating on the mildew-stained carpet. *Danger Level Two.* Was two more dangerous than one? How many danger levels were there?

Oliver recognized that he was wondering these things to avoid concentrating on the unfolding horror show.

"Ah!" Mike Knudson cried. "Oh no! I needed that hand!"

Oliver could smell blood. It smelled like the way metal tastes in your mouth.

Danger Level Two had sounded so innocuous. Like it was the second most harmless of all the danger levels. But the scale must be inverted! Danger Level Two was... like... *a lot* of danger!

"Oh gosh!" Mike Knudson's voice sounded weak. His face grew pale. "Oh shoot!"

"That's...pretty gross," Bob said as an arc of arterial blood fountained out of Mike Knudson's stump and streamed over the writer's shoulder, spattering on the wall behind him.

The pig-faced man feebly kicked at the Mayhem. Mayhem dodged and retreated to the doorframe—where he turned to face the constable. The dog's mouth yawned wide, showing off the ghoulish serrated fangs once again. An intense jet of hot emerald light exploded from what Oliver could now only think of as "the were-terrier."

The brilliant green flame sliced soundlessly through the room. Oliver felt a tingling electric shock sensation, as though he'd touched the lead of a battery.

For a second, the pig-man wore a dazed expression. Then his eyes rolled back in his head, and the top half of his body slid sideways off the bottom half.

The upper three-eighths of Mike Knudson hit the floor in a splash of entrails and internal organs. Mayhem had severed the constable as cleanly as a razor-sharp guillotine.

Oliver spun away from the gore. His gorge rose in his esophagus. "I—I need some air!"

Mayhem, once again in his normal, seemingly harmless domesticated canine form, sat in the doorway panting.

"This is...not good," Irena said. "He would have been wearing a monitor."

Over the shrieking wind, a new sound rose.

A siren wailed, the klaxon loud enough that Oliver would have covered his ears if his hands weren't zip-tied behind his back. It reminded him of the heavenly trumpets he'd experienced earlier on a very different plane of the multiverse, but this sound, though of a similar volume, was digital and dissonant.

"We need to go!" Irena exclaimed, heading for the front door.

"Wait!" Oliver said.

There were *enough* variables at play here. *Too many,* in fact. The tiki bar should work as a stepping-off point. It was a proven entity. That meant if they *could* travel from the tiki bar, they *should* travel from the tiki bar.

He knew he was probably overthinking it, but overthinking it, at that moment, helped him forget the slopping noise Mike Knudson's ruptured small intestine made when it uncoiled on the wet carpet. Aside from that, the severed corpse was blocking his path to the front door.

"Out here!" He pointed to the patio and darted out the ruined back door, sprinting for the bar just as the thatched roof gave in to the wind and blew off its posts and into the inland waterway.

"Irena, can you cut us loose?" he shouted.

"No," she said. "No knife!"

Oliver reached into his butt pocket and produced the Cast Master 4000.

Between the abandoned homes, he saw headlights converging at the end of the road. Black shadows and harsh xenon light raced over the patio in sequence as vehicles barreled toward the twenty-seventh level of hell's version of Bob's house.

Oliver stopped dead in his tracks, skidding in the muck that had pooled on the patio stones. Irena and Bob banged into him.

"What?" Irena said. "What now?"

"My banana!" he screamed. "Where's my banana!?"

"No time!" Bob said. "In fact, I'm kind of surprised you're hungry after what just happened in there."

"No..." Oliver cursed. Now wasn't the right moment to be explaining the technical ins and outs of interdimensional risk management. "I'm eliminating variables. The banana is a known entity!"

"I have no idea what you're talking about!" Bob shouted over the storm.

"Just look for the banana!"

Over the cacophony of the howling storm and the screaming sirens, Oliver heard screeching brakes. Doors thumped closed. Someone barked orders.

"They're here!" Irena shouted.

Oliver was tempted to sarcastically thank her for narrating the blatantly obvious, but decided there was no time, and besides, just because the situation was tense, it was hardly an excuse to act like a jerk.

"Get the dog!" Oliver said.

"What?"

"The dog! Get the dog!"

Irena grabbed Mayhem, who, despite the chaos, seemed perfectly calm, if somewhat nonplussed to be back out in the cold rain.

Oliver nosed through the shambles of the tiki bar, using his swollen fore-head to push debris aside. The usually quiescent reptilian portion of his brain realized that he could point the device at literally anything at all and it would probably work, but the logical part of his brain that was supposed to listen to advice from the reptilian part had turned off and decided to go on strike the moment the pig-faced police officer had been cut in half by his dog.

The banana, he thought, was a proven entity. The banana must be recovered!

"Aha!" he exclaimed, squatting low and turning so his zip-tied hands could grab the fruit from the ground where the storm had blown it.

A shot rang out. The countertop just above his head exploded in a shower of splinters.

He tossed the banana on the patio stones, aimed the Cast Master 4000 from behind his back, and fired. Immediately the banana was transformed into the rotting skunk carcass.

"Ew!" Bob said.

Another deafening rifle shot cracked from the side of the house, and this time Oliver swore he felt the bullet whiz by, brushing the small hairs on the back of his neck.

He ran full tilt past the end of the bar and shouted, "Grab hands!"

He and Bob both turned sideways, so they were butt-to-butt. They grasped hands. Irena reached between them with a free hand and locked her grip onto Oliver's arm. Following Oliver's cue, they lunged headlong into the stinking skunk.

— *Fourteen* —

The journey was over in a flash. Oliver materialized lying on his back. His clothing still felt sopping wet, but the patio stones upon which he lay were thankfully warm and dry. He pressed himself against the ground, his body hungry for the heat.

He felt a little strange. Not sick, necessarily, but off-kilter.

From his vantage point, he stared up at a magnificent painting of Bob's tiki bar.

"Weird," he said.

His voice sounded tinny, as though it were coming from a phone's speaker.

The canvas before him was huge, filling his field of view, and obscuring everything else. The artist had certainly captured the essence of the structure. All the drinks were there, rendered perfectly in two dimensions, only, the painter had drawn them from an atypical perspective. The light reflected incorrectly off the right side of the glass bottles, and the shadows fell to their left side, but it should have been the other way around from where Oliver lay, and he couldn't put his finger on why it was so disorienting.

He remembered a painting he'd seen in a long-ago high school art history class—*The Ambassadors*, by Holbein. It was one of only a handful of artworks he could recall, and this was chiefly because the artist had included a strange, anamorphic skull that could only be seen when the viewer looked down on the painting from atop a flight of stairs.

The piece before him brought *The Ambassadors* to mind. He was looking at it from the wrong angle, he was sure, and it would all make sense if he could find the correct vantage point.

Aside from the unusual perspective of the rendition of the tiki bar, the details were astounding. The bananas, the book Bob had been reading (*She Sang to Them, She Sang,* by W.D. Clarke), the blender, half full of now melted daiquiri (seeing this, his stomach did a flip), even the overhanging palm trees had been captured perfectly, to the point of photorealism.

He turned to see how the massive painting was being displayed, and he gasped.

Bob's house, too, looked like a painting.

He sat upright and stared at his legs, which would better be described as "drawings of his legs."

"Oh," he said. "This can't be good!"

He was flat. Flat as a pancake? No. Flatter than a pancake. Flat as a crêpe, was more like it. He tried to inspect his hand, but his flat arms were still somehow bound behind his flat back with Irena's flat plasticuffs.

The experience, he imagined, was like something out of an extraordinarily terrible acid trip.

Picturing all the things that could make one flat in the secular world—steamrollers, falls from tremendous height and being sat upon by large, sub-Saharan mammals, to name a few, Oliver's primary concern was that being flat was not a survivable condition.

He rubbed his flat back, with flat, tethered hands, and tried to assess whether or not his flat internal organs were still functioning. He guessed that they must be, because he wasn't in any pain. Still, he suspected that any human being who had ever been flattened would immediately recommend against it.

He looked at Bob. Bob looked like a halibut.

"Ahhh!" Oliver screamed.

"You look like a halibut," Bob said, his voice digital and trebly.

"So do you!"

"You both look like halibuts!" Irena said, getting awkwardly to her feet.

"And you look like a red halibut with horns," Bob said.

"Where's the dog?" Irena asked.

Mayhem whined and, turning sideways, appeared to materialize from nothing. The not-exactly-a-dog was as thin as a sheet of paper.

"What's going on here?" Bob asked.

"We are between tiers of the multiverse," Irena explained. "The third dimension is immature."

"Immature? What does that mean?"

"Have you ever been around a teenage boy? They joke about flatulence all the time. They are very annoying."

"What?" Bob looked very much like a bewildered halibut wearing pink drugstore glasses.

"Well, the third dimension is immature in a completely different way."

"Oh."

Oliver squinted into the night, but he could barely see anything. Only when he maneuvered around the patio was he able to reconcile the appearance of the tiki bar with the ambient evening light. The entire structure was roughly as thick as a manhole cover.

He tried to cast away thoughts of immature third dimensions, and impossible physical phenomena, and instead focus on his primary mission.

"Teddy? Bert?"

There was no reply. Maybe they were in the house.

He turned until he could see the two-dimensional structure of Bob's house. Walking to the back door, his thighs chafed, as he was unable to separate them.

"This is really uncomfortable."

"What is?" Bob asked.

"Thigh friction."

"Agreed," Bob said.

After a few steps, Oliver realized the best way to get around was to hop with his right foot always ahead of his left, the way he'd seen Neil Armstrong and Buzz Aldrin do it on the moon.

When he moved, he felt like a construction-paper-cutout character from the original season of *South Park*.

"This is ridiculous," he complained.

The red woman nodded her halibut-like head in affirmation.

Oliver entered the house through the patio door, which was no more than a slit in the wall. Bob, Irena, and Mayhem followed.

"Did you know the dog could zap people in half?" Bob asked as he tried to manipulate a light switch with his nose.

"You know what? I did not," Oliver said.

Since first materializing in the celestial multiverse, Oliver had assumed the role of a new pet owner getting to know his dog. It couldn't be helped. He was now in the unique position of being a new pet owner who just learned that his dog was capable of extraordinary violence using cosmic superpowers. He didn't want to think about what had happened to Constable Mike Knudson. It made his stomach turn. He didn't feel particularly guilty, per se; the man had, after all, tried to kill him twice. But still, the punishment seemed a little extreme, given the ineptitude with which the crime had been committed.

He wondered if the dog could use its powers for other tasks, and then he had an idea. He called Mayhem. The two-dimensional terrier happily sauntered over, apparently unconcerned about its lack of three-dimensional substance.

"Mayhem, can you use your sci-fi, telekinetic laser powers to cut these zip ties?" Oliver asked.

The dog flopped on the disconcertingly linear ground and chewed furiously at its two-dimensional tail.

"Never mind."

Bob finally succeeded with the wall switch. The switch flipped with a click, there was a dull hum, and they were gradually bathed in an ethereal blueish-purple glow.

Oliver was sure he'd seen light like this somewhere, but he couldn't place it. Maybe in a physics lab, or maybe—.

"Um... what's with this?" Bob asked. "Why are the lights blue?"

"Interesting," Irena said. "This is Čerenkov Radiation."

"Radiation!?"

The writer looked very much like a startled halibut.

Now Oliver remembered! The blue glow—it was the same light seen around nuclear reactors as photons from the fission process hit the surrounding water. "It's light that's made when photons move through a medium faster than the speed of light in that medium. It means that light and the atmosphere here must be out of sync. Either light moves faster, or the air is somehow denser."

"Is it dangerous?" Bob asked.

"No."

"Good."

Bob made his way to the kitchen, but stopped at the threshold. "Irena, honey, I can't exactly fathom what it is I'm looking at here, but could you see if there's a knife in one of those drawers, so you can cut these zip ties?"

In the place where the kitchen was supposed to be, there was a swirling vortex. It appeared to contain hundreds of millions of stars and galaxies. It made a faint buzzing sound, like a worn-out fluorescent lightbulb. Oliver did not know exactly what it was, but his intuition told him that to stare into the vortex was to invite unrelenting madness into one's soul.

"Hmm," Irena said. "That's pretty weird."

She fumbled around the edge of the now-pulsating cosmic wormhole in the kitchen. She vanished.

"Oh my God!" Bob screamed. "Irena!"

"What?" Irena said from behind the wormhole.

"Oh," Bob said. "You didn't get sucked into the cosmic portal thing?"

"No. But don't stare at it. I suspect it may trigger some kind of unrelenting madness of the soul."

"Hey," Oliver said, "that's exactly what I thought."

"Yes, it would obviously be psychologically devastating," she said. "Don't look at it, Robert."

"OK."

When she reappeared from the edge of the wormhole, she brandished a kitchen knife.

She cut the restraints off their wrists.

"Thanks," Oliver said. "I'm sorry, by the way, that I almost turned you into an interdimensional portal back there in your home tier of the underworld. I thought you were going to turn us in, and that we would be tortured."

"Don't mention it," she said. Her voice wavered a little.

She was obviously anxious. Oliver wondered if she'd stared too long at the portal.

"Everything OK?"

"I thought for a second I had cut off your thumb when I was cutting the zip tie," she said. "The flatness is freaking me out. Everything just kind of looks like lines back there."

Oliver checked his thumbs.

"Still attached," he said, smiling. "See?"

He wiggled them for Irena to see.

"Oh... please don't smile," she begged. "You look like a happy halibut. It gives me weird feelings."

"Sorry."

He turned to the hallway that led to the bedrooms and bathroom. "Bert? Teddy? Are you guys here?"

"Maybe they're outside," Bob suggested.

Oliver did his best to search the rest of the house, but he kept banging into walls. As soon as an object was out of plane, it simply looked like a line that blocked his vision. It was almost impossible to gauge distances.

On his way to the front door, Oliver came across a large structure that blocked his path.

"What's this?" he asked.

Irena shimmied past him. "A Chesterfield," she explained.

"Oh."

He backed up, then tried to follow her around the object. Once facing it, it did look like a worn-out brown-velour Chesterfield. The problem was that the Chesterfield was really almost no more real than a painting of a Chesterfield. From one angle Oliver could see the seat and the cushions and the back, but from another angle, the couch appeared to be no more than a thin, beige tube. It was surprisingly difficult to convince his legs to walk beside the object, instead of directly into it.

Mayhem, panting, tried to jump on the Chesterfield, then yelped as he ricocheted off, and landed in a two-dimensional tangle on the floor.

Losing his balance, Oliver reached out to grab the seat cushion.

"Ouch," he exclaimed, pulling his hand back and inspecting it.

"What?" Bob asked.

"It gave me... well... I want to say a paper cut," Oliver said. "I miss the third dimension."

"I guess it's like Joni Mitchell said. 'You don't know what you got 'till it's gone,'" Bob mused.

Oliver frowned. "I read a book by Andy Weir once. It was about waking up on a distant space station. He talked a lot about how humans can basically adapt to any situation, and will just manage to get on with things, regardless of whatever craziness is happening in their environment."

"Yeah?" Bob said.

"I'm not sure Andy Weir ever tried living in two dimensions though."

"Probably not."

Irena ran into the door frame on her way out to the walkway.

"Son of a bitch," she said.

There was no car in the driveway, which was just as well. Driving would be a suicide mission.

Oliver decided he hated the ethereal plane. He wasn't very keen on hell, either, for that matter. As soon as they found Bert and Teddy, they were getting the heck out of Dodge.

He banged his shin on the mailbox post at the end of the driveway, and stooped to rub it.

"We've got to find Teddy and Bert," he grumbled through clenched teeth. "I hate this place so much."

"How do we find them?" Bob asked. "They could be anywhere. Given how flat everything is, would we even see them?"

It was a good question. Oliver had no idea where they might be, and there was a very real possibility that he could walk right past them without seeing them, since in all probability they were no more substantial than a sheet of cardboard.

Two things worked in their favor. The immature third dimension made getting around so difficult that Oliver guessed they couldn't have gotten too far. And secondly, sound, though altered, still seemed to work.

"We could... ah... I don't know—try yelling, maybe?"

"Gotcha," Bob said.

"Teddy! Bert! Can you hear me?" Oliver called.

His voice echoed back to him, from houses that appeared to be painted onto a backdrop of night sky.

They were about half way to Gulf Boulevard when a temblor struck. The quake was strong enough to send them sprawling to the pavement.

"Oof." Oliver somehow managed to elbow himself in the stomach.

He sucked wind.

Before he could get up, the ground lurched again, and then, oddly, the chunk of atmosphere that surrounded them seemed to swirl away. It wasn't wind, exactly. It was more the sensation that the world was a jigsaw puzzle and one critical part had just been inhaled into the turbine of a hairdryer.

Oliver gasped. "Something weird is..."

Mayhem yipped, and then, to Oliver's astonishment, lifted off the tarmac and floated past, toward a streetlamp, the dull, greasy blue light from which began to blink on and off. The not-precisely-a-dog pawed helplessly at the air.

Mayhem was... what? Flying? Not exactly. It looked more like it was... *falling up.*

"Hey!" Oliver said, reaching for the celestial being.

As soon as he extended his arm, *he* floated off the ground. It seemed like the ground was falling away from him into some kind of sinkhole, and he was simply stagnant in space. He couldn't help but think of the coyote in the Roadrunner cartoon, suspended in mid-air after running off the edge of a cliff.

Whipping his two-dimensional head back and forth, he established that the ground was relatively immobile, and he was somehow rising away from it. He screamed.

"Did anyone just hear a child scream?" Irena shouted, craning her two-dimensional neck in an apparent effort to locate the source.

"I... I heard it too," Oliver said, sheepishly, as he wafted another two feet above the earth's surface.

"What's happening?!" Bob shouted. His body tumbled in an unwieldy somersault.

"It's gravity!" Irena said. "It's stopped working! Try to grab my hand!"

She was also floating, though, of the four of them, she was the only one who appeared to be managing her sudden buoyancy with any sense of grace.

Oliver stretched toward Mayhem, but it was hopeless. The dog was too far away.

Irena accelerated past. He missed her hand and grabbed her ankle instead. He felt himself suddenly jerked upward. The best he could figure, she'd managed to push off something when she felt herself lifting. They were on a straight path to Bob and Mayhem.

Irena reached out for the writer and caught him by his hair just as Oliver finally caught Mayhem by his hind leg. Bob's somersaulting momentum threw the whole group into a slow, awkward tumble as they ascended into the overcast night sky.

"Try to grab the light pole!" Irena said.

Oliver tucked Mayhem under his arm, and reached for the pole. He was too late, missing it by roughly six feet.

"I missed it!"

"You sure did!" Bob said. "Wow."

They continued their trajectory, tumbling steadily through the two-dimensional sky, like a tangled flatfish pretzel.

Oliver resigned himself to the fact that they were probably going to die. He didn't want to die. He especially didn't want to die without at least finding Bert, Teddy, and Emma. But floating off into the sky, it seemed he wasn't going to have much say in the matter.

He wasn't terrified of death, per se. He'd seen heaven, after all. It was a pretty nice place, though he'd hoped to have at least five or six more decades before taking up permanent residence.

All this reflecting on his certain impending doom did raise a question. Could he get there from here?

"Irena," he said, "when we run out of oxygen, or when gravity kicks back in and we fall to the ground and splatter, what happens to us? Do we actually die here?"

"In the underworld? Yes. In ether? I am not sure. Keep in mind, I am a physicist, not a theologian."

"Oh." He was a little bit disappointed that she didn't know, but now that he thought about it, he didn't think he would be comforted by an answer either way.

"The pig-guy certainly seemed to die," Bob observed.

"Yes, Robert," Irena said, "you have made a good observation. But that was not the ether. That was the regular underworld."

"I'm very observant," Bob said. "It's an attribute that all full-time writers develop."

"Oh yeah?" Irena challenged. "Then what is this young man's name?" She nodded towards Oliver.

"Um. Give me a second." He closed his eyes in obvious concentration, looking exactly like a floating halibut lost in deep thought, and Oliver had to look away because a floating halibut in deep thought is a very unsettling thing to look at. "Phil?"

"Close enough," Oliver said. He expected no better.

They watched the lights of the small, flat, Floridian community grow distant below them, and then they were in the cold, damp, flat clouds.

Oliver's ears popped.

He wasn't a particularly big fan of heights. Now that he was dangling in the sky, suspended by nothing at all, he felt very much unnerved. It was such a strange way to die. He tried to imagine what Gerald, his postdoctoral supervisor, would have done in the same situation. He was quite certain that Gerald would have absolutely soiled himself.

Despite everything, Oliver smiled.

Irena started shivering.

"Are you OK?" Oliver asked.

"I have poor cold tolerance," she explained.

Oliver pulled himself up along her pant leg and jacket until he was alongside her. Bob, getting the idea, did the same on the other side. With Mayhem in the middle, clutched to Irena's chest, they squeezed together to preserve body heat.

Even through her clothing, Irena radiated warmth. Oliver could see why the writer found her physically appealing. That feverish warmth was strangely exotic.

Her teeth chattered, and Oliver tried hugging her tighter, pressing the wider part of his two-dimensional frame against hers to increase the surface area. He felt Bob do the same.

"Any better?"

"A little. Thank you."

On the ground, there had been a background humming sound that was no longer present. Their ascent was completely silent. The stillness of the atmosphere was one more factor that made it hard to judge just how high they had climbed. Oliver tried to guess by the temperature. It had, after all, been warm back at the tiki bar. But the heat radiating from Irena made it difficult to judge just how cold the air had grown.

"You're hot!" Oliver said.

"Thank you."

Oliver blushed. "I mean…"

"She knows what you mean, kid," Bob said. "And stop blushing. Blushing halibuts look really messed up."

In a rush of air, their ascent quickened.

"Whoa! Did you guys feel that?"

"We're speeding up," Irena said. "Entropy is winning."

"Hey. I've been meaning to ask," Bob said. "How did you end up in hell?"

"You've never asked?" Oliver was amazed.

"It never occurred to me," Bob said. "I mean, you said yourself, she's hot. I didn't really need the whole back story."

Irena laughed at Oliver's discomfort. "Do you remember Chernobyl? I was the nuclear physicist who suggested we could save money by tipping the boron rods with graphite."

"Really?" Oliver said. "But there's no way you could have known that would cause an explosion. It was a freak accident."

"I knew there was some risk. In an emergency, the graphite might accelerate the reaction. I never imagined it would actually happen."

"And you got eternity in hell for that?"

"I had the best intentions," Irena explained.

"So the old adage is true," Bob said to himself. "Remarkable."

"What adage?"

"You know… the road to Hell…"

Irena shook her head. "What road?"

"It's paved…" Bob said, circling his two-dimensional wrist, presumably waiting for her to finish.

"There is no road," Irena said. "It's a different dimension."

"With good intentions," Bob said.

"Dimensions don't have intentions. They're inanimate."

"Never mind."

"Still, eternity in hell for an accident? That seems kind of harsh," Oliver observed.

"Well, I also had a thing for married men," she shrugged.

Oliver's ears popped again. Now he could feel the cold. Anywhere his skin was exposed, it was starting to freeze. He shivered. "How high up would you guess we are?" He sounded a little bit drunk, and he was getting a headache. He understood this to mean he was developing altitude sickness.

"Somewhere between fifteen and twenty thousand feet," Irena said. "It could be more, of course. If gravity fails the atmospheric molecules too, they may be following us up here. At twenty thousand feet, assuming gravity is only affecting us, and not the air, we will run out of oxygen."

"It *is* getting a little tough to breathe, now that you mention it," Bob wheezed.

He stuffed his hand into his pocket and produced a vape pen. He clenched the device between halibutesque lips, as he first inhaled deeply, then exhaled an extremely flat stream of thick white marijuana smoke.

"That's better."

The vape pen triggered something in Oliver's mind. "Hey! The Cast Master 4000!"

"Won't it just deposit us way up in the air on some different plane of existence?" Irena asked.

"It has an altitude setting!" Oliver said, pulling the device from his pocket.

He started to adjust the altitude dial on the device, but his frozen fingers wouldn't work. He huffed a two-dimensional stream of warm air on his hands to loosen his joints, but due to his reduced tactile feedback, and two-dimensional state, he hadn't been holding the Cast Master 4000 as tightly as he'd thought. His breath was enough to push it out of his unclenched hand. It floated in space for a second. He fumbled the grab and sent it flying. He could only watch as it floated away, tumbling end-over-end.

He thought about pushing off from the group and going after it, but that would do no good. He would have no way of getting back to Bob, Irena and Mayhem. He could save himself, but what about them? He couldn't just leave them.

There were no options. The Cast Master 4000 was gone.

He realized with horror: he had just killed Bob and Irena. Mayhem, the celestial Host, had just been relegated to an eternal existence floating through the ether. And Teddy, Bert, and Emma were stuck here for the rest of their lives.

What a colossal dumb-ass he was!

He wanted to wallow in self-pity for a moment, but the situation demanded otherwise. Sure, he could act emotionally and irrationally. He could maybe even have himself a little cry. He certainly felt like it. But when, in the history of human existence, had an emotional breakdown solved a crisis? Psychologists might tell you not to bottle up your emotions, and that catharsis is somehow good for you. But when had a psychologist ever confronted a sudden, life-threatening shortage of gravity?

His mind reeled. No immediate solution was apparent. What else did he have at his disposal?

He had companions. Maybe they would have an idea.

"So, uh..."

Bob apparently noticed the Cast Master 4000 tumbling off into the distance.

"Did...you happen to drop the life-saving device just now?" Bob asked.

"Yes, I did."

"I'm going to go out on a limb here and guess that you didn't play a lot of sports as a child."

"No, sir, I did not," Oliver confirmed.

"Can the dog fix this?" Bob asked.

Oliver looked at the terrier. "Mayhem? Any ideas buddy?"

Mayhem blinked meaningfully back at him.

"No," Oliver reported.

Back in his days as a curious high-school student, Oliver had read about test pilots and astronauts who would pass out in the centrifuge during training, due to cerebral hypoxia. All their blood would pool in their extremities, and the G-forces they experienced could not be overcome by their circulatory system. They described the experience as a greying out of their peripheral vision, with the grey curtain getting larger and larger until it was all they could see.

Oliver didn't want to give up, but he was greying out.

He realized that either they had ascended somehow faster than the oxygen molecules in the air, or else all the oxygen in the atmosphere was simply floating off into space like Helium. Either way, the end was imminent.

Thinking about astronauts triggered a memory. Hadn't Bob said Irena almost shot him when they first met?

"Irena?" Oliver gasped. "Do you have a gun?"

"I don't think suicide is the answer," she wheezed.

"No... I'm thinking more Newtonian physics."

Her eyes widened in understanding. "Yes! Equal and opposite reaction!"

It took her a moment to rummage through her two-dimensional jacket pocket. She produced what looked like a paper cutout of a semiautomatic pistol.

"Which way?" she asked.

"The device is over there!" Oliver pointed to the place where he'd last seen the Cast Master 4000.

She pointed the pistol in the opposite direction, and took a moment to manually override the two-dimensional safety.

"Hold on!" she said.

Oliver gripped her tighter and felt Bob do the same.

When she pulled the trigger, instead of a bang, the gun made a sizzling sound. Smoke and sparks poured from the barrel, giving the effect of some kind of dollar-store firework.

A lazy, flat copper-plated projectile slowly spun from the end of the muzzle. Oliver plucked it out of the air.

"Newton is turned off too," Irena said.

They really were screwed.

"Frig."

They burst through the stratospheric layer of cirrus clouds and suddenly the sky above them was a brilliant curtain of stars.

Oliver realized he had stopped shivering and actually felt warm. He remembered something he'd read about climbers stranded in the death zone of Everest. Even though they were literally freezing to death, they often described feeling overheated. Bodies were found semi-nude. The phenomenon was called "Paradoxical undressing."

Oliver thought that this was a very weird thing to think about as his final coherent thought, and that it had been very statistically unlikely that such a final thought would be his own.

Bob, gazing up at the stars, sighed. "At least *that's* 3D."

"It's beautiful," Oliver said. "I'm finding it a little tough to oxygenate my brain though, if I'm being honest."

"Yeah. Cool way to go, though, you have to admit."

"I am hallucinating," Irena said.

"Lucky you," Bob said, squeezing her as best he could around the waist, and taking another deep pull from the vape pen.

"A giant man-moth is in the sky."

"A mammoth?" Oliver said, craning his neck to see the stars. He assumed she was referring to a constellation of some kind.

"No," Irena said, sleepily. "A man-moth."

She dropped the impotent gun and it floated away.

The grey curtain spread over most of Oliver's vision, and he gawped, halibut-like, at the air that was no longer there.

"Whelp," Bob panted. "It's been groovy."

Oliver felt Bob relax his grip, and then he let go of the others.

The last thing he saw was Mayhem, floating into the stars.

— Fifteen —

Oliver came around gradually, as if waking from a dream. Cool wind rushed through his hair, and the collar of his paisley shirt flapped against his cheek, gently slapping him back to consciousness. He opened his eyes to find he was descending through the two-dimensional clouds.

He shifted slightly. Something rigid, prickly, and pinchy had made its way down the back of his pants and seemed to be gripping him by his gluteal cleft.

In a daze, he panicked and grabbed at the thing. It was as thick and as solid as a two-by-four, and was, to his horror, covered in bristly, coarse hairs that brought to mind Jeff Goldblum's transformation in *The Fly*.

The hairy thing retracted from his pants and Oliver fell freely back toward the earth. He had time to gaze upward and see a gigantic creature—part moth and part human—hovering above. His friends' lifeless, two-dimensional bodies dangled below the creature's carapace, each individual suspended on an extended, articulated limb.

The moth-man glided effortlessly, its enormous and very three-dimensional bulk dwarfing the flat shapes of Irena, Bob and Mayhem. Oliver estimated its wingspan at twenty-five feet.

The creature was nude, which Oliver supposed most creatures were, but the human characteristics of the thing made its nudity a particularly striking feature. The head, for instance, was human. Its hair was pulled back in a greasy ponytail. From the neck up, it looked like an actor in a movie about an outlaw biker gang. From the Adam's apple down, however, things got pretty weird. Its thorax and abdomen were segmented like those of a moth or a butterfly, and multi-jointed, insectile appendages extended from its flanks. Below the beltline, it had human legs. It was obviously male, and it was obviously not too bothered with personal grooming.

One appendage held each of Oliver's halibut-like companions, a fourth gripped a small metal device Oliver recognized as the Cast Master 4000.

Tumbling earthward, Oliver could only watch as the moth-man disappeared into the sky. Gravity had obviously come back on, full blast.

Swinging his arms crazily as he dropped, he hoped to prevent himself from somersaulting, not that it would make a heck of a lot of difference. From this height, no matter how he impacted the ground, he would end up roughly the consistency of a fruit smoothie.

Sure enough, his flailing limbs did little to dampen his two-dimensional body's awkward, adverse yaw, and he pitched and rolled helplessly, screaming the very specific type of scream screamed by people falling from the sky without a parachute.

Rolling faster and faster, Oliver caught a glimpse of the winged beast as it burst through the clouds. It dive-bombed toward him, wings tucked back, ponytail flapping crazily in its wake turbulence.

The monster plunged past him, then, using its enormous wings as an airbrake, matched his fall. Pulling alongside, it flared its body as a professional skydiving man-moth hybrid might, and inched closer.

Using its wing as a hammock, it guided Oliver into a relatively stable, face-down position, before sliding its hairy arm down the back of his pants, and gripping the top of his butt crack.

Oliver fought the instinct to wrestle himself free of the moth-man. If he wanted to avoid leaving an impact crater somewhere on the ethereal Floridian soil, he was just going to have to go along with the situation.

The creature beat its wings again, and they picked up speed.

Oliver eyed the Cast Master 4000 in the moth-man's opposite appendage, and wondered if he could somehow get to it. He was unable to formulate any meaningful plan, however, before the creature changed course, and Oliver's attention became entirely focused on the G-forces transmitted to the crack of his butt.

They entered a downward spiral.

Where were they going? A lair, probably, populated by the moth-people of the ethereal realm, where he and his friends would be cooked and eaten as a rare delicacy in this otherwise meat-devoid realm. Did moths eat meat? In the heat of the moment, he simply could not remember.

He shifted his weight, angling toward the Cast Master 4000, but the moth-man's appendage pinched down tighter and he yelped in pain.

The idea of being eaten was terrifying enough, but the idea of being eaten by a gigantic insect-human hybrid who was intent on playing a high-altitude game of grab-ass was even worse.

The hairy appendage adjusted its grip as they pitched to the right. For a second, Oliver thought he was going to slide off. His stomach lurched.

When Oliver involuntarily screamed, Bob woke up. They met one another's gaze in the shadow of the creature's thorax.

All things considered, Bob seemed to be dealing with the situation quite well. He fished the vape pen out of his bathrobe, inspected it, then took a long, thoughtful drag, before adjusting his glasses.

"Which thing happening are you screaming about?"

"The moth-man!" Oliver shouted. "Mostly."

The moth-man craned his head to look at Oliver. "I prefer the term 'Man-moth,' if it's all the same."

"Ahh!" Oliver screamed again, startled. He immediately felt foolish. "I'm sorry. I didn't know you could talk."

"Of course I can talk."

"So, are you, like, planning to eat us?"

"Come again?"

"I don't know," Oliver said, "I've never been captured by a... er..."

"A man-moth?"

"Yeah."

"No. I'm not planning to eat you."

"Well, that's good," Bob said. "I'm Bob, and this is Phil."

"Oliver," Oliver corrected him.

"Right. This is Oliver," Bob said over the sound of the rushing wind.

"Ahh!" Irena screamed as she regained consciousness.

"And that's Irena," Bob added.

"Hello," the man-moth said. "I'm Fixeloclastes Hatchoo."

"Gesundheit," Bob said.

"No, that's my last name," the man-moth explained.

"Oh."

"Why aren't you wearing pants, Fixeloclastes?" Oliver asked. Their descent had picked up speed and Fixeloclastes' hairy genitals flapped loudly against his thighs.

"For the same reason Aristophroces here doesn't wear pants," the man-moth explained.

"Who?" Oliver said.

"Aristophroces... the dog," Fixeloclastes said, hoisting two-dimensional Mayhem for them to see.

"Dogs usually don't wear pants," Bob said. "Pants would interfere with the... um..." Bob took a second as if searching for a tactful way to say the thing he was thinking about... "crapping process."

"No," Fixeloclastes said. "Aristophroces isn't wearing pants because he wasn't wearing pants when he materialized here."

"Right…" Oliver said, having no idea what the man-moth was getting at.

"Because he was an extracorporeal being in the secular world," Fixeloclastes continued.

"I smell what you're cooking," said Bob, who in all likelihood did *not smell* what Fixeloclastes was cooking at all.

"Because the dog is a celestial entity…" Fixeloclastes said.

"Of course." Oliver nodded enthusiastically, despite having no idea what the man-moth was getting at.

"He is Host," Irena said.

"Oh!" Bob and Oliver said in unison.

"Specifically, I'm the Host that goes along with your friend, Teddy," Fixeloclastes explained. "Humans refer to me as 'Goodness.'"

"It sounds like you prefer Fixeloclastes," Bob said.

"I do indeed. Aristophroces, however, prefers Mayhem. There was an incident at a Greek shipping port a few thousand years ago. It's a long story."

This was huge! Oliver had found Teddy's Host! Well, technically, Teddy's Host had found him. Either way, that meant that Teddy must be nearby. He wanted to shake his fist in excitement, but worried if he did, Fixeloclastes' appendage might somehow violate his rectum.

Gulf Boulevard came into view below. To Oliver's surprise, they were circling toward the bright yellow Angler's Cove condominium complex.

"Hey," he said. "I was just here."

"It's a vestigial place…" Fixeloclastes began.

"Yeah, I know," Oliver said, "but how do *you* know about vestigial places?"

"I'm a Host—we are eternal beings. We know these things. Also, it was the only three-dimensional structure within a hundred miles of Bob's house. We figured it would make for a good meeting place."

"Oh," Oliver said.

Wafting his majestic, three-dimensional moth wings, Fixeloclastes alit on his human-like legs in the parking lot.

Oliver was about to do the awkward two-dimensional moonwalk toward the building when Fixeloclastes stopped him with an appendage on the chest. He handed Oliver the Cast Master 4000. "You dropped this."

Oliver grabbed the device and, with some challenging two-dimensional wrangling, stuffed it into his front pocket. "Thank you!"

"Don't mention it."

"Hey!" someone shouted from the balcony of one of the apartments.

Oliver looked up and saw Teddy waving. The rush of relief that he felt, seeing his friend, made his knees weak. His heart thrilled in his chest.

"Hey Teddy!" he shouted, waving back.

"Yah!" Teddy screamed.

"What?"

"You're flat! Like a flounder!"

"We prefer 'halibut,'" Bob said.

"Wait, why aren't you flat?" Oliver asked, feeling suddenly self-conscious.

Teddy shrugged. "No idea."

"Follow me," Fixeloclastes said.

He led them through the main door of the condominium complex. As Oliver crossed the threshold, there was a loud popping sound, followed by a flash of excruciating pain as each of his internal organs seemed to explode. He assumed he'd been shot, and fell to the ground.

"Oof," he said.

"What?" Fixeloclastes asked.

Oliver looked up from the floor to see Mayhem cross the threshold. There was a similar popping sound, and the two-dimensional Host animal puffed into its three-dimensional form. Mayhem wagged his tail and licked Oliver's face.

Oliver, realizing he may have overreacted slightly, got to his feet.

"We're 3D!"

He was about to warn Bob and Irena, but before he had a chance they too crossed the dimensional threshold, and expanded into the Z-axis. Bob tripped and fell, and Irena stumbled over him.

"Geeze!" Bob said, rubbing his knee. He patted himself down, noticing the change. "Hey, wow! I'm deep again!"

Irena worked her jaw to equalize pressure in her inner ear. "That was unpleasant."

Fixeloclastes had to crouch to keep his greasy hair from hitting the ceiling. He led them up the stairwell, to the second level, and, to Oliver's complete lack of surprise, to apartment 203—the same unit where Oliver had been earlier that day, only in the nineteenth tier of the celestial multiverse, with his father. Actually, now that he thought about it, he had also briefly visited that same apartment, on the eighteenth celestial tier of the multiverse, where a woman was putting away her groceries.

Fixeloclastes knocked before announcing "It's us!"

The door flew open and Teddy barged through, pulling Oliver into a bear hug so tight that Oliver's spine cracked.

"Hey Buddy!" Oliver wheezed.

"We thought we lost you!"

Teddy's face beamed.

"Fixeloclastes—he sensed you. Until then, we figured it was something like a one-in-a-billion chance we'd ever see you again! But here you are!"

Straining to see over Teddy's muscular deltoid, Oliver peered into the kitchen. To his enormous relief, Emma leaned one hip against the island, and wore the widest smile Oliver had ever seen. He smiled back.

He turned his gaze to the living room, where Bert and a large, cobalt-blue animal that looked very much like a wallaby sat on the sofa. Bert waved. "Hey kid!"

Oliver's voice came out shaky and weak. Tears of relief threatened, and he choked them back. "Hey... hey Bert. Hey Emma."

When Teddy finally released his grip, Emma lunged across the room and folded Oliver into another snug embrace. He tensed, anticipating a Teddy-like vice-clamp of a hug, but unlike her companion she seemed to sense just how tight was tight enough. She was a wonderful hugger.

"Olly! I can't believe it!" she said. "You were so brave! Teddy told me all about the glamour, and the caster... uh... Bob."

"Hi," Bob said meekly, waving from the hallway.

Releasing her embrace, Emma held Oliver at arm's length and studied his face before pulling him close again. "I can't believe you! I just can't believe you took this on."

Now the tears did come, tracking gleaming channels through the dust on his face. "I couldn't do that to you, without, you know—trying to fix it."

She hiked an eyebrow. "Do what to me?"

"You know—the glamour that sent you here. That was meant for me."

She pushed him away. "Hon, are you serious? How on earth were you supposed to know?"

"I just..."

"Did Teddy give you that idea? That this was your fault? Because if he did, I'm going to give him a piece of my...."

"No, no, no," Oliver interrupted, hands up, palms facing her in surrender. In that moment he realized that being on Emma's bad side was perhaps a scarier prospect than going to the underworld in the first place.

Her face relaxed and she grinned. "Well, none of this is your fault. I knew it was a glamour. I figured it would take me some place or other."

"What happened to the guy?"

"The communist?"

"Yeah."

"Funny you should ask. Rick left. He was disgusted by my brand name yoga pants and by my sympathies for capitalism."

"His name was Rick?"

"Yeah. He was kind of a dick. Anyway, he decided that whether or not I could find a way out, he wanted to stay here. Since nobody else exists, he reasoned it was an ideal, egalitarian society."

"You mean he's still out there, somewhere?"

"I guess."

Oliver sighed. All thoughts of moth appendages, bisected security agents with pig snouts, and two-dimensionality were gone, replaced with the deepest sense of relief he'd ever experienced.

He pressed pause on his emotional rollercoaster of triumph, disbelief, and elation and remembered his manners.

"I'm...uh... gosh..." he blushed. "I should really be thanking you, Emma. You saved my butt back at the trailer park riot."

She used her thumbs to swipe the tears from his cheeks. "All in a day's work, kiddo."

Bert ambled over and shook Oliver's hand, and then eyed Bob and Irena.

"Where were you guys?" he asked. "And who is this?"

"Most recently, we were about thirty-five thousand feet in the atmosphere, on our way to low-Earth orbit," Bob explained, "and this is Irena."

"They were caught in the gravity quake," Fixeloclastes explained. His voice was low and resonant, the way a person with acromegaly's voice sounded. It made Oliver think of the bad guy from *Silence of the Lambs*.

Oliver turned to the man-moth. "I guess we all owe you a big thanks too."

Bob and Irena both nodded and mumbled their thanks, but Oliver continued, "Having said that, I'm not fully clear on why you had to grab me by the butt crack."

"Look, as you humans would put it, it was 'no great shakes' for me, either," Fixeloclastes said, using one of his long, hairy appendages that ended in a rudimentary claw to make air-quotes, "but I don't have opposable thumbs."

Oliver examined his own hand. "Why aren't we flat anymore?" he asked the man-moth.

"To be honest, I'd only be guessing. Three-dimensional structures are inconsistent in the ethereal plane. You know what that is, correct?"

Oliver nodded.

"Good. I brought Teddy to this building when we first materialized, because it was the only three-dimensional structure I could find. It might be due to its status as a vestigial place, but his tiki-patio is probably also a vestigial place, and it was flat, so it's hard to say. In any event, it seems everything inside has a third dimension. We dimensionalized upon entering, and then even after I left I stayed 3D. Go figure."

"How did you find Emma?" Oliver asked.

"I didn't. I found Bucky, her Host. Host are able to locate one another. It's one of the ways we coordinate. I'm quite good at it, as you may have noticed when I found Mayhem and yourselves hurtling toward the mesosphere."

"And Bucky would be...?" Oliver eyed the blue wallaby.

The wallaby stood up and scratched its belly. It hopped over. "Howdy," it said in a cartoonish lilt. "Pleased to meet you. I go by Bucky or Forbearance. Your choice."

"It can talk," Oliver marveled.

"What can talk?" Bucky asked. "The dog?"

"Never mind," Oliver said, shaking Bucky's paw.

"How come you don't have an ancient Greek name like the other Hosts?" Oliver asked.

"Well... I'm not Greek," Bucky said. "I'm from Grand Forks."

"Oh."

"Yeah."

Mayhem plodded across the living room and took his place on the couch.

Oliver turned to Fixeloclastes. "What are the odds that Emma and...er... Bucky would be on this same level of the ethereal plane? There would have to be an almost infinite probability against that happening."

"Maybe not," Fixeloclastes said.

Oliver, unsure of how good a read he could get from a greasy-haired celestial humanoid moth monster, nonetheless suspected Fixeloclastes was anxious about something. He was going to inquire about this, but was interrupted by someone pounding on the door.

"Hold on... Are we missing someone?" Bert asked.

"No," Fixeloclastes said, "this is everyone."

Teddy opened the door. Oliver peered out over his shoulder.

An odd, doll-like thing sat in the hallway. It appeared to have been made by a mad taxidermist, sewing various bits of different stuffed animals together. It was roughly the size of a domestic cat.

It had a set of forelegs like a dog, except they somehow ended in hands like those of an ape. The furry torso disappeared into a shiny purple bathrobe with white star and moon patches sewn into the satiny material, but out the back end came the diamond-patterned hind section of a fat snake. It had an owl's head, adorned with a Napoleonic tricorne hat.

Teddy laughed in delight. "Look at this weird thing!"

Oliver assumed the unfortunate object was a strange type of ethereal children's toy. "The hat is a nice touch."

"Thank you, Mr. Bell," the thing, which was not, as it turned out, an inanimate doll, said in a breathy voice.

"Ahh!" Oliver jumped back.

The creature pushed and slithered its way past Teddy and into the kitchen, where it struggled to climb onto a tall chair and then onto the table itself.

"Excuse me," Emma said. "What's going on here?"

"I'm glad you asked, Emma," the snake-owl-dog-ape thing said. "First of all, I need the two of you... Well, I suppose it's the three of you, now—" at this, the creature nodded toward Oliver "—to stop trying to kill me."

Teddy furrowed his brow. "Kill you? We don't even know you."

The snake-owl-dog turned its gaze to the man-moth. "Fixeloclastes?"

Fixeloclastes cleared his throat. "This is, uh, Amon," he said.

Oliver backed away from the creature. He imagined the little snake-dog-owl thing performing a vivisection on his brain. He pictured those strange, ape-like digits digging around in his hippocampus while he lay strapped to a medical gurney, screaming. He wanted to believe that such an idea was complete nonsense, and yet, upon inspection of the corrupt little beast, it seemed somehow plausible.

Oliver backed directly into Bucky, who caught him before he could fall to the floor.

"That's...Amon?"

Bucky nodded. "It's true. We used to hang out."

Teddy stiffened, squinting hard at the creature. "This weird little troll is captain of forty legions of hell-spawn?"

"Uh..." Fixeloclastes said.

"You're telling me this ugly spud is the great destroyer? A lord of the underworld? The renowned defiler?"

"Well..." Bucky said.

Fast as lightning, Teddy snatched a potted cactus from the kitchen counter and hurled it at Amon.

Amon lifted a monkey paw. The cactus jerked to stop in mid-air, hovering as though time had simply stopped around it. The demon nodded, and the plant settled gently on the table.

Teddy bellowed and launched himself at the demon, but before he'd made a full stride his body came to a jarring halt. He rose six inches off the ground. His muscles swelled and he grunted in a futile effort to resist an unseen force that manipulated him into a sitting position. He was planted, unceremoniously, into a kitchen chair.

"Hmph," Teddy said angrily.

Amon fixed the lapels of his bathrobe with the tip of his snake tail. When he spoke, his voice was calm—he sounded almost bored. "Please relax, Teddy," Amon said. "I'm not here to hurt you."

"He's a master of lies!" Teddy managed to say through gritted teeth.

"Oh, come now. I'm only here to... what do the humans say these days... 'Speak *my* truth.' All I ask is for you to hear me out."

While Amon was distracted by Teddy, Emma snuck up from behind and stabbed at him with a kitchen knife. The blade bent double and snapped a full six inches from the demon's hide before clattering to the tile floor. Emma, too, was lifted from the ground and peaceably floated into a chair at the table.

"It's really no use," Bucky said. "He's got this telekinesis thing. So long as he anticipates a threat from a secular being, you can't touch him."

"It's like the Force, from *Star Wars*!" Oliver observed in awe.

"From what?" Teddy asked. The veins in the big man's face and neck engorged as he flexed against the unseen power that held him motionless.

"*Star Wars*! The movies. You know. Obi-wan Kenobi? Light sabers? Mark Hamill?!"

"Does anyone know what he's talking about?" Teddy asked.

Oliver turned to Bob, his face pleading. "Bob?"

"Sorry. I'm not really into that Dungeons and Dragons mumbo-jumbo," the author said.

"Oh my God!" Oliver leaned against the wall, exasperated.

"Whatever power this thing has, I can take him," Teddy said confidently. "I have a thousand years of combat experience! I beat every arm wrestler in Tampa during the summer of 1932. I broke one guy's wrist!"

"Teddy," Amon sighed, "I admire you. You're motivated. Loyal. Committed to the cause. I get it. However, my friend, a thousand years is but a minute to me. There have been a million warriors before you. They come and go. I, on the other hand, am eternal."

"Nothing lasts forever," Teddy mumbled.

"No? What about God?"

"Well...maybe."

Amon swished his robe and turned to address the room. "See there's the problem! You guys go on and on about the 'Great Balance,' but does that sound very balanced to you? An eternal God, and everyone else is just here on a temporary visa? Sounds like a load of crap to me. And that sort of segues into the reason for this meeting."

"Are you saying we're here because of you? That you brought us to this weird place?" Bert asked.

"Let's just say I put things in motion, and I'm happy with the way they're turning out. I knew if I could trap one of you, the rest would come looking. I only meant to take Oliver. He's sort of the main thrust of all this, but I'm thrilled to have the greater audience. I could really use all of you."

He rotated his owl head until he could lock eyes with Emma, who set her jaw and stared straight back at him. If she was afraid, her face did not betray it.

"Emma, I must admit, grabbing that glamour was unpredictable. Very brave. Not to mention fortuitous. Here we are after all! But it certainly threw me for a loop. In fact, if it hadn't been for that ASMR Cutie channel on YouTube, I likely would have never had a chance to meet the rest of you. So, Emma dear, as an adversary, you have my utmost respect."

"I appreciate that," Emma said. "That way there will be no hard feelings when I kill you."

Amon tilted his head in a manner suggesting that if he could roll his owl eyes, he would.

"God's eternal nature is an issue," Amon said. "Because it inherently fails to serve the Great Balance. That's why we're all here in the ethereal underworld's version of Florida this evening."

"Because of God?" Bert asked.

"Because of eternity," Amon said.

Oliver backed into the kitchen and ducked behind a column. He needed a second to think. If his father and Peter were correct, then Amon wasn't really after *him*, or his friends. The demon was after the code. Anything else was just an afterthought.

If it were as simple as turning himself over and taking whatever licks he had coming, well, that was one thing. But with the consequences of handing over the code potentially leading to a nuclear apocalypse, he felt the weight of the world on his shoulders.

His only option was to escape.

Was Amon aware of the Cast Master 4000? If not, maybe he could jump a few levels up in the multiverse, and when Mayhem said it was safe, come back here and rescue his friends. It wasn't an ideal situation, but it just might work. After all, it had worked once already. Mayhem and the other Host could probably find one another again.

Mayhem!

Oliver peaked around the column and saw the dog, still sitting on the couch, scratching itself furiously behind the ear.

"Oliver," Amon said, "would you stop trying to distance yourself from this situation and join us please? It's not like I'm going to vivisect your brain. I think if you'll just hear me out, you will at least come to understand my perspective."

"I'd rather not," Oliver said. "I'm feeling a bit freaked out."

"Fine. Listen from the kitchen if you prefer. All I ask is that you actually pay attention. It's important."

Amon turned back to Teddy and Emma. "Mathematicians always get uncomfortable when you bring up eternity."

He then swiveled his head almost one hundred and eighty degrees to face Irena. Oliver, watching from the kitchen, couldn't help but think of *The Exorcist*.

"Irena, my darling demon-physicist. Could you explain the Big Bang to Teddy here? His life partner already understands it. But I think Teddy could use some background."

She studied Teddy's strained face. "No. He is not an academic."

"Just in general terms," Amon coaxed, "as if you were explaining it to a child."

Irena sighed. "The Big Bang theory of the origin of the universe states that all matter exploded outward from a single point, smaller than an electron."

"Good," Amon said. "And what led physicists to that conclusion?"

"They observed that the universe is expanding, as well as the rate of expansion."

"Excellent," Amon said. "What would happen if the universe were to stop expanding and start contracting back to that single point?"

"I don't know," Irena said.

"Speculate," Amon encouraged.

"Well, things would begin heating up, for one. Collisions would become more frequent. Solar systems and galaxies would collide and merge. Black holes would form, and then begin accreting together into supermassive black holes.

Eventually the universe would contract back into a singularity."

"Do you know why this doesn't happen?"

"No," she said.

"To protect sentient species like human beings. The entire universe is kept in a constant state of expansion to save animals that are too stupid to stop killing one another over differences of opinion.

"For some completely opaque reason, we're supposed to protect these idiotic species at all costs, even to the point of intervening in the multiverse, as though their rudimentary consciousness is an entity worth preserving at enormous expense.

"Because of that, we continue down the unbalanced path of a flawed, eternally expanding multiverse, and we can never hope to achieve better.

"You might be surprised to hear that I, too, pursue the Great Balance.

"But the path we're on—the path that we are supposed to pursue—well, just look at it! Does it look balanced to you? Because to me it seems absolutely crazy. Just because we wrap our interventions in the word 'balance,' does not a true balance create."

Oliver had to admit that Amon had a point.

His scientific pragmatism demanded that he always question everything. His sources for all his newfound cosmic knowledge had obviously been firmly in the "Protect Humans at all Costs" camp. But did that mean he had introduced bias into his own understanding of the grand scheme?

In his new role, he could see the trees, but not the forest.

Every time he thought he understood a solution, it only meant he faced new problems. He supposed such tunnel-vision understanding was a limitation of the human condition.

And, to Amon's point, humans were problematic when you got right down to it. When humans invented currency to stop killing one another for food, they started killing one another over currency instead. They simply could not get out of their own way. They were fundamentally flawed.

As a species, *Homo sapiens* were hopeless, doomed to generational repetition of missteps, failures and self-destruction. How on earth could they warrant such an elaborate cosmic intervention as to which he had borne witness?

Then he remembered his mother reading at his father's funeral.

He wasn't much of a Biblical scholar, but the verse had resonated with him:

"As the heavens are higher than the Earth,
So are My ways higher than your ways
And My thoughts than your thoughts."

This wasn't a scientific journey. He was wrestling, not with a mathematical construct, but rather, with faith.

It wasn't his job, in these circumstances, to understand the greater plan. It was his job to act on faith. He was not the main character in this story. He was a small cog in a big machine. He simply had a job to do. And his faith told him that Teddy and Emma were on the right path. That he was supposed to hitch his wagon to their cause. His purpose might be unknowable, but by following the course he was on, thanks to Teddy, Emma, and even his father and Peter, he was fulfilling it nonetheless.

But Amon's words bothered him. They burrowed worm-trails of doubt through what had been quickly turning into Oliver's certainty.

There really was something ridiculous about a universe hinging on the whims of a primitive species like his own, when you laid it all out. Humans fought one another over trivialities all the time. They burned down libraries to protest the fact that the books inside were written by omnivores, for heaven's sake! Could they really have a significant role in the future of the universe? Should they?

He couldn't help but wonder if his entire ethos had always been backward.

He shook his head in an attempt to clear it. Hubris, he knew, was also part of the human condition, and questioning the Great Cosmic Deity's plan after a snake-owl-dog monster appealed to one's sense of academic pride was pretty much the pinnacle of it.

Had Teddy not warned him the demon was a master of lies?

On the other hand, just because he liked and trusted the big man, did that mean he should accept his paradigm of thought?

He remembered an MIT study that had concluded there was no objective truth. Were beings like Teddy and Amon therefore destined to lock themselves in an eternal struggle, since they perceived reality from different archetypes? Certainly, the two realities, one in which the human race was paramount, and the other in which it shouldn't exist, were diametrically opposed.

"Oliver," Amon said. "I perceive that you are beginning to comprehend the problem."

"Uh..."

"You understand that we have a natural, constant struggle. An endless battle forced upon us by oppositional, ingrained points of view, yes?"

"I guess."

"Do you at least believe me when I say my goal is a balanced universe without such opposition? A universe that can evolve and progress with an objective set of principles?"

"Well... I mean, we just met."

Amon snickered.

The creature hopped down from the table and slithered and pawed its way to the balcony, telekinetically sliding the door open before walking outside. Teddy and Emma floated behind him, still fighting the invisible force gripping them. Everyone except Oliver followed.

Oliver needed more time. He hadn't anticipated Amon's nature. He'd imagined facing off against fire and fury, not... logic.

He watched them from his place in the kitchen.

The landscape outside still looked much like a painting, but it was beautiful in an eerie way.

From the balcony, the demon waved his ape-like hand at the heavens. The strange clouds parted, revealing a brilliant night sky bursting with stars. He made a gesture with his tail, and all the surrounding buildings, and the streetlights with their eerie blue halos, went dark, leaving just the radiant cosmos.

"Examine the sky please," he said.

"No," Teddy grunted. "You'll poison our minds!"

"Oh, come on," Amon said. "You believe everything you've ever heard? You want to serve the Great Balance, but you only subscribe to a single stream of information?"

"Evil... don't listen," Emma grunted, her voice strangled.

"Ah, thank you," Amon said. "We can get to that if you could just be patient a moment. You'll note that the harder you struggle, the harder it will be to talk. It's my way of keeping our discussion civilized.

"As you just heard, the universe is constantly expanding. This creates a stable setting for life to exist. Collisions amongst the celestial bodies are rare enough to allow evolution to proceed.

"I trust that when I use the term the Great Balance, everyone, save for Mr. Quinn, is familiar with the term?"

"I've heard some grumblings," Bob said.

"Wonderful!"

Bob smiled proudly and produced the vape pen from his bathrobe.

"Would it surprise you to know that I, too, have been pursuing this balance?"

"You spoke about this a long time ago," Fixeloclastes said.

"That was long ago indeed, my friend," Amon sighed.

"How do you guys know one another?" Bert asked.

"I was a Host," Amon explained. "Before humans became sentient."

"He was Conquest," Bucky said. "He had some pretty big ideas."

"They weren't so much 'big' as they were different," Amon said. "Would you say that's a fair assessment?"

"You wanted to destroy the multiverse," Fixeloclastes said. "I suppose you could call that 'different.'"

Amon nodded. "A few hundred thousand years ago, the Great Balance began bothering me. Specifically, the arbitrary point we were pursuing, which, from how I saw it at least, wasn't in any semblance of balance at all. We weren't aiming for a balance point—we were aiming for a state of constant progress, endless evolution and technological innovation. We were aiming to give intelligent species, and I use that term lightly, the powers of celestial beings."

Oliver found himself nodding, as though he'd heard all this before. The reality of it was that even in the short time he'd been familiar with the idea of the Great Balance, he'd struggled to understand what, exactly, the balance point was supposed to be.

He realized he was agreeing with a lord of the underworld and stopped nodding. The others might be on the balcony with Amon, but he had the distinct impression that this sermon was meant specifically for him. Could the demon poison his mind, as Teddy said? Or was Amon simply able to tap into something that already existed within him? By saying it out loud, could Amon crystallize the doubts Oliver had developed through his own observations?

The demon slithered up on the patio table and gestured at the surrounding buildings. "Imagine, if you will, human beings, with all their inherent flaws, with their pettiness, short-sightedness and narcissism, having the technological power to live forever in the secular plane. Aside from the fact that spiritually, we already have a multiverse that allows them to exist in perpetuity, imagine allowing them to inhabit the lynchpin, secular universe, endlessly—to expand across the cosmos, like an out-of-control virus, infecting other civilizations and planets with their meanness and self-centeredness.

"The human spirit should never have been allowed to flourish in secular life. It has been nothing but trouble. And yet, we've committed all the celestial resources in existence to maintaining such a species. To preserving this flawed universe."

"So what?" Bert asked. "You want to wipe us out?"

"It's nothing personal. It isn't your species' fault that things are the way they are. It's the natural progress of the evolution of a civilization that's brought you to where you are today. To fix this issue, we would need to do more than simply destroy the human race. We would have to bring an end to all sentient or presentient life. We would have to start again, with a clean slate. Eliminating sentience will take away the celestial incentive to keep this multiverse going. It will fail, and a new consciousness will arise. One that understands *real balance*."

Oliver understood exactly where this was going. Amon was talking about the "Humans as a pathogen" theory. It was an intriguing, if somewhat terrifying school of thought. The whole concept was that the human race was a flaw in an otherwise perfect universe.

If indeed sentient species were the reason the Universe was being maintained in a stable state of expansion, then by all logic, without them, it would collapse. Amon wanted to use Oliver's code to that end. To get it, he was playing at Oliver's own concerns about his species—specifically, that they were mostly idiots; himself, more often than not, included.

He had to be real about this though. They were talking about the end of the world. If Amon truly wanted to use Oliver's code to end humanity, even if it was toward the goal of some ultimate, cosmic greater good, Oliver had no interest in being the architect of the destruction of civilization. Despite his feelings about mankind—and yes, he hated to admit it—those feelings were often contemptuous—he knew good people when he met them. Teddy was good. Emma was good. Bert and Carmella were good. Bob... well... Bob was good-*ish*.

Even the people he didn't much care for had their lives to live. Who was *he* to decide that their existence was not worth saving? The communist accountants who had tried to burn down Bert's trailer—each of them was surely loved by somebody. The naked man with the rifle he'd met at the entrance to the Vagisil Autonomous Zone was *somebody's* son.

Oliver wasn't going to casually make a pact with a lord of the underworld and take away what wasn't his to take.

Despite his cynicism, he rejected the premise of Amon's argument.

Then, standing in an ethereal condominium, watching a toy-sized demon deliver a speech to an audience of telekinetically entrapped humans, a retired cardiologist, a stoned writer, a red woman with horns, and Host beings from a different plane of the multiverse, Oliver experienced what he would later think of as a lightbulb moment.

For the briefest of moments, he intuited the bigger picture. Humanity was probably not the end goal of the celestial force that kept the universe from collapsing. More likely it was the byproduct of humanity that was most important. The thing that had so eluded him until now. It was the essence of human connection that brought people together and inspired them to be good. The thing that gave them hope.

When you boiled it all down, the essence of humanity wasn't the people themselves, rather it was the force that connected them. Their connectedness was their real value. Their altruism—the way they would lay their lives on the line for one another—Oliver understood that this was the unique end product of human life. *Homo sapiens* were more or less the yeast that fermented the wort of existence then died away. Somewhere in the long-distant future, perhaps, there might exist a true balance point—a progeny species that produced the product—call it interconnectedness—call it love—whatever, in a purer form. The human race was just a means to a better end.

That conclusion felt incredibly cheesy. But it felt right.

For some unknowable reason, Oliver had been allowed a glimpse of the grand scheme.

Only a week ago, he doubted he would have been able to comprehend it. But he had friends now. He understood love—at least in some new way. It wasn't roses and passion and "Romeo, wherefore art thou Romeo?" It was a network of goodwill. It was the willingness to help one another despite sometimes terrible inconvenience. It was so much bigger than what Amon, even in his ancientness, could fathom.

Oppositional paradigms aside, Oliver now knew without doubt where he stood.

He was not going to help Amon. Not in a million years.

This sudden bout of moral clarity put him in an awkward situation. It was obvious that Amon had some semblance of telepathy. The demon, he was quite certain, had read his thoughts just minutes earlier. To counter this, he willed himself to think of anything at all that was not the subject at hand.

For a moment he imagined the Stay Puffed marshmallow man. He guessed this was probably not the best idea, and he put it aside.

An image of Jessica, Bob's earthly girlfriend, popped into his mind. She was brushing past him on the walkway, only this time, instead of jamming his hand into her belly, Oliver imagined a smoother interaction. He imagined them having a conversation about Russian literature.

He didn't know a lot about Russian literature, so he was only going to be able to keep this going for so long.

He had to get out of there. This was his chance.

While the forefront of his mind recited lessons he'd learned in his Intro to English class, aptly including the idea that Leo Tolstoy's work focused on the Christian doctrine of non-resistance to evil, the hidden substructure of his consciousness tried to conceive of an escape strategy. He would have to wait for a chance to grab Mayhem. He set the Cast Master 4000 to a half-level up. Whatever awaited him on the twenty-sixth tier of hell, it was better than being manipulated into revealing the doomsday code.

The only problem—Mayhem had followed everyone else out to the balcony.

Oliver crouched low and observed them through the open patio door.

"Mayhem!" he whispered.

Mayhem didn't even turn.

"Mayhem!"

Amon was still proselytizing in his strange, breathy voice. Bert stood on the corner of the balcony, his arms folded on his belly. Oliver thought he was scowling, but then he saw Bert nod begrudgingly in agreement, conceding points to the demon.

Bob leaned on the railing, and stared out at the painting-like two-dimensional landscape, smoking.

The Host creatures stood behind Amon, and stared up at the weird night sky.

"Mayhem!" Oliver whispered again.

Mayhem cocked his head slightly, without turning. It was a meaningful cock of the head.

"We need to get out of here!"

The terrier's ears twitched. Oliver interpreted this to mean, "Not yet."

All things considered, the non-verbal terrier was quite good at communicating with body language.

"Oliver?" Amon said.

Oliver ducked back into the kitchen. It was stupid, but he wasn't ready to go out there. Not when the stakes were so high.

"You know," Amon said, "I can sense you in there, just as well as if you were standing right here beside me. I could just drag you out here."

An invisible squirming coil wound around Oliver's chest and, just for a second, pulled taught. Along with having existed in mostly two dimensions, it was the most unsettling sensation he'd ever experienced.

"I realize that," he said, willing himself not to freak out about the invisible boa constrictor wrapping around him while still maintaining a mental facade in which he fervently discussed the virtues of Isaac Babel's Benya Krik with the beautiful Jessica, "but if it's all the same to you, I'm just going to listen from here."

"Suit yourself," Amon said. The squirming thing let go.

He breathed a sigh of relief, patted his chest where it had been, and of course felt nothing at all. He watched through the patio door, focusing his attention on the not-exactly-a-terrier. Why was Mayhem refusing to help? Was the Host buying what Amon was selling? If so, they would have to part ways, and the thought of this hurt Oliver's heart.

A few days ago, he didn't know how in the world he could survive with the celestial being. Now he couldn't fathom existence without it.

Amon turned to face his audience. "You heard Emma refer to me as 'Evil' a moment ago. The truth is, there is no good and evil. Those are relative terms. There is only balance. When you see an ever-expanding universe, with an ever-flourishing semi-sentient population, you intuitively know you aren't looking at balance. Balance is stability. Balance is the knife's edge tipping point between yin and yang."

"Wait," Bob said. "Is Satan here a Buddhist?"

"Satan? I'm not Satan," Amon huffed, waving a dismissive monkey paw through the air. "That guy is such a prick."

"Sorry," Bob said.

"It's fine, it's fine. I have to remind myself that modern humans know practically nothing about the underworld. Bob, beings like me predate Buddhism by billions of years. I was just trying to express things in terms you could understand."

"Gotcha," Bob said.

The creature slithered and wriggled up the railing, grunting loudly with the effort, then finding a perch closer to eye level. It wrapped its tail around the rungs for support, and leaned forward, stretching toward the absurd quasi-dimensional landscape. Gazing over the empty streets, Amon waved his strange upper limb and a thunderous roar filled the air as all the two-dimensional buildings and structures popped into their three-dimensional forms.

"Think of me as a fallen angel. I asked too many questions. I studied too much. I had, as Bucky said, controversial ideas. My power grew too strong. And suddenly I was no longer welcome amongst the divine. I was cast down here, into the underworld.

"But I continued to study. I continued to grow my strength. I discovered the ether, and how to move through it. I discovered power, not just in the underworld, but in the keystone universe. The cosmos themselves have urged me on. The balance, the true Great Balance, must be restored. And I need you to help me restore it. Specifically, I need your friend Oliver—who is for some reason hiding from me in the kitchen and thinking about Dostoevsky. I need your help convincing him to help me."

At the mention of his name, Oliver tensed for more telekinetic bondage. But nothing happened. He knew the moment was almost at hand. Amon would ply him for the code. He was unarmed, and Mayhem was still on the balcony.

Something caught his eye. The drawer under the stove was half open, the handle of a cast-iron frying pan angled out. It was the only weapon he could find. It was ridiculous—if Teddy and Emma couldn't hurt Amon, what chance did he have? But he picked it up anyway.

He crept to the living room, then toward the balcony, belly crawling with the Cast Master 4000 in one hand, and the frying pan in the other. If Mayhem wouldn't come to him, he would have to go to Mayhem. If Amon caught him... well... he had the frying pan, at least.

Amon and the host were gathered at the rail, gazing into the ethereal Floridian night sky. "That's it," Amon said. "That's the pitch. Let's join forces. Let's redo the multiverse the way it's supposed to be. Let's stop the human virus before it spreads. Let's release Mr. Bell's code to the world, and let the humans do what humans do best! It's not like it will happen all at once. The humans will have years... decades even. But we need to let them come to their natural conclusion. To intervene like we have been doing is beyond tragic. It helps nothing. You know it. I know it. Oliver knows it. So let's make things right."

A long silence ensued. Finally, Fixeloclastes sighed. "What if we can't?"

"Then forty legions of hell-spawn will descend upon you and your human companions."

"What happens after that?" Bob asked, taking a toke.

"I mean...it won't be good."

"Amon, I'm sorry man," Bucky said. "I'm sorry for what happened to you. You weren't a bad guy. Maybe just a little mixed up is all. But come on, dude. We can't exactly destroy humanity. We love them. To hurt them... it's against our essential nature. We're their guardians."

"Humanity will eventually destroy itself anyway," Amon said. "I have foreseen it. The reason I am here, however, is to ask if you could kindly ensure they take the rest of the secular version of Earth along with them when they go."

The demon turned his owl head, looking toward the kitchen. "In fact—Oliver...? Where is Oliver?"

Oliver sprang from his position behind Fixeloclastes' giant moth wings and smacked Amon with the frying pan. He hadn't expected it to actually make contact, but the pan hit the lord of the underworld in the face with an audible *clang!*

Wearing a look that, even for an owl, would have to be described as "wide-eyed," Amon tumbled off the balcony and into a hedge below. As the creature hit the bushes, a vortex opened in the ground and Oliver found himself staring once again into a swirling, pulsating hole in the multiverse like the one he'd seen in the two-dimensional version of Bob's kitchen.

Teddy and Emma fell to the concrete floor.

"Whoa," Bucky said.

"Uh oh," Fixeloclastes said. "Did you seriously just smash him in the face with a frying pan!?"

Oliver examined the thing in his hand. "Yeah. I guess I did."

"He is going to be seriously *pissed!*"

Oliver set the frying pan on the patio table. He spun the wheel on the Cast Master 4000, pointed it, and depressed the red button. The rotting skunk carcass appeared.

"Ew," Emma said. "What's with the skunk?"

"Glamour," Oliver said. "You first, Irena. It's set for your home world."

"Wait," Fixeloclastes said. "She helped us. Add twenty-six levels."

Oliver made to do as instructed, but Irena placed her warm red hand over his own. "It's OK," she said. "I want to be where Robert can find me."

"Really?" Bob said. "You'd stay down in hell on my account?"

"What can I say?" Irena said. "I have a soft spot for you. You have your charms."

Bob stared at her over the rims of his drugstore glasses. "I don't know what to say, honey."

She crossed the room and pulled him into an embrace. She gave the writer a peck on the cheek. "Come visit me soon, yes?"

Bob stuffed the vape pen back in his pocket and tenderly touched the place on his cheek where she had kissed him. "Of course."

Oliver wondered if he would ever see Irena again. It made the most sense to hope that he wouldn't. Despite hardly knowing her, it stung a little to watch her ongoing tragedy unfold. He was no great judge of character, but he felt she deserved better, or at least deserved a second chance.

Without ceremony, she grabbed the carcass and disappeared.

As Oliver fiddled with the dials, hunting for the 26.5 setting that would send them to the secular world, a faint electrical hum filled the air.

"That's weird," Bert said. The old man tapped his hearing aid.

The buzzing grew, followed by the loud crackles and snaps of static discharge. It was like the sound Oliver would attribute to a power transformer on the verge of catastrophic failure.

A rush of hot air blew in from the Gulf of Mexico. The air shimmered and stars turned a dazzling bright blue.

A blinding light like that of a flashbulb briefly bathed the grassy patch of lawn under the balcony in daylight, and when it faded, a new dimensional vortex appeared in its place. A four-foot-tall weasel-like animal, wearing chainmail armor and carrying a poleax, jumped out of the space-time hole. It stood on its hind legs and sniffed, finally turning its gaze to their balcony.

More vortices opened. The stench of ozone filled the air, as the loud buzz of interdimensional portals coming online drowned out all ambient sound. Out of each cosmic threshold a strange beast appeared. Some were furry, others slimy or scaly. Some looked like men, and others like reptiles, or birds. Flames erupted from one of the buildings down the street. The earth shook. The misshapen creatures moved, en masse, toward the Angler's Cove condominium complex.

"What the hell is that?" Bert asked, dumbfounded.

"That would be the forty legions of hell-spawn," Bucky said.

Oliver, distracted, screwed up the setting on the Cast Master 4000 and overshot the setting on the finicky dial. "Gah!"

A vortex opened in the living room, and a penguin wielding a broad sword between its wings waddled awkwardly through.

"Aw," Teddy said, "I love penguins."

Without any hesitation, the flightless bird swung the sword in a hard arc at Teddy, who dove to the side, crashing into a rattan-style end table. The glass tabletop shattered.

The big man, his eyes bulging, touched his throat. His finger came back bloody.

The penguin raised the sword and lurched toward him. Teddy barely had time to roll out of the way of the bird's powerful thrust.

"Oliver, whatever it is you're doing, you should hurry. This adorable penguin has murder in its eyes."

Teddy rolled hard and gripped the armrest of the couch. He grunted, slid the large piece of furniture between himself and his attacker.

"Wow," Bob said. "He's pretty strong."

Moving quick as a flash, the penguin spun away from Teddy and pounced on Bob's back. It was about to plunge the blade into the writer's skull when Mayhem scrambled up Bob's chest, opened his mouth wide, and a jet of white phosphorous flame erupted from the terrier. The blowtorch-like fire pierced through the penguin's winsome head, and the animal crumpled to the floor in a smoking heap. Mayhem pounced on the carcass, and growled.

Bob patted out the smoking shoulder of his fuzzy bathrobe. "Well I'll be a monkey's uncle."

"Grab the dog!" Oliver shouted.

Emma scooped Mayhem off the carcass. Oliver pointed the device at the closest object he could find on the patio, which happened to be a deflated beach ball. There was no time for controlling the variables. All hell was literally breaking loose.

Just as the glamour materialized, the large propane tank that supplied the building's gas-powered range-tops exploded. The skunk carcass bounced off the patio table and tumbled over the balcony, narrowly missing the vortex below.

Teddy kicked hard at the railing, snapping it clean off its support posts. He herded the group to the edge of the patio.

"OK, on three," Teddy said.

A new vortex opened in the living room behind them. A grizzly bear, grasping a sputtering World War Two-era flamethrower, stepped through.

"Three!" Fixeloclastes shouted, thoroughly skipping one and two. Wrapping the group in his wings, he pushed them off the edge.

They landed in the hedge on top of the skunk carcass.

Their trip to the secular world happened in the blink of an eye. A loud pop accompanied their landing.

Teddy, who outweighed Oliver by at least a hundred pounds, landed on top of him.

"Oof!" Oliver said.

"My back!" Bert complained. He tried to roll out of the hedge only to land face-first in Emma's cleavage.

"Excuse me!" Emma protested.

Bert got to his knees, flustered. "I'm sorry, dear. That was unintentional."

"Pretty great though, right?" She wore a cruel smile.

Bert grinned. "Yeah. Pretty great."

Oliver stood and brushed himself off. It was a cool evening in secular Florida. A gentle breeze blew in from the gulf. He was home. Sort of. He'd found his friends. He'd brought them back. He hadn't revealed the doomsday code. All in all, it had been a successful adventure.

He realized he was hungry. He needed a snack. Then a nap.

"Is everyone here?" he asked.

"I think so," Teddy said.

"What about the dog—and the moth guy? And the kangaroo?" Bob asked.

Oliver felt Mayhem's presence.

"They're here," Teddy said.

Bob nodded. Squinting at Emma, he adjusted his glasses and smiled. "Back to normal! You've got your aura back!"

"I can tell." Emma smiled.

Bert, getting slowly to his feet, wearily scanned left and right. "Are we safe?"

"Yes—I think so," Oliver said. "I'm pretty sure Amon needs a very specific set of conditions to come to the secular world."

"*Pretty sure?*" Emma said.

Oliver nodded.

"That's what my dad told me. His friend Peter said human sacrifice is involved. I think we're OK."

"Your *dad's* friend Peter?" Teddy asked.

"I was in heaven," Oliver began. "It was—" He stopped short. What it was, was a long story.

"Can we, maybe, get some food and go back to Bob's? It's complicated, and I'm starving."

"Sure!" Teddy said. He slapped Oliver on the back so hard that Oliver almost fell into the hedge.

He smiled and rubbed his back where Teddy had whacked him. "Man, it's good to be back in the secular plane," he said.

A fraction of a second later, a smooth calcite stone, hurled from the vicinity of Gulf Boulevard, hit him in the ear.

— *Sixteen* —

Oliver's knees buckled and he sat hard on the pavement, pawing awkwardly at his injured ear which bled freely all over the tight paisley shirt he'd been growing to like.

"Hey! My ear!" His voice came out monotone. Everything felt fuzzy and slow. His cognitive functions, he dreamily guessed, must have scrambled by the blow to his head.

Everything was topsy-turvy and off-axis as though gravity had suddenly decided it should work at a forty-five-degree angle. The world yawed and pitched and he couldn't get his bearings.

His first semi-coherent thought was that he'd been shot, but then he saw the stone on the ground, not two feet away, and he pieced together that he'd been hit in the head with a rock, like a caveman.

God, he was dizzy!

He closed his eyes for a moment to let things settle. If this was another concussion it would be his third or fourth in as many days. He was having trouble keeping track.

"Look out!" Teddy called. Another rock sailed over the parking lot, narrowly missing Bob, who was desperately trying to get his vape pen working again.

Oliver managed to focus his eyes. Plumes of smoke billowed skyward from the main road. The familiar call-and-answer rhythm of a protest chant came from somewhere nearby.

Oliver remembered the protests he'd seen on Bay News 9. What had it been? Something about salad dressing? Was this the same rally, or was this something new? That had to have been at least a day ago... or had it only been a few hours? How long had he been out there in the multiverse?

The angry crowds blended together in his mind. The vegans—the communist accountants—the salad dressing thing—it was all one big, angry, self-righteous blur.

He couldn't make out what anyone said. The caller's megaphone was turned too loud, and it squelched with static. The answering crowd was therefore off cue, and no more intelligible than a crowd of basketball fans in an ESPN broadcast.

"Oh frig," he sighed. "Here we go again."

A brick hit the red Honda Civic parked closest to him, and the car alarm blared.

A bottle shattered on the nearby asphalt, and he was drenched in a fragrant perfume.

It was actually kind of nice. Floral, yet masculine. Still in a daze, he leaned forward to examine the label-bearing shard.

Issey Miyake (For him).

Teddy had apparently had enough. He scooped Oliver up and threw him over his shoulder. "I'm going to get you somewhere safer, kid."

The big man dashed toward the hedgerow that separated the parking lot from the main road.

Oliver, suspended over Teddy's shoulder, remembered the protest-turned-riot in Halifax. "Hey, this is how we met."

"Just like old times."

Teddy plunked him down in the grass, and Emma herded Bob and Bert across the tarmac. She wove expertly between parked vehicles, ducking for cover and timing each leap forward with breaks in the onslaught of incoming projectiles. Bert tried to emulate her every motion. Bob simply bumbled along behind, fiddling with his vape pen.

Emma sidled up next to Oliver and moved his hand out of the way so she could inspect his ear.

When she touched it, he winced. "That's pretty tender."

"Just hold on," she said, then, "Hey, you smell great!"

"It's Issey Miyake for Him."

She prodded his ear again, and this time he had the very specific sensation of two pieces of cartilage that were supposed to be attached to one another being distinctly not attached to one another.

"Yikes," she said.

"Yikes?"

"Your ear is kind of messed up. It's OK. Teddy's good with stitches.

"It's still attached, right?"

"Mostly."

Oliver wanted to be upset by this new mutilation, but he was still too busy trying to convince his vestibular system which direction was down.

Emma peeked through the bushes.

"They look really mad," she whispered over her shoulder. "Something about preferred pronouns."

Bob looked through a space in the hedgerow. "Uh oh," he said.

The convenience store across the street erupted into flames. The crowd on the other side of the hedgerow burst into ecstatic cheers.

Bob looked scared. Until that point, the only time Oliver had seen Bob look even remotely concerned was when the writer couldn't find his vape pen. That included the time when they faced certain demise as gravitationally challenged two-dimensional bio-structures. The PEN-Award-winning author had been one cool halibut. But now, chewing on his lower lip, eyes darting hither and yon, Oliver read genuine fear on the man's face. This new development was cause for concern.

"What is it?" Oliver asked.

Bob just shook his head.

Bert, too, seemed to pick up on the sudden change in the writer's disposition. "We were just attacked by a demonic grizzly bear with an M1A1 portable flamethrower, and you didn't bat an eye. Why are you so afraid of a bunch of people whose biggest concern is what gender they identify with?"

"It isn't them I'm afraid of. Gender dysphoria is a pretty common, openly discussed issue on campus these days. I teach college-level creative writing, for Pete's sake. I practically have to pledge allegiance to the trans community to get in the door every morning. We've got a much bigger problem on our hands." Bob pointed and Bert followed his outstretched arm. Oliver strained to focus.

A massive throng of young and middle-aged hipsters, bearing rainbow-themed placards that read "Ally!" stood packed shoulder-to-shoulder along Gulf Boulevard. One Ally in a "Peace, Love and Progress" T-shirt hurled a Molotov cocktail at a parked Pinellas County Sheriff's cruiser.

Interspersed amongst the horde of allies, were a few actual transgendered individuals who, for the most part, appeared to be entirely bewildered by the unfolding chaos.

"The allies—those are university people." Bob's voice trembled. "They have nothing better to do. They latch onto an issue of semantics, usually appropriated from some other group. Then they exponentially amplify their outrage by trying to one-up one another's moral superiority on social media, erasing all nuance and forcing their social media contacts into with-us or against-us camps. Because humans are social animals, they all want to be seen as being on board, no matter how crazy and extreme the demands become, because to be an outsider is emotionally devastating and can exclude them from job opportunities, and, from an evolutionary behavioral standpoint, from the mating pool. And suddenly an easily solved problem becomes a powder keg. They even try to quantify how righteously outraged they are on their resumes! It's an endless feedback loop! The outrage just builds and builds! No hill is too small to die on. Believe me..." he shuddered... "I've led seminars."

As if to accentuate this, a third-edition hardcover of *Shakespearean Reduction; an Analysis of the Lesser-Known Works of the Problematic Bard, through the Lens of Inter-Sectionalism* sailed over the hedgerow and through the windshield of a Chrysler Pacifica with Alamo stickers on the bumper.

"Oh no," Bert said. "Do you think Carmella's safe at your house?"

"Definitely not," Bob said.

"Now how could you possibly know that?" Teddy asked. "She's at least a mile from here."

"The university people... I recognize some of them. I have reason to believe they're heading that way."

"To your house!?" Emma exclaimed. "Why!?"

Bob looked ashen. "I may have given a guest lecture last week, during which I accidentally misgendered the head of the student union."

"Oh, Bob," Emma said, shaking her head.

"She had a beard!" Bob said in his defense.

"And this protest—?" Teddy began.

"There are multiple buildings on fire," Emma said. "I think you can call it a riot now."

"Don't—!" Bob trembled. "It's a *Peaceful Protest*. You *must* call it that when university people are involved. No matter what! You have no idea what they'll do if they hear you say the word 'riot' at one of their protests. You can think it, but don't say it out loud."

Bob was right. Oliver had spent almost a decade in university. At least in so far as one could speak openly, the "R" word was reserved only for causes oppositional to those the university people supported.

The situation was dire. If the protestors really were after Bob, it would take more than a little finesse and double-speak to navigate the writer to safety.

"OK," Oliver said, shaking off the cobwebs from his most recent traumatic brain injury. "This...protest... You think it's heading to your house?"

"I'm positive!"

"And Carmella's still there?"

"As far as we know, yes."

"Is there a landline at your house?"

"Sure."

Teddy produced a cell phone and handed it to the writer.

Bob examined it.

"Bob?" Teddy asked.

"Uh huh."

"Call Carmella."

"Oh. Right. Yes."

Carmella picked up on the first ring. Like so many elderly individuals, Carmella suffered from the affliction of assuming you had to yell at the receiver, and Oliver heard her clearly through the phone's tiny speaker.

"Hello?"

"Hi," Bob whispered. "You need to get out of there."

"What? I'm hard of hearing."

"You need to get out of there!" Bob hissed.

"What?"

Bert snatched the phone. "Carm! It's Bert! How are you?" Bert, too, yelled at the receiver.

A lantern-jawed, very musclebound protester wearing a snappy ensemble composed of Docker brand Khakis with rolled cuffs and a tight-fitting Lacoste Golf shirt accented with a rainbow pin, turned toward the sound of Bert's voice. He clutched a placard in one hand, and something else in the other. Oliver squinted. It looked like a golf club—a nine-iron! The placard read "Ally!" on one side, and "Call my friend 'Him' And I'll Break your Shin!" On the other.

"Bert! I was starting to worry!" Carmella's voice was as clear as day.

"Don't fuss about me, dear," Bert said. "I just need you to get in the van, and drive away from Bob's house as quickly as you can."

"That's going to be a problem."

"Why? What's wrong?"

"I think Oliver has the keys."

Bert cursed.

"Can you speak louder?" Carmella said. "I can't hear you."

Bert cleared his throat, and shouted into the receiver, "I said, 'Oh Shit!'"

The lantern-jawed protester jumped back from the bushes. "Hey! There are people back here! And they aren't wearing Ally paraphernalia!"

A small crowd of allies, bearing gasoline bombs and baseball bats and the other trappings of peaceful protestation, began assembling on the opposite side of the hedge.

Oliver did not like where this was headed.

"Oliver! Do you have the keys to the van in your pocket?" Bert hissed with some urgency.

Teddy grabbed him by the armpits and stood him up. He patted him down, reached into his front pocket, produced the key to a rented Dodge Caravan, and three envelopes—one silver and two white. He showed the keys to Bert, who cursed again.

"Hey," Oliver said. "Those white ones are from my dad. They're private."

"Who is the other one from?" Teddy asked.

Oliver didn't actually know who the silver envelope was from. Hadn't his father said something about a higher-up?

"God, maybe."

"God?"

"It wasn't fully clarified for me. Dad just said to open it when we returned to the secular plane."

"Do it," Emma said, looking serious.

"Now?"She nodded.

The hedgerow that separated them from Gulf Boulevard rustled, and Oliver suspected it was the lantern-jawed protestor with the golf club.

Working quickly, he tore open the letter that wasn't from his father. It was written on official letterhead and in Helvetica font. The header read, "From the Office of the Archangel Derrick."

"Archangel Derrick?" Oliver asked, hiking an eyebrow.

"No idea," Teddy said.

Bert covered the receiver with one hand. "Very nice paper stock," he observed.

Oliver, Teddy, and Emma crowded over the hand-written letter, which read:

Dear Oliver,
Instead of fighting the waves, become the wind.
Yours,
AA Derrick Purdy

PS There's a pretty good chance you may end the universe. Best of luck.

End the universe? He assumed Archangel Derrick was referring to his computer code, but some more specifics in terms of how to avoid ending the universe would have been helpful. Some wishy-washy advice and a "Good luck" didn't quite cut it.

"Become the wind?" Oliver said. "What the hell does that mean?"

"Hmm," Teddy said. "Something to do with driving really fast would be my guess."

Oliver turned to look meaningfully at Teddy, who met his gaze.

"OK, it probably isn't that," Teddy said.

"I think Derrick might be a Buddhist," Emma said.

The hedgerow shook again, accompanied by a series of loud cracks as branches gave way.

The lantern-jawed protester with the Dockers rolled at the cuffs crashed through. A small, half-terrified balding person wearing a striped shirt followed, urged forward by another "Ally," who wore very fashionable horn-rimmed glasses and a crocheted rainbow-pattern hat. The second Ally wielded a rather expensive-looking putter.

Casting their placards aside, the two Allies brandished their golf clubs in a two-handed stance. They were shouting, clearly furious, but they were so loud that Oliver couldn't decipher what they were saying.

The small, balding person in the striped shirt looked embarrassed and held up a hand to mollify the two allies, but the lantern-jawed Ally slapped the balding person's arm back down, while the Ally with the crocheted hat made to shush him by placing her open palm over his mouth.

Still on the phone with Carmella, Bert held up a finger, a "give me a second" gesture. When he did, the Allies shouted even louder. A vein pulsed from under the crocheted hat of the Ally with the horn-rimmed glasses. The Ally with the crocheted hat was rage personified.

Bob turned away, hiding his face. He struggled to roll a joint using a torn zig-zag paper he'd found in his wallet. His hands shook, and he dropped the bulk of his crumbled marijuana. He had obviously given up on the broken vape pen, which sat in two discarded halves at his feet.

When the lantern-jawed protestor recognized the writer, and raised his nine-iron overhead, Teddy sprang into action.

The big man's brusque movement telegraphed that the aggressors would not maintain any semblance of meaningful neurological function once he had done whatever it was he was about to do. They would be lucky, in fact, if they weren't about to spend the rest of their lives in special care homes, receiving nutrition through surgically implanted tubes.

It was at that moment that Oliver, who had been considering the note from the Archangel Derrick, became the wind.

He quick-stepped between Teddy and the Allies. "Calm down, please," he said in a firm voice. "My friends are prone to sensory overload."

The lantern-jawed Ally in Dockers with rolled cuffs stopped screaming. "Oh!"

"This is the guy!" the Ally with the horn-rimmed glasses and crocheted hat exclaimed, pointing the putter excitedly at Bob. "This is the guy we're supposed to beat up."

"Please don't beat him up," the small person in the striped shirt said in a meek voice. "I thought you were taking me to a concert."

"Shut up," the Ally in the horn-rimmed glasses and crocheted hat hissed. "There will be music in due course! Right now, though, this son-of-a-bitch needs to pay for what he did to your intersectional cohort!"

"Here..." the Ally in the crocheted hat handed her cell phone to the lantern-jawed Ally in Dockers with rolled cuffs. "Get my picture whacking him. I'm going to blow up the 'Gram tonight."

"Hold on," Oliver said, pointing to Bob. "Did you just assume my friend's gender?"

"Uh..." the Ally with the horn-rimmed glasses and crocheted hat said.

"I'm sorry. What?" Bob asked. He looked up from his rolling paper and seemed to notice he was on the verge of having his head split open by a hipster in a crocheted hat, wielding a TaylorMade Spider X7 putter. He took a step back.

"This person just assumed your gender," Oliver said, making a face he hoped would convey "Go along with this."

"Why is your face like that?" Bob asked. "Are you having a seizure or something?"

Bert clued in. "Olly's talking about your, um... you know...adjectives."

"My what now?"

"You know. He, him; she, her."

"Oh that." Bob finally seemed to understand. "You assumed my pronouns?"

Caught off guard, the Ally in the crocheted hat shifted from foot to foot, looking suddenly sheepish. "Well I...uh..."

The lantern-jawed Ally in Dockers shook his head. "We're not falling for that! You're just appropriating our cause!"

"Appropriating your cause?" Bob straightened, looking indignant. "You're accusing *me* of appropriating *your* cause? First of all, this all started out as a really specific issue, which you, as the progressive movement's version of the Gestapo, have appropriated as your own. Secondly, after coming to beat me up or kill me for failing to use the language you demand, now that I insist on the same courtesy, *you* are accusing *me* of appropriating *your* cause?"

"That's how it works!" the lantern-jawed Ally in Dockers said, shrugging in a *what can you do* gesture.

"No!" Bob shouted, and both protesters took a step back. "That isn't how appropriation works. You can't force me to use your language, and then accuse me of appropriation when I do."

The tension was palpable. The situation was riding on a knife's edge. One wrong move and Bob's accidental politically incorrect foible would end in significant bloodshed. But Oliver was the wind!

"Do you want to know who's really appropriating your cause?" he asked, calmly sliding between Bob and the Allies.

"Who?" asked the small man in the striped shirt.

"Navy Outlet!" Oliver said.

"Oh... Uhh..." said the lantern-jawed Ally in Dockers. "We're not supposed to talk about—"

"Yeah," Oliver said, cutting the protestor off. "You've seen the commercials. Navy Outlet puts all the social justice stuff in their ads. Pride flags, Black Lives Matter signs. They get to sell their shitty sweatshop clothes using your logos and your cause to make everyone think that they're socially conscientious, but in reality they exploit child labor in China and Bangladesh to make crappy jeans that stretch out the first time you wear them."

"We are *really* not supposed to talk about Navy Outlet," the Ally in the crocheted hat said. "They're sort of our corporate sponsors for this beat-down."

"My beat-down has a corporate sponsor?" Bob asked.

"Of course it does!" the lantern-jawed protestor in Dockers said. "It's expected to get airtime, isn't it?"

Oliver held up his hands. "Folks—I mean, people! Don't you see what's going on here?"

"Point of privilege," the Ally with the horn-rimmed glasses and crocheted hat said. "This is Steven, it-slash-its," she said, then gestured at the small balding person in the striped shirt. "It identifies as an android. You can't refer to it as people or folks."

"It's really OK," Steven said. "I mean, not everyone is going to immediately change their understanding of grammar and vocabulary just because of me."

"No it isn't!" the lantern-jawed protestor exclaimed. "If you prefer it-slash-its, this... uh...person," the protestor nodded towards Oliver, "should not be including you in the term 'people.'"

"An android?" Bert asked confused. "How does that work?"

"It had a pacemaker put in and everything," the Ally with horn-rimmed glasses, wearing the crocheted hat said. "So you'd better respect its pronouns!"

"Wait," Bert said. "Pronouns aside, are you telling me you had a pacemaker inserted, not because you have a cardiac arrhythmia, but because you want to be more android-like?"

Steven shrugged. "I know it sounds weird. It's weird to me too, but it's just the way I am, I guess. Actually, it used to be kind of fun being different and unique, but lately..."

"It isn't weird!" the two Allies shouted in unison.

"It's completely normal!" the lantern-jawed protestor continued. "Saying it's weird to you is super robophobic!"

"*Hitler* would say it's weird!" added the Ally in the crocheted hat.

"But—" Steven started to protest, only to have the Ally in Dockers clamp a hand over its mouth.

"You'll have to excuse our friend," the Ally in the crocheted hat said; "Steven hasn't had as much inter-sectionalism and critical theory coursework as we have. It can be kind of a troglodyte sometimes."

Steven rolled its eyes.

"I didn't mean any offense," Bert said. "It's just that... well... a pacemaker! That's a pretty risky procedure."

Steven started to respond, but the Ally in Dockers shushed it.

The Ally in the crocheted hat took a step toward Bert. "You're causing him—I mean, *it!* Oh my God... I am *so* sorry! It! You are causing *it* distress!"

"I'm not sure you *can* cause an android distress," Bert said.

Steven nodded in agreement from behind the Ally in Dockers' hand.

"I don't like the tone of your voice," said the Ally with the crocheted hat.

Sensing the situation was about to spiral out of control, Oliver intervened again. "Hey, no. This is Bert. He's cool. You'd never know he was born with a vagina, would you?"

The Allies took a step back and gave Bert's crotch an appreciative look. Bert thrust it forward, as if to help.

"Is that true?" asked the Ally in Dockers.

"It is," Bert said. "I had a vagina."

"A huge one," Bob added, making a rude gesture with his hands to signify the size of Bert's vagina.

"Huh," said the Ally in the crocheted hat. "Neat."

"OK," Oliver said. "Forget Bert's vagina for a second. This is important.

I'm telling you, your emotions, your anger, it's all being manipulated and exploited to distract you. Navy Outlet wants you to be angry at old men like Bert here, who wouldn't harm a fly, so that you don't focus your anger on their appropriation and monetization of your cause, their exploitative labor practices, and their terrible, terrible clothing."

"Come to think of it," Steven said, "I was in Navy Outlet the other day, and they did not offer any android-friendly facilities."

"And they don't sell dresses in sizes that would fit a more traditionally masculine frame!" exclaimed the lantern-jawed Ally in Dockers. "I think a dress would really help demonstrate that I'm a terrific Ally!"

"That's right," Oliver said.

"They're exploiting community movements to sell those T-shirts that have make-believe brands on them, but the material is too thin and you can see your nipples through them!" the Ally in the crocheted hat said.

"Exactly!" Oliver said.

"How far is the nearest Navy Outlet?" the Ally in Dockers asked.

"Just across the bridge," Bob said, pointing.

"Let's go!" the Ally in the crocheted hat exclaimed.

They crashed through the hedge once more, and this time Bert, Teddy, Emma, Bob and Oliver followed. The once-bloodthirsty crowd now parted way and made room.

Moving through them, Oliver took a moment to consider human behavior. The protestors thought they were on the verge of witnessing a human sacrifice. Most of them probably identified as atheists and ridiculed religious beliefs. He wondered if any of them knew they were in the process of starting a religion of their own, with doctrine, and language rules, and forbidden fruit, which in this case appeared to be a sense of humor.

Amon wasn't entirely wrong about the species.

The Ally in the crocheted hat grabbed a megaphone. "Excuse me, everyone! Excuse me! Point of privilege!"

The crowd quieted.

"Thanks. Tanya. She, her... We've recently been confronted with a problematic issue..."

As Tanya revealed her new truth about the ridiculously transparent corporate practices of Navy Outlet, Teddy pulled Oliver and Bob back to the edge of the crowd.

Bert was still struggling to hear Carmella. He had Teddy's phone pressed tight to his ear.

"Carm, I don't know who Jessica is, but if you can hear me, meet us at Navy Outlet," he said before hanging up.

They followed the crowd. Teddy stayed close to Bob, on high alert to any potential threat. Oliver walked with Emma.

The anger amongst the Allies palpably swelled as the protest changed course and crossed the bridge to Seminole.

When Oliver saw the Navy Outlet sign in the distance, he shuddered, remembering the story of Frankenstein's monster turning on its creator.

Emma put an arm around his shoulders. "Just out of curiosity, was that you or Mayhem talking back there?"

Oliver thought about it. "Me, I think."

"Way to become the wind," she said.

He smiled. A compliment from a friend was a wonderful thing.

— *Seventeen* —

A popular Wikipedia entry would later describe the peaceful protest that ended in the destruction of the St. Petersburg/Seminole Navy Outlet as the first known instance of common ground discovered between protesters and counter-protestors from opposite ends of the political spectrum.

As it happened, the Navy Outlet Protest for Pronoun Progress ran headlong into the Mr. Pillow Protest for the Preservation of Existing Pronouns just outside the parking lot of the Seminole Mall.

The protesters on the political left were infuriated at the appropriation of their slogans and mottos for blatant profiteering, as well as Navy Outlet's lack of non-binary bathroom facilities and trans-friendly sizing.

The protesters on the political right, meanwhile, had had enough of Navy Outlet's use of cheap, unethical overseas labor, both for its lack of workplace safety standards and for the blow it struck to North American manufacturing.

Both groups agreed that Navy Outlet jeans were overpriced, and that the brand's T-shirts were made of too thin a material, through which one's nipples were far too apparent.

It was a small miracle that nobody perished in the conflagration, which the Seminole Fire Department refused to extinguish until they could be absolutely, one hundred percent certain that all the men's stretch-fit khakis, which caused a phenomenon known as "Camel Tail," had been fully incinerated.

Oliver, for his part, took a pair of jeans and a new T-shirt. His paisley shirt had been reduced to a bloody rag, and his pants were filthy and torn from his fall off the balcony. Being the only peaceful protester to break into a till, to leave money in it, caught him some odd looks, but he felt that as the human host of a celestial, divine entity, it was his duty to try to pay for his clothing. He had, after all, pretty much caused the demolition of the store.

A moment after he put his money in the till, it was ripped from the counter by a protester with blue hair, who ran away cackling like the Wicked Witch of the West.

Standing beside the ruined till, as a nearby rack of very poorly made men's retro chest-stripe style T-shirts toppled to the tile floor with a *crash*, Oliver felt guilty. Wanton property destruction was something he considered generally abhorrent. His intention had been to simply redirect the focus of the protest. He hadn't meant to cause the complete annihilation of a retail outlet. But when Bob had been facing imminent death by golf club, it was the best idea he could come up with on the fly.

By the time he exited the building, his new jeans had stretched out and sagged in the butt.

Teddy met him in the parking lot.

"Just so you know, I can see your nipples through that T-shirt."

Intentional or not, Teddy's remark eased his conscience a little.

Together, they made their way back from the crowd toward the roadside, where they could watch the chaos unfold from a relatively safe distance.

A Molotov cocktail exploded against a display of folded High-Waisted Megasoft 5/8-Length 5-Pocket Leggings for Women, and the first big cloud of black smoke roiled from the smashed storefront windows.

An Ally in spandex bike shorts and a counter-protestor in a leather jacket joined forces to hoist a heavy wooden crate from the back of a pickup truck. They charged into the burning structure, and a moment later a frenzy of explosions followed. Contrails spiraled from a hole in the building's roof; brilliant flashes of green, blue, and crimson lit up the late-afternoon sky.

"Wow," Oliver said. "Are those fireworks?"

"They sure are!" Teddy squeezed his shoulder. The big man wore a grin of paternal pride.

"You're enjoying this, aren't you?"

Teddy inhaled deeply, drinking in the violence and chaos. "I hate Navy Outlet," he said.

Several police vehicles converged on the storefront and were swarmed by angry protestors. White chemical clouds billowed from the cruisers' windows, and Oliver tasted the now-familiar tang of capsaicin-laced tear gas.

Teddy licked his finger. "Hmm. Combined Systems Inc. Very nice."

"You can distinguish brands of tear gas from one another?"

"Oh yes. CSI is the best. Note the faint musky nuttiness behind the smoky, picante layer. Once you get past the initial sting, there are some very pleasant umami undertones. And the mouthfeel is tremendous!"

The big man took a deep, appreciative breath.

"Look out!" Emma shouted. She grabbed Oliver and Teddy as an open-top Jeep careened over the curb. It skidded, tires squawking, over the exact spot they had been standing.

Horn blaring, the Jeep spun in a half circle, kicking up a cloud of dust.

Oliver saw a wild maelstrom of hair caught in the whirlwind of the driver's frantic maneuvering.

Was the driver wearing a sundress?

He squinted. It was Jessica, the woman he'd met outside Bob's house. The one with the Russian literature. The one he'd imagined talking to, to prevent the Amon from reading his mind back in the ether.

She wore a look of determination and was breathing hard, clearly jacked up on adrenaline.

By God, she was hot!

She worked the gear shift with her right hand, sawed at the steering wheel with her left. The Jeep drifted in a reverse J-turn, bringing the passenger side around.

Carmella rode shotgun. The older woman had the grab-handle of the Jeep's A-pillar in a white-knuckled death grip.

"Hey!" Oliver called. "Over here!"

Carmella, despite her affliction with presbycusis, must have heard him. She scanned the crowd in his direction, her face full of worry until her eyes found Bert. She put a hand to her chest and breathed a deep sigh of relief.

Jessica waved wildly. "Come on! Get in!"

Oliver didn't need to be told twice. None of them did.

A firework exploded on the small patch of pavement between Oliver's group and the Jeep. His ears rang and he nearly choked on the hot cloud of cordite smoke. Charging forward, he kicked aside a tear gas cylinder that landed at his feet.

The peaceful protest had turned extraordinarily dangerous.

They piled in, a tangle of flesh and limbs. Bert squeezed himself next to his wife, while Bob, Teddy, and Emma scrambled into the back seat. Oliver was last, throwing himself onto Teddy's lap.

"Go!" he shouted.

Jessica stomped on the gas, spinning all four wheels before the Jeep found traction and jolted forward. They bounced back over the curb before drifting onto the road.

Oliver glanced over his shoulder. The burning mall and chaotic protest receded into the distance.

Just like that, it was over.

He'd done it! He'd rescued his friends! Rescued them from another dimension, no less! He'd gotten the better of Amon and escaped the ancient demon's trap!

His heart swelled with pride. Against all odds, he'd pulled it off. His team had won!

"What are you smiling about?" Teddy asked. "It isn't because you're sitting on my lap, is it? Because I don't want you to get used to this arrangement. Special circumstances only."

Oliver laughed. "I'm just happy to have everyone back!"

Teddy smiled. "Yeah... me too. You did great, kid."

His heart swelled even more. "Praise from Caesar!"

Jessica swung into the driveway of Bob's bungalow. She hadn't even come to a full stop before Bob leapt from the back seat and charged through the front door. "Home sweet home!" he exclaimed.

He slipped on a stack of bills in the entryway. His bathrobe caught on the doorknob, and he fetched up like a junkyard dog at the end of its chain, only to fall directly onto his bony backside.

Oliver bent to help him. He couldn't help but admire the sizable collection of bills, most of which were stamped "Final Notice."

Bob picked up a power bill and squinted at it, adjusting his glasses. "Say, Jessica, honey. How long were we gone?"

She checked her watch. "Just under two days."

Oliver jerked. "Two days?!" He'd lost all sense of time. "We were gone for two whole days!?"

"Actually, that feels about right," Bob said. "Time goes faster when you're down there."

"No kidding!"

As the others filed in, Bob scooped up handfuls of unpaid invoices. "If it's only been two days, what's with all these bills?"

"Good question. They must have come yesterday. I uh... I'm going to be couch-crashing at a friend's place for a while. We can talk about it later."

Bob picked up another bill and examined it. "Some of them are months overdue!"

"You didn't happen to have your agency dealing with your mail, by any chance, did you?"

"Well—yeah. I did, why?"

"Chantelle?" Jessica hiked an eyebrow.

"What about Chantelle? She isn't dropping me, is she?" Bob asked.

"No. She's dead. Remember?"

"Really?"

"Yeah. Three months ago. You wrote the eulogy."

"Oh yeah! Well... shit. She was nice."

Jessica rolled her eyes. "How long was she your agent, Bob?"

"I don't know. Since... like... 1996 I guess."

"So twenty-eight years!?"

"Give or take."

"And you forgot she was dead?"

"I guess I must have."

Jessica swore under her breath. "You know, they called me after the funeral to ask why you didn't go in person."

Bob frowned. "What did you tell them?"

"That you were probably stoned and forgot."

He nodded. "Fair enough."

"I'm going to water the plants," she said, turning on her heel and walking back out the front door.

Bob sighed and dumped the armful of unpaid invoices into the kitchen recycling bin, before settling on the couch in front of the typewriter.

"Man... Chantelle," he mumbled. "How did I become such a self-absorbed prick?"

He shook his head one more time, obviously dismissing whatever deep revelation he'd been on the verge of experiencing. He cracked his knuckles and picked up the top paper on the gigantic manuscript. He adjusted his glasses and got down to what Oliver assumed to be the serious business of figuring out what his book was about.

Oliver wanted to leave the writer to his work. He was about to make his way to the patio when he abruptly stopped. He stared hard at the living room floor, wondering if there would be any trace of the things that had transpired in the underworld. He didn't know what he was expecting—maybe a magical psychic echo of some kind, but he got nothing.

"What are you staring at, champ?" Bert asked.

"My celestial dog cut a policeman named Mike Knudson in half right about here. At least, he did in the underworld version of this house."

Bert cocked his head and followed Oliver's gaze. "Hmm. You don't say."

"You won't find anything," Bob said absently. "The structure stays. The pig guy doesn't."

"Pig guy?" Bert asked.

"Yeah," Bob sighed. "It's going to be a hell of a mess. I'm half inclined to list the place if I go back again."

"If?" Oliver asked. He was thinking of Irena. Irena who chose to stay in twenty-seven-layer-deep hell because of Bob.

"Yeah. It's always 'if.' But I always seem to find my way there, one way or another."

Bob gave Oliver a pleading look over the top of his manuscript. It was a look that said, "I know I'm a philandering bastard, but please don't talk about it right now."

Oliver nodded. He had no intention of inserting himself into Bob's love triangle. He'd had enough drama for a lifetime or two.

In fact, as far as this chapter of his biography went, his quest appeared to be at an end.

He wanted just four things, but he wanted them very badly. He wanted a shower, he wanted a snack, he wanted a snooze, and, despite not having much of a taste for alcohol, at that moment he wanted a cold, carbonated beverage, preferably of the beer variety. After one or two of those, he would ask either Bert or Teddy to sew his ear back together.

While he rummaged through the kitchen refrigerator and failed to find any beer, Jessica sidled up next to him and fiddled with the dial of an old clock radio that occupied the counter space next to the toaster.

"That was really something back there," she said. "Do you think it'll be on the news yet?"

Oliver smiled. "I guarantee it."

"Oh, here we go," she said.

She'd picked up an AM talk-radio station. The announcer, in a deep southern drawl, reported that what had been coined "The Navy Outlet Rebellion" had now turned against the adjacent Walmart, where a bonfire fueled by George brand Women's Mock-Neck Quilted Fall-Style Jackets was consuming one of the cart-corrals in the parking lot.

Oliver excused himself. He didn't want to hear any more. He was done with protests. He was done with fires, and with everyone's outrage. He was done with violence and drama. He was essentially done with anything that wasn't a shower, a snooze, a snack or a cold beer.

He made his way down the hall to the washroom, where he caught a glance of his soot-covered face in the bathroom mirror. He tentatively fingered his swollen, scabby ear. It was tender as hell, and a one-inch gash had sliced through the cartilage on the top. He gritted his teeth and rinsed the wound with soap and warm water. He kept doing this until the dripping water came off clear.

Rifling through the vanity drawers, he found a box of waterproof bandages. He stuck a few over the wound and tested them. They held well.

Soot and dried blood covered his forehead and neck. He eyed the shower, and decided it would be the first thing to tick off his wish list.

He hunted through the bungalow in search of the linen closet.

Bert and Carmella sat holding hands on the patio by the tiki bar. Teddy and Emma were both in the living room, nodding off on the worn, wicker chairs, while Bob sat on the couch and hen-pecked at his typewriter. How a man could write so often and yet have to hunt for each letter on the keyboard was a mystery.

At the end of the hallway was a room, which on a different plane of the multiverse was the first and only place Oliver Bell had ever witnessed a bright-red nude demon administering a sensual backrub to a writer with fidelity issues. Next to that room, he found what he was looking for. A half-width door hung partly open, revealing a neatly folded pile of unmatched bath towels.

A moment later, he stood under Bob's shower head, rubbing shampoo into his greasy locks, concentrating entirely on not touching his disgusting ear wound. The scent of charred, shoddily made T-shirts and Pert Plus filled the steamy air.

Oliver breathed a sigh of relief. The hot water drumming against his bruised forehead all but lulled him to sleep.

He was very much trying not to remember the football-sized rat he'd seen in hell's version of this bathroom, when someone knocked on the door.

"Are you decent?" Jessica asked.

"I'm just in the shower," he said. "I'll be five minutes."

"I have to pee. I'm sorry. I'm coming in anyway."

"Ah... OK. Just a sec."

Oliver stepped out of the shower and grabbed the towel from the counter, planning to wrap it around his waist so he could safely unlock the door. He had no way of knowing that the lock on Bob's bathroom door was more decorative than functional.

When Jessica opened it, Oliver found himself standing in her direct line of sight, dripping, soapy, and very naked. He scrambled to wrap himself in the towel and fumbled it. The towel landed in a heap at his ankles.

While in some far-off future, he might well have self-consciously imagined himself in an intimate nude encounter with Jessica, the particular circumstances of such an imagined encounter would have been very different than the soapy, horrified, bloody-eared, scrambling disaster that was now unfolding.

"Ya!" he shouted. Then, "Oh... dammit. I'm so sorry!"

He threw himself into the shower and yanked the curtain closed, but he was moving too fast and slipped in a puddle of shampoo, nearly falling back out into the bathroom and only by the grace of God managing to catch himself by the backs of his calves against the lip of the tub. He felt the cold white shower curtain cling his soapy butt cheeks, and he knew with absolute certainty, that Jessica could see every detail of his ass through the translucent vinyl.

He struggled to correct the situation, and somehow overcompensated, such that, for a moment, he gave her a full-frontal blast.

"Ah... Oh my God!" he said.

His feet squeaked and squawked on the wet porcelain as he twisted this way and that, trying to right himself without pressing any more of his anatomy against the shower curtain.

After what seemed like an eternity, he finally regained his balance, if not his poise.

"The... the... lock," he stammered. "It... it must have..."

"Yeah... it doesn't work," she explained.

"Oh my God. I am so sorry! Again! Sorry!" It was all he could think to say.

Imagining what would come next, a dozen scenarios played out in his head at the same time, most of which ended up in at best, humiliation, and at worst, handcuffs. He desperately hoped she knew it had been an innocent mistake.

Jessica laughed. "I should be the one apologizing. It's hard to be a proper hostess in a single-bathroom house."

He heard the sound of the toilet seat opening. "Promise not to look, OK?" she said.

"I'm not a perv, I swear."

"That's exactly what a perv would say though, isn't it?"

This was the first time he'd ever shared a bathroom with a woman. It was also the first time anyone suggested he might be a pervert. He had no idea how to respond. He was a fish out of water in the situation. "I... uh..."

"Relax," she said. "I'm just messing with you."

The toilet flushed and the water in the shower became suddenly piping hot. Oliver yipped.

"Oh right. Sorry," Jessica said. "The plumbing is pretty old."

He ducked into the dry space subtended by the scalding stream. "No problem."

He listened for a minute, but did not hear her leave or the door close again. He risked a peek out the side of the shower curtain.

She had closed the toilet and was sitting on the lid, in her happy floral sundress, with tears tracking shining trails down her cheeks.

Had he upset her? While his display had been truly horrendous, he could not imagine it would have been particularly traumatizing. Was it something to do with Bob? Had she guessed what he was up to? Was it Irena?

"Are—are you OK?"

"Ah... good question." She gave her nose a swipe with the back of her hand. "I don't know."

"You look pretty sad," Oliver observed.

"You've made quite an astute deduction," she sniffed, trying a smile that never quite made it all the way.

She had lovely white teeth, Oliver could not help but notice. They were incredibly straight. He self-consciously ran his tongue over his own teeth, and noticed he had chipped one of his canines. He probably looked like a backwoods yokel.

"Could you... ah... pass me that?" Oliver asked, pointing at the floor where the towel that had so betrayed him lay in a pile.

She picked up the towel, offering it to him, but when he reached for it she held it back, just out of his grasp. "Where does he go, when he disappears like that?"

"Who, Bob?"

"No. David Copperfield." She rolled her eyes a little. "Yes, Bob."

"You don't know?"

"No."

She handed him the towel.

Oliver liked Jessica. He liked Irena, too, for that matter. He really didn't want to get into it. He had sort of promised Bob he wouldn't say anything in exchange for the writer's help back on the negative-twenty-seventh tier of the multiverse. "It's complicated. You should really talk to Bob about it..."

"Is he seeing someone?"

Oliver hated the idea of hurting this woman. He instinctively did what so many men before him had done when faced with such circumstances. He changed the subject.

"You and Bob... are you guys, like...?"

"Together? It's hard to say. I mean, not really. I'd been seeing this guy, and he's kind of Bob's boss at the university, but... well... it's complicated. You know writers."

"I'm an introverted mathematician," Oliver offered. "I hardly know anybody."

"So lucky." Jessica sighed. "You get to deal in absolutes."

"Not always," Oliver said. "We used to hear this joke all the time—what's two plus two?"

"Four."

Oliver smiled. "Three if you're buying, five if you're selling."

"Hilarious."

She rolled her eyes again, and in doing so, ever-so-softly twanged one of his heartstrings.

"The thing is, though, I had this professor, Dr. Friedman, who was convinced you could theoretically prove the joke was true. He hypothesized that if you modeled a simple formula through a series of quantum probability filters you could demonstrate that occasionally, two plus two *is* five—in the right set of circumstances. Other times it's three. The ramifications would be enormous. Everything from nuclear power generation to carbonated beverage dispensers could be changed by this new probability framework. The theory could even unlock the basic premise of space and time, opening up possibilities like time travel, or trans-galactic wormhole creation. He spent seventeen years researching it."

"Was he right?" Jessica leaned forward.

"Nobody knows. He got one of his grad students pregnant and quit his job to work at a General Motors dealership."

"Oh."

"But the point is, regardless of whether he was right or not, nobody could have predicted that the man would end up slinging Chevrolet Equinoxes to retired couples for a living. Even when you work in a world of absolutes, things will still go non-linear. In fact, absolutism may just be the way our un-evolved brains comprehend the universe around us. It allows us to put things in some semblance of order. But that doesn't mean it's real.

"So in a way, you can look at all human behavior as a spectrum of probability, instead of a binary process. Like if someone has a habit that you aren't crazy about, it doesn't necessarily mean that they'll repeat that behavior ad infinitum. Given the spectrum model of behavioral probability, there will be times when any person will display attributes that you like or dislike, so much so that in the fullness of time, were we able to exist infinitely, all people would do all things. So my point, I guess, is that we should try to be patient with one another."

"Equinoctes," she said.

"Pardon?"

"The plural of equinox is equinoctes." Jessica sniffed, and this time her smile made it a little further.

If Oliver had been asked to set a new life goal at that moment, it would have been to never make a woman like Jessica cry.

He grinned, conceding the point. "You study literature. I almost forgot."

She pulled the shower curtain aside—he was grateful he'd wrapped himself in the towel.

"Thanks, Olly."

She pressed herself against him and kissed him on the mouth. Her lips lingered on his for a long second. Her warm breath cascaded over his tongue. Wrapping her arms around his shoulders, she squeezed harder, grinding against his pelvis.

"Oh God," he whispered.

She kissed him again, letting her lips linger on his longer this time, and then sliding the tip of her tongue against his own. He tentatively placed a hand on the small of her back, pulling her closer.

This was crazy! They hardly knew one another! But in the moment, it felt perfectly right.

She slid a hand up the back of his neck, playing her cool fingers through her hair, and massaging his scalp until she playfully tugged at his earlobe.

He winced and she recoiled.

"Oh my God!" she said, her eyes like saucers. "Did I just rip your ear open?"

He stepped back, bringing his hand up to the wound and inspecting it. It came back bloody.

"Uh... no, no. That happened earlier."

"Oh... it's really bad, Olly."

"Yeah. I've been meaning to get it fixed."

She stepped out of the shower and rummaged in a cupboard until she found a facecloth, which she brought up to the side of his head.

"I guess I kind of ruined the moment, didn't I?"

"No! No! The moment's great! Best of my life, in fact! Still one hundred percent in the moment!"

"I can see that," she said, glancing at the towel.

"Oh... right," Oliver covered his crotch with his hands. "Sorry. I uh..." he had no idea how to finish that sentence.

"You're sweet," she said, taking one of his hands and bringing it up to the makeshift dressing. "You'd better hold pressure on this."

Noticing the splotches on her sundress where she'd pressed against his body, he said, "You're all wet."

He then realized what words had just come out of his mouth and turned the approximate color of a pickled beet.

"Another fine deduction, Sherlock."

She winked and turned away, casually calling over her shoulder "Thanks for the talk, Olly. You're a peach."

Then she left, closing the door behind her.

He stood motionless in the shower for a full minute, sensing the warm places where she'd touched him, and wishing that the warmth would never fade. He delicately fingered his lower lip where she had kissed him, imagining that if he pressed the spot too firmly, his first real kiss would disappear from the history books. His heart thrummed in his chest, and it took him a few tries before he managed to accept what had just transpired.

Eventually he recovered his wits.

"A peach?"

He dressed quickly and brushed his teeth.

He needed sleep. He pushed everything else out of his mind. He could deal with his feelings for Jessica later. He could deal with his father's letter later. He could call his mother later. His need for unconsciousness was immediate.

He made his way through the living room.

Jessica had perched herself like a cat on the armrest of the couch and was reading a dog-eared copy of *The Old Man and the Sea*. Her bent knees leaned against Bob, who peck, peck, pecked away at the typewriter. It made Oliver a little jealous. But that was OK. Jealousy was something new for him. A raw emotion he had never felt before. In a weird way, he was glad for it.

But still, it hurt.

Their encounter hadn't been ten minutes ago, and yet it was like he was old news. She didn't even offer a smile, or any acknowledgement of his existence. She just sat there, reading, and touching Bob with her beautiful knees. He supposed it must be this way with creative types. His only option was to play it cool.

Jealous or not, he knew that he would carry the happy memory of his shower encounter with Jessica to his grave.

He slid out to the patio, where a spare lounge chair beckoned him.

"OK if I sit?" he asked.

"Be our guest," Bert said, smiling. "Want me to look at that ear?"

"Is it still bleeding?"

Oliver removed the facecloth. Bert squinted. "No. It looks like it's stopped. We could just leave it. It'll heal in two parts. It'll look very cool. Punk rock, if you know what I mean."

"You should suture it," Carmella said. "It won't match the other side."

"Can we do it later?" Oliver asked.

"Sure!" Bert seemed perfectly happy not to get up.

Too tired for small talk, Oliver put his feet up, closed his eyes and fell instantly into a deep sleep.

Minutes later a terrific ruckus from the living room woke him. He scrambled from his lounge chair, assuming Bob's bungalow had come under attack from sword-wielding penguins. This was not the case.

Beloved and celebrated author Stephen King had arrived. Beloved and celebrated author Stephen King had then placed lesser-beloved and lesser-celebrated author Bob Quinn in a headlock, and appeared to be angling for an arm bar.

The two skinny, out-of-shape authors slapped at one another, cursing.

"When Stephen King invites you to dinner, you show up for dinner, you stupid dick-weed!" King shouted in a brassy New England accent.

"I had important affairs to attend to, you self-aggrandizing blow-hard!"

"You're a bum! You don't do anything! How can you have important affairs to attend to?" King yelled.

"Oh, go write about a washing machine that kills people, you hack!" Bob yelled back.

Jessica threw herself between them. Veins popped up on her neck as she pried with both hands at the entangled authors, but she wasn't much stronger than either of the old men. The entire scene looked like a mime-troop acting out a story about an un-shuckable oyster.

Apparently realizing that she had no chance of breaking King's grip on Bob, Jessica darted to the kitchen, returning a second later with a bottle of Windex, which she sprayed at Stephen King's face. The blue mist hit him directly in the philtrum.

"Ah!" King shouted, using his free sleeve to wipe his upper lip. "Is that Windex?"

"Down!" she cried, as if speaking to a dog. "Get down!"

Bob waved her off. "It's OK, honey," he said.

"You sexist piece of crap!" Stephen King said, before landing a ridiculously pointy elbow on the bridge of Bob's nose, which would have broken were King built of anything more than loose white skin hung over a frame of osteopenic bone and wispy sinew.

Oliver didn't know what to do. Part of him felt he should intervene. Given the physical condition of the two wrestling writers, however, he suspected the most serious injury that might happen would be a rolled ankle, and maybe it was best to just let them have it out. He was also slightly torn, in the sense that he wouldn't completely mind seeing Bob get bopped in the nose once or twice more for upsetting Jessica.

He twisted around, hoping there was a "phone-a-friend" option, but Teddy and Emma were nowhere to be seen.

He allowed the fight to continue for another fifteen seconds before finally shoving his way between the winded and huffing emphysematous authors.

"Guys! Relax!"

King stumbled backwards and fell into a chair, wheezing and clutching at his chest. "Tabby's pissed!"

"I'm sorry, Steve," Bob said, panting.

"Don't apologize to me. Apologize to her."

"I will."

"She made a casserole."

"The one with the mushrooms and cheese?"

"Uh huh."

Oliver cleared his throat. "Can I, uh, get you guys something to drink?"

"Beer," Bob said. "In the bar-fridge."

So *that* was where Bob kept the beer.

"I don't drink," King said. "I don't like to lose control of my emotions."

Oliver returned to the patio, where Bert and Carmella, still holding hands, were snoring on adjacent lounge chairs.

He found a Landshark Lager and a bottle of water in the fridge, and then fussed for a moment finding a bottle opener. He inhaled the humid, Floridian air and wondered once again at the series of cosmically unlikely events that had brought him here. It started, he supposed, with his thesis, then the Halifax riot, then the police officer human host who saved him from the library, then the Vagisil Autonomous Zone, then Detective Jennings, then Mayhem, then Teddy and Emma, then the would-be gunman at the IHOP, then Bert and

Carmella, then Bert's dead neighbor, then the communist accountants, then the glamour that sent Emma to the underworld, then Miami, then the Influence-Ah conference and Cindy, then Bob, then the nineteenth divine tier of the multiverse, then of course he'd seen his dead father and his dead father's new friend, Peter. After that it was the Cast Master 4000, then the underworld and Irena, then Mike Knudson being cut in half by Mayhem, then the ether, then the gravity quake, then Fixeloclastes and Bucky, then Amon, then the grizzly bear with the flame thrower, then the Navy Outlet riot, then his first kiss, then breaking up a fistfight, and now getting a bottle of water for Stephen King. Who could have predicted?

When he returned with their drinks, the two authors had hunched next to one another on the couch, and were busy pouring over the type-written pages of Bob's sophomore novel.

King took the water bottle absently and chugged half of it down, muttering a thank you but refusing to look away from the page he was reading. Bob tipped his beer toward Oliver, making his own absent gesture of thanks.

"Dammit," King mumbled. "This is good."

"Is it always like this?" Oliver asked Jessica.

"Third fistfight this month," she said.

While the two old writers engrossed themselves in Bob's book, Oliver attempted to catch a few more minutes of sleep on the patio, but the adrenaline dump of waking up to a fistfight had overwhelmed his system and he couldn't relax.

Instead of sleeping, he closed his eyes and thought more about Jesicca, and about that kiss. He'd been through a lot lately, but sometimes it was the simple things that demanded one's attention.

After a while, he got up and perched on a barstool. He sipped at a beer and played with the envelopes from his father. He pressed the paper between his thumb and forefinger. Were these really from a different plane of the multiverse? From the place where you go after you die?

The longer he sat at the bar, the more he marveled at the idea. An endless string of universes. An answer to the great unknowable question.

Where do you go when you die?

Florida, in his father's case.

He spun the envelope on the countertop. Opening it would truly end this chapter. He understood that. It was the last thing he had to do. And after that, what? Go where the wind carried him? He just hoped whatever the next chapter was, he would face it with his friends.

He spun his letter around and around.

Each envelope looked and felt the same as any other he'd ever handled. The shape was the same. The paper felt the same. That meant they must have pulp mills in the divine multiverse. Who wanted to go through life only to die, and assume the position of a janitor at a pulp and paper mill?

And yet, it seemed there was an economy up there in heaven. That would mandate a need for materials, for construction, and yes, for paper.

He realized he was just delaying things.

He slid his thumbnail under the corner of the envelope. He paused. He took another look over his shoulder. Bert and Carmella were asleep. Bob and beloved author Stephen King were completely absorbed in Bob's manuscript. Jessica was lost in her Hemingway.

The sun had dipped behind the big, western-facing condominiums on the far side of the main road.

Maybe he really was alone enough to do this.

Still, he hesitated.

After his father died, Oliver had spent hours rummaging through the man's office, checking the document folders on his desktop and laptop, looking for a goodbye note, or a set of instructions. He'd marveled at the fact that the man who was normally so pragmatic and practical had not taken the time to write a letter. Had he just been too damned hopeful?

Jack loved his family. So why had he not written? The answer was in Oliver's hand, but he just... wasn't ready to see it.

He wasn't ready to relive his grief.

He slid the envelopes back into the pocket of his stretched-out jeans.

It could wait another day or so. It could wait until he'd had some rest.

He was considering whether to phone his mother when Teddy and Emma rushed onto the patio. Emma was pale, her eyes wide.

He leapt down from his perch. "What's wrong?"

"Olly, we have to go."

Carmella sat up suddenly. "What's going on?"

"Amon," Emma said.

It was supposed to be all over, wasn't it? They were supposed to be safe now. He'd saved his friends! His job was done!

"But—he can't do anything here. Dad said he would need a human sacrifice, and the sacrifice would have to be possessed by this specific type of demon—"

"Well..." Teddy said, interrupting.

"There might have been a *slight* miscalculation in that regard," Emma finished for him. "The conditions, apparently, are now adequate for his return to secular earth."

"How do you know?"

"Do you remember the simp we met in Miami?" Teddy asked.

"The what?"

"The simp. The man who pays physically attractive women to pretend to like him?"

Oliver gawped. "The fax machine guy?"

"That's the one."

Teddy produced his phone and opened a CNN YouTube video. The title of the video was "Florida Man Ruins Internet Influencer Conference," followed by a graphic content warning.

Shaky cell phone footage from the Influence-Ah conference at the EAST Hotel, Miami, showed a man standing in a broken window frame, leaning out of his room. He appeared to be on the sixth or seventh floor.

Oliver adjusted his glasses. The man in the window did, indeed, appear to be the fax machine guy.

The narration began: "Oh my God, you guys, I think he's going to jump. Oh my..."

Teddy silenced the phone with the volume button. "The narration is grating and obnoxious. He uses the term 'You guys' over seventy times. I counted."

The fax machine guy leaned further out the window, and on the white exterior wall he wrote, in a brownish-purple smear, the words "AMON RETUNS."

"He meant to write 'Returns,'" Teddy explained. "He forgot the second R."

The man disappeared back into the room. A moment later, a white object sailed out the window and landed on the pool patio, sending the crowd scattering in all directions.

The image zoomed in on the thing, which turned out to be a female hand with a wrist and approximately half a forearm attached. Bright yellow happy faces adorned the blood-stained fingernails.

Cindy!

Oliver cursed. He'd somehow forgotten about Cindy. Bert had even *told* him she'd brought a demon back with her! *Of course,* it would be the specific subtype of demon that Amon would need. *Of course,* Amon had been planning to visit the secular universe! It was the only thing that made sense. With tensions kicking off in Eastern Europe and the Middle East, Amon wanted to end it all now! All he needed was Oliver's code—he could simply slip it into the wrong hands and set off the cascade of mutually assured destruction.

He returned his attention to the video. The cameraman back-pedaled from the gruesome severed limb and tripped over a lounge chair. The picture went crazy as the camera skittered and tumbled across the pool patio. When it was picked up again, the shaky footage showed the scattering crowd running from the pool area, through the hotel lobby and into the street beyond.

The camera's perspective spun back around to the hotel and to a swirling maelstrom of dark clouds gathering in the sky above it. Lightning flashed through the sky, and the video ended.

"This is not good," Teddy said.

"Not good?" Oliver stammered. "This is like... The Book of Revelations. Like... the end of humanity... possibly of Earth as we know it! Not just that— if Amon gets his way he'll destroy the whole multiverse. We're talking about complete dimensional destruction! Total spiritual death! The collapse of the cosmos! The end of all things, past, present and future!"

Teddy stroked his chin. "Like I said. It's not good."

Oliver tried to think. His father had warned him not to face off against Amon—that he had no chance of success. But then, his father hadn't met Teddy and Emma. As a team, they'd already faced the demon once—and lived to tell the tale. Maybe there was a chance they could do it again.

"What do we do?" he asked.

"We destroy him," Teddy said.

"Only that didn't turn out to be very easy back in halibut-land."

"Ah! But in halibut land I didn't have the armory."

Oliver blinked.

"The armory," Emma said, tossing Oliver a phone. "Look it up on the way."

He tried to get his head around the idea of going toe-to-toe with Amon again, on so little sleep. A faint alarm sounded in the recesses of his memory— something he was supposed to tell Teddy and Emma.

Bert cleared his voice. "So... back to Miami, then?"

"You don't have to come if you don't want to," Emma said. "It's going to be very dangerous."

"In fact, Oliver will probably die," Teddy added.

"What!?" Oliver said.

Teddy shrugged.

Oliver didn't like the look of that shrug. It was the kind of shrug that suggested he should get used to the idea of imminent demise.

Bert climbed from his lounge chair and stretched. "In for a penny, in for a pound, right Carm?"

"If you're in, I'm in," Carmella said, fumbling through her purse.

She produced a tube of Rub A535, squeezed a dollop into her palm, and proceeded to reach down her waistband and massage it into her right hip.

"We're in," Bert confirmed. "But first, have you seen my back pills?"

Carmella dove back into the purse, this time retrieving a bottle of muscle relaxants.

Bert dry-swallowed one, made a face and then pounded on his chest, presumably to help the pill work its way down his esophagus.

"Let's go," he said.

"What about my ear?" Oliver asked. "Should we like... do something about it?"

"Ah. Right! Just a sec."

Bert charged into the house and returned a moment later, his hands suspiciously behind his back.

"What's in your hands?" Oliver asked.

"Nothing. Now let me see that."

Oliver turned his head, wondering how Bert was going to fix his ear, and then wondering if Bert was even remotely qualified to fix an ear, since he wasn't a plastic surgeon. The old doctor pressed something cold to the gash in his ear, and he flinched.

"Hold still," Bert said. "Right... about... there!"

There was a loud click, followed by excruciating pain.

"Yah!" Oliver yelled. He fell to his knees and brought his hand up to the ravaged meat of his helix and antihelix. His skin was tacky with blood. His probing fingertip brushed against something hard, and the pain flared again.

Bert, smiling, set the stapler on the tiki bar. "That ought to do it."

"You stapled me?"

"Yeah. That's what they would do in the hospital."

"They would staple my ear?"

"Probably. To be honest, I'm not an ear doctor. I'm a cardiologist. But staples are great. Way faster than sutures."

"Did you staple people in the heart?"

"Sure. All the time. Let's go kid."

Bert took Oliver's hand and helped him to his feet.

They filed through the living room, past Bob and Stephen King, who never looked up, and out the front door.

Oliver, last in line, was about to climb into the van when Jessica called out. He stopped and she rushed to meet him. "You're leaving?"

"Yeah. It's a bit of an emergency."

She put a hand on his chest. "Will I see you again?"

"I hope so."

"Probably not," Teddy said from the driver's seat. "He's almost definitely going to die within the next six hours or so."

"Hey! You don't know that for sure," Oliver said.

Jessica worried her lip. "Is that true? Are you going to die?"

"I don't know. Maybe."

She leaned in and kissed him one more time. Her lips pressed hard against his for a long moment before she pulled away. "Try not to die, OK? I kind of like you."

"Uh. OK."

Teddy leaned back from the driver's seat. "Let's go, Romeo."

"Uh... yeah. Sorry about that," he said to Jessica, cocking his thumb at the big man. "You know Teddy. Anyway, I probably should get going. In the meantime, don't worry. I've been with these guys for days, and I haven't died yet, have I?"

She smiled, and this time the smile made it all the way to her shining eyes.

As they pulled from the curb, Bert slapped Oliver on the shoulder. "You definitely could have... you know..." he made a now-familiar obscene gesture with the index finger of one hand and the circled thumb and forefinger of the other again.

Oliver didn't even flinch this time. "You know what? I think you're right!"

"Our boy is growing up!" Carmella announced.

"There will be plenty of time for fornication later," Teddy said, his voice full of encouragement. "On the odd chance you survive the next twelve hours. But just to be clear and to avoid disappointment, that's statistically extremely unlikely."

— *Eighteen* —

The Comprehensive Guide to Hosting a Celestial Entity describes "The Armory" as a loosely affiliated network of scientists, pharmacists, gunsmiths and accountants who, in the interest of preserving the Great Balance, play a supporting role to human hosts.

According to the guide, "*The role of armorer is hereditary in nature, passed down through generations. Where most armorers are laypeople, the armory is considered amongst celestial entities to be one of humanity's best-kept secrets.*"

The Guide goes on to detail the best method of locating an armorer.

...in recent decades, the armory network has developed a clever model to make access for hosts much simpler. By exploiting trends toward both online shopping and antioxidant content in fruit smoothies, armorers have found a way to set up shop in plain sight, with practically no concern for exposure to the public. Specifically, the armory network has taken over most of the world's Orange Julius franchises.

"Hey," Oliver said from the backseat of the minivan. "It says here that Orange Julius is just a front for the armory?"

"Yes, that's true," Teddy said.

"But I love Orange Julius. I think I'd notice if there were arms dealers hanging out at mall kiosks."

"Yeah?" Emma said. "And when was the last time you had an Orange Julius?"

Oliver thought about it for a second. "August twelfth, 1997."

She nodded sagely.

"Oh," he said. "I see."

The faint alarm in the back of his mind grew stronger. It was something Jack and Peter had told him on the nineteenth tier of the divine multiverse. It was something about Legion... maybe something about Amon. His mind flashed on an image of a BB gun.

He remembered!

"Uh... now would probably be a good time to tell you guys something."

"What?" Teddy asked.

"Amon can't be killed with conventional secular weapons. It might even be impossible to kill him by any means. He's an infinite being, just like the Host."

"How do you know that?"

"My dead father told me."

"I see."

Teddy pinched his chin. "I accept your weird explanation. I suspect, though, that we'll still need conventional weapons to get anywhere close to him. Remember, he'll have forty armies of Legion-possessed foot soldiers at his disposal."

"Right, but how are we supposed to *destroy him*, even if we do get *to him*?"

Teddy squinted in deep thought. "Well, I could try to strangle him, I suppose. If that fails, I don't know. Maybe you could try hitting him with a frying pan again."

Oliver rubbed the bridge of his nose.

"What?" Teddy examined him in the mirror.

"Nothing."

"No, not nothing. You were about to say something. Something, nerdy, would be my guess."

"Well, it's just that last time you couldn't get within five feet of Amon."

"I knew it," Teddy said.

Emma put a hand on the big man's shoulder. "He's right."

"So how are we going to kill him without conventional weapons, knowing you can't get close enough to strangle him?"

"I'll be better prepared," Teddy said.

"How?"

"I'll do some extra pushups when we stop for gas."

"That's not how it works!"

"So what's your plan then, brainiac?"

"Well, I was thinking I could agree to hand over the computer code."

Emma and Teddy spun to face him. They shouted in unison, "No way!"

"I won't actually give him the code. I'll just distract him until you..."

"Smash his head in," Teddy finished.

"Well..."

"Well what?"

"That won't work. Well, it certainly won't kill him."

"Maybe we can't completely destroy him. But at least we can give him a concussion. I'd consider that a W." Teddy smiled.

Bert cleared his voice. "You have to use the spirit light."

"Huh?" Oliver cocked an eyebrow.

"The spirit light. Didn't you read anything in that guide? Remember on the boat, when we found out you were hosting Mayhem?"

"Yeah. Sure."

"Remember how it got dark all around us?"

"Uh huh."

"It wasn't really dark. The three of you sort of became light. That's the spirit light. It comes from the Host when they're directly summoned."

"The spirit light is dangerous?" Emma asked.

"It's dangerous to demons," Bert said. "And that's why you have to take me with you when you go to see him."

"No," Emma said. "It's way too hazardous. You and Carmella are our support crew. You can help us get into the city, but there's no way we're taking you to see Amon himself. Just tell us how to make the light happen."

"Sure... how's your ancient Hebrew?"

"Congratulations," Teddy said. "You're officially on the 'People who are going to see Amon' list."

The nearest Orange Julius was located at the Tyrone Square Mall. The drive back took them past the charred remains of the Navy Outlet and the Walmart Supercenter. Smoke curled from the rubble where the two brick-and-mortar giants had so recently stood.

Teddy shook his head. "The human race is nuts."

"The pandemic didn't help," Oliver said. "It pushed people into spending more time on social media. Everything is so polarized now."

"No," Teddy said, "it's always been like this. We just *hear* about it more now."

He reached over and turned up the volume on the stereo.

The broadcast was all about the events unfolding in Miami, reports of armed militia groups roaming the streets, violence erupting in the downtown core, the National Guard being called in to take control, and pleas for residents to remain home. And if that wasn't bad enough, there were reports of supercells developing throughout Miami-Dade County. A category-three funnel cloud had already touched down, leveling the popular Cantina La Veinte.

It was like the world was unravelling. Things had been grim before, but this was uniquely terrible! This was apocalyptic kind of stuff, which was fitting, since an ancient demon was here to destroy the multiverse. Oliver actually found himself missing the simpler days of nude, militant vegans and armed communist accountants.

He rubbed his temples. Urban warfare in a major US city, wandering militia groups, tornadoes. What else? Nuclear explosions was what else. And because he hadn't offered up the code in the ethereal realm, Amon was going to have to make do without those.

So overall, things could be worse.

He allowed himself a half smile. At times like these, the small victories mattered.

Teddy switched the radio off, and a heavy silence settled on them like a funerary shroud.

It was uncomfortable. Silence was OK when one was alone. It was even alright when you were with a friend or two. But between all of them, the quiet diffused like a toxin, dashing their hopes.

Oliver was about to broach it with an inane question about the traffic into Miami, but Bert, clearly on the same wavelength, beat him to it.

"Hey, did you guys know I'm allergic to latex?"

Oliver turned to look at him. "What?"

"Latex. It gives me a rash."

"I'm not sure how that's relevant."

"Oh, it isn't relevant. It's just a thing we older folks do—we fill uncomfortable silences with complaints about our health."

"Oh," Oliver said.

The uncomfortable silence returned.

"I had a polyp in my rectum," Carmella said. "The doctor said it was the size of a man's thumb!"

"That sounds... uncomfortable," Oliver said.

"Oh heavens no. I couldn't even feel it. The gastroenterologist caught it on a routine colonoscopy."

"Well, that's lucky."

"Yes, indeed! It was very lucky! In fact..."

Teddy turned the radio back on.

Emma smiled at Oliver in the vanity mirror. He smiled back. For a group of five people determined to end the life of an extremely powerful, eternal Lord of Hell, they were quite a rag-tag posse.

Emma flipped through the stations until she found one called Rock Classics 96. Oliver recognized the song as "Nookie" by Limp Bizkit, which he didn't consider to be old enough to be a classic, until he did the math and realized that the time span between 1999, when the album "Significant Other" was released, and the present was similar to the timespan between 1971 and his own childhood, when the Classic Rock stations would play songs from the fourth Led Zeppelin album.

Bert nodded his head with the pounding rhythm. "I always liked this song," he said to Oliver's surprise. "It reminds me of a course I took in college called Evolutionary Biology. It turns out, it really is all about the nookie."

Carmella chuckled. "It reminds me of that camping trip we took to the Smoky Mountains. Remember?"

"Oh yeah," Bert said. "You had that little thong, and you let me..."

Teddy accelerated hard, pushing the engine revs to drown out the conversation. He swung the van into the mall parking lot, chirping the tires as they bounced over the speedbumps.

A congregation of what Oliver guessed were Uber drivers had parked their vehicles in a tight circle near the building's main entrance, but other than that the lot was empty. The drivers reclined in their seats, smoking cigarettes and staring at their cellphones.

Teddy brought the van to a crawl and drove past the group before turning a corner and pulling into a spot near a side entrance, where they would be shielded from view.

"I hope they have something good," he said.

Emma smiled. "Only one way to find out, big guy. Let's go."

She hopped out. Teddy followed. Oliver tried to open the sliding rear door, but found that he couldn't.

"What gives?" Bert said.

"I... I don't know."

Teddy returned, grinning. He opened the door from the outside.

"I pranked you!" he cheerfully said. "Since your life expectancy is so incredibly short, I engaged the child lock to lighten the mood!" He stared into the vehicle. "Is your mood lighter?"

"Sure," Oliver said. "Light as a feather, Teddy. Thanks."

"Great! Let's hope they have some weapons of mass destruction. Then we'll all be able to maintain our good spirits!"

Teddy turned and trotted off after his life partner.

"He's joking, right?" Oliver asked. "About the weapons of mass destruction?"

"It's hard to tell, sometimes," Carmella said.

Bert just frowned.

In the mall, which was almost entirely empty, and was clearly in a state of advanced financial distress, Emma jogged ahead, past dozens of empty storefronts, before dodging into a luggage store, one of the only operating businesses along the main thoroughfare. Before Oliver could catch up, she reappeared wearing a red backpack.

They reconvened at the food court, which, along with an Orange Julius, had a Chinese takeaway kiosk manned by a woman who appeared to be the world's oldest surviving methamphetamine addict.

"OK Olly," Emma whispered. "What do you know about guns?"

"Uh... " Oliver didn't want to admit that he knew absolutely nothing about guns, so he wracked his brain for any firearms-related information he could think of. "You're supposed to, uh, assume they're loaded at all times?"

"Right. I think maybe let Teddy and I do the talking, OK?"

"Sounds like a good plan."

At the Orange Julius counter, Teddy cleared his throat and addressed the young man across from him. "Excuse me. Do you have any special menu items available?"

The young man looked Teddy up and down before examining the determined faces of the others. He squinted, in a near-perfect imitation of Clint Eastwood. "What, exactly, did you have in mind?"

"Butternut squash."

"Right this way, please." The young man in the Orange Julius smock lifted the swinging countertop gate and ushered them into the back room. It was dark and cramped, and no larger than a broom closet. Oliver bumped into something and twisted to catch it. It was a broom. This, he realized, made sense.

Teddy started to speak, but the young man held up a hand to stop him.

"Wait. Can I make you an Orange Julius first?"

"We're sort of pressed for time," Teddy said.

"It'll only take a second. I've been dying to make one. I haven't had a customer in, like, forever. It would really mean a lot to me."

"OK," Oliver said. "I mean, if it's not going to take that long, I'd actually like an Orange Julius. I'm pretty thirsty. Plus, I'm probably going to die sometime this evening. I don't mind putting it off for five extra minutes"—he searched his friends' faces—"you know, if it's all the same to you guys."

"I'm thirsty too," Carmella said.

"Might as well make it five," Teddy said.

"OK. Awesome! Wait here a sec."

The young man had to check a recipe card before filling the blender. Bert,

Teddy, Oliver, Emma and Carmella stood shoulder to shoulder in the cramped broom closet and watched.

"I didn't realize they still made Orange Juliuses," Teddy said.

"Julieia?" Emma offered.

"Julii," Bert said.

The young man turned on the blender, then started opening and closing cupboards. "Where the heck are the cups?" he muttered.

"I don't think they make a lot of them," Emma said.

Five minutes later, Bert, Carmella, Teddy, Emma, Oliver and the young man who worked at Orange Julius, whose name was Dirk, stood crammed like sardines in the broom closet of the Tyrone Mall Orange Julius. They slurped loudly at their beverages. Dirk, who admitted to having always been curious, had made himself a drink as well.

"These are really good," Teddy said.

"I forgot how much I like the texture," Bert admitted. "Foamy."

"They're so smooth," Oliver observed. "And, like, sweet, but not *too* sweet."

"You're right!" Emma said. "It's amazing that people don't drink these more."

"It's because of the marketing," Bert explained. "They use point-of-sale marketing, relying on customers who are already at the mall seeing their sign, and being mentally cued to buy a drink. Add to that, the color scheme of the sign is garish and jarring. They use orange and blue on purpose—opposites on the color wheel—in order to grab your attention. But modern mall shoppers, or what's left of them, generally prefer muted tones. More often than not they're here for a technology product like an iPhone case, and the stores that attract them the most are the ones that adopt an Apple Store aesthetic. So, the only customer base they're really appealing to are the folks who came to the mall for a haircut, but psychological studies show that after looking at their own fat faces in a mirror for half an hour, haircut customers are extremely unlikely to shop for fast food products. And even aside from that phenomenon, there's the unappealing prospect of getting prickly little hairs in your food or beverage after going to the salon or barber."

"Wow," Oliver said. "You sure know a lot about Orange Julius."

"He was one of the investors in a big mall in Tampa," Carmella explained. "It went tits up."

Dirk made an "ahem" sound. "So, uh... What can I get for you guys? I assume this is for the issue in Miami?"

"It is indeed," Teddy said. "What do you have in terms of nuclear weapons that can be deployed by a three-person team?"

"What?!" Oliver exclaimed. "I thought you were joking about that!"

Teddy fixed Oliver with a look that said he was definitely not joking about that. But then his eyes softened ever so slightly. "I'll only deploy one in a worst-case scenario."

"Unfortunately, we no longer carry anything that might show trace decay. The proliferation of drone-borne detector technology has sadly made discovery of such armaments highly likely. Especially the Soviet-era warheads that we may or may not have previously had access to. Those things leaked *a lot* of radioactivity."

"Frigging Obama," Teddy said, shaking his head. "Frigging drones."

"Could I interest you, perhaps, in a chemical agent?"

"A chemical agent!?" Oliver couldn't believe what he was hearing.

"Hear the man out," Teddy said.

Was Teddy smiling?

"What do you have?" Emma asked.

"Let's see," Dirk said, pulling a large Tupperware container from one of the shelves and setting it on the floor. He opened it. It held six clear containers. Bright orange liquid sloshed inside.

Dirk held one up to inspect it. A drop of the orange liquid splashed down to the floor.

"Oh my God! It's leaking!" Oliver shouted.

"Hmm..." Dirk said. He touched his finger to the liquid then gave it a cautious taste. "It's Orange Julius mix."

He replaced the leaking container and snapped the lid back on. "Wrong Tupperware."

He toed the drink mix under a utility cart, then stood on his toes and searched the top shelf. "Ah!" he exclaimed, reaching up for an identical Tupperware.

He placed it gently on the floor. Inside were six olive green metal cylinders. Each cylinder had a yellow stripe running around it. There was a pin and spoon-handle mechanism on the top of each device, and Oliver realized he was looking at gas grenades.

"This is rapid-diffusion tranquilizer gas," Dirk announced.

"What's the dispersion area?" Emma asked.

"Indoors, you'll get a roughly forty-foot radius per round. It will obviously be diluted by the... uh... barometric event that's occurring in Miami, so try not to use it around open windows or doors."

He handed three of the grenades to Emma, who stuffed them in her backpack.

"What else do you have?"

"I have paralytic curare darts from the Amazon basin—"

"We'll take them," Teddy said.

"Are you comfortable with a blowgun?" Dirk asked.

"I survived four years in the jungles of Angola, hunting colobus monkeys with one," Teddy explained.

"Like that monkey from *Friends*?" Carmella asked.

"There was no monkey in *Friends*," Teddy said definitively.

"Yes there was. It was Ross's pet. Remember?" Emma said.

"No."

"She's right, dude," Dirk said.

"Why don't I remember that?" Teddy asked.

"His name was Marcel," Emma said.

"It was actually a female," Oliver offered. "And she was a white-faced capuchin, not a colobus."

"Wow," Emma said. "*Friends* fan?"

"Incredible Daily Facts app," Oliver said.

"I love that app!" Dirk exclaimed.

"What do you have in the way of anti-armor Javelin missiles?" Teddy asked.

"Not much," Dirk admitted. "Another group cleaned me out the day before yesterday."

"Any guns left?" Emma asked hopefully.

"Sure."

He retrieved another Tupperware box. "We have the usuals. Glock 17, Colt 1911. Let's see…" He rummaged through the small handgun cases inside the Tupperware. "Ooh! I have a Ruger Blackhawk 357 magnum."

"I'll take that one," Emma said, popping the latches on the case. She loaded the revolver with a box of cartridges that had been stored with it, then put both the gun and the remaining cartridges in her backpack with the blow gun and gas grenades.

"Do you have anything bigger?" Teddy asked.

"I believe I have a Desert Eagle 50," Dirk said. He began stacking the handgun cases beside the Tupperware box, but Teddy stopped him.

"I mean, a lot bigger."

"Like... how big?" Dirk asked.

"Like vehicle-mounted big."

"Vehicle-mounted?" Oliver asked. "Like in the Middle East?"

Dirk ignored the question and addressed Teddy. "Can you follow me to my shop?"

Teddy checked his watch. "How far?"

"Two-minute drive."

"Is it worth it?"

Dirk smiled. "Oh yes."

"Then sure."

Dirk closed the Orange Julius kiosk.

On the way out of the mall, at Teddy's insistence, they stopped outside a Dick's Sporting Goods.

"I'll just be a sec. Wait here," Teddy said.

"What's he doing?" Oliver asked Emma.

"Baseball bat," she said. "Guaranteed."

A second later, Teddy jogged back to them grinning. He was carrying a Louisville Slugger.

In the parking lot, Dirk jumped into a blue Ford Fusion and spun the tires as he hurtled onto the main road. He turned right at the first light and disappeared.

"Oh for crying out loud," Emma complained. "He knows we have to follow him, right?"

They got stuck behind a transport truck at the light, but when Emma made the right turn, Dirk had parked up along the street and was waiting for them. She pulled up beside him.

He looked sheepish.

"Sorry. I was a little excited."

"It's fine," Emma said. "Let's go."

They followed him into a subdivision. He parked in the shrub-lined driveway of a small bungalow, and Emma backed the van in behind his car.

Dirk sprang from the driver's seat, and rolled up the garage door, revealing an arsenal that could have adequately provisioned a force intent on the takeover of a small European nation. The young man beamed with pride. On each wall hung row upon row of rifles, shotguns, mortar tubes and grenade launchers.

"Aha!" Teddy said, making his way to a large black gun that stood on a tripod in the back corner of the room. "Is this a—"

"Mark Nineteen, forty-millimeter belt-fed automatic grenade launcher," Dirk finished for him.

Teddy stooped to pick up the gun.

"Be careful of your back," Dirk said. "With the tripod and the ammo-can that's at least a hundred and fifty pounds."

Teddy hoisted the grenade launcher easily, and slung it over his shoulder, grinning.

"Whoa," Dirk said.

Obviously keen to show off, Teddy made his pectoral muscles twitch and dance. He smiled wide, waggling his eyebrows at Emma. "Pretty strong, right?"

"Alright, alright, that's enough, hotshot," she said, opening the rear lift-gate. Teddy folded the rear seat down, and mounted the gun, pointing it out of the back.

Oliver lifted an eyebrow, puzzling at the arrangement.

"It's so you don't shoot me with a grenade," Teddy explained. "Or Emma... I don't want you shooting her either. She's very important to me."

"Aw," Emma said.

"I love you," Teddy said to her, "and I very much enjoy fornicating with you. It would be tragic if Oliver were to accidentally frag you."

Teddy jogged to a far wall, where he grabbed a pair of black shotguns and two boxes of buckshot. He tossed one of the shotguns to Emma, who caught it by the pistol grip and expertly racked a round into the chamber.

"Benelli M4's! My favorite!"

"Should I get a gun?" Oliver asked. He oddly found himself wanting one. He was going into a war zone after all. He felt he should be armed with something more dangerous than a very thorough understanding of calculus.

"No," Teddy said.

"A knife, or something?"

Teddy looked around. He found a small red Swiss Army knife next to a crate of .308 rounds. "Here you go." He handed Oliver the pocketknife.

"Oh... that's for cutting packing tape," Dirk said.

"Yes. And Oliver can use it to defend himself," Teddy explained.

Oliver fiddled with the knife. "Ouch."

"What?" Teddy asked.

"Nothing."

"Did you just break your fingernail trying to open the blade?"

Oliver felt himself blush. "Yes."

"Is that blood?"

Oliver examined his finger. "Yes it is."

Dirk squinted at the instrument. "Technically, the thing you're trying to open is the flat-head screwdriver."

"Be careful," Bert said. "The edges of those screwdrivers can cause quite a scrape."

"Shouldn't I have something a little bit more... uh... dangerous?"

"No," Teddy said. "Absolutely not."

"You'll get to use the grenade launcher," Emma said cheerfully, "in the event that you're the only surviving occupant of the minivan. Everyone else will have guns. You'll be fine as long as you stick with us."

"Wait! Bert and Carmella get guns?" Oliver asked. "They're practically octogenarians."

"That reminds me, Carmella," Teddy said. "Do you know your way around a Heckler and Koch PSG1?"

"What do I look like, a Canadian?" Carmella asked. "Of course I know my way around a PSG1."

Teddy handed her a large sniper rifle with a black stock and wooden pistol grip. A long scope, branded *Nightforce*, had been mounted on the top rail.

"That looks like something out of a video game," Oliver said.

Dirk nodded at the weapon. "She saw some action in Iraq and Yemen, but she runs as clean as the day she came out of the factory."

"Is this sighted in?" Carmella asked.

"Zeroed at one hundred yards. She'll shoot sub-MOA groupings all day long. That's a Hart, custom competition fluted 4140 chrome-moly bull barrel. She gets even more accurate when she heats up. No need to let her cool. She'll eat fifty, sixty rounds without drifting a millimeter."

With casual, practiced smoothness, Carmella removed the magazine and checked that it was loaded before inspecting the chamber and ejecting a round, which she caught midair. "Any spare mags?"

Dirk handed her a fifty-round drum magazine. She slammed it into the magwell and pocketed the smaller magazine. It made an unsightly rectangular bulge in her khaki stretch-fabric leisure pants.

"Are you kidding me?" Oliver squeaked. Nothing, leading up to now, had indicated in any way that Carmella knew her way around a military sniper rifle.

He turned to Teddy. "Why can't I have a gun? I feel juvenile and pathetic."

"Because it would be against the law," Teddy said. "Unless you have your possession and acquisition license. And even then, we'd still need a special permit."

"What!?" Teddy had killed people. And now he was going to fuss about paperwork!?

"I'm trying to be polite," Teddy said. "The real reason is that you're clumsy, and I think you would accidentally shoot one of us."

"But..." He wanted to protest, but then he remembered the Cast Master 4000 tumbling away into the atmosphere of the ether during the gravity quake.

"Relax, Oliver," Bert said. "You're the only one of us who's ever gotten close enough to Amon to actually hurt him."

"I hit him with a frying pan," Oliver explained, as an aside to Dirk who nodded appreciatively.

"If you go in there looking like Rambo, he's going to get his back up," Bert continued. "Your whole schtick is that you're unassuming. If anyone can get close enough, it's you."

"If you do get close, don't fight any compulsions you might experience," Emma said. "Mayhem is probably our best chance at surviving this thing. If anything can summon the spirit light, it's that dog."

"What dog?" Dirk said.

"Don't worry about the dog," Teddy said. "It's a Host thing."

"The thing is," Emma continued. "You be you. Be sweet. Be harmless. Be helpful, even. You're our best chance."

"Emma's right," Teddy acknowledged. "Having said that, there's about a ninety-seven percent chance that if you get anywhere near him, Amon will just kill you and collect Mayhem, trapping him in one of the in-between layers of the underworld for eternity. So, if it looks like things are going that direction, go ahead and use the Swiss Army knife."

"Terrific," Oliver said, not feeling terrific at all.

Teddy made to hand Bert a rather lovely walnut-stocked pump-action shotgun with an extended magazine tube. Bert held up his palms. "Do no harm, remember? I'm still a doctor."

"Not killing Amon and allowing Legion to spread across the continental United States will most likely result in three hundred thirty-seven million deaths in this country, and almost seven billion worldwide," Teddy assured him.

Bert took the shotgun.

"Here," Dirk said, strapping canvas webbing with two ammunition pouches around the old man's waist.

"Hey. It's like a fanny pack," Bert said, admiring the setup.

"I had a feeling you'd like it."

Dirk then dumped a box of clear shotgun shells into each of the pouches. "Double-aught buck," he said. "Be careful... it makes a mess."

Bert slid ten rounds into the magazine, and then racked the action to draw a shell into the chamber, before thumbing the safety.

"You guys really know your way around guns," Oliver observed.

"I used to shoot clays at the trap club," Bert explained, "before that prick lawyer, Jeff Mickelson, had me kicked out for unsportsmanlike conduct."

"What did you do?"

"I shot the tire of his car. We were having an argument about frivolous medical malpractice suits. I might have been a little hot-headed in those days. But I don't regret it. The guy was a slime-ball."

"Lawyers, right?" Oliver said, trying desperately to sound like he at least knew something about the world, even if his understanding of weaponry fell drastically short.

"My mom's a lawyer," Dirk said.

"Oh," Oliver said. "Sorry."

Nineteen

Save for an occasional military convoy, the southbound lanes of Interstate 27 were empty.

Teddy kept the radio on for the first leg of the drive. The news was all about tornadoes, chaotic firefights, mounting casualties and a phenomenon in which organized gangs of individuals armed with "military assault-style weapons" were opening fire on civilians, the National Guard, and anyone else crossing their makeshift checkpoints. The news anchor on the radio referred to these gangs as "Right-wing militia groups," though it was unclear exactly how the radio station's journalists had determined the political leanings of the murder squads.

Regardless, the downtown core of Miami had devolved into a war zone.

Oliver would have much preferred the silence, but Teddy explained that he was waiting for the traffic report, which could help him and Emma formulate a plan of ingress. "We want to avoid any checkpoints or blocked roads until we're close enough to walk, carrying all this gear," Teddy said. "Otherwise, prepare for major inner thigh chafing."

Oliver secretly suspected the big man just didn't want to hear any more of Bert and Carmella's health complaints.

According to the news anchor, the major highways in and out of the city were gridlocked, and the National Guard had set up checkpoints at all ingress and egress routes. They were turning away anyone crazy enough to enter Miami, and were searching exiting vehicles for firearms.

All lines of communication were jammed. Cellphones had completely stopped working, and there had been next to no new information for over an hour.

When it became clear that nobody knew what was happening, the talk radio politicos took over. They battled it out regarding the cause of the chaos. It was pure speculation, but they could certainly take up airtime. While some excitedly theorized that an Islamist terrorist attack was at the heart of the matter, others referred to the footage from the EAST Hotel and argued that it could all be the result of a satanic death cult uprising. Still more wonks were convinced that the entire thing was the result of Russian disinformation.

The intense squabbling, combined with the sweet benzene aroma of gun oil, gave Oliver a headache.

The existential anxiety he experienced would be comparable to that of a death-row inmate watching a delivery van carrying the lethal dose of barbiturates pulling up at the warden's office. He didn't fight the feeling. Whatever was in store for him, he was just going to have to accept it.

If this was the end, he could think of worse last meals than an Orange Julius.

Finally, Teddy pulled over on the side of the highway and climbed out. He slid Oliver's door open. "You're up."

"Huh?"

"You're driving. Emma and I have to oil the guns."

"They're already oiled."

"Sure... by that Dirk guy. Never trust a gun you didn't clean and oil yourself."

Oliver shrugged. "Can I turn off the radio?"

Teddy studied Bert and Carmella, who stared straight back at him. "No."

After pulling back into the middle lane, Oliver's next order of business was changing the dial to an oldies channel. Rolfe Harris sang "Tie Me Kangaroo Down Sport."

"If I'm going to die, I'd really prefer not to have to listen to any more talk radio. OK?"

Teddy nodded sagely. "He was a pedo, you know."

"What?" Oliver said.

"Rolfe Harris. He did time for it."

"No—no way!" Oliver refused to believe it.

Teddy pulled out his phone and looked up Rolfe Harris. He showed Oliver the screen.

"Son of a bitch," Oliver said. "I used to love this song. My dad knew all the words."

"Even the verse about the Aboriginals?" Bert asked from the back seat.

"What?"

"You know 'let me Abo's go loose, Bruce.'"

"What!?"

"They changed the lyrics later," Teddy said.

"Why does everything seem to get worse when you look into it?" Oliver asked.

Teddy sighed. "Try living for a thousand years. People can be pretty disappointing."

"So Amon was right? We're out of balance?"

"Oh he's not wrong," Emma said. "He's just aiming for something that we can't reconcile with."

"Still... should we just... I don't know... let it all burn?"

"Because of Rolfe Harris?" Teddy asked.

"Among other things."

"No," Teddy said. "It's out of balance, but I want you to think for a second about how it's out of balance. Rolfe Harris was a pedo, right?"

Oliver nodded.

"Are you a pedo?"

"What?! No!"

"Don't get upset, Oliver, I'm just making a point. So, you're not a pedo. That's Oliver, one; Rolfe Harris, zero. That's balance."

Teddy turned around.

"Bert, are you a pedo?"

"No, sir."

"Now we're at two non-pedos to one pedo. Do you think I'm a pedo?"

"No."

"So now we're at three to one, and I don't think Carmella or Emma are pedophiles either so that's five to one. Not very balanced, now, is it?"

"I guess not."

"While people individually can be disappointing, overall they're generally good. The people who rise to positions of power or fame are generally the most disappointing of all of us because the successful pursuit of such earthly delight favors traits like narcissism and sociopathy, so we get a skewed representation of how bad things are when we consume media."

"I guess I see—"

Teddy held up a hand. "But think about it! If we rebuilt humanity, and balanced good and evil so that for every good person there was an evil one, it would turn to absolute chaos. You wouldn't even make it to tribalism. In fact, you probably wouldn't make it to the second generation."

"So the Great Balance is...?"

"Loosely defined," Teddy said.

Teddy used a traffic app on his phone to help Oliver find the least congested route to the city center. The rain began in Sebring, and by the time they crossed the Kissimmee River it was hammering down in sheets, whipped by a brutal, unrelenting wind.

They stopped to fill the minivan in Okeechobee. Teddy got a few sideways looks, standing in the driving rain in a soaking white tank top. Other drivers, all of whom were going north, away from the chaos, gawped as he started a warmup routine with the baseball bat slung over his shoulders. He did a round of jump squats, his giant muscles flexing and swelling with each movement. Oliver knew, of course, that Teddy was strong, but he hadn't realized just how strong before that moment. The man was a freaking colossus!

At the South Florida Chinese Bible Church on Griffin Road they hit a government checkpoint. Uniformed National Guardsmen milled about under a flapping tarpaulin. Oliver slowed to a stop at the boom barrier, and a young guardsman, one hand outstretched to protect his face from the rain, hustled out to meet him.

Oliver rolled down his window, feeling flustered. He'd known there would be a checkpoint, so why in the name of all things holy hadn't they come up with a plan to get through. He tried to think of something that would make sense.

Teddy leaned close. "Let Mayhem do the talking."

Just as Teddy said it, he was seized by a compulsion.

"Folks, this is an exclusion zone. I'm afraid that in the interest of national security, civilians aren't allowed past this point," the guardsman shouted over the howling wind.

"We aren't civilians. We're with the National Meteorological Service," Oliver said. "We're here regarding the supercell."

"Uh..." the guardsman poked his head inside the window. He took his time, first inspecting Oliver, who probably looked like he might be some kind of scientist, then Teddy, who looked like Dwayne "The Rock" Johnson and who had a Louisville Slugger propped between his legs, then Emma, who looked like some kind of fitness instructor, then Bert, who looked like an eighty-year-old retired Jewish cardiologist, and finally Carmella, who looked like a sweet grandmother, who happened to be cradling a massive Heckler and Koch sniper rifle with a drum magazine.

"Can I see... a badge or something?" the guardsman asked.

"Badges?" Oliver said. "We don't need, uh, badges. We're meteorologists."

The guardsman poked his head back inside the van. Rivulets of rainwater sluiced down the creases in the hood of his raincoat and into Oliver's lap.

"Is that a Mark Nineteen forty-millimeter belt-fed grenade launcher?"

"Yes," Oliver said. "We use it to fire sensing equipment into funnel clouds from a safe distance."

"And the rifle?" he nodded to Carmella.

"An even safer distance."

"I don't know..." the guardsman said.

"Look—how the hell would we get our hands on a belt-fed grenade launcher if we weren't with the government?" Oliver asked, feigning impatience. "We really need to get in there before the storm breaks up."

"It's going to break up?" the guardsman asked.

"Of course it is."

The guardsman picked up a clipboard and wrote their license plate number in pencil on a soggy sheet of paper.

"You folks stay safe," he said.

"You too," Oliver replied, rolling up his window.

They idled forward into the exclusion zone.

— *Twenty* —

What their plan lacked in thoroughness, it made up for by being easy to remember.

The idea was to infiltrate the Miami EAST Hotel by whatever means necessary, and then to get as close as possible to Amon, at which point Bert would utter an ancient Hebrew incantation and the Host would hopefully take over and send out some sort of interdimensional death ray. Ultimately, the hope was that it would work like the face-melting ghosts at the end of the first Indiana Jones movie, but Bert couldn't specifically promise that result.

Failing victory by spirit light, the next best hope was that Mayhem would speak through Oliver and deliver some sort of profound, timeless wisdom to convince Amon to abandon his plan to end the universe and release whatever Celestial Host beings he had trapped in the ether.

If both those plans failed, they would try to beat the little bastard to death.

"If it comes down to Plan C, it's best to improvise," Teddy said. "If we're too specific, it might not be manageable depending on the situation on the ground. Plus, it will make for a better story that way."

The first two minutes of the drive went surprisingly smoothly.

Oliver allowed himself a sigh of relief. Maybe this wouldn't be as bad as they'd anticipated.

Then, with an eardrum-splitting crack, the windshield burst into a fractal pattern of spiderwebs. They were just outside the guitar-shaped Hard Rock Café and Casino.

Oliver slammed on the brakes. "What the hell was that? Did we get hit by lightning?"

The driver's-side window exploded, spraying safety glass all over him.

"Back, back, back!" Teddy shouted.

Oliver put the van in reverse and hit the gas hard. "What's going on?!"

"Gun!" Emma yelled, pointing at the casino.

Oliver frantically looked where she was pointing, but he didn't see anything. Then a tiny flash illuminated one of the windows.

Whump! The hood caved in.

"Turn!" Teddy yelled.

Oliver, without thinking, whipped the van into a J-turn. The tires squealed, skipping over wet tarmac.

"Did you guys see that?!" he shouted. "Did you see that J-turn? I can't believe I just did that."

"Nice driving, Schumacher," Bert growled from the back seat. "But could you get us the hell out of here?"

Emma scrambled over Carmella's shoulder, and flipped herself into the trunk. She booted the lift gate hard, and it flung open as bullets ripped through the thin sheet metal of the sliding door. Foam exploded from the mid-row seats.

"Do you see him?" Teddy shouted.

"I have them!" Emma called. "Two on the third floor!"

Oliver craned his neck crazily to see what was happening. Teddy reached up and grasped Oliver's chin in his palm, before pointing the younger man's head forward. "Eyes on the road."

He nodded that he understood, but couldn't help but steal glances at Emma in the rearview mirror.

She manned the grenade launcher, her legs splayed around either side of the tripod. In one smooth, practiced motion she slammed the top cover assembly down on the ammunition belt and racked the charger.

"Firing!"

She sent three rounds downrange as Oliver sped back the way they'd come. The big gun made a mechanical *cah-chunk cah-chunk cah-chunk* as it fired. It was so loud, Oliver felt the concussion in his chest. A second later three blasts echoed back.

"Got them," Emma announced. "Two dead."

"Dead?" Oliver asked. "They're dead?"

"Ker-splat," Emma said, pantomiming the motion of a human body being blown in half in the rearview mirror for his benefit.

"Oh God."

Of course, he knew there would be violence. But intellectually conceptualizing it and blowing people up with a grenade launcher were very different beasts. "Who were they?"

"They were the people shooting at us," Emma said.

"Legion-possessed," Teddy said. "Like the guy who was going to shoot you in Halifax."

"Right. OK," Oliver said. "They were shooting at us. They were *shooting...* at *us*. Oh man. But they're dead. Legion."

Adrenaline coursed through his bloodstream. He was talking a mile a minute. He could hear it. His voice sounded high and tight. His mouth tasted like copper.

The crazy thing was, he wasn't particularly scared—just...wired! *Too wired*. He tried to imagine his father patting him on the back, and after a second managed a deep breath.

He swerved to avoid a pair of burning sedans in the middle of the road.

"It's OK," Teddy said. "You can slow down."

He glanced at the speedometer. He was doing nearly seventy. He brought the minivan to a more reasonable forty-five.

"Everyone alright?" Bert asked.

"I pissed my pants a little bit," Carmella admitted.

"Me too," Bert said. "Isn't getting old great?"

"It beats the alternative, they say."

An upcoming side street ran into a subdivision. Oliver swung off the main road. Only once he was out of range of the Hard Rock Cafe and Casino did he pull over.

"What are you doing?" Teddy asked.

"I, uh..." Oliver got out of the car and put his head between his legs.

"Take some deep breaths," the big man suggested.

"I am," Oliver said.

"Are you hit?" Bert asked.

"Nope."

"I think he's trying not to vomit," Carmella said.

"Bingo," Oliver said, snapping his fingers and pointing at Carmella, without looking.

When he was moderately confident he wasn't going to upchuck, he got back in the van.

"Congratulations," Teddy said.

"For what?"

"Not puking."

"Thank you, Teddy," Oliver said.

"Let's find somewhere safe and inspect the damage," Emma suggested.

Oliver cruised through the subdivision until he found a small playground. He eased the minivan into the parking lot. With plenty of foliage to give them cover, it seemed as good a spot as any.

He popped the dented hood and jumped out to see if the engine had been damaged. Aside from a crack in the plastic cover, it looked like it was OK. He took a knee and peered underneath. No fluids leaked out. No ominous oily puddles had formed.

Bert stood guard with his shotgun while Teddy and Emma plotted a new route to the hotel.

"We're going to have to creep through the subdivisions," Teddy said. "The main roads will be full of ambush spots."

Ambush spots? Oliver had thought he understood what he'd signed up for. It was turning out to be a little more intense than he'd imagined.

Teddy pointed through the rain toward the downtown core. "I suspect we'll see more abandoned and burned-out vehicles as we get closer to the city center. They make for natural bottlenecks, and if you see vehicles across the road ahead, expect incoming fire. I'm thinking that won't be as big an issue if we stick to subdivisions and side streets, but, I'll be honest with you guys, I have no way of knowing for certain. I just imagine that if I were Amon, and I were establishing my choke points, I'd start with the main roads. Those are the roads the big, armored vehicles will need to use."

"We do have a few things working in our favor," Emma said. "The weather is terrible. It will give us some cover. The side streets will have more exit options, which means we can keep moving. Even a top military sniper would have trouble hitting a moving target in a downpour like this. And these people aren't in the military. They're just regular Floridians who were unlucky enough to be possessed by interdimensional hell-spawn. They aren't strong. They aren't tactical. They aren't necessarily intelligent. Their only big advantage is that there are a heck of a lot of them."

"Where are they getting their guns?" Oliver asked.

"They probably have an armory system, just like ours," she said. "But there's no point in worrying about it. They have them. That's all that matters."

Teddy spent a moment consulting Google Maps before setting the route into the GPS. According to the new directions, they would sweep south of the hotel and flank in from what Oliver agreed would be the least-expected angle. Amon would be expecting an attack over land, and that meant he would shore up the approach from the north. If they could come at the hotel from the south, they might meet less resistance.

Everyone climbed back into the vehicle. Oliver, despite being soaking wet, didn't feel the least bit cold, but he shivered uncontrollably all the same.

"It's the adrenaline," Teddy said. "It'll pass."

"Why aren't you shaking?" Oliver asked.

"My adrenaline levels are normal."

"Normal! How can they be normal? We almost died back there!"

Teddy laughed. "Almost died? Don't be so dramatic. I hardly even puckered my sphincter."

Oliver shook his head. "Unbelievable."

Teddy's upper lip twitched.

"OK, listen up," he said. "I want everyone to watch for anything weird on the side of the road. Sandbags, wrecked cars, people picking up a cellphone when you drive by... stuff like that."

"I can hardly see anything through the broken windshield," Oliver said.

Teddy brought his knee up to his chest and kicked the windscreen. It clattered down across the hood and onto the ground.

"Better?"

Everything went blurry, and Oliver, out of instinct, pulled the wiper stalk. Blue washer fluid sprayed through the empty space, directly into his and Teddy's faces. The wipers wiped crazily at nothing at all.

"Oh. Right."

Teddy used a massive forearm to squeegee the liquid from his eyes. "Are you done?"

Oliver took a second to pat his lenses on his shirt, then turned off the windshield wipers.

"Yep. That should just about do it."

He put the van in gear. "Onward and upward."

Creeping forward, he kept his head on a swivel, hypervigilant to any possible threat. He followed the directions on Teddy's phone. Every thirty seconds or so, Teddy called back from the passenger seat. "Anything?"

Emma answered. "Nothing."

When they came to the next subdivision, Oliver hit the gas, not wanting to offer any potential amateur snipers an easy target.

Teddy put a hand on his shoulder. "You're doing great. Keep it under fifty."

Oliver still shook like a leaf, but he was managing. He was no Rambo, but he could play his part in this thing with relative competence. Two weeks ago, he never would have guessed.

Bravery, he now understood, didn't mean you weren't scared. Bravery was working through something despite your fear. And now that he was doing it, he knew in his heart that he had grown. Or maybe *matured* was a better word for it. If he survived this day, he would emerge from it, changed. This was the kind of experience, his father would have told him, that puts hair on one's chest.

He remembered Hemingway. "A man can be destroyed, but not defeated."

Despite everything, he smiled.

He noticed Teddy looking, and when he turned, Teddy just nodded thoughtfully, his deep brown eyes, for the first time, soft and understanding as though he knew exactly what Oliver was going through.

For the first time, he was an integral part of a team, and Oliver, despite facing pretty steep odds against survival, was kind of enjoying himself.

Approaching a corner, he slowed and craned his neck to see two parked pickups facing one another, blocking the road. He eased to a stop.

The distant *rat-tat-tat* of automatic gunfire echoed through the neighborhood.

He raised an eyebrow at Teddy, but Teddy, who must have known what he was about to ask, shook his head no. "Drive around them on the lawn."

"But what if it's—"

"It's the homeowners," Teddy said. He gestured at the houses on opposite sides of the street. Both garage doors were open, both bays empty. "They're trying to keep people out of the neighborhood."

"Won't they be pissed off if I drive on the grass?"

"It's the least of their worries."

Oliver drove over the curb, across the sidewalk and over the lawn, circumventing the choke point. Nothing happened.

"How did you know?"

"I have—or I suppose I should say the moth-guy has—a pretty good sense for Legion," Teddy said. "That wasn't Legion."

At the end of the subdivision, Oliver slowed to a stop at an intersection. He didn't like the look of the road ahead. It was too open. There were trees on one side that would provide a perfect hiding spot for an opposing force. Smoke billowed from burning cars just out of sight, and he intuited that those vehicles would create a bottleneck. His intuition screamed.

A dark shadow caught his attention. Movement! *Something—no— someone* was moving. *Running.* He pointed and whispered, "Hey!"

"What is it?" Teddy asked.

"A guy just ran across the road, up there. He ducked into the tree line."

"You sure?"

"Yeah."

"Stay here."

Teddy quietly clicked open the passenger door and dropped to the tarmac. Crouching low, he darted behind a nearby gas station.

"He left his baseball bat," Oliver said.

"He has the blow gun," Emma said. "He's a crack shot."

"In this kind of wind?"

"He'll account for it. You'll see."

Oliver's world paused. Fat raindrops hammered at him through the broken windshield. Cold water pooled in his crotch. He felt exposed but didn't dare move the van and inadvertently screw up whatever it was Teddy was doing.

After what felt like an hour, but was, in reality, only two minutes, he turned to Emma. "Should I go look for him?"

"He'll be fine."

Another agonizing five minutes passed.

Something had obviously gone wrong. Oliver reached for the door handle. Lightning flashed and thunder rumbled—just as Teddy's face popped up out of the gloom at his window. The big man was drenched in blood.

Oliver screamed.

Teddy slid around to the passenger side and climbed in. The seat cushion squished when he sat on it. Deep crimson stained nearly every stitch of his clothing.

He looked like something out of a horror movie. Oliver gawped.

"It's OK," Teddy said. "It's transmission fluid."

"Transmission fluid?"

"They had a pickup truck. I dismantled it."

Oliver breathed a sigh of relief. "So, you didn't have to kill anyone?"

Teddy laughed. "No, no. I killed eleven men. I also paralyzed a woman with a curare-tipped dart. I didn't have a choice. She was going to shoot me. I'm hoping she'll survive, but of course, without access to a ventilator, that seems pretty unlikely."

"Oh my God," Oliver said.

Eleven people! Serial killer Jack Unterweger had killed eleven people over a lifetime. His friend had just matched that record in less than ten minutes.

Teddy snapped his fingers, breaking Oliver's trance. "You're good to go."

"Eleven people?"

"Twelve if you count the woman. Let's move."

As they drove past the disabled checkpoint, Oliver couldn't help but notice a white Toyota pickup with a large gun mounted in the back. Hanging over the side of the bed was what appeared to be a human arm.

Teddy followed his gaze.

"That Tacoma is a great truck. The bed will hold ten and a half human bodies and a Soviet heavy machine gun almost perfectly."

Oliver tried not to think too hard about what Teddy had just said.

They drove south and east until they arrived at a tall condominium building called the Four Ambassadors. According to Google Maps, they were within a mile of the EAST Hotel.

"Stop here," Teddy said. "We need to go inside."

Oliver eased the van into the parking lot. Vehicles of all kinds were placed helter-skelter in the parking lot and loading zone. Many of them were heavily dented and missing glass. One Volkswagen had burned to a husk, the only recognizable feature being the emblems on the fire-oxidized alloy wheels.

Oliver climbed from the driver's seat and crouched beside the sliding door. After Bert, Carmella, and Emma disembarked, he took a moment to inspect the bullet holes along the panel.

"We got lucky," Emma said, prying a flattened chunk of copper and lead out of the B-pillar behind the driver door. "It was just a nine-millimeter."

"Speaking of that, if Legion has an armory network, should we assume that they have grenade launchers too?"

"Oh, definitely. You saw the gun truck, right? That DShK machine gun is a heavy hitter. Sort of a classic Middle Eastern technical weapon. It's long been postulated that their armorers are affiliated with world governments, which means we're most likely going to be severely outgunned, since our armorers are only affiliated with Orange Julius."

"Great," Oliver said. "The news keeps getting better and better."

"Don't worry. We still have something they don't have."

"And what's that?"

"We have *you*. So, we'll just have to use that big brain of yours to outsmart them."

She sounded confident. Not wanting to dash her hopes, Oliver nodded.

Teddy led the way and jogged through the parking lot, sprinting from one vehicle to the next and ducking for cover until reaching the entrance of the Four Ambassadors. He left a crimson trail in his wake.

Oliver, Bert and Carmella followed, and Emma brought up the rear.

Once inside, Emma leap-frogged past Teddy. She took point, revolver at the ready. She whipped around the first corner and swept the muzzle left to right. "Clear!"

Teddy then bypassed her position to the next hallway, and checked it.

The two moved with a natural rhythm that reminded Oliver of every movie he'd ever seen about Special Forces.

Bert ambled past with his shotgun over his shoulder, and Oliver had the distinct impression that the old cardiologist had no desire, whatsoever, to fire it in anger.

Carmella, on the other hand, hustled into the lobby in a bent stoop, carrying her sniper rifle low and looking like a First World War combatant charging through the trenches.

Oliver offered to carry the heavy gun, but she cocked an eyebrow and said, "No thanks, Olly. No offense, but I don't want to have my ass accidentally blown off today."

"Fair enough."

Teddy and Emma cleared the rest of the lobby, and then did the same for the small office behind the reception desk. Emma relaxed, dropping the handgun to her side.

"We're OK. Let's take a breather."

"I could use a second," Carmella said, setting the Heckler and Koch down with a metallic *thunk*. She put her hands on her hips and stretched her back. Her spine creaked loud enough for Oliver to hear.

"How are you with stairs?" Teddy asked.

"Uh... not great, to be honest," Carmella answered. "Bum knee—and hip. And the other knee. And the other hip. Oh, and also my back, obviously."

"We can handle it," said Bert.

Teddy took Carmella's gun and slung it over one shoulder. Then he stooped low, scooped the woman easily up on the other.

"Bert—get the door," he said. "Then follow us and say goodbye to your wonderful life partner in case one of you gets killed."

Bert opened the door to the staircase.

"Emma, Oliver, you stay here and guard the stairwell."

A second later the big man, with the matronly lady on one shoulder and the sniper rifle on the other, disappeared up the stairs. The old, shotgun-wielding Jewish cardiologist huffed and puffed at his heels.

"What's going on?" Oliver asked. "Why are they going upstairs?"

"They're setting up a sniper nest on the roof."

"Right... because—"

"Because this is a war zone, and we need supporting fire."

"Supporting fire... is good?"

"Yes."

"Good," Oliver said, not feeling very good at all.

The revolving door to the lobby made a clattering racket as it spun over shards of safety glass. Oliver and Emma turned at the sound.

A man with severe burns on half his face, a smoking hairpiece and clothing that hung from his body in ragged tatters stumbled into the lobby. Emma drew her revolver and pointed it at him.

"Uh... hi," he said.

"Hello," Emma said.

"Do you guys know if the Delores-But-You-Can-Call-Me-Lolita restaurant is open for takeout? My wife sent me out to get some food, and I can't seem to find the place."

"It probably isn't open," Oliver said. "You should shelter-in-place."

"We will, once we get some appetizers," the man said... "Only, I think I got turned around. There was this... well... I guess you'd call it an explosion, see, and I kind of got discombobulated."

"It's on Brickell, by the mover station," Oliver said. "But it's going to be closed. If not for the armed conflict, then for the tornadoes."

Emma gave him a look.

"What? I noticed it last time we were here. It's a unique name."

"Thanks, buddy," the man said.

"You should get those burns looked at," Emma said. "Half of your hairpiece has melted."

The man looked confused, and touched his smoking toupee, which indeed had partially melted to his scalp. He winced. "Yeah... maybe," he said, before walking back into the storm. His hairpiece sizzled, emitting puffs of steam in the torrential rain.

Emma armed Oliver behind a concrete column in the lobby.

"What?"

"Listen," she whispered.

Distant gunfire echoed from north of their location.

"That sounds like it's pretty far away," Oliver said.

She nodded.

"Do you think we actually circumvented them?"

"What I think is that Teddy has the best military mind the world has ever known. Take Winston Churchill, Hannibal, and Alexander the Great, roll them all up into one, and you're still not even close to Teddy."

"You have that much faith in him?"

"Y'ar—I'd follow that man ta' Hell and back, I would!"

"Was—was that, like, a pirate voice?" Oliver asked.

"It was an attempt, yes."

"Very nice."

A terrific blast shook the building. Oliver stumbled, grabbing the column for support. He gripped the Swiss Army knife in his pocket with all his strength and wished, once again, for an instrument with a little more stopping power.

A moment later, a very dusty Teddy and Bert clambered out of the stairwell, followed by a cloud that reminded Oliver of 9/11 footage.

Bert, watery-eyed and huffing, leaned forward with his hands on his knees. He spat a gob of concrete dust/saliva slurry on the floor.

Teddy had carried the shotgun for him, and now handed it back so Bert could wedge the barrel into the corner where the wall met the floor and lean against the stock.

Teddy then patted him on the back, until Bert held up a palm. "Osteoporosis," he wheezed. "Your hands are like meat tenderizers."

"Sorry."

"Are you OK?" Emma asked.

He held up his arthritic index finger. "Just need a minute."

"You have to be mindful of Bert," Emma lectured Teddy. "He's an old man."

"I'm not that old," Bert protested. He stood up, and even over the sounds of the storm and the distant gunfire, his hip made a loud pop. "Well, I guess I'm pretty old."

"What can we do to help?" Emma asked.

"A drink of water would be nice."

Oliver had spotted a fitness center earlier, when Emma had pushed him behind cover. He jogged to the glass door, and pushed, but it wouldn't open. An electronic key-card reader mounted on the wall blinked red.

He was about to give up when he noted a decorative potted fern in the hallway.

He grinned.

With Bert fully rehydrated, they hunkered low, zigzagging across the parking lot. They were almost back to the minivan when the old cardiologist froze.

"Oh," he said. "Hold on. Duty calls!" He made a beeline for a burned-out pickup truck on the street.

"Bert!" Emma hissed.

They changed course so they could follow him to the road, where the man with the burned hairpiece lay gasping for breath. Blood bubbled from his mouth and nose.

Bert crouched. "He's been shot. Stay low."

Oliver tried to will himself smaller, kneeling on the wet asphalt against the driver-side front tire of a Chevrolet Malibu.

When he looked back, he could see the man with the burned hairpiece, but Bert was gone.

"Bert?" he called.

Nothing.

Then, faintly, like some kind of apparition, Bert was there again, mumbling quietly over the dying man. The old man was semi-opaque. Oliver could look right through him and make out details of a red Toyota. He tried to think of the right word for what he was seeing, and he guessed it was "incorporeal."

Oliver wiped his glasses on his shirt. When he looked back, Bert was whole again, but the man with the burned hairpiece was obviously dead.

Bert used the barrel of his shotgun like a walking stick and leaned on it to pull himself back up.

"Did I do the ghost thing?"

"Yeah you did the ghost thing! What the hell was that all about!?"

"Sorry about that. I always prefer to work in privacy. It can kind of freak people out."

"You were... like... translucent!"

"That's death duty," Bert said. "It never takes a holiday."

A loud thump shook the street. The concussion beat the breath out of Oliver's lungs.

He turned to see fragments of their Dodge Caravan raining down on the parking lot. Oliver and Bert rolled under the Malibu just in time to avoid the smoking hulk of the passenger seat, which slammed to the asphalt with enough force to blow a jet of high-density foam from the torn upholstery.

Shimmying to the other side of the car, Oliver craned his neck to the sky, where a quickly dispersing contrail led to a building across the street.

"What the hell was that!?"

"RPG," Teddy shouted from the next vehicle over. "Damnit! My baseball bat was in there!"

"So were most of the weapons!" Oliver called back.

"Don't remind me!"

Emma crawled out from under an SUV and hustled, head down, to Oliver and Bert. "Looks like we're on foot from here, fellas."

"What about the guy with the RPG?" Oliver asked.

"Don't be sexist," Emma said; "it could very well be a lady with the RPG."

"Ah, right. Sorry."

She smiled. "I'm messing with you."

"Oh."

A rifle cracked from the vicinity of the rooftop garden of the Four Ambassadors condominium complex, and a rag-dolling body and tubular object Oliver assumed to be a rocket launcher tumbled silently off the rooftop of the hotel across the street.

It happened so fast he almost missed it.

"That's my girl," Bert said proudly.

"She shot him? The guy—or the, uh—person with the RPG?"

"You bet your ass she did!"

"Let's get moving," Teddy called from the next row of vehicles.

Following his lead, they ran, semi-stooped, toward the main road.

Oliver caught a momentary glimpse of someone running toward them from the direction of the hotel, before Teddy shouted, "Get down!"

Deafening gunfire erupted from their eleven-o'clock position. It was so close, Oliver could smell the sulfuric powder smoke.

"Up there!" he pointed.

Another volley of shots followed, and the passenger-side mirror of the F-150 under which he was taking cover shattered, raining shards of glass in his hair.

Teddy stood, and with one foot against the rear panel of the pickup truck, grabbed the door handle and pulled, grunting with effort.

Oliver was about to tell the big man that the door was obviously locked, when the metal groaned, then bent, and finally cracked as the lock gave way.

"Holy moly!" Bert said.

Oliver heard running footsteps and turned to see three men, armed with rifles, charging toward them.

"Look out!" Oliver cried, turning back to where Teddy stood exposed, but the big man was gone.

In unison the men, who wore balaclavas, raised their guns.

Oliver resigned himself to his fate, and didn't bother raising his hands. This, it seemed, was the end of the road.

Then, in what he would later calculate to have been less than a tenth of a second before he was murdered, Teddy launched himself at the men from the far side of the truck, knocking the first into the other two.

Before the first man could recover his balance, Teddy sprang from the ground and slammed a metal pipe hard into the man's arms.

The bones cracked and the man screamed.

Teddy grabbed the gun with his left hand, and just as the second assailant opened fire he flipped the first man over his back using the sling. Three consecutive bullets hit the first assailant in the back as the big man side-stepped the projectiles and returned fire with the gun, still attached to the quickly dying, broken-armed attacker.

Bullet holes stitched their way up the second attacker's legs, crotch and gut as Teddy unloaded the entire magazine.

Meanwhile, the third man had regained his balance and raised his own gun, but Teddy, in a batter's stance, swung the first attacker by the rifle loop, and released.

The body knocked the third man off course, and his shots went wide, giving Teddy just enough time to sprint, crouch, and spring from the ground, driving the black metal pipe through the bottom of the man's chin and up through the top of his skull.

Teddy held him up in the air by the pipe as the body twitched and kicked.

He stayed that way for a few seconds, until he was satisfied, then dropped the body in a heap.

Oliver had never seen such violence. He examined the twitching body.

"Is that..."

"The tire iron," Teddy said, catching his breath. "Crew Cab F-150s have them under the back seat."

Oliver thought he might pass out. The adrenaline shakes returned with a vengeance.

"That was—I mean—like..."

"Pretty crazy, right?" Emma said.

"Yeah..."

"Sort of like John Wick, wouldn't you say?" Teddy grinned.

"John who?"

"John Wick. You know. Dead dog. Assassin. Keanu Reaves? John Wick!"

"I have no idea what you're talking about," Oliver said.

"Unbelievable."

Bert busied himself for a few minutes, administering death duty to their fallen attackers. Oliver couldn't help but watch as the old man did "the ghost thing."

The universe was infinitely more mysterious than he'd given it credit for.

While Bert worked, Teddy and Emma huddled in conference. Oliver couldn't quite hear what they were saying. The wind, which had briefly quieted, picked up again, whistling through the cars and buildings, and he worried about the tornado warning, and whether he might be about to experience one firsthand.

Teddy spoke in his direction and pantomimed a person walking with his index and middle fingers, but Oliver could only shake his head to indicate he couldn't understand. The big man shouted, "I'll lead, you and Bert follow. Emma brings up the rear."

He nodded.

The wind escalated further until it howled like a freight train. Oliver saw the beginnings of a funnel cloud forming in the distance, over the harbor. The experience gave him all kinds of cheesy B-movie vibes.

He pointed at the supercell, and yelled to Emma, "This is like *Shark-nado!*"

"It's more like Exorcist-nado!" she called back.

"Are we going to—like—survive the tornado part?"

"No idea!" she called. "Best not to worry about it!"

"OK."

Oliver tried not to worry about the tornado part.

Zigzagging between cover, he felt silly, pretending to play soldier.

They were almost at the driveway of the Miami EAST Hotel when an Asian man in jeans and a Billy Joel shirt, armed with a Kalashnikov, popped up from behind a cement parking barricade at the bistro directly across the street. The man fired wildly, and Oliver dove to the tarmac, skinning his knees and elbows on the wet pavement. Bert fired two quick shots over Oliver's head.

The shotgun reports left Oliver's ears ringing.

He twisted off the ground and scrambled behind a burned-out Subaru Forester. He glanced over the hood just in time to see Emma drawing her revolver. Before she could take aim, however, Carmella's rifle cracked once again. A pink mist sprayed upward from behind the cement barrier.

Oliver could barely hear the wet, meaty *smack* of the body hitting the pavement over his tinnitus.

"What a shot!" Emma exclaimed.

"Carm used to spend a lot of time at the range, when I was working," Bert said. "It helped her burn off steam."

"I'm really not comfortable with all this death," Oliver said. "I kind of hate violence."

"You get used to it," Emma said encouragingly, patting his shoulder.

"It's us or them," Bert said. "This isn't a quantum equation. Try to think of it as a more binary proposition."

"Are you using those terms because I'm a mathematician?"

"Yes, I am."

"Thanks."

They continued advancing toward the hotel, and as they approached, the wind ebbed, and the atmosphere calmed. The rain slackened, then stopped entirely. Oliver looked to the sky, and to his surprise saw a patch of blue above them.

The distant cacophony of urban warfare was still audible, but the gunfire and explosions were much further to their north. The hotel itself appeared to be in relatively good shape, and unlike the Four Ambassadors building, the ground-floor windows were intact.

Teddy ducked behind a floral arrangement delivery van across the street from the EAST Hotel pool patio, and Oliver pressed into him. Bert and Emma weren't far behind.

Oliver risked a glance around the side of the vehicle.

To his surprise, an orderly line of people stood along the side of the hotel. The queuing people were silent and appeared almost reverent, craning their heads to gaze up toward the broken window where "AMON RETUNS" was still marked in blood. The rain, it seemed, had never touched this place.

The queuing people reminded Oliver of tourists in a grand European cathedral.

Most wore civilian clothes, but some were in police or military uniform.

"What do we do now?" Oliver asked.

"Get in line, I think," Teddy said.

"Won't we get shot?"

"Hard to say for sure."

Without waiting, Teddy stood and jogged around the front of the delivery van, exposing himself to any potential combatants.

Oliver's heart leapt into his throat. "What the hell's he doing? He's going to get himself killed!"

Nothing happened.

Casually, as though he perfectly belonged there, the big man strolled toward the line of people—people who paid him no attention whatsoever. Once he'd assumed his position at the end of the line without being shot, he waved for his friends to follow.

"This feels really weird," Oliver said.

"They're protecting the perimeter," Emma said. "We must be behind their line of defense."

"It's still freaking me out."

"You want to go back?"

He looked over his shoulder, back the way they'd come. Destruction and debris dotted the landscape. A black scorch mark on the Four Ambassadors building marked the place where it had been hit by an RPG. That was what awaited the world if they failed. Chaos and death.

"Nope. I'm seeing this through, one way or the other."

"Then let's do this. Try to act natural."

Despite his screaming instincts, he stood and followed Bert and Emma across the street. He expected a bullet to penetrate his head any second, and was overall pleased when this didn't occur.

Nearing the line of people, he was overcome with an awful, sickening sensation. It felt like he was being pounded by hot, nasty pulses of pure misery. The feeling emanated in waves from the queuing crowd, only to wash over him like a riptide, threatening to pull him under.

"Ugh," he said. "What *is* that?"

"Legion," Emma explained.

"All these people?"

"Yup."

"Why aren't they attacking us?"

"I have no idea."

"So, we can sense Legion?"

"Sort of. The Host can. Our nervous systems, as you've probably figured out, are integrated with theirs, so that means we can experience what they are experiencing to some extent. It's especially bad when Legion are all together like this."

"Will the wonders ever cease..." Oliver marveled.

"I believe the saying is 'Will wonders never cease,'" Bert said.

"Does it change the meaning?" Oliver asked.

"That's not the point," Bert said; "the idiom is 'Will wonders never cease,' and it was first recorded in print in 1775."

"You seem a little testy, Bert," Teddy said.

"Did you just call me 'a little teste?'" Bert asked. His face turned red, and a vein swelled and pulsed on his forehead.

"Hmm," Emma said. "I think you're having a reaction to Legion."

Bert cocked his head in consideration. "You know what? I think you're right. I'm feeling really unreasonably pissed off. These pricks are worse than latex."

"Legion has that effect on people," Teddy said. "In fact, I saw a man club his own horse to death during the Storming of the Bastille in 1789."

"No shit," Bert said. "I can see how that could happen. In fact, if I had a horse right now..."

Bert raised his shotgun, but Teddy grabbed the older man's forearm and locked eyes with him. "Stay frosty, buddy. We're going to need you."

The man in front of Teddy turned and loudly sighed. "Excuse me," he said.

"What?" Bert grumbled.

"I'm Karl. Sagittarius, if you're wondering. Yes, I believe in the horoscope. So sue me. Anyway, I just need to tell you, you're giving off a really libertarian, tacti-cool, gun-nut vibe, and I, for one, am very uncomfortable welcoming you into the new world order. I think it might be best if you—"

Bert hoisted his shotgun, thumbed off the safety and pointed it at the man's forehead.

Karl, the Sagittarius, went silent, and turned around.

Oliver thought he might be on the verge of a complete and total nervous breakdown. "For the love of Pete! What the hell, Bert? We're so close!"

"He should have shot him," Teddy mumbled.

"He was just being an asshole," Oliver said. "That isn't a death sentence."

"There are times when I think it should be," Teddy said. "Especially for Legion."

"I, for one, feel a lot better," Bert said, thumbing the safety back on. "Like maybe things are going to work out. Like maybe, people like Karl Sagittarius here might be capable of learning something after all."

Karl's head twitched slightly, but he didn't turn around.

The line slowly wound its way around the pool patio and into the hotel lobby. Oliver craned his neck to see the AMON RETUNS window but it was now obscured by the sunshades that overhung the pool area.

Someone had moved Cindy's severed arm from the spot where it had landed on the patio in the CNN video. It now rested on the swim-up bar and someone had placed a bottle of Sol in its hand.

Emma followed Oliver's gaze and shrugged. "They thrive on chaos."

"But isn't that... like... order?" Oliver said.

"I don't know; it's frigging gross, whatever it is."

Inside the lobby, the line snaked its way around the fashionably retro art-deco furniture toward a stairwell. Oliver had been half expecting some kind of resistance once through the door, but instead he was met with more of the same quiet nonchalance he'd encountered outside.

He kept track of the number of individuals crossing the threshold to the stairwell, and timed it on his watch. "One minute, thirty seconds per person on average. There are seventy people in front of us."

Red in the face, Karl turned around once again. "Really, this is a place for quiet, somber introspection. Nobody here appreciates your—"

Before he could finish, Bert clobbered him on the side of the head with the butt of the shotgun. Karl crumpled to the ground.

Oliver gasped. "What happened to 'Do no harm'?"

"It went out the window when I met Karl. Now it's 'Do no harm, except to Karl.' I think it has a nice ring to it."

Bert toed the unconscious Sagittarius, lifting his chin with his orthopedic shoe. Karl snored. "He'll be fine."

Oliver braced himself, expecting everyone in the line to attack now that Bert had broken the peace, but nobody even looked their way. They were like automatons. He imagined the Heaven's Gate cult members placing the purple velvet bags over their own heads. He shuddered.

Teddy hoisted Karl over his shoulder and excused himself. "Hold my place," he told Oliver.

He jogged behind the reception desk and dumped the unconscious astrology enthusiast on the floor. A few of the people who had joined the line behind Oliver wore blank expressions and looked in every possible direction other than the one in which a giant man resembling Dwayne "the Rock" Johnson was hiding the limp body of an unconscious asshole.

"OK, there are sixty-nine people ahead of us," Oliver said, picking up where he'd left off. "That still means we're going to be here for another one-point-seven-two-five hours before we reach that stairwell."

"Right," Teddy said.

"And though we're not exactly sure what these people are here for, given that they're hosting Legion, we can assume it has something to do with helping Amon, right?"

"That's true," Emma said.

"So what I'm wondering is, should we maybe consider, uh, skipping the line?"

"Oh," Emma said.

She reached into her bag and produced two gas grenades. She handed one to Teddy, then squeezed the spoon and pulled the pin on her grenade. Teddy did the same. "We should probably step outside," she said.

Teddy shoved his way past the individuals who had just lined up after them and motioned the group back through the door. As Oliver hustled by, Teddy threw his grenade toward the stairwell. Emma lobbed hers into the center of the room.

Two loud *cracks* followed, and clouds of dense white smoke filled the lobby. The previously calm line of Legion-possessed Floridians broke into panic. Teddy held the door shut while bodies began piling up on the other side. The crowd struggled frantically to leave, but Teddy was too strong. The frenzy quickly subsided, and fifteen seconds later a corpulent man in a Hawaiian shirt, who was the last holdout of lucidity, gave up his half-hearted attempt to wrench open the door and slid, comatose, face-first down the glass.

"They aren't dead, are they?"

"No," Emma said. "But they look like they're pretty messed up."

"That's basically your bog-standard anesthetic," Bert said. "They should be fine. A little hungover, worst-case scenario. And no doubt a few will soil themselves. I hope Karl soils himself. If ever a man deserved to shit his pants—"

"How are we going to get back in?" Oliver asked.

"Can I borrow your shotgun?" Teddy asked Bert.

Bert handed it over, and Teddy used the butt to smash the glass out of the door. He then methodically moved window to window, smashing out the glass, allowing the breeze to rush through the lobby. The white gas cloud dispersed quickly, leaving no trace of the anesthetic fog. "I think we're good."

They picked their way through the foyer, mindful not to step on any bodies.

"What floor is Amon on?" Teddy asked Oliver.

"The sixth, I think."

They climbed the stairs without meeting any resistance, but Oliver's instincts began tingling at the fourth floor, and by the time they reached the doorway to the sixth floor, his intuition of danger was outright screaming.

"Do you guys feel that?"

Teddy smiled. "Oh yeah."

"He's here, isn't he?"

"Let's hope so."

"Ready?" Emma asked.

"Ready," Oliver said.

Teddy eased the door open and slid into the hallway. Bert followed, shotgun at the ready. Oliver emerged next, a death grip on the little Swiss Army knife in his pocket.

Emma brought up the rear.

Oliver felt a ripping sensation inside. It was like the part of him that made him Oliver was being twisted apart.

"Ugh. What is that?"

"Remember in the underworld," Bert said, "when the moth guy, and the kangaroo and the dog were all separate from you guys?"

"Sure."

"Well, if Amon is here, he probably brought some of that underworld with him. Maybe the Host are going to—I don't know—rematerialize or something."

"But will the spirit light work? If they aren't part of us?"

"I have no idea."

They turned a corner and finally met the resistance Oliver had been expecting. The form of that resistance, however, he had completely failed to anticipate.

A raised, partitioned Formica desk had been set up in the center of the hallway. Behind it sat two extremely bored-looking women in pant suits. A short glass panel separated the women from anyone encountering them, and a small divider ran between them, presumably to give the illusion of privacy to anyone bringing their business to the desk.

The women stared absently at their phones, not bothering to look up. They didn't appear to be armed with anything more sinister than stand-offish attitudes. The setup reminded Oliver of the last time he had to renew his driver's license.

One of the women chewed a wad of bubblegum. Her nametag read "Hi. My name is Lisa."

Oliver, approaching the desk, took the lead.

"Hello."

The woman on the right, whose nametag read "Hi. My name is Stacy" held up her index finger.

Oliver looked up.

There was nothing on the ceiling.

"Oh. Do you mean wait a second?"

She gave him the blank stare Oliver guessed she reserved for only the stupidest of people, then returned her gaze to the phone.

"It's just that, we're uh, anxious to get going," Oliver said.

The woman said nothing.

"I'm sort of hoping you could point us in the right direction. You see..."

The other woman, to Oliver's left, made a big deal of angling a plastic blue placard so he could read it. The placard read "On Break."

"Oh. I see. How long, usually, does your break tend to—um..."

"What's the hold-up?" Teddy asked.

"They're on break, apparently."

"On break from what?"

"I don't..."

"Name?" said the woman on Oliver's left, between chomps of gum. She had removed the placard.

"Oh. Uh—Oliver Bell," Oliver said.

The woman went back to looking at her phone and chewing. The other woman continued to not to pay any attention to them. She was apparently still on break.

"Ah... excuse me," Oliver said.

"What?"

"Where do I go?"

"I have no idea," she said.

"I mean... to see Amon."

"You aren't on the list, Oliver Bell."

"He'll want to see me," Oliver said. "I have the code for the destruction of the multiverse."

"Good for you," the woman said.

"He needs it," Oliver said. "I want to give it to him."

"It sounds like you're very special," the woman said, in a tone that made Oliver feel like he wasn't special at all.

"So how do I get it to him?"

"You don't. You aren't on the list."

She went back to her phone.

Oliver willed a compulsion from Mayhem... something he could say that would convince her to direct them to the lord of the underworld. He got nothing.

"Just go," Teddy said. "We'll find him."

"What about..."

"Forget these bitches."

He gave Oliver a gentle shove past the desk.

They didn't get far.

The woman with the bubblegum moved fast. Too fast for Teddy or Oliver or any of them to react.

Leaping from the desk, she somersaulted over her chair, managing a full double backflip with a half-spin, only to land flat on her back in front of Oliver. Loud pops and cracks echoed in the hallway as her elbows and knees first hyper-extended, and then inverted completely.

"We will not tolerate abusive language like that!" the thing that recently looked like a bored DMV employee, and now looked like a videogame horror with a backwards head, roared in a deep, rasping voice.

"OK," Teddy said. "What am I looking at here?"

"I don't know," Emma said. "She's like, a crab or something?"

"More like a spider," Bert observed.

Spider-Lisa's neck made a series of crunching pops as her head twisted in a one hundred eighty-degree arc. Staring at Oliver, she spit out her gum.

Oliver stood frozen in shock.

Spider-Lisa skittered toward him. He emitted a short, shrill scream. Teddy jumped between them, but with the swipe of a backwards arm she smashed him into the desk. He tumbled over it, full force, shaking the hallway when he landed.

Stacy, who also wasn't a run-of-the-mill service desk employee, leapt from the reception desk to the wall. She clung to the vertical surface. Her fingers, which only a moment ago had appeared perfectly normal, and which Oliver had noted bore a French manicure, were now tipped in wide, fleshy cups lined with waving organic needles.

Oliver recoiled at the sight of those awful hands.

She scrambled up the wall and then along the ceiling, hissing at him as she approached. Her mouth snapped open and shut, like an angry snake. Instead of teeth she now had row upon row of shark-like denticles. Even her tongue appeared to be covered in the sharp, scaly plaques.

"Uh... I think there's been a misunderstanding..." Oliver backed down the hallway, not daring to turn his back on the hell-spawn.

"You're on video, you know," the Stacy-monster rasped. "Calling us bitches. That is completely inappropriate behavior and we do not tolerate it in the workplace."

In an explosive burst of insectile motion, the Stacy-monster caught up to him, detached from the ceiling and pounced, knocking him to his knees.

She was incredibly strong. She grabbed him by his open mouth, probing inside with her cup-like digits. He felt sticky, prickly hairs run over his taste buds, and gagged.

Emma grabbed his arm, but he was wrenched away by the Stacy-monster, who dragged him further down the hallway as though he weighed no more than a doll. His elbows rubbed painfully as she hurried his flailing body over the rough carpet, and he howled in pain.

When she finally stopped at the corner, she pried his mouth wider open, and pressed her own mouth to his. Her breath was like old seafood, and Oliver guessed why the Lisa-creature had such an affinity for gum.

He tried to twist away, but some kind of proboscis latched onto his tongue. His scream was swallowed up in the monster's mouth.

With all his strength, he tucked his legs between them and shoved. The monster detached and a long, brown worm-like thing with a mouth full of razor-sharp teeth retracted into its mouth.

"What the hell is that!?" he cried.

The Stacy-monster grabbed fistfuls of his hair and wrenched his head to the side, attacking again. This time, it latched onto his neck.

"Not the neck!" he screamed.

Just then, the Lisa-monster pounced, latching onto his crotch.

"The neck!" he cried, "You're supposed to go for the neck!"

Bert was first to reach them. The old man raised his shotgun. "How firm a grip does that one have on your... you know?" he asked.

"Just shoot her!" Oliver said.

"I don't want to risk taking your tallywhacker off," Bert said.

"My tallywhacker?"

"I've got it!" Emma raised her revolver and fired three shots into the side of the Lisa-thing's head.

The beast let go of her purchase on Oliver's crotch. Thankfully, she hadn't made it all the way through the mouthful of sagging, stretchy denim.

The Lisa-thing, still very much alive despite the new bullet-holes, charged at Emma, who fired again, emptying the cylinder of her Ruger. Bert followed with two point-blank blasts from the shotgun. On the second shot, the monster's head popped like a water balloon. Blood, bone and brain tissue exploded in every direction. Pieces of the monster rained down from the ceiling. The remains of the creature twitched on the floor.

The Stacy-monster on his neck convulsed, and Oliver felt something warm and wet slide out of its mouth, into his neck. "Um—if it isn't too much to ask..."

Bert slammed a round into the chamber of the shotgun.

Something slimy and wriggling slithered deeper into his flesh. He thought of that worm-like thing. He thought of it inside his circulatory system. He thought that it would probably be bad to have a worm like thing inside one's circulatory system.

"Please hurry," he gasped.

"Cover your ears," Bert said.

Oliver covered his ears.

Bert pressed the muzzle of the shotgun against the Stacy-creature's head, pinned it against the wall and pulled the trigger.

The creature's head exploded into ragged chunks. Its body fell to the floor in a thrashing pile of contorted limbs.

A gout of dark purple blood fountained out of Oliver's neck where the thing had latched. Instinctively, he brought his hand to the place, and pressed.

He didn't know how much blood he'd lost—it had obviously been a lot. He felt woozy.

Plunking himself down on the floor, he looked at Teddy. "What were those things? Were they vampires? Like actual vampires?"

"Who knows," Teddy said. "Whatever they were, I stand by my assertion that they were bitches."

"Am I, like, going to turn into a vampire now?"

"Do you feel like you're turning into a vampire?" Bert asked.

"Not really. I just kind of feel like I might pass out."

"That's probably just the blood loss," Bert said, his voice full of optimism. "You're young. You'll be fine. You don't have any chest pain, do you?"

"No."

"Then yeah, nothing to worry about."

Oliver turned to the convulsing body just feet away. "That thing is dead, right?" he asked.

"I think so," Bert said. He kicked the twitching remains. They continued to twitch. "So much for the element of surprise. Maybe I should have a look at your neck."

Oliver removed his hand; dark blood flowed from the wound and soaked into his already saturated translucent T-shirt.

"Hmm," Bert said. "Looks like she got your jugular pretty good. Probably best to keep pressure on it." He guided Oliver's hand back to the spot, and pressed firmly.

"Am I going to die?" Oliver asked.

"We're all going to die," Bert said whimsically.

"I mean, in the next five minutes," Oliver clarified.

"Yeah, so do I."

Teddy grabbed Oliver by the elbow and helped him to his feet. "No time to die right now. Which room?"

Oliver thought about the pattern of the building, and tried to remember the layout from the outside. He counted the rooms from memory, and reconciled his count with the hallway before him.

"Wait..." He wobbled. "Which way is east?"

Teddy pointed.

"OK, it's that one." Oliver indicated a door.

They piled up in a tight line against the wall, beside the door, the same way Oliver had seen Marines do in footage from Fallujah. Teddy turned to face them. "Ready?"

Oliver nodded and felt dizzy.

Teddy knocked.

"Wait. We're not busting it down?" Oliver asked.

"How would I bust it down? It's a very robust door."

"Oh."

"You look disappointed."

"No. No... I just—"

"It has a deadbolt," Teddy explained.

He knocked again. "Hello?"

The door opened. The simp who had been unable to use the fax machine greeted them. "Uh... hi."

"Hey!" Teddy said. "You're the guy! You killed that poor woman."

"That 'poor woman' was the demon that heralded Amon," the simp said. "All I wanted was to send a fax. And now look at me. I'm a possessed slave of one of the upper-tier lords of the underworld."

"That sucks," Teddy said. "But you shouldn't have been such a simp."

"Tell me about it," the simp said.

Amon's breathy voice sounded from deeper in the suite. "Is it them?"

"Yes," the simp called back.

"Send them in, Mitchell!"

Mitchell, the simp, stood aside and waved them into the room. Just as Teddy crossed the threshold Oliver heard a familiar popping sound, and Fixeloclastes materialized beside him.

"Whoa," Fixeloclastes said.

"Hey!" Teddy said. "How are you, buddy?"

"I've been better," the man-moth replied. "I wasn't expecting to materialize."

"Oh shit," Bert said, in a way that Oliver did not like hearing.

Fixeloclastes nodded. "Yup."

Emma followed Teddy into the room, and Bucky suddenly appeared at her side.

Bert followed Emma, and when Oliver came through the door, he felt his soul tear in half, and Mayhem popped into existence at his feet. He reached down to pat the dog, who licked his hand. When he straightened, the room went dark, and he felt like he was in a tumble-dryer for a moment. He made a mental note to avoid any more deep bends while in a state of hypovolemic shock.

"Whoa there," Fixeloclastes said, gripping Oliver by the elbow with one of his moth appendages.

Oliver limped into the room. A humid breeze washed through the broken floor-to-ceiling window above. It felt surprisingly nice. Spattered blood droplets marked the walls and ceiling. Oliver remembered from watching *Dexter* that the droplets made "an arterial spray" pattern.

Poor Cindy. She was a bitch, but she didn't deserve this.

On the floor, extinguished candles surrounded smears of blood in the shape of a pentagram.

Amon sat perched on a chair in the corner wearing a child-sized stark-white EAST Hotel bathrobe, which was much too large for him. The strange creature watched Oliver approach, and motioned for him to sit.

Oliver flipped a blood-stained cushion on the sofa with his free hand, and sat down hard. His neck felt swollen. It throbbed. He wasn't sure if it was the bulging hematoma, but for a second he imagined he could feel something slither under his fingers. He decided to hold more pressure.

He remembered his basic lifesaving training from a long-ago swim class. When in doubt, press harder.

Mayhem jumped up on the couch beside him, pressed his face into Oliver's side. Yes something inside Oliver moved. The slithering thing.

"I know," Oliver whispered.

Mayhem pressed again, and the thing moved further. The worm-like thing was inside him.

Mayhem nipped at his side.

"Ouch," Oliver said.

The Host looked at him with sad eyes and blinked. He was saying goodbye. Oliver petted him. "It'll be OK," he said, blinking away tears.

The not-exactly-a-terrier nuzzled against him once more, this time gently.

"Love you, buddy," Oliver whispered.

Amon, once he had ushered everyone into the room, waved one of his ape hands. Bert's shotgun, Emma's revolver and remaining gas grenade floated over his shoulder and out the window before dropping into the swimming pool.

"Dammit," Teddy swore.

"Hello again, Teddy. That was very impressive, you folks fighting your way up here."

"The creatures in the hallway are dead," Teddy said.

"That's too bad," Amon clucked. "Interesting, weren't they?"

"Vampires?" Bert asked.

"We call them 'lampreys.'" He nodded at Oliver. "It looks like they gave you quite a spirited contest."

"Yes," Emma said, indicating the torn crotch of Oliver's jeans, "They hurt Oliver quite badly."

"I'm sorry, Oliver," Amon said. "I really didn't intend for them to injure you. But they are entirely brainless attackers. Once they become aggravated, they'll attack friends and foes alike. I've even seen them turn to cannibalism. It's a serious weakness, but I thought they could at least work the reception desk. I miscalculated."

"Why *was* there a desk?" Oliver asked. "And who were all those people out there? Why were they lining up to see you?"

"They were getting their assignments, paying their tributes, and the like. You know—Legion stuff. It isn't often that I get to visit secular earth. It's kind of exciting for my foot soldiers. I'm sure you can understand. After all, you hosted one for a while, if you remember."

Oliver did remember. He'd been thinking about that possibility for a few days now. It was that period in his life—his *former* life—when he'd been convinced he should turn over his thesis to his supervisor.

"You resisted. Even then, you were tougher than you gave yourself credit for. And now look at you!"

Was that a compliment?

"Hopefully we can get our business out of the way quickly. As I'm sure you can imagine, I'm a bit busy," Amon said. "But not for too much longer, thankfully. I want you to see something."

Amon waved once more, and the television turned on, showing a scene shot from a helicopter. It hovered over a foreign city Oliver didn't recognize. He could just make out what the camera was focusing on—bodies lying on the sidewalks and in the street. The news scroll read "Deadly New Respiratory Illness. Chongqing in lockdown."

"Pestilence," Amon said, pointing at the screen, before waving and changing the station to a local Fox affiliate: a convoy armored vehicles rolled along the streets of an eastern European city.

"War."

He changed the channel again. A shot from yet another circling helicopter showed the smoking wreckage of the port of Miami, where black smoke and roiling orange flames billowed from thousands upon thousands of shipping containers. "Famine."

Finally, the small creature used one of its forelegs to pat himself on the chest. "Conquest. Do you see?"

"The four horsemen?"

"Exactly."

"Is this the apocalypse then?"

"As you know, I consider it more... a return to balance."

"You're going to kill billions of people!" Emma cried.

"Don't be so dramatic. They will still exist in the multiverse."

"Until you collapse that too," Fixeloclastes said.

"Well, there is that," Amon admitted, "but that will take eons."

The long, slithering thing under Oliver's skin squirmed its way down to his beltline.

He groaned, and for a second, lost his grip on his neck. When he did, only a trickle of slick blood came from the wound. It was slowing down.

Oliver wasn't sure if slowing down was a good thing or a bad thing.

"Ah! I suspect you're starting to understand what makes the lamprey so particularly revolting," Amon said.

"It's occurring to me, yes," Oliver said.

Oliver couldn't help but think of the movie *Alien.* He very much hoped that whatever the parasite was, it wasn't going to explode out of his chest.

"I'd offer to help," Amon said, but you really hurt my beak when you hit me with that frying pan."

"Would—would it help if I apologized?"

"Not really."

Oliver tried to think—it wasn't easy given the circumstances. There had to be a way out of this. He thought about the Cast Master 4000 and whether he could use it to send Amon back to the underworld. The device would not work on secular earth. He knew that. But the Celestial Host, Amon and the demonic lamprey people should really not exist in the secular world, either. Yet here they were. Hadn't Bert said something about Amon bringing the underworld with him?

Perhaps instead of managing to alter his own existence in the universe to inhabit secular earth, Amon had instead created a portal to the underworld.

And if that were true...

"Are we in a portal?" Oliver asked.

"Very good!" Amon said. "Yes we are. But don't get any big ideas of tossing me out like a sumo wrestler. The ethereal portal follows me wherever I go."

Oliver looked at Mayhem. He was about to ask the dog if it had any useful ideas, but the parasite in his abdomen coiled around his bellybutton.

"*Argh!*" Oliver gasped.

Amon bellowed a cruel laugh, and turned to Fixeloclastes.

"The larva in your friend is preparing to feed, it would seem."

A funny thing happened then.

To Oliver, the entire world flickered. For the smallest of seconds, he found himself standing in the hallway, as if watching the scene unfold from a crack in the doorway.

Then he was back.

Mayhem jumped on his chest and barked frantically. Oliver smelled something.

Skunk.

Amon waved a hand, and with a flash of light the dog disappeared.

Oliver felt half his consciousness collapse. "Oh God!" he cried.

Fixeloclastes pounced at the demon, the pincers at the ends of his insectile arms open wide. Just as quickly, the man-moth blinked out of existence. Teddy bellowed in pain and fell to the floor.

The skunk smell grew more intense.

What the hell was going on?

"Oh no!"

Emma turned to Bucky and gripped the arm of the extra-dimensional marsupial. With a flash, he was gone. She sobbed.

"You prick!" Teddy hurled the wooden desk chair at Amon. It almost hit home, smashing against the wall just over the creature's shoulder.

Amon jumped from his perch, and hissed. He waved his arm, and Teddy collapsed to his knees, clutching his chest. His face went scarlet and Bert and Emma rushed to his side. The big man's eyes rolled back. He went limp.

"What the hell did you just do?" Oliver shouted.

"I gave him a heart attack," Amon said. "Ventricular fibrillation, to be exact. I hear it's quite unpleasant."

"Stop it!" Oliver cried. "Please!"

Teddy couldn't die! He was supposed to be invincible!

"I'm sorry, Oliver. That's out of the question. He's too dangerous."

"Save him!" Emma screamed. "Save him for God's sake!"

"Let Bert save him," Amon said. "He's a cardiologist, after all."

"That isn't fair," Bert said. "I—I don't have my stuff. I don't have any drugs!"

"Try anyway," Amon hissed. "Who knows. Maybe you'll get lucky."

The old man got painfully to his knees. "I can do this," he whispered to himself. He started giving Teddy chest compressions. Emma dropped to her partner's side.

Oliver kept his eyes on the demon. The spirit light hadn't worked. Perhaps there was another way...

"What if I give you the code? Will you save him?"

"No!" Emma shouted. "Don't do it!"

"The thing is, Oliver, I'm not sure I really need the code anymore. Look around you! Civilization is ending with or without active engagement. Those nukes are going off one way or another."

"Don't!" Emma pleaded. "Teddy wouldn't want you giving him the code!"

Oliver ignored her. "I can end it quicker. You save Teddy, and I'll give you what you need. A nuclear apocalypse! Imagine it! It all ends in one big bang. I could be, sort of, the unofficial fifth horseman, if you will."

Amon paused a moment. "I really can't have him running around trying to kill me."

"I understand that. But Teddy's just Teddy now. He isn't a human host anymore. You sent Fixeloclastes where? Into the ether? What could a human being possibly do to you, an eternal lord of the underworld? He's going to die anyway, just like the rest of us. But you—you're immune to secular weapons. What would you have to worry about?"

"You make a good point."

Pain flashed in Oliver's abdomen. The parasite thing felt like it was biting him. He did his best to ignore it.

He had a plan—the odds of working were something like one in a million. But something Amon had said was echoing in his mind.

"Listen, I have the only copy of the code on the USB key in my pocket. If I give it to you, will you save Teddy?"

Amon glanced once more toward the big man on the floor. Oliver knew it was a pathetic scene. "I could just take it. You know that."

"Sure. But there's something else. You know I can be an asset. Aside from all this violence," he waved out the window, "you know I agree with your plan. The human race is a colossal failure. Worse, they're selfish, petty, quick to anger and generally stupid. They've replaced faith in God with faith in themselves. It's like a cult of narcissism. Do you know how hard it is to be a smart person living in a society of idiots and jerks? Just today, for example, I learned that Rolfe Harris was a pedophile! The human species doesn't deserve to progress any further. I want it to end—maybe almost as much as you do."

"I knew it!" Amon whispered.

"I'm going to reach into my pocket, now, and hand you the USB key. OK?"

"Oh, Oliver!" Emma wailed. "Don't!"

Amon slithered closer. The demon held out a monkey hand.

Oliver reached into his pocket, and produced the small Swiss Army knife. He banked his plan on the fact that Amon hadn't been to the secular world in centuries, and had almost certainly never seen either a Swiss Army knife or a USB key. "It works like this."

He opened the blade. Amon cocked his head.

Oliver lifted his shirt and plunged the point of the knife into his own abdomen, just above his bellybutton, where he could feel the worm-thing chewing. The sharp metal point found the wriggling flesh, and he stuck it in deeper, cutting into the worm thing, not stopping until he felt the hilt press against his skin. He gagged.

The worm stiffened.

Amon lunged, his ape-hands tearing at Oliver's arm and wrist, but Oliver refused to let go. With his free hand, he grabbed the demon by the owl head, and pulled it toward his stomach.

Amon, seemingly realizing what was happening, writhed, but Oliver's grip was firm.

He pushed the knife harder, prodding the parasite, hoping against hope that he wouldn't simply kill it. The lamprey larva thrashed its way through the fascia and muscles in Oliver's abdomen. It coiled under his skin, and to his horror, he realized it was the size of a large eel.

Whispering a silent prayer, he prodded the thing once more, then swiftly pulled the knife from his flesh.

When he did, the lamprey exploded out with such force that it knocked the air from his lungs. Oliver fell over backwards into the couch cushions.

The parasite latched onto Amon's face and pumped frantically at the little demon's eyeball. Its tail stood straight up in the air, and then wrapped around and around Amon's head.

"Yargh!" Amon screamed.

The slimy, wriggling creature pumped faster and faster. The slurping and sucking noises were so loud they made Oliver feel physically ill, and he clambered back, away from the demon and its brainless attacker.

Amon struggled to grab the beast, but its slippery skin slid through his hands over and over again.

Oliver then remembered what his father had said—Amon was impervious to secular weapons. Whatever the worm thing was, it wasn't secular. It was more like the stuff of cosmic nightmares.

Amon frantically waved his arms. One by one, the lightbulbs in the room exploded. Sparks and tiny shards of glass rained down from the empty sockets.

A telekinetic wave pounded Oliver, blasting him off the couch. Bert flew off the floor and crashed into the desk.

Mitchell, the simp, was lifted off the ground, and his head bumped off the ceiling. He had a fraction of a second to scream before hurtling out the open window.

None of this had any effect on the attacking lamprey. The wet slurping gave way to grinding and crunching as the creature penetrated Amon's thin, bird-like skull.

Amon's arms stopped waving. His tail thumped a few times, then went still, and when it did, something fizzed in Oliver's brain. He felt an unusual sensation of lightness, and though someone had poured sparkling wine all over him.

It took him a moment to realize what was happening.

"He's looking for a host!" Oliver cried.

"I've got this!" Getting to his knees, Bert spoke in Latin.

The light from outside the broken window thickened, and the feeling of transference went away.

"I think that worked," Oliver said, but Bert muttered the incantation over and over, each time more quickly. "*Spiritus, hic donum non habes!*"

"It's good, Bert. It worked!"

Amon's body fell flat on the floor, and the lamprey uncoiled from his neck. It turned to face Oliver.

"Oh—no—never mind. He's in that thing."

It whipped over the carpet, and up the arm of the couch, before launching itself at Oliver's face. Oliver swiped a protective arm through the air, and in doing so, the Swiss Army knife sliced cleanly through the lamprey, separating its head from its body. The body landed in a squirming mass in Oliver's already-bloody lap, and he emitted a rather girlish scream.

He shoved it to the floor, where it coiled and uncoiled in spastic contractions.

The head, meanwhile, had gone over his shoulder and landed in the wastebasket next to the broken desk.

He could hear it thrashing in the white kitchen-catcher style garbage bag.

Oliver rushed to Teddy and fell to his knees. Teddy's bulging eyes stared straight ahead, unblinking, and unseeing.

"Teddy!"

Bert pushed Oliver out of the way.

He allowed himself to be pushed. All he could do was watch as Bert started compressions again, counting to fifteen each cycle before pinching the big man's nose and giving two breaths of mouth to mouth.

"Emma," Oliver whispered. "I'm so sorry!"

She was on her knees on the opposite side. Tears streamed down her beautiful face as she whispered in Teddy's ear. Oliver didn't need to hear what it was she was saying. He already knew.

He felt in his pocket. It was still there. The Cast Master 4000.

He chanced a look over his shoulder. The lamprey's body convulsed on the filthy carpet. The bin liner beside the desk twitched.

He could still smell skunk. That had to be a good sign.

"Bert," Oliver said. "Bert!"

"What!? You're making me lose count!"

"Stop!"

"No! He'll die!"

"Can you really save him? With just CPR I mean?"

Bert looked at Emma and hesitated. But it was obvious that she already knew the answer. He stopped the compressions. Emma let out a soft sob that tore Oliver's heart into pieces.

"But you aren't Death right now? I mean... your death duty, or whatever it is, you don't sense it?"

Bert cocked an eyebrow. "Actually, no."

"If you had medical equipment, a defibrillator, and drugs... could you save him?"

"Sure. He's otherwise healthy. It's just your standard V-fib arrest. He's only been down a few minutes."

Oliver yanked the Cast Master 4000 from his pocket.

He flipped the yellow safety latch and spun the time dial to negative five. He had no idea what the units were. It could mean five minutes, five hours, five days, or five orbital transits of Uranus.

"Emma," he said. "Unlock the door. Push the bolt so it stays open."

"I…"

"Just do it!"

Oliver's voice was shockingly firm.

"And don't look into the hallway. No matter what!"

She jumped to her feet and ran to the door.

He aimed at a striped throw pillow that had been knocked off the couch and pressed the button. The rotting skunk carcass appeared.

"Ha! I knew it!"

He was going to save the big man.

"Listen," Oliver said. "When Archangel Derrick said I might end the universe, he wasn't talking about the computer code. He was talking about *this*. This glamour takes us back in time. Nobody knows what happens. There's a chance it could collapse the multiverse. There's a chance we would be giving Amon everything he wanted."

"But there's a chance it *won't* end the universe, right?" Bert asked.

"Yeah! There's a chance it will send us back, and we can get medical supplies. I think it's more than a chance. Did you guys smell it, earlier? The skunk, I mean?"

They both nodded.

"We can show up here at…" Oliver glanced at his watch, "Exactly nine-forty-three pm, with the medical supplies you need. We can save Teddy."

Emma stared at him. "Teddy wouldn't want Amon to win," she said. "He'd give his life to stop him. You know that! He's had over a thousand years. He'd be OK with dying."

Oliver put both his hands on her shoulders and met her eye to eye. "I think we can save him."

A tremendous gust of wind roared through the broken window. A bolt of lightning flashed, and thunder peeled behind it.

The glamour flickered.

"What's happening?" Bert asked.

"The portal is collapsing. If we're going to do this, we have to do it right now!"

They held hands, approaching the glamour.

Oliver was beyond pain. The wounds in his abdomen and neck were a distant, gauzy sensation. He was ready to fulfill his destiny.

He knelt next to the skunk. Bert took a knee beside him on one side, and Emma did the same on the other.

Bert put an arm around Oliver's shoulder, and Emma hugged him tight around the waist.

The glamour flickered again, this time taking the shape of the throw pillow.

"This has to be your choice!" Emma shouted.

"You know more about it than either of us!" Bert said. "You decide!"

Oliver closed his eyes. He pictured the elaborate structure of the multiverse, tier upon infinite tier. The planes of existence seemed so incredibly fragile, like thin panes of glass held together by silk.

He imagined himself punching a hole through the entire beautiful thing.

He became the wind.

The Comprehensive Guide to the Multiverse's

Incredible Daily Facts

Polar bear liver contains so much vitamin A that eating it can kill you.

The largest known prime number has 24,862,048 digits.

John James Audubon shot all the birds he painted. Furthermore, five of the birds he painted don't seem to exist: specifically, the Cuvier's Kinglet, the Townshend's Finch, the Carbonated Swamp Warbler, the Blue Mountain Warbler and the Small-headed Flycatcher have never been spotted by anyone.

An Australian woman was pecked to death by a chicken. The bird hit a varicose vein and she exsanguinated.

Snails have up to fourteen thousand teeth called radula. Snails also carry Shistosoma, a parasite that causes 200,000 deaths per year.

As of 2021, Ketchup flavored chips are only available in Canada. So is pink cream soda.

Fruit Loops all taste exactly the same, regardless of color.

The pattern of seeds in a sunflower is a Fibonacci sequence.

In any group of twenty-three people, there's a 50% chance that two of them have the same birthday.

Children of genetically identical twins are genetically siblings, not cousins.

Clouds typically weigh millions of pounds.

The comb jellyfish has a transient anus.

A dentist invented the electric chair.

To write out a googolplex on paper would take more space than exists in the known universe.

High-heeled shoes were originally designed for men.

Cats can have an allergy to humans.

3% of the ice in Antarctica is frozen penguin urine.

Orange was a fruit before it was a color.

Titan, a moon of Saturn, has an atmospheric density twice that of Earth's.

A snail can sleep for three years.

A sloth can hold its breath longer than a dolphin.

Lobsters and butterflies have taste buds in their feet.

The tongue of a blue whale can weigh more than an elephant.

The depiction of God and the angels on the ceiling of the Sistine Chapel is enshrouded in the shape of a human brain.

Two grapes, side by side in the microwave, will create an arc of visible plasma.

The earliest record of dentistry dates back to 7000 BC.

John Quincy Adams kept a pet alligator in one of the White House bathtubs.

Jockey Frank Hayes won a horse race at Belmont Park in 1923 after dying mid-race. His body stayed in the saddle. His odds were 20-1.

The place where a flamingo bends its leg is the bird's ankle, not its knee.

Due to its lack of light-scattering atmosphere, shadows are darker on the moon.

A flock of ravens is called both "an unkindness," and "a conspiracy."

The largest organism on earth is a fungus called Armillaria ostoyae that occupies 2384 acres of soil in Oregon.

Poison dart frogs are not poisonous when raised in captivity. It is thought that the toxins found in their skin are synthesized from insects they eat in the wild.

Because Mercuric Nitrate was used to remove fur from animal skins, those who were exposed to the process (often hat-makers) frequently suffered from mercury poisoning, hence the term "Mad as a hatter."

Continental drift occurs at the same speed that fingernails grow.

Mt. Thor on Baffin Island has a vertical drop of 1250m, which angles inward at 105 degrees, making it the world's tallest overhang and longest drop.

If all the gold in the world's oceans were collected and evenly distributed, every person on earth would be given nine pounds of it.

Gadsby by Ernest Vincent Wright is a fifty thousand-word novel that does not use the letter "e." A composition in which the writer purposefully omits a letter is called a "lipogram."

"The Bloop" is one of the loudest ocean sounds ever recorded. Nobody knows for sure what made the sound.

Every human has a unique smell, save for identical twins who smell the same.

A decapitated human head maintains consciousness for 15-20 seconds.

The human genetic code is 70% similar to the genome of a slug.

There is no official language of the United States.

Tennessee Williams choked to death on a plastic bottle cap he was using to ingest barbiturates.

The world record for breath holding is 24 minutes 3 seconds, by Spanish freediver Aleix Segura Vendrell.

The most common color of toilet paper in France is pink.

Henry VIII introduced a beard tax in 1535.

A question mark, followed by an exclamation mark, is called an interrobang.

The fortune cookie was invented in San Francisco.

The friendship paradox refers to the fact that on average, most people have fewer friends than their friends have.

The Vatican Bank has the only ATM with a Latin language option.

Japan has one vending machine for every twenty-three people.

A day on Venus is twenty Earth-days shorter than a year on Venus.

The Greenland Shark lives an average of 272 years.

Turkeys can reproduce asexually through a process called parthenogenesis. The offspring are always male.

Silly Putty is a non-Newtonian fluid.

One cubic meter of the material in a neutron star would weigh the same as the Atlantic Ocean.

The smallest thing ever photographed is the shadow of an atom.

Humans can detect the difference in sound between hot and cold water being poured.

Albert Einstein married his cousin.

Ants can live twenty-nine years.

In the Middle Ages, chess pieces were usually red or white.

Every planet in the solar system could fit, side by side, between the earth and the moon.

The cheetah makes the same sound as the domestic cat.

Lighters were invented before matches.

Two twelve-inch pizzas contain less pizza than one eighteen-inch pizza.

There are more variables for the order of a deck of cards than there are atoms on earth.

Charlie Chaplin once lost a Charlie Chaplin lookalike contest.

Cans were invented forty-eight years before can-openers.

The girlfriend of the founder of match.com left him for a man she met on match.com.

From the time it was discovered, until it lost its status as a planet, Pluto did not complete one orbit of the sun.

The original footage of the Apollo 11 moonwalk was accidentally taped over to record satellite data.

Elephants are the only animals that can't jump.

Koala fingerprints are so similar to human fingerprints that the two have been confused at a crime scene.

Slugs have four noses.

Musicians have a shorter lifespan than the general public.

Hyperion, a moon of Saturn, is charged with a particle beam of static electricity that flows out into space.

There are roughly seven octillion atoms in a human body.

Fuchsia is not a real color and does not appear in the rainbow. It is your brain's interpretation of full-intensity red and blue light combined. It is also indistinguishable from magenta.

The sun contains 99.86% of all mass in the solar system.

Cicadas have evolved to use a prime-numbered lifestyle, which, it is hypothesized, puts them in contact less often with predators who use a round-numbered life cycle.

Random data follows patterns. In general, 30% of random numbers in a data set will begin with the digit 1. The probability of digits starting a number decays in a linear fashion until 9. Only 5% of random numbers will start with a 9. The more orders of magnitude the data set incorporates, the stronger this pattern will be.

From zero to one thousand, the only number that has the letter "a" in it is one thousand.

"Eleven plus two" and "twelve plus one" both contain thirteen letters.

The longest-running hotel in the world has been in business since 705 A.D.

The ashes of Fredric Baur, the inventor of the Pringles Can, are interred in an original flavor Pringles can.

There are roughly two thousand thunderstorms happening at any given moment.

Hawaiian pizza was invented in Ontario, Canada in 1962.

Hudson Bay in Canada has lower gravity than the rest of the planet.

There are more pyramids in Sudan than in Egypt.

Oranges are not a naturally occurring fruit. They are a hybrid of tangerines and pomelos.

Stop signs were yellow until 1952.

Researchers using the CERN supercollider created a temperature of 5.5 trillion degrees Kelvin. The interior of the sun is thought to be roughly 15 million degrees Kelvin.

The Mpemba Effect describes a quirk in nature in which hot water freezes faster than cold water in the same sub-zero environment. There is an ongoing debate as to whether it is real.

Dolphins have names for one another, denoted by a unique whistle.

Boanthropy is the psychological disorder in which a person believes they are a cow.

A daddy longlegs is not technically a spider, as the males have a penis.

Bullfrogs never sleep.

No two tigers have the same pattern of stripes.

Wonton Food Inc. produced a fortune cookie in 2005 that correctly foretold lottery numbers.

Himalayan honeybee honey is hallucinogenic.

The man who discovered "The Iceman," a 5000-year-old frozen mummy, was also found dead, frozen in ice.

The James Blunt hit song, "Goodbye My Lover," was recorded in Carrie Fisher's bathroom.

Your brain shuts down the sneeze reflex when you sleep.

Dead people can get goosebumps.

Iguanas have a third eye at the top of their head that perceives brightness.

On Good Friday, 1930, the BBC reported "There is no news" and played piano music.

Squirrels are the most common cause of power outages in the United States.

Sunglasses were originally invented to hide Chinese judges' facial expressions in court.

The diameter of a blue whale's aorta is large enough for a human to swim through.

Your tongue print is as unique as your fingerprint.

Female kangaroos have three vaginas.

Grooves were added to the tarmac of Route 66 by New Mexico's Department of Transportation, such that your tires play "America the Beautiful" when you drive over them.

Paper bags require four times the energy of plastic bags to create.

In a 2007 survey, 62% of Icelanders claimed to believe in elves.

Casu marzu is a cheese that contains live maggots.

A balloon full of xenon will fall faster than a balloon full of nitrogen in atmospheric air. A basketball and a bowling ball will fall at the same speed.

A duel between three people is called a truel.

Humans are capable of echolocation.

The particles in a sneeze can travel up to 100 miles per hour.

In a Major League Baseball game, up to 120 individual balls are used. The average lifespan of a single baseball is less than three minutes, or roughly seven pitches.

In 2006, an unusual-looking Arctic bear was confirmed to be a hybrid between a grizzly bear and a polar bear.

Dentures were once made of animal or human teeth.

All the landmasses on Earth combined are smaller than the Pacific Ocean.

Pez dispensers are shaped like cigarette lighters because the candy was originally designed to help people stop smoking.

Cheese is the most shoplifted food in the world.

The electrical activity cycle of sleep happens in various parts of your brain when you are awake, suggesting parts of your brain are always sleep cycling.

Pointing your key fob at your head will increase the range of the radio signal by using your brain as a transmitter.

The plague killed so many people in the 14th century that it took until the 17th century for the world to return to pre-plague population levels.

Vesna Vulović, a Serbian flight attendant, survived a fall from 33,330 feet when her aircraft broke up after a bomb on board exploded.

Dartboards are made out of horsehair.

A Las Vegas hospital suspended workers for running a betting pool on when patients would die.

The Bible is the world's most shoplifted book.

More than one-fifth of all calories consumed by humans are in the form of rice.

The first toy to be advertised on television was Mr. Potato Head.

Marmite had to make smaller containers specifically for travelers as jars of Marmite were the most frequently confiscated items at UK airports.

Warner Bros, not wanting to spend $14 million on the film Home Alone, *cancelled it. It was then picked up by 21ˢᵗ Century Fox, who continued the production, which grossed $476 million.*

In 1862, the King of Siam offered Abraham Lincoln elephants, on the grounds that "A country as great as the United States should not be without elephants."

The incidence of women giving birth to twins is increasing.

As of 2021, the world's hottest chili pepper, the Dragon's Breath Chili, could kill you if consumed, by inducing an inflammation cascade in your airways. The pepper, which measures 2.48 million Scoville Units, is hotter than the previous hottest pepper, the Carolina Reaper, which measureds 1.6 million Scoville Units. A Jalapeno, in comparison, measures up to 8000 Scoville Units.

The coldest outdoor temperature recorded on Earth was -144 Fahrenheit, in Antarctica. Breathing air that cold can be fatal.

The combined weight of all the ants on Earth is roughly equal to the combined weight of all the people on Earth.

More than 60% of the original Soviet space dogs suffered from constipation and gallstones after returning to Earth.

Neutron stars can spin at 600 revolutions per second.

John Chapman was the real Johnny Appleseed. He planted apple trees across the United States in order to exploit a rule at the time that allowed a person to claim land upon which they grew a permanent orchard. He would later sell the land. The apples from the trees he planted were not good for eating, and instead were used to make cider.

Bears are known to grieve.

Rats laugh when tickled.

Mosquitoes urinate on you while they feed.

Bananas are slightly radioactive.

In an experiment, a bright light was shone on the backs of people's knees. This was shown to alter the subject's biological clock by up to three hours.

In whales and dolphins, only half of the brain falls asleep.

In 1954, Beulah Hunter gave birth after being pregnant for 375 days, or 12.5 months.

The earth's rotation is gradually slowing down, such that in 150 million years a day will last twenty-five hours.

Acknowledgements

I wrote the first draft of "Oliver Bell and the Infinite Multiverse" during the COVID outbreak in 2020. Working as a doctor, I really needed a laugh, and so I decided to create a satire about what seemed to be a developing, society-wide case of borderline personality disorder.

The book was never intended to be more than a novella, but once Teddy entered the scene one thing led to another and a universe with its own rules exploded in my brain. I would write the rules and the history of Oliver's multiverse as I would go on my long, rebelliously mask-free walks during the day, and then work on the story at night.

I'm not a particularly great writer, but once that first draft was done, and I read it through, I realized other people might actually enjoy the story. The problem was, I had no idea how to go about making it right.

Initial salvation came from Terry Armstrong. Terry was as much a writing coach as an editor and he helped me get the book to a state of readability. Under his tutelage, I rewrote the entire thing six or seven times, and each draft was better than the previous.

Abby Teed-Walton, a fellow writer from Saint John, who possesses significantly more talent than I do, read the first chapter and helped me hone it down from a garbled mess.

Finally, this book wouldn't exist without Lee Thompson. For some reason, Lee decided to help me further edit what was still a pretty rough story, bringing it to its final, polished form. He also thought it was funny; an encouraging sign.

Lee was starting a new press at the time, but told me to send the book around first, which I did, and after endless rejections from agencies and publishers, he, alone, is the reason that this book exists. I owe him an enormous debt of gratitude.

I, of course, have to thank my wife, Chrissy, and my son, Jack, for giving me the time to pursue this endeavour, knowing full well it would be unlikely to ever put food on the table.

Finally, thank you, dear reader, for giving me a shot at entertaining you. I hope this book made you smile.

Humbly yours,
Jake

Jake Swan is a writer, physician, occasional fisherman, and all-around dumbass.

He is of the unpopular opinion that margarine is superior in both flavour and texture when compared to natural butter.

Recently, he gave up eating beef jerky from gas stations after checking his blood pressure. He describes the reading as "Stratospheric" and considers himself fortunate that neither of his eyeballs exploded like eggs in a microwave.

While watching the news one evening, Jake saw a story about a protest autonomous zone. In the footage, the protestors were spreading roughly one inch of topsoil on an asphalt parking lot next to a sign reading "Autonomous Zone Community Garden," and therefore he wrote this book.

Jake lives in New Brunswick, Canada, with his wife, Chrissy, their son, Jack, and Stella, their rescue mutt from South America, whose biography would undoubtedly be more interesting than this one, which Jake, coincidentally, wrote in the third person.